Happily FOREVER After

A NOVEL

THE FINALE TO THE FOREVER SERIES

MARY A. WASOWSKI

Copyright © 2016 by Mary A. Wasowski
Cover Design by Sara Eirew
Editing by Joe Marron
Formatting by JT Formatting

First Edition: July 2016
Library of Congress Cataloging-in-Publication Data

http://authormaryawasowski.com/

Wasowski, Mary A.
  Happily Forever After (*Book Four in The Forever Series*) / 1st ed
    ISBN-13: 978-0-9969605-5-7

  1.   Happily Forever After—Fiction.   2.   Fiction—Romance
          3.   Fiction—Contemporary Romance:

To Reese,

You are my forever.

Walker

To Jackson,
When I saw you
I fell in love,
and you smiled
because you knew.
Riley

A NOTE FROM THE AUTHOR

THANK YOU, READERS, for taking the time to read **Happily Forever After.** Please consider leaving an honest review.

So now, here we are! What an amazing adventure it has been getting to know Walker and Reese, and all the characters we love from the **Forever Series.** Every great love story has to come to an end, and in this finale, I sure hope you love how I have concluded all the happily ever after endings for the Forever family.

I will always be thankful that I trusted my heart while writing my first series. Writing has changed my life in more ways than I can ever explain. By the way, today marks my three-year publishing anniversary. Eight novels later and I am still chasing the dream...one book at a time. I truly hope I will continue to write for many years to come, to share my voice with you, and create many super couples for you to love.

Sparkle with smiles,

Mary

PROLOGUE

Finding our Forever

LIFE HAS A way of coming full circle in one's life. For me, Walker Reed, it has. As I sat here with my sleeping daughter in my arms, I reflected on how my life had changed over the past year. I was holding a living, breathing, and so perfect little version of the love of my life, Reese.

I always knew our child would be gorgeous. Our little baby was the combination of the both of us, but I had a feeling that this daddy's girl was going to rule the world someday, as I did from behind my desk at Reed Global.

Oh, to reflect on how far I had come in such a short time since reuniting with Reese! We went through hell, literal hell, to be together. We survived my father, Henry Townsend, and nearly lost my son, Jackson, to the same fate that took his mother. Talk about coming full circle! Yeah, we made it through and came out stronger on the other side.

I swore to myself and to God that if Jackson survived, I would change and finally give my son the freedom to live his life on his own and on his terms. Giving up control was never an option for me, but I promised Jackson that I would try. Reese always had faith in me and knew and understood all of my intentions when it came to the well-being for my son.

I trusted my son and saying goodbye to him and Riley was probably the hardest thing I had to get through, but I did it. I let him go but reminded him that I would always be here if he ever needed me. He hugged me tightly and said he knew without question. Reese was there to comfort me as they drove away to their new life in New York.

I was a hard man to love, and by choosing to love a man like me, that commitment took unconditional acceptance. Reese loved all parts of me, and knowing that made me a better man for her and for Jackson. The Reed men had been through hell and back, and we were both still standing with new promises of Forever with the ones we loved.

We are all trying to find our Forever; it just takes some of us a little longer to find it. I am living proof of that.

CHAPTER 1

Walker

Family

BEFORE LEAVING OUR very warm bed where my angel was sleeping, I leaned in ever so gently to kiss her goodbye. It would be another long day spent at the office and away from the most important women in my life: my Reese—my wife, my life—and our precious daughter, Fallon. She was my princess. Was there ever any doubt on how much she would be spoiled by me?

Whenever I had to leave early before my princess would wake, I would quietly tip toe into her nursery and just sit by her crib and hold her hand. I would tell her how much her daddy loved her and how his day would not be complete until he returned home to her. Reese sometimes would listen to me on the baby monitor and wait for me outside the door, not interrupting my private time with our daughter. Reese's expression was always the same. She would smile, and all I saw was love in her eyes for me. I so easily was lost every time our hearts connected with the other. I was a man in love and so incredibly blessed.

My heart ached when I was away from them, but if I wanted the perfect Christmas with my girls and Jackson, who would be coming home for his holiday break with Riley, then I knew all of my work commitments had to be completed. Christmas this year would be spectacular in every sense of the word. With Fallon being born and her first birthday approaching, I truly had everything a man could ever want in ten lifetimes.

I had planned on taking an extended vacation and leaving my right hand men, Donovan and Tom, in charge of the office with my assistant. Jenny was the other woman in my life, who kept me on my toes at work and not flat on my ass when I pushed myself too hard, *not living life*, as she so bluntly reminded me from time to time. I hadn't wasted a day since Reese came back to me, when I instantaneously came back to life.

"Good morning, baby. You should be in bed," I whispered as I took Reese into my arms.

She happily sighed. She hadn't been sleeping well the last few nights and I was beginning to worry, but Reese would always say or do something to distract me from questioning her.

"I could say the same for you," she said as her eyes danced with desire for me. "What do you say you free yourself from this suit and come back to bed to have your wicked way with me?"

She's going to be the death of me, I thought to myself.

I responded, "A tempting offer love, but one I have to refuse...for now, but will collect when I get home."

"Promise?" she asked as if she didn't already know my answer.

"Always," I whispered as I crushed my lips down onto her delicious mouth.

She was intoxicating, my drug of choice. Reese lit a fire deep inside of me that on most days I had difficulty containing. She knew me like no other, and we were always in a synchronized rhythm with one another. Her deep gaze into my eyes was pulling me in, and I was slowly losing all that was left of my control.

"I need to go to work baby," I told her.

"And I need you," she argued in return.

Her demand almost sounded feral and desperate on a deeper level. This was what I meant about Reese deflecting. But no matter how her requests sounded coming from her delicious mouth, I always submitted. She was the only one that could ever hold that much power over me. Well, her and our daughter.

Fuck it! There was no way I was going to leave her now and with my raging hard-on she was responsible for. I swiftly picked her up and carried her back to our bedroom. We only had a few precious moments left before the baby would interrupt and beckon Reese.

Reese was breathless as I placed her in the middle of our bed. I could see her gorgeous body through her barely there lingerie. Her nipples pebbled beneath my fingers as I raked them over her sensitive flesh, inviting me in to suck on them until she screamed my name.

"You are so fucking sexy, you were always meant to be mine, and I love you so much." I could barely get my words out, once again lost to her beauty.

"I'm yours, Walker, always. Make love to me."

Another desperate plea, but I shrugged it off. She never had to ask me twice for anything, especially when it came to fulfilling her desires. Sex between us was always amazing. It fed a deep hunger between us, but never really sated us. We always desired it, and most times fucked until we passed out. Yeah, I was one lucky son of a bitch.

We began our lovemaking gently, and then we fucked so hard that I saw stars. Beads of sweat were glistening on her forehead, and she was mine forever.

"I love you even though you are a devilish vixen that now has made me late for work."

"I love being naughty with you."

"It's the only way I know, baby," I replied breathlessly.

I kissed her one last time and then pulled out of her body. Reese always winced a bit. I knew I was probably too rough, but she never stopped me nor did she complain. Our connection to the other could never really be broken.

I gathered my clothes and quickly got dressed. Reese was now sitting up against the headboard and eye fucking the shit out of me, making me hard again.

"Stop it," I told her. "I'm already late, thanks to you and your sexy teasing."

"It was sexy fucking, and you loved it," she said with a wink.

"That I did, my love, but I really need to go," I said as I fixed my tie and took one last look in the mirror.

"I didn't hear you complaining," she said, stifling a laugh under her breath.

"Never, but I have much to do today, and I am very late."

She just smirked at me. What was she thinking when she did that?

"Will you shower when you get to the office?" she teasingly asked while the sheet fell away a bit.

"No," I firmly stated, surprising her. "I always want you with me, and if I can't physically be here, then your scent will be with me until I can make precious love to you again."

"Savage. You look amazing and devilishly handsome, but I can smell our lovemaking on you. What will your colleagues think?"

I loved it when she blushed and hid her smile. One thing Reese should know about me is that I wanted to see all of her, all the time, and it turned me on like nothing else in the world.

"Walker? Did you hear what I said?"

"I did my love, every single word. And the answer to your question is that I do not give a fuck what my staff will think or whisper behind my back. They wish they were lucky to have what I have, but they can dream all they want because you are mine."

One more kiss and then I left, but not before I saw her smile and sigh. God! I loved her and thanked the universe every day for this life I had.

I met Stephen at the car and he took my briefcase from me, but not before looking down to his watch. I bristled by him and stepped into my car. He remained silent and closed my door behind me. He was smiling in the rearview mirror, and I hit the button to raise the privacy screen. I wasn't going to defend the lateness of the hour to Stephen, or anyone for that matter. Sometimes matters of the heart took precedence over everything else.

We arrived at my office, thankfully avoiding the morning traffic. Jenny was waiting for me as I stepped off the elevator.

"Good morning, sir. Coffee is on your desk. Can I bring you anything to eat before we get started?"

"Good morning, Jenny. Coffee will be fine for now. Hold my calls for the next couple of hours, and then we will status around eleven."

"Yes, sir."

I sat down at my desk and took a few deep breaths. This time last year Reese and I were newly married and preparing for the birth of our daughter. After surviving her brutal attack from Townsend and all we went through with Jackson, I knew in my heart that I had to make every effort to give Reese the surprise of the year. I needed the best, and only one person came to mind to help me accomplish all I wanted to do. She was a fiery pain in my ass, but truly worth her commission. I had her on speed dial, and she answered on the second ring. She greeted me with her usual saccharin tone.

"Good morning, Mr. Reed. How are you? And what can I do for you?"

Seriously? Fourteen words to greet me before I've had the opportunity to speak? And people wonder why I get right to the point of my business...It's so I could skip all of this useless banter.

"Ms. Baker."

"Oh, Mr. Reed, please call me Rosalyn."

"Ms. Baker, are you going to give me a minute to speak? Or shall I pick the next event planner whose name is sitting on my desk?"

She let out a gasp but remained silent to take in my threat. I so enjoyed making her squirm, as I had no intention of calling anyone else. She was a pain in the ass but amazing at what she did.

"I'm sorry, Mr. Reed, please go on," she said in her most professional tone.

"Thank you. Ms. Baker, I have a list of requests for you. Are you ready?"

"Yes, sir."

"Good. The first thing I need is the exterior of my estate decorated for Christmas. I want the grounds covered in lights and decorations. I also want the interior decorated to whatever my wife wants. I will need several fresh Christmas trees delivered by the 23rd, and all decorated, excluding our personal selection that my family will decorate on Christmas Eve. Are you with me so far?"

"Yes, sir, go on."

"The section of the property that I have designed as my daughter's play area, I would like to turn that into a winter wonderland fully equipped with snow."

She sighed on the line, breaking me out of my thought process.

"Problem, Ms. Baker?"

"No, sir, no problem. It's just that we live in California and, with the warmer temps, providing snow may be an issue."

"Not to me, Ms. Baker. Anything can be accomplished, and it will be if you want to continue to work for me."

"I will work it out, Mr. Reed. No worries here."

"Good. As I was saying, snow is necessary. My daughter loves the Disney characters, namely the princesses. I want a carousel assembled and moving figurines all around, the bigger the better."

She sighed again on the line, irritating me to the point where I was about to disconnect the call altogether, but not before I questioned why she wasn't immediately agreeing to my requests.

"Ms. Baker, that is the second time you deeply sighed. Do we have a problem?"

"No, sir, we don't, and I will do anything you request. But I do have some concerns to what you have in mind."

"Which are?"

"Sir, your daughter is not even a year old yet. Although I do not have children of my own, I do have nieces and nephews, and they never took to bright lights or loud noises at that age. I fear all of it may overwhelm her. It's just my *professional* opinion."

She stated the word "professional" very slowly to get the message across to me. It didn't fall onto deaf ears, and I did listen and reconsider.

"Okay, Ms. Baker, being that you so clearly stated your *professional* opinion, what do you have in mind?"

Silence. I think I stunned her, which was no easy task on my part, considering the way she usually carried on.

"Mr. Reed, all you have suggested pertaining to decorating the property for Christmas is doable and wonderful. My suggestion for your daughter's play area is simpler. Do you play music for her? What does she respond most to?"

"She loves music; we play a variety of classical to nursery songs."

"Great. I suggest a selection she is familiar and comfortable with. We can choose a mix of nursery songs for the carousel as long as it is not too loud where it will frighten her. As for the moving figurines, I can stage them in the background so as you take her around the property, you can show her the displays without again being too overwhelming. Mr. Reed, are you still there?" she questioned.

"I am, Ms. Baker. I'm just processing all you have recommended. From all you have just mentioned, it sounds like you are speaking from experience. Have you planned many children events?"

"Only personal, Mr. Reed. I have a large family with many little children, and let's just say that my favorite Manolos didn't go unscathed from time to time at one of my niece's birthday parties. Or the time my nephew met Santa and threw his grape juice all over my white Chanel suit."

"So noted, Ms. Baker. I will take everything under advisement. Please design a theme based on what we discussed and send it over to me by the end of business today. I will be in touch."

I ended my call and sat back to take in all she had said. I hated to admit it, but she was right. It would be a complete disaster for any child to have that much stimulation all at once. But my Fallon was a Reed, and I somewhat convinced myself that my princess would be fine and love it all.

On cue, Jenny was standing before me with my coffee. She tried and failed at containing her smile.

"Daddyzilla," she said. She got me there. I smiled as she left me to my planning.

For the better part of the day, I revised my original plans for the play area and came up with something that I knew Reese would love and Fallon would enjoy for years to come. I wasn't too keen on a treehouse even I knew she was too young for that. I designed a play-house for her. It was going to re-create the Disney castle, but I quickly changed my mind. I wanted to build something she could grow into. Then the idea hit, and I began sketching what would be her surprise birthday present. I was dying to tell Reese, but this was for her too. I envisioned Reese playing tea party with our little girl, and me in costume as I did the voices of all the characters in her favorite stories.

I never loved Reese more than when she told me she was carrying my child. I almost missed it and longed for more babies with Reese. Would she want to? We never discussed not having anymore, and still to this day did not practice safe sex. If it happened, it happened.

Should I ask her later tonight when I get home, I asked myself. *What will she say? Do I want to tempt fate and want more than I already have? The universe has been guiding us from the minute we reunited, what's one more dream for us to share?*

Yes! I would definitely bring this up to Reese in the one place she could never say no to me...in bed.

"Reese, I'm home," I called out as I entered our quiet home.

Priscilla was always the first to greet me as she took my coat and briefcase, and then Reese would always join me, but not tonight.

"Welcome home, Mr. Reed. Can I get you anything?" she asked.

"Yes, where's Mrs. Reed?" I nervously asked.

Her face had fallen a bit and then she answered my question. "Mr. Reed, Mrs. Reed is upstairs in the nursery with your daughter. Fallon is under the weather with a cold, and she's giving her a bath."

"What?" I almost shouted as I gritted my teeth. Priscilla took a step back, and my face immediately softened. I was just taken back at this news, wondering why Reese hadn't phoned me earlier.

"Thank you, Priscilla," I quickly said as I made my way up the stairs to the nursery.

"Reese, Reese!" I called out, and that's when she appeared with her fingers over her lips to quiet me.

"Walker, please no shouting. I just put her down."

She reached for my hand and led me away from Fallon's room with the baby monitor in her hand. We went to our room, where Reese turned on the video monitor to watch our daughter sleep. Fallon looked so peaceful and cozy under her blanket.

I silently counted to ten in my head and then took Reese into my arms to hold her. She looked exhausted, no doubt over worrying about our sick baby. I got myself into check before speaking to her. She must know that I would have come home immediately if she had phoned me, but this was Reese keeping me at bay and doing everything on her own when she didn't have to. I had an entire staff here at the house plus a nanny, but Reese rarely depended on them for help. She was completely devoted to our daughter as I was, but I still wanted Reese to have some time of her own and be herself.

"Reese," I whispered into her ear, "why didn't you phone me about Fallon? What's going on? She was fine this morning when I left."

Still in my arms she said, "I didn't want to worry you, Walker.

Babies get sick, and sometimes no matter what you do to prevent it, it happens anyway."

"What's wrong? Did you take her in to see Dr. Sutherland?"

"No, I thought that would be worse to leave the house with her running a temperature, so I had our pediatrician come here.

That's my girl. Although she didn't call me, that's exactly what I would have done. Reese knew me so well.

"After you left, we carried on throughout our day, and then after her walk she seemed hot. I took her temperature, and that's when her fever was nearly 101.2. It just happened so quickly. I gave her medicine and cooled her down. She was restless for most of the afternoon. I would have thought she would be the opposite, but something was bothering her. And then she vomited all over her crib. Once she did that, she seemed a little bit better. Dr. Sutherland diagnosed her with a virus, and to just keep her hydrated. She finally fell asleep after the soothing bath I gave her."

Reese let out a deep breath and looked deeply into my worried eyes.

"I'm sorry, Walker," she said.

"For what, baby?" I asked as tears formed into her eyes.

"I should have called you the minute she began running her fever, but I thought I could handle it on my own, and I didn't want you to worry. It's been a long time since I had to take care of an infant, almost toddler. It's quite overwhelming after all of these years."

To see Reese upset because she believed she has disappointed me gutted my insides. She was the best thing in my life and a wonderful mother. I was the beast that she married and I knew not to show this side of me every time something happened, especially something so natural as a baby's cold.

I nodded my head in agreement and remained silent, remembering what Rosalyn had told me earlier. I led Reese over to the bed, where I knelt down to remove her shoes. I rubbed each foot as she leaned her head back in relaxation. She let out quiet moans of pleasure as I massaged her. I knew I could take this further in a heartbeat, but I was not that much of a selfish bastard to recognize that my woman was tired. In the next few moments, my angel was soundly asleep. I tucked her in under the duvet. Reese did not move an inch. I placed a kiss onto her forehead and dimmed the lights.

I walked into our closet and quickly changed into a t-shirt and track pants, taking the monitor with me, but looking once more over to where Reese was sleeping. The sight of her in her angelic state made my heart beat faster for only her. I declined dinner and went straight to the other angel in my life…our daughter.

CHAPTER 2

Walker

My world

I MOVED THE rocking chair closer to Fallon's crib so I could be near her. She had beads of sweat on her beautiful skin. I gently wiped her forehead trying not to wake her. Her puckered lips formed a perfect O as she let out little puffs of air.

My heart was aching to hold her but knew she needed her sleep. No parent ever wants to see his or her children sick, not even for a cold. Sitting vigil by her crib brought back memories of Jackson when he was fighting for his life last year.

The situations were entirely different, but the feelings were the same for me. I couldn't bear to see my children sick or hurt in any sense of the word. I would take it all on myself if I could, but that's not rational, so I did my best to protect them from harm. The thought of baby Fallon suffering just destroyed me, and the fact that it was a common occurrence that all babies went through didn't make me feel any better.

She always slept with her little hand outreached, as if she were waiting for me to hold her hand and make it all better. That is what daddies are supposed to do. I took her small hand in mine and gently kissed it.

"I'm here, princess. Daddy's here. Please get better so I can see you smile again."

My mind drifted back to my earlier thoughts about having another child with Reese. Maybe it was foolish thinking on my part. We already had the perfect family, so why tempt fate? My son was thriving and doing well in New York. I had a second chance with our perfect daughter, but I still wanted more. And that more was with Reese. I wanted to fill this home with the laughter of children and happy memories with all who loved us.

It was not a dream for me anymore; it was a reality and one I could make happen again with another child. Or at least have fun trying.

As I closed my eyes, I envisioned Fallon running through our meadow of wild flowers, trying to catch butterflies, while Reese tried valiantly to keep up with her. She was beautiful, wearing a summer dress, her belly swollen with our child.

"Dada... Dada..." I heard in my dreams as I fought to stay asleep. I was having the best dream until I heard those lovely words again.

"Dada. Dada. Dada."

I blinked my eyes open to see Fallon sitting up and trying to reach for me through the bars of the crib. She was awake and looking so much better. Her cheeks were rosy pink as she smiled and raised her little arms for me to hold her. She was babbling with baby coos and blowing raspberries at me. I loved every amount of attention she was giving to me.

I quickly reached to take my princess into my arms. I felt her forehead, and it appeared that her fever had broken. Always airing on the side of precaution before I could rejoice, I took her temperature to make sure. It read 98.6 degrees, a perfect reading. Fallon happily bounced in my arms as I held her and began talking to her.

"Hey, princess, daddy is here. How are you feeling? You look perfect to me, but daddy is not taking any chances. No tumbling today for you. I promise double tummy time tomorrow when you are 100% better. Oh, do you understand what daddy is saying? Your eyes are so bright but sad at the same time. I'm sorry, baby, but we need to take it easy today."

She drooled all over my face and tried to shove her tiny fingers into my mouth. I kissed every one of them and then changed her diaper and pajamas. She wiggled all over the changing table and made more sweet babbling sounds. It was always music to my ears, but nothing measured up to when she said, "Dada."

I wasn't sure if I should try to feed her, so I left that up to the boss. By the time I reached our bedroom, Fallon was nestled comfortably against my chest. For a moment I had thought she had fallen back to sleep, but this was just what she did. My little baby would pick a comfy spot and plant herself there, just like her mother.

Reese appeared to be sleeping, but clearly she had moved from the shifting of the blanket. I placed Fallon beside her, and then our little girl tapped her hand on Reese's cheek. I wished I had my camera to capture this moment. Fallon's hand was on her cheek, and our daughter was quiet as a mouse, waiting for her mother to wake.

I quickly felt another pang to my chest, remembering all the years I was lost without her in my life, but I quickly shoved that aside to take in the new memory in front of me. Reese opened her eyes and smiled. She placed a kiss on top of Fallon's hand and then kissed her nose.

"Hello, my sweet girl," she said softly. "Come here to mama. No more fever, and your smile has returned. Oh, princess! Don't scare mommy like that again."

I watched silently and listened to Reese talk to our daughter and look relieved that she was better. I snuggled between them and held my girls close to me. Fallon continued to coo and now kiss raspberries on her mommy's cheeks. My girls. My world. I let out a sigh of relief and then Reese's eyes met mine.

"She's fine, Walker. We will all be fine. I just know it," Reese whispered as her eyes were on Fallon.

I wasn't sure about what she meant by "we will all be fine," but I held off questioning Reese about it. It was a long day for her and the baby. I nodded and smiled back at Reese. I wasn't sure if she was trying to convince herself or me, but I wasn't going to push the issue. I, of all people, understood overprotectiveness when it came to a child. I also understood loss, and that's why even the common cold scared us. There was no point trying to dispute it.

"Are you hungry, baby?" Reese asked.

"Yes, I'm famished...and not for food," I said with a wink.

"I was asking our daughter, but thank you, Walker, for letting me know. I will feed our daughter, and then I will feed you."

That's my girl! A witty comeback, I love it. This was a good sign that her much-needed nap had helped her.

"Oh, Reese, I would rather eat *you* if that's okay. You are the tastiest delicacy my palette has ever tasted."

"You have no shame, Walker. No sex talk in front of Fallon."

"Me? No shame? You are a walking contradiction. Your mouth says no, but your body says yes. It always says yes, you sexy minx. What's a man to do but try to keep up as best as I can."

She left our bed with our precious daughter wrapped up in her arms and turned to me.

"You know I love you, right?" she said to me.

"I never doubt it, but I love you more."

"Impossible, but thank you for saying it."

I quickly rose from the bed and led Reese back to it, where I saw my opportunity to say what was on my mind.

"I mean it, baby. I love you more. You brought be back to life when I thought I would always be in perpetual darkness. You are my light, the sun that rises and sets on all of my days. To see you hold our daughter lovingly in your arms makes my heart nearly beat out from my chest. I can hardly contain the thousands of emotions I feel for you both. I want more, Reese, so much more. Please, my love, say yes. It is the perfect time to give Fallon a brother or sister. Reese, please? Say yes to more."

My girl was silent and did not give anything away. I hated and loved this about her. Reese leaned in to kiss me, and I kissed my girls back. Then she left to feed our daughter. I remained hopeful that she would say yes.

It was very rare that Reese denied me of anything, but the decision truly had to lie with her. She protected our daughter throughout her entire pregnancy and kept me above water during the crisis with Jackson. We survived Henry and all he tried to do to destroy us, and we came out so much stronger. We could conquer anything life challenged us with. Our family was proof of that.

I never doubted Reese, not ever. I walked outside to our balcony. The stars were out on full display tonight. I closed my eyes and spoke aloud to our first child, our son, our angel in heaven.

"You are never too far from our minds and hearts, Thomas. One day I will see you, son, but for now will you continue to watch over us from the sky? We love you always."

I wiped a falling tear and cleared my mind from the pains of our past. I had so much more control over it than I ever had. The reason? Because of Reese and what she brought to my life. My wife had filled all of the dark holes in more ways than I could ever imagine. I once told her that in every chapter of our life together, there were steps to climb. We had survived so much together and were blessed with more. Having another child would be another step to take together.

It didn't happen too often, seeing a falling star here in California. I remembered a long time ago when one fell over the shores of the Hamptons. I had never experienced that before, and I longed to see one again. Tonight, I realized that the wish I had made so long ago in the Hamptons came true. Not one to let an opportunity pass, I prayed on the falling star and made a new wish.

My newfound respect for prayers and faith was discovered through reuniting with Reese, and then those revelations were tested when I feared I would lose Jackson. I waged an internal war within myself and my relationship with God. I begged him for mercy for my son, to give him a chance at life, to keep him with me.

My prayers were answered, and I hoped they would be again. Having another child would only grace our lives even more. I was a selfish man, I always had been, but even selfish men deserved love. I found that when I met Reese, and again when I held our daughter in my arms. Was I satisfied with what I now had? Yes, of course I was, but she made me want more. I always wanted more with Reese. Fortunately, everything in my life always had a way of working out.

But no matter what was next in our story, I would always have Reese, and that meant I already had everything.

CHAPTER 3

Walker

More

REESE DID NOT come back with Fallon to our bedroom or to the nursery. I called out for her, but I heard no answer in return. I was about to check the video feed when Priscilla told me where my girls were. Reese had taken Fallon for a walk on the grounds.

One of her favorite spots on the property was our gazebo. We made love in there more times than I could count, and best of all…we got married there. We sealed our souls and entwined our hearts forever to each other. It was an incredible day I would remember always. It was also a place where Reese would go when things weighed heavily on her mind. My request to have another baby may have shocked her, but I was not sure why. I could not overthink it any longer and decided to just find her and ask her myself.

I quietly approached the gazebo and remained silent while I listened to my beautiful wife sing to our daughter. I closed my eyes to take in the melody that Fallon was blessed to hear in her mother's arms. Reese was singing "If tomorrow never comes" by Ronan Keating. She played this particular song quite often when she was pregnant, but to listen to Reese sing it now to our baby was incredible. She had to know I was nearby; I could see a hint of smile on Reese's lips. I leaned against the doorway as she sang the last verse to Fallon, who closed her eyes and drifted off into sleep.

This woman had the power to unman me with just a look, touch, and the sound of her voice. I never stood a chance of resisting her. Now, with our daughter being born, I was outnumbered. I would give them everything I had just to see them smile and know they're happy.

"That was lovely, Reese. Thank you for not stopping when you saw me eavesdropping on your private time with our daughter."

"You can eavesdrop as much as you like, and I certainly did not mind. I was actually waiting for you."

"Then I'm glad I didn't disappoint," I said.

"Oh, Walker, that is one thing you never do."

"Happy to hear that, my love. She looks so precious sleeping in your arms," I said as I lovingly looked down to our daughter. I placed a kiss on her forehead. She was beautiful just like her mother. "Do you wish to stay out here much longer? I can have Priscilla come for Fallon, and put her down in her nursery."

"That's okay," Reese replied. "I'll put her to bed."

"Are you okay, Reese? Talk to me."

"Not here, Walker. In our bedroom…in our bed."

She said nothing more and walked back toward the house. I kept a few steps behind to give her space. She seemed off, and I did not want to push her. Was it too soon to bring up more children with her? On the other hand, was it something else? I found myself doing what I always accused Reese of: overthinking.

I met her in the nursery, where she was tucking in our daughter.

I leaned down to kiss Fallon goodnight, and then I reached for Reese's hand. She looked as if she were going to cry, but her tears never fell. She accepted my hand, and we walked back to our room.

Please, baby, do not pull away from me, I was thinking those words on repeat to calm myself down. Reese was beyond exasperating when she would shut down on me, but she did invite me to our bed so that was a positive sign.

I wanted nothing more than to tear her clothes off and make love to her. She was an enigma of elusiveness, and it was killing me. Reese walked over to our bed and unfastened the buttons to her blouse. She extended her arms to her back and let the fabric slide off her body. She then unzipped her slacks and let them fall down her silky legs to the floor. Always graceful, Reese stepped out from her clothes and then turned to look at me.

The moonlight shimmered off our floor length windows, and Reese was my Aphrodite basking in the glow of it. Her eyes were hypnotizing me and drawing me in closer and closer to her. I could feel my dick press hard against my pants so constricting to almost the feeling of pain. I wanted nothing more than to fuck her into the mattress and stay there for days, but Reese was leading me and I went willingly.

She shook her long tresses as she untied her ponytail, where it draped over shoulders and down her back like a veil. She was so fucking sexy and knew exactly what she was doing to me.

Like the vixen she was, she crooked her finger, beckoning me to come to her. I took a few steps forward, and then she asked me to stop. She then unhooked her bra and tossed it aside. Her breasts were perfect, and her nipples were pebbled and waiting for me to take them into my mouth where I could feast on and devour them. I wanted to rush my goddess and take her, but again, this was me showing incredible restraint. Reese was in control, and I fucking loved it.

"Come to me, Walker," she said as she extended her arms out to me.

I was there in a second, and then my mouth found hers and I

was begging for entrance. She bit down on my bottom lip, and my dick nearly exploded from inside of my pants.

Pushing her pelvis against mine, Reese was thrusting up against me. My hands were in her hair and pulling her toward me, while she unbuckled my pants. She dropped to her knees and took me into her warm, naughty mouth. She took all of me in one fast moment. I could do nothing but lean my head back and release my pleasure down into her throat. She was taking all of me; I was so lost to Reese. She looked wickedly at me as she rose from the floor to meet my heated gaze.

"Fuck me Walker, and don't hold back…I won't break."

She never ceased to amaze me. And with her request, I did exactly what she wanted me to do. Picking her up and placing her in the center of our bed, I feasted on her breasts, and then made my way down to her glistening sex. She was so wet for me, I could see the evidence of her arousal drip down from her pussy, only igniting my fire even more.

Parting her legs with my hands, I leaned in and entered her with my tongue. She lifted her pelvis hard against my mouth and then screamed my name repeatedly as I made her orgasm and come all over my face. I lapped up all of her juices as her body continued to contract. I did not give her a moment of rest and swiftly flipped her to her stomach and took her from behind.

Her glorious ass was in the air as I fucked her deeper, slapping her skin to the rosiest shade of pink. Reese cried out, clenched the sheets, and took in all of me. We were always in perfect harmony with the other, and we were close to coming together. Reese went first, and then I quickly followed, releasing every drop of my seed into her. I gripped her shoulders and her back was upright to my chest. My hands were covering her breasts as I kissed my way down her neck.

"You. Are. Forever. Mine. I love you, Reese. Always."

I could not help but smile as I thought we could have just conceived at that moment.

Panting in between breaths, she agreed with three words, "Yours. Always. Yours."

Her words satisfied me. It was something I still needed to hear, especially in the throes of our lovemaking. Reese never held back when it came to our intimacy. She craved the hunger just as much as I did.

We settled in for the night with Reese turning away from me, another act I hated, but I simply wrapped my arms around her and held her close to me.

"Reese, are you okay? Please talk to me? You know how I love to be silenced by sex, but I'm also smart enough to know that it's a distraction weapon you use not to talk to me, so I will ask you again: what's wrong?" I whispered close to her ear.

"I'm fine, Walker, just tired. Can we talk tomorrow?" she asked.

Clenching my jaw to the point of pain, I reluctantly said yes. I felt shut out when she closed herself off like that. I wanted to make her talk to me, but I stopped myself and held her while she drifted off to sleep.

"Tomorrow, Reese. Tomorrow you will talk to me." I whispered in her ear. I knew she heard me, but still she said nothing.

The hours of sleep I did manage to have were torturous on my mind. I tossed and turned and battled through the night on what was bothering Reese. Clearly by her actions last night, she did not appear to be troubled, but looks and actions can be deceiving. I could be looking into things that were not there, but when it came to Reese, I hardly did anything rational.

I knew something was off. I could feel it the moment I mentioned having more children. I reached over to touch her, and her side of the bed was cold—too cold for my liking. Did she sleep? Was she as troubled as I was?

I was not going to lie here one more minute and put myself through anymore unnecessary worry. It was time to talk to Reese. After my shower, I dressed and made my way downstairs. I purposely took my time and thought perhaps Reese would have joined me, but she did not.

"Good morning, Mr. Reed. Can I serve your breakfast now?" Priscilla had asked as my eyes scanned the room with Reese nowhere in sight.

"No, thank you. Where is Mrs. Reed?"

Her eyes fell a bit with concern.

"Priscilla?" I questioned. "Where is my wife? And my daughter? I will not ask again."

"Mr. Reed, Mrs. Reed left early this morning, taking baby Fallon with her. She left you this note. I'm sorry, Mr. Reed, that's all I know."

Not wanting to take my anger out on Priscilla, I told her, "Please leave me."

"Yes, sir."

She quickly scurried off and left me with the note that Reese had left. Why a note at all? I begged her to talk to me last night, and she promised we would this morning, so why was she not here? *Where are you, baby?*

I felt as if I were going to faint. I was rendered speechless by Priscilla's words: "Mrs. Reed left early this morning, taking baby Fallon with her." What the fuck? I did not understand this at all. I was about to phone Stephen and order him to find Reese at once, but I took a breath and opened up her note instead.

There was no way Reese would ever leave me again. She said she would never run again and certainly would not take our daughter from me.

Stop this line of thought right now, I said to myself. I was going out of my mind, and I had not even opened up her note. I took another breath, and then I tore open the envelope.

Dear Walker,

Please do not be angry with me for leaving this morning without talking to you first. You must be confused by my actions and are probably already plagued with worry. I am so very sorry for causing you one second of pain. I have to work out a few things on my own, and I cannot do that while in the close proximity of you.

Fallon is well and misses her daddy. I promise with all of my heart that I will be home in a few days. I promise, Walker, and I am not running.

I love you more.

Reese

WTF? "A few days?" Like hell, a few days. I could barely stand being away from her for hours in my workday, let alone a few days. *What is she thinking?*

I crumbled her note in my hands and then fell to my knees. Reese had left me and taken our daughter with her. Why? What had happened to make her do this to me? And to us? *Hell fucking no if she thinks for one minute that I am just going to sit on my hands and not do everything in my power to bring her home.*

I pulled out my cell phone and saw no messages or missed calls. I called her immediately, and my call went directly to voicemail. Fuck! Where are you Reese? Please, baby. Come back to me.

I hit Stephen's number on my cell and requested his presence to the house immediately. She could not have gone far. Reese knew how protective I was of what was mine. Our phones and cars were tracked. The property was under surveillance for our protection. I calmed myself down and met Stephen at the door.

"Mr. Reed, I received your 911 text. What's happened?" Stephen asked.

"Mrs. Reed...she's gone and has taken my daughter with her."

"Gone? That's impossible, Walker. There is no way she would have just left and without my knowledge. The feed has been running all night. I checked it this morning, and there were no red flags. I would have notified you immediately if there were."

"Stephen, she's gone and the reason why I know she's gone is because she left me this note. Her side of the bed is cold, and Fallon's nursery is empty. Priscilla was the one that handed me this paper. Find my wife. Find my daughter. And bring them home to me."

I nearly collapsed at just saying those words.

"I'm on it, sir. I will find them," he said, and then he was gone.

I called Reese repeatedly on her cell phone, but my calls were sent directly to voicemail. I left her a message this time.

"Reese, please come home. You are right, my love. I am plagued with worry and you cannot even begin to know what is going through my mind right now. Please, baby. Come home. I am sorry for anything I may have said or done to cause you to run. Please come home. I cannot live without you. Please, Reese, come home."

I ended the call and fought the urge not to smash my phone. I felt paralyzed by my own fear of the unknown. I was not a man known to be patient, but without knowledge of Reese's whereabouts, I was forced to go against my nature and hold back my emotions.

Priscilla knew to keep her distance. I locked myself away in my study and while I was holding onto my senses and control, I phoned Jenny and told her that I would not be in today. She seemed a little shocked by it, knowing how full my schedule was today and for the rest of the week.

Jenny knew better than to question me. She knew me like no one else and I was sure my tone was not going unnoticed, but she remained professional and did what I asked of her.

After my call to Jenny, I paced my office holding Reese's picture in my hands. I was angry and hurt by her absence. She fucking knew she could tell me anything. I may not like it, but I would always listen. And to take Fallon? *WTF!?* The baby was ill yesterday, and now she's God-knows-where, and I was left here with my own devices to just think the worst possible scenarios in my mind.

I placed the photo carefully back to its rightful place on my desk and did something that I swore I would never do again in my lifetime. Today I felt I deserved a pass. I fixed myself a double scotch and just...waited.

CHAPTER 4

Walker

We will always find our way

"SIR, WAKE UP."

I heard Stephen try valiantly to wake me, but after losing count on how many doubles I knocked back, my head was fuzzy and the room was spinning. After Reese came back into my life, I swore I would never drink scotch again. It was my father's drink of choice, and I wanted nothing that connected myself with him. If Stephen touched me again, it was likely that I would throw up all over his Ferragamo shoes.

"Sir, can you hear me? I've located Mrs. Reed."

That got my attention. I opened my eyes to the blinding sun coming through the windows. Trying to stand proved to not be a good decision as I nearly fell over my own feet. My stomach retched. Stephen already had his arm around me as he led me to the nearest bathroom. I hugged the toilet for the next ten minutes, successfully expelling all the liquor I ingested. Great decision on my part, considering I had skipped dinner last night and two meals to-day.

Stephen handed me a towel as I wiped my mouth. The room was still spinning, but at least my vision was beginning to clear and I could actually focus on Stephen. I washed my face with ice-cold water and then turned to face Stephen.

"Where is she?"

"She's in Malibu," he responded.

"Malibu! Of course she is!" I exclaimed.

She was with Freddy Mac, her go-to person when she could not talk to me, or when she was making the choice to shut me out. The only other person she trusted other than me was Freddy, her best friend and keeper of all her secrets.

Her decision to leave and take our daughter gutted my soul and shredded me to ribbons. All she had to do was talk to me when I begged her to. Once again, she had run and hidden from me. No matter what her note said, it was what my heart believed. Mac should have been my first call, but I was out of my mind discovering she had left and never got beyond that.

I asked, "What else do we know?"

"We were only able to track her to Malibu; we don't have any-thing in-between. I should receive some reports soon."

"That won't be necessary, Stephen. I will take it from here. I am going upstairs to shower and change. I'll be ready in ten minutes."

"I'll be outside, sir."

I stood under the cold shower to wash away the remnants of my reckless decision to drink my troubles away. The last time I drank that heavily was when...*on second thought I will not go back to that time. That part of my life is in the past, where it will remain. I will never touch scotch again.*

I walked into Fallon's nursery, and my heart ached with her ab-sence. This house was too quiet without Reese and our daughter. I looked down to her crib, where my eyes found her teddy bear. Jackson gave this to his baby sister on the day she came home from the hospital. She loved it, and Reese left it behind. Why did she do this?

It had been hours since discovering Reese had left me without any word of her whereabouts. We were fine yesterday morning. What could have changed from yesterday to today? And to take our daughter without me knowing was just unconscionable to me. Reese knew how madly I loved them both. What could she possibly say to right this wrong? I needed to know and could not wait another second sitting here in my daughter's empty nursery while my family was out there without me.

I sat in silence in the backseat of my car as Stephen drove me to Malibu. My mind entertained all sorts of crazy scenarios to why Reese ran. I did not want to alert Mac or Reese of my arrival, but I had passed the point of rational thinking and was ready to break down his front door.

Before getting out, I asked Stephen if he received any reports from our security team, and he looked at me with a crestfallen expression.

"Hand me the file, Stephen."

"Sir, it's not what you think, so please don't go there."

"Where am I supposed to go then, Stephen? Is my wife leading a double life, and if so, then how did I not know any of it? Am I fucking blind and so in love that I don't see what is happening right in front of me? So if she is not cheating on me, then what the fuck? Why did she run? I want answers, and I damn well am going to get them. I don't care if I have to tear down Mac's house to get to my wife."

"You're not going in there until you calm down and let me talk."

"You work for me, Stephen, not the other way around. Let me pass."

"No!" he yelled back.

"No? Are you fucking kidding me right now?"

"No, sir, this is no laughing matter. I am well aware of who signs my paychecks, but I am not your employee right now. I am your friend, and I am going to talk to you as a friend. That woman in that house loves you more than her own life. I am so sure of it that I would bet my own life on it. My God, man! She went up against a crazed lunatic and survived, all in the name of loving you and protecting her child."

"My child!" I interrupted. "Stephen, I have not held my daughter since last night. What the fuck do you expect me to think? I am out of my mind, and I've never felt so helpless than right at this moment. It is even worse since the first time she left me. I have so much more to lose this time, and I swore I would never allow myself to feel this type of pain again. So I ask you again, Stephen, how am I supposed to behave when I don't even know what I'm facing once I knock on that door?"

"You're angry and have a right to be, but you need to calm down and listen to your wife. Please, Walker, go to her and listen. I swear you will find the answers you need, and the last ten hours will not even matter."

"What's in the file, Stephen?" I asked again, but he still did not hand it over to me.

Whatever it was, I knew what it did not contain: evidence of Reese cheating on me. She would never ever betray me; I own her, body and soul. I felt sick for even entertaining that thought, but I was lost and crazed with worry.

I took a breath and knocked on the door to see Freddy standing on the other side of it, holding my daughter. My heart nearly stopped at the sight of Fallon. The minute she saw me, she excitedly began bouncing in Freddy's arms and reached for me.

Without hesitation, Freddy handed me my daughter, and I held her close to me, kissing the top of her hair, and then kissing her rosy cheeks. The sweet sound of Fallon saying "Dada" resonated throughout the entryway of Freddy's home.

I could not move from where I was standing. I was so happy to just see her again. I kissed my daughter once more, and then I handed her over to Stephen, but not before giving Freddy a death glare. There was no way in hell that I was leaving here without my daughter or Reese.

"Where is she, Mac? Whatever game you have going on here is one you do not want to play with me. Where is my wife? I will not ask again."

He replied, "First of all, no game. You do not have a clue as to what is going on, and in typical Walker-Reed-fashion, you lead and destroy before seeking out and asking questions first. I do not care how much you threaten to blow my house down or beat the hell out of me; there is no way you are seeing Reese right now until you calm down. Okay? Please come in and sit. She's resting in the guest room."

"She's resting? Do you even know what I have been through today? And you calmly tell me that she is sleeping? Freddy, if you want me calm, then please…tell me what the hell is going on."

"Walker, she's my life, and you know I love her too. You know I would never say no to anything she asked for. I wanted her to tell you herself, but in typical Reese-fashion, she put you first. She did it twenty years ago, and she is doing it right now. She never wanted you to ever find out, but because she got scared, this drama you both went through today could have been avoided if she had just talked to you."

"Tell me what? Freddy, please? Please tell me Reese is okay."

"She is now, but the last few weeks have not been a picnic for her. Walker, I am begging you…please just go in there, take our Georgia Peach in your arms, and just love her. She needs you more than ever before. Take a breath first, and go in. She's in the last bedroom on the left."

I said nothing more to him and walked down the long hallway to find my woman. A thousand crazy scenarios ran through my mind. I felt sick to my stomach knowing that for even a second how I mistrusted her and immediately drew the worst-case scenario instead of keeping myself in check.

I have been where she is right now, and it is not a great place to be. Here I was, trying and convicting her without ever asking her one single question. Reese would never hurt me…hurt us. I will get on my knees and grovel at her feet if I have to. I need her forgiveness for how I behaved today.

As quietly as I could, I walked into Freddy's guest room, and Reese was still asleep. Crumpled up tissues were surrounding her, and I saw her cell phone beside her. It was turned off. I only prayed she did not listen to my frantic voicemails. I pocketed her phone to wipe it clean and leave no trace of those messages.

She looked so tired but always beautiful. Her eyes were red and puffy, probably from crying. I did not want to wake her, but I needed to touch her and feel her against me. I kicked off my shoes, climbed into the bed, and pulled her to me. She moved slightly with my touch, and then her hands covered mine.

"I'm sorry, Walker. I'm so sorry," she whispered.

The sound of her voice cracking through her tears nearly broke me. I turned her around and kissed her madly. I did not know what she would tell me, but I had to show her how much I loved her and that no matter what, I was not going anywhere.

"Reese, I love you. Please, talk to me. What was our deal? No more running. No secrets. No hiding. No matter how crazy I am, you vowed to never leave me and to love all parts of me. Baby, you had to know what running away again would do to me. Why? Why did you do it?" I begged, while more of her tears fell away.

"Walker, I'm a foolish woman, I know this, but not when it comes to loving you. I would cut off my arms for you. I would never do anything to cause you one second of hurt, but clearly my plan backfired because I did everything wrong. I should have told you the minute I found out my results, but then the baby got sick. You had come home so happy like you did every day. In addition, you tell me that you wanted more children. But I was barely holding it together. I could not let you see that there was anything wrong, so I hid it from you. I should have never left this morning without you knowing the truth. I was so scared of the unknown, and I made matters worse by behaving the way I did."

"Reese, can we please take a breath and just back up for a god-damn minute? You are not making any sense to me, because I am only hearing parts of this story. You mentioned results, so if that is the case, then you must have had tests done for something you still have not told me about. What is going on? Reese, tell me now!"

My arms around her tightened and my eyes flared with anger waiting for her to tell me what was wrong. Reese let out a deep sigh, and I took a few calming breaths of my own. She was not afraid of my ever-changing mood swings; she was the only one that could handle me. I tried with all my might not to lose it, but I was hanging on by a thread. I gently kissed Reese to show her I was ready to listen.

"Walker, do you remember about a month ago when I went in for a check-up with Rachel?"

"Yes, of course I do. You told me everything was fine, was it not?"

"At my appointment, she ordered a full panel that included urine and blood work, and I had a Pap test performed. It had been a couple of years since I had one done, and she felt it would be a good time to check. I have no medical history of anything pertaining to cancer, but I am over forty now and have to be proactive when it comes to matters like this. After all the tests were performed, Rachel called me back into her office and sat me down. They found something, Walker, and it was a complete surprise to me."

"What Reese? What did they find? You are scaring the hell out of me."

"I'm pregnant."

Two words I longed to hear again! *Is this a bad thing? How can it be? This is what I wanted, and now it is no longer a desire. It is very real and growing inside of the love of my life. Another child.*

"You are?" I said. "Oh my God! I cannot believe it. I have been dreaming about this moment for months now, and it is real. You are pregnant again! I am so happy. Are you?"

I suddenly pulled back from Reese, who just looked at me.

I asked her, "Do you not want another child?"

Oh my God, the thought of Reese not wanting this baby made my stomach hurt. No way would I ever allow her to terminate the pregnancy.

"Walker, please let me finish. Of course, I want more babies with you. How can you even ask me that?"

Oh, thank God. Forgive me, my love, for ever doubting you.

"We never really discussed it before, and then out of the blue last night, you come home and declare it. I was a bit taken aback and was still dealing with another issue. When Rachel told me the news, I was completely thrilled. Yes, there are complications for women my age, but I am in great shape and it would probably be an issue if I were not. I was prepared to pull out all the stops and tell you our amazing news, but then she phoned me later that night with an update. My test came back abnormal. The readings were high, and it showed I might have precancerous cells on my cervix. Rachel suggested I schedule a Colposcopy. It is a test to look for problem areas when a Pap test is abnormal. It's perfectly safe during pregnancy, but I still have to be careful."

Reese continued, "Rachel was concerned because of my history with miscarriages. When she was performing the procedure, she found some abnormal tissue and proceeded to do a biopsy. With me having cysts before, she did not want to take any chances. Right before you came home last night, Rachel had called to tell me the results were in, but she wanted to see me in person. I was so scared and overtired because I was tending to Fallon and making sure she was okay. I did not know how to broach the subject with you. I quickly called Freddy, and he took me to my appointment today. Please say something, Walker? Your silence is scaring me."

"My silence? Reese, I cannot even begin to process what I am hearing, and you still have not told me if you are okay or not. What about our child growing inside of you? Are you still pregnant?"

"I am, and as of right now, the baby and I are fine," she responded.

"Fine? You are fine. Well, that is fucking great, Reese! You should have told me the minute you found out you were pregnant, or the minute Rachel called to tell you something was wrong. Instead, you sate me with sex! You should have told me, Reese. I love you with all my heart and soul. Reese, we are supposed to be partners in all areas of our life together. Why would you keep this from me? And to destroy me even more, you confide in Freddy, who is not your fucking husband. I am!"

As I said this to her, I couldn't help but wonder: *Was I so blind with love, lust, desire, and constant need that I completely ignored any warning signs that something may be wrong with my wife?*

I continued, "The days of you keeping anything from me are over. They were over the minute you walked back into my life. Your actions back then were justified, and I understand you did what you had to do, as you swore you understood the choices I too had made, but this? Reese, we are so past that shit. We vowed every single day since we have been back together that we would not run…not ever. Nevertheless, you did, Reese, and you cannot use me as an excuse to why you did it. I will always be there for you, and we will face everything and anything life throws our way. Jackson's illness taught us that! Motherfucking Townsend showed us that! We will survive anything together, but you damn well have to trust me!"

I was shouting as my heart was breaking with all of Reese's revelations. I knew I had to calm down, but she sat there saying nothing, allowing me to vent.

"Reese, after what Jackson kept from me, how could you repeat that same mistake? You of all people knew what that did to me."

She finally responded, "I was scared! That is the truth. I may have not been there when Elizabeth died, but I know what losing her did to you. When I found out that I was going to have another baby—your child, Walker—I was on cloud nine. But then I was faced with something I couldn't possibly be prepared for, and it stopped me where I stood and scared me. We have a child who's not even a one-year-old yet. I have another child beginning her life as an adult with an amazing future to look forward to, living on the other side of the country with the love of her life. Then I am told I am pregnant and may have cancer on top of it? I know I hurt *you*, but can you just step away from your anger for one fucking second and put yourself in my shoes? How do you think *I* feel, knowing that something could happen to me and worrying about where that will leave you? Or our kids? And this new miracle that I'm carrying?"

Ouch. Shot through my heart. I could not speak. I felt like my heart was going to burst. I had more emotions going through me than I knew what to do with. All I could do was hold her and cry with her. It would have destroyed me if I lost Reese. I didn't know if I could survive it. I continued to hold her as she held me. Her nails were clawing into my back as she cried out all of the fears she was bravely trying to keep from me.

"I'm so sorry, Reese. Please forgive me. Please, baby, I need you to forgive me."

She paused and pulled back to look at me. She said, "I will…if you forgive me."

"There's nothing to forgive."

"Yes there is, Walker, and I need to hear the words from you. I need to know that we are okay. I love you so much and I know I should have trusted you enough to tell you the truth, but I let my fear guide me instead of trusting my heart that all would be okay."

"*Is* it okay, Reese? What happens now?" I asked.

"The results showed no infection, and the compromised tissues were remnants of a past cyst that left some scarred tissue behind. I will have to be closely monitored throughout the pregnancy and follow up with more tests about six months after the birth. The risks are small, and as long as I follow the doctor's orders, there's no reason to believe that I won't have a healthy pregnancy."

"You're really okay?"

"I swear it, Walker, I'm okay. Our baby is safe and growing inside of me as he or she should."

"I love you so much, Reese. I will never stop telling or showing you. I never thought you could make me happier than I am right at this moment. You have made all my dreams come true. You have made my dark soul shine brightly with sun radiating through it. I am so sorry I mistrusted you. My mind drifted back to dark places that I never ever want to revisit. Promise me right now that you will never put me or us through this again? You must always talk to me, Reese. I'm your husband. I know I can be crazy, but you know it comes from the deepest depths of my soul for the love I have for you. You promised me once, please promise me again?"

"I promise, Walker, I promise. I will not keep anything from you. I love you," she said.

"I love you more...so much more."

I held her in my arms, I let my tears fall, and then a thought hit me like a freight truck running me over. My anxiety and the combination of no food, no sleep, and too much scotch were getting the better of me.

"Reese, I was so rough with you yesterday. How could you let me make love to you the way I did? Are you okay? Should we abstain from sex until after the baby is born?"

"Walker, I'm not made out of glass, and you weren't rough. You were being you, and I loved every part of it. I am fine. It is safe to have an active sex life while pregnant...maybe we can tone it down a little, but we do not have to completely stop. I will be the first to tell you if I cannot handle something. I swear I will tell you, okay?"

"Okay," I said to her.

With Reese, it was literally impossible to keep my hands off her, and now that she was pregnant again, I saw many cold showers in my future. I didn't care what she said; I would not put her or the baby at risk.

My anxiety level was still extremely high. My natural instinct would be to just tear her clothes off and have my way with her, but I knew I was still too raw for that. I had to discipline myself and find my center of control.

"Let's go home," I told her. "I want you in our home, our bed, and in my arms. I need to just hold you and feel you breathing against me."

"Let's go home," she agreed with no argument.

I picked Reese up, carried her through Freddy's home, and out to my waiting car. Freddy just waved from the window. He knew me too well and was smart enough to know not to challenge me any further than he already did.

Fallon slept throughout the entire car ride home. I put Reese to bed, and then tended to our daughter. I fed and bathed her, and then read three stories to her before tucking her in for the night. Today was a complete blur, one I wished to forget.

"I love you, sweet girl. You dream of beautiful things tonight, my princess. I will see you in the morning."

I kissed Fallon once more and then quietly closed the door behind me. Reese was waiting when I returned to our bedroom. She had finished her soup and said she was full. I could tell she wanted to talk some more, but I was mentally exhausted and could take no more for today. I silenced her with kisses and settled us into our bed for what I hoped would be a restful sleep, but not before whispering to her, "We will always find our way."

She silently smiled and found her spot on my chest and remained there for the rest of the night. All I could do was watch her when I knew she was down. My mind replayed the events of today, and my heart ached from all of today's ups and downs.

Reese was back in my arms, but my worry was still the size of Texas. Before I wished on my falling star last night, I was already blessed with a miracle. Reese was pregnant again and carrying our growing child in her belly. I had missed sight of that. There is nothing sexier than knowing that the woman you love is carrying your child…a child made from pure love for the other, and now another blessing for our family.

Sometimes I sounded like a pathetic fool, a dreamer from another time, but I could not help myself when it came to Reese. My feelings for her hadn't changed since the first moment I laid eyes on her in our college library all those years ago. She was my only love, The One. It took my father nearly destroying us to realize that the love I had for Reese would never just burn out and fade away. Our love had sustained over the course of time, even when we were separated and I didn't know if I would ever see her again. My feelings for Reese had evolved to a deeper level and eventually healed every bit of my broken soul when she came back into my life. These feelings still drove me forward throughout my life. And now that we had it all, we were faced with another testament to our love...a health scare.

She ran away today to not worry me, but that had the opposite effect. I was not going anywhere and neither was she. She knew I would move heaven and earth to make sure she and our unborn child were safe and well.

As I closed my eyes and held her closer, I silently prayed on my falling star. Just one more wish, please?

"We will always find our way. I promise you, Reese...always."

I kissed her and breathed my beauty in. And then finally, sleep beckoned me as well.

CHAPTER 5

Walker

Every day is a blessing

THE FOLLOWING DAYS were spent at home with Reese and our daughter. I cancelled everything on my calendar, throwing my office into complete chaos. Thankfully that lasted only five hot minutes, and then Jenny reined in my team and got everyone back to neutral, including me.

I had a very limited close circle I could confide in when things weighed heavily on my mind. I was very lucky to have Jenny as an amazing assistant and blessed to also call her a friend. She reminded me of Reese's grandmother, Lila, but a younger version.

Without going into detail of my absence, I simply instructed Jenny that she would run the office and I would filter everything through Donovan and Tom. Stephen would also be at the helm, keeping everyone in his or her rightful place.

The morning after was a bit emotional for Reese. She was embarrassed at what Priscilla may have thought of her, but I put that to rest very quickly. Priscilla was a trusted member of our staff. She did not have a harsh word in her vocabulary, and if she did, I would dismiss her at once. This was Reese going through her stages of guilt. As much as I assured her that we were okay, seeing my empty scotch bottle in the trash did not put her fears at ease. I swore on my life that I would never drink that poison again. I prayed she believed me.

Although I wanted to surprise Reese with the perfect Christmas, she also needed to be cheered up right away. I had gone into my study to prepare for our holiday celebrations. Lila and Thomas would not be able to join us for the holiday, but they assured me they would be here for Fallon's first birthday. My mother would also miss Christmas. She was on a six-week trip around Europe with friends she met last year while on holiday in France. I suspected that one of those friends was male, but I kept that suspicion to myself until she was ready to tell me. She would always love my father, but she was the one that was still alive and I wanted her happy. It was a welcomed sight to see. Smiles looked amazing on my beautiful mother.

Now it was time to make Reese smile again. She had been experiencing morning sickness again, but not too bad. I opened up my Mac laptop to find seven emails from no other than Rosalyn Davenport Baker. I phoned her immediately and tried with great effort to hold my tongue. She was the best, and I needed her to pull off the party of the year for the special women in my life.

"Ms. Baker, Walker Reed here."

"Good Morning, Mr. Reed, I hope you are not too upset over the correspondence I sent you. I wanted to give you an array of choices for the holiday and birthday themes."

"I'm not upset, Ms. Baker. On the contrary, I am very pleased with what you have in mind. My only request is that your team be very respectful of my grounds. The meadow is very special to my wife, especially the area that surrounds the gazebo. You may decorate the structure with exterior lights, but be mindful of the flowers and plants that surround it."

"Mr. Reed, I can assure you I oversee every last detail of each and every event I plan, as you should well remember from your wedding."

"I do, Ms. Baker, but there is nothing wrong with reminding. Now, tell me more about this theme you have in mind."

"The winter wonderland will include an ice rink for skating. The surrounding area will be snow-covered. All the trees will be lined with twinkling lights. The carousel will be set up in the play area, and I would like to have a baby gym playground geared for any children that are crawling to nearing the age of one and older. It will rather be like a Gymboree baby class meets winter town. I've done it before on a more personal level for my family, but all the children seemed to have a great time," she said.

"I approve of your plans, Ms. Baker. You have a direction. I would like this project to be completed by December 18. Our grown children will be arriving that weekend, and I would like the festivities to begin the week of Christmas. In your email, you will find an added request for the 23rd. It is my wife's birthday, and I want to do something special just for her without including it with the holiday festivities. Birthdays should always be celebrated, and my wife's birthday is one of the best days on my calendar. The closing celebration will be with the tree lighting on the 24th. Are we clear on everything?"

"Yes, sir. I will be in touch."

"I'm sure you will be," I said as I ended the call. Surprisingly it was not too torturous for me.

Rosalyn and her over the top persona had grown on me. She was truly worth every dollar that I paid her. With all I was planning for Fallon's birthday, holiday celebrations, and with Reese's health scare, my heart sank when I looked at my calendar and saw the 23rd circled with a red heart. Once my brain reconnected with the circled event, I knew what I wanted to make this year's birthday the very best for her. *Wait until Ms. Baker reads my email. If she pulls this off, she will get the biggest bonus she could ever dream of receiving.*

After my fury had passed with Freddy, I phoned him to give him an update on Reese. He was thankful for the call, and I thanked him for his continued love and support he had for Reese and me. I knew that committing to Reese would also mean accepting her friendship with Freddy. I was human and insanely jealous at times, but I vowed never to get between her friendship with Freddy. She needed him, he was there, and then ultimately he was there for the both of us. I could not ask for a better friend than Freddy, and he was a wonderful uncle to Fallon, as well as a terrific husband to Fabrizio. My little princess had the best wardrobe in all of Beverly Hills, thanks to her fashion designer uncle. I laughed because every time he would visit, he always had a box or two in hand. Fabrizio promised to make sure our daughter was fluent in Italian. He loved to speak to Reese in his native tongue, which only infuriated me because I only partially understood what they are saying. They had fun at my expense, as I expected my Fallon would eventually too, unless I learned with her.

Reese was breathtakingly beautiful, and after she had Fallon, Mac wanted her to model with our daughter, but that was one thing I would never concede on. I was too high profile to publicly put my daughter out on display and risk her safety. He knew never to ask me again, but I did okay a private photo shoot at our home, where the mother and daughter photos are now prominently displayed. They melt my heart every time I walk past them. Every month of her life has been captured, leading up to her first birthday. I was so excited to ring in another amazing New Year and celebrate our daughter's special day.

Holed up in my office for practically the entire day got many tasks accomplished, but I needed to complete one more thing…call my son and confirm his itinerary. The last time I had spoken to him, he was very excited to be coming home. He and Riley were growing into their New York lifestyle. However, their plan of moving into an apartment with friends fell through when the bachelors of their circle—or what Riley called them: "man whores"—decided to settle down with girlfriends, causing their spacious living quarters to be too cramped for my son. Despite how I felt, he originally decided not to live in my apartment in New York when they first went out to the East coast. But now that things were different, he broached the subject with me carefully, and I did not give him the "I told you so" as my father always enjoyed giving to me. I conceded and supported him. In the end, I was happy they were living in my apartment, always under the watchful eye of my security team with Richard leading the charge. What Jackson did not know would not hurt him, but it would put me at ease. With all we went through last year, I needed to always know my son was safe. It was not just about him anymore; he had Riley to care for too.

I checked the time and knew Friday's was Jackson's early class day. I was just about to hang up when he answered on the last ring.

"Hey, dad," he said in a breathless tone.

"Hey back. Why are you out of breath? Wait, don't answer that."

He laughed at my attempt to be funny.

"Get your mind out of the gutter, pop. I was just coming in from my run."

"How many miles did you get in?" I asked.

"Almost 6, but it's really getting cold out and the wind was whipping at my face. I'm sitting in front of the fireplace now, and the feeling is slowly returning to my nose and cheeks."

"Jackson, I hope you are not pushing yourself too much. I am all for exercise, but do not go overboard. How was your check-up with Liam?"

"Don't you know? I would have thought you still get reports on me," Jackson said a bit sarcastically, but probably warranted with how I still monitored him.

"For the record, I have not spoken to Liam, nor received any reports. You are a grown man now, and I trust you to take care of yourself."

"Is that so? Is this why an unmarked car was on my trail

throughout Central Park? Way to go on trusting me, dad."

"Jackson, securing your safety is entirely different than medical records. Our family is high profile, and I do have enemies. I will not hesitate in protecting what I safeguard, so please try to cooperate and understand why this is necessary."

"Okay, dad, I'm sorry I snapped at you. It's not you who I'm angry with these days."

"What's wrong, Jackson? You know you can tell me anything."

"I do, but it involves Riley and school. I'm really not ready to discuss anything right now, but I promise I will once I have some time with you over the holiday break."

"Fair enough, son. I look forward to seeing you and Riley under this roof again. The house is not the same without you. We miss you terribly, but you already know that."

"I know, dad. This is me agreeing. Can we leave it at that?" he said.

"Yes."

"Thank you, dad, I love you."

"I love you more. I'll send the plane for you and Riley, and we'll see you both on the 18th of December."

The phone was silent on the other end.

"Jackson, are you still there?"

"I'll see you then, dad. I have to run."

And just like that, our call ended. I wanted to call him back and find the underlying cause of what was troubling my son, but this was me giving him room to be an adult and handle things on his own. I hated it, but I vowed to allow him to live his life on his own terms. Knowing all this, though, did not stop me from placing a call to Richard. He worked for me, and it would not be out of the norm to status with an employee of mine.

I phoned him with all intents and purpose to receive a status, but he surprised me with information I did not see coming. He had told me that Riley had not been back to the apartment in three days. The thought of Jackson and Riley having problems raised alarms with me on a completely new level. I also wondered if Reese was aware of anything and chose not to tell me. This would not be her keeping things from me per sé, but if it involved Jackson, then it involved me.

After Richard disclosed everything he knew about Riley and Jackson, I had more questions than answers. For the most part, he explained that before all this, they were having no issues that were visible to Richard, or anyone else in the building. Jackson and Riley both maintained a very busy class schedule, which left little time for anything else. They each took online courses while Jackson recovered, and then took more throughout the summer. They were both eager to begin their careers and passionately pursue their dreams in the film industry.

The only thing was that I was not sure if Jackson wanted that anymore. He did not have the same light in his eyes when I would ask. He always shrugged it off anytime I questioned him about it and blamed it on long studying hours, another soul in my life that kept closed off and in the name of sparing my feelings. It seems like they all knew how I would react and take control over any situation I was faced with, but it only came from my love for them.

When I was married to Elizabeth that was only for a short time, and I had to take on fatherhood all on my own. But now I was married to Reese. She was my guide throughout the life we shared. She was amazing and now not only has blessed me with our daughter, but maybe even a son. Seeing her pregnant with my child was an experience I truly could not articulate into words. Every day I would just show them how much I loved them. As a father, I could only hope that when he was ready, Jackson would share with me what was bothering him. I had come a long way in the listening department, another thank you to Reese for showing me the way to do that.

"Is that really the time?" I said aloud.

Reese was smiling in the doorway holding Fallon in her arms.

She said, "Yes it is, and you nearly missed dinner. Care to join your daughter and me? Or do we eat alone?"

She rocked our daughter on her hips as Fallon bounced and let out happy sounds.

"Absolutely! I am sorry, love, but time just got away from me today. Forgive me?"

"Stop it, Walker. No need to apologize. I was just teasing you."

"I'm serious, baby. If you ever feel neglected by me at all, you need to scold and punish me…fiercely."

I enunciated the last word very slowly for Reese to catch my meaning. Oh, she knew and smiled as we joined hands and walked to the dining room.

Reese handed me Fallon while she checked with Priscilla about dinner. I placed the baby in her high chair, and she drummed her little hands on the tray. I could not help but to laugh at her thousand expressions. She smiled, laughed, pouted, and then her eyes would brighten, all at the same time. God! This little baby could bring me to my knees. She was amazing in every sense of the word, and I could not even begin to express how grateful I was to Reese for giving me a second chance at fatherhood.

"Penny for your thoughts?" Reese asked as she watched me stare at Fallon.

"Just a penny? I may need a hell of lot more than that. How did I get so lucky?"

"It wasn't luck, Walker. It was fate doing the work for us and making us whole again. You are not the only one that feels this way. I say my thanks to God every night for the life he has given me with you. I do not ever want to think about the past and how much we lost. I need to live for today, tomorrow, and for the rest of my life…with you. Time is so precious and you never know what it will challenge you with from one day to the next. We have zero control over it, and I will not waste a minute trying to figure it out. I just want to live it, and live it with you."

"Hey, where is this all coming from? Are you okay?" I questioned.

"Walker, that's just it. Of course I am okay, I am better than okay. I am just telling you how I feel. This is what you want, right? For me to be an open book and share everything with you? This is me being an open book. Never doubt my feelings for you. I love you with everything I have. I swear I will never keep one more secret from you. When I was faced with the cancer scare and now this new pregnancy, I just checked out for a minute and could not breathe. Confiding to Freddy was not a slap in your face nor was it me going back on my promises. I was just not ready to see the look in your eyes and feel the fear behind them when you held me. Do you understand?"

I responded, "Yes. I swear I do, baby and if you are worried that I am angry, please rest assured that I am not. I will not lie and tell you that I was not out of my mind when you left, but I got past all of it the minute I saw you. I am so sorry for making you worry about my reaction. We both made mistakes, but at the end of the day—this day—you are fine. My beautiful wife is healthy and carrying our child. I love you."

I took Reese in my arms and felt her tremble beneath my touch. Tears fell from her eyes, and I quickly wiped them away, kissing every inch of her face.

"No more tears, baby," I told her. "We are fine. Our family is fine. I love you."

With that, Fallon slammed her arms on the tray, looked at us, and said, "Dada. Dada. Hmm, ma, ma, ma."

And in an instant, all was righted in our world. Our daughter made it that way. I guess she was feeling left out of the conversation.

"And that, my love, is Fallon telling us to chill out. Don't you agree?" I asked.

"I do. Let's eat. I'm starving."

"Me too. We will have dessert later in our room," I whispered.

"Counting on that, Walker," Reese said with a wink.

She kissed me on my cheek and began feeding Fallon as Priscilla entered with our entrees. My heart was bursting with love for my girls. What a way to begin the New Year. I could so easily fast forward to the summer when Reese would be having our baby.

I would spend the rest of the weekend enjoying our private time together but also looked forward to going back to the office to begin the surprise for Reese. I debated on telling her some of it, but ultimately chose not to. She loved surprises, and for what Rosalyn had envisioned, there were no doubts here, as Reese would love what we had planned for her.

We ate our dinner and listened to our daughter make all of her baby sounds. It was almost time to ready her for bed and read her a story. Tonight was my night to choose, and I picked the perfect one to make Fallon smile. It was a story I had been telling her since she was nestled safely inside of Reese's belly. It was our story…the story of our life.

Fallon babbled and wiggled as I changed her into pajamas. She was happy and smiling throughout our time together. Reese kissed Fallon good night and gave me my time with her. After I covered her with a blanket and placed her bear beside her, she was ready for her story.

I pulled up a chair and spoke softly about meeting Reese for the first time. Every time I mentioned her mother's name, her eyes would sparkle. I guess she got it from me, because my eyes did the same thing. She listened intently until her eyes began to close. A few more sighs and our little princess was down for the night.

I kissed her little hand and watched her for a few more minutes before joining Reese. Before leaving each evening, I would always end our stories the same way.

"…And they all lived…happily forever after."

How true those three words were.

CHAPTER 6

Walker

Countdown to Christmas

IT WAS MONDAY again, and I was ready to head into the office but wanted to check in on Reese one more time before leaving for the day. Fallon was already fed and changed by me, and Priscilla was under my strict instructions not to disturb my wife. When I finally went to bed last night, Reese was asleep but awakened when my hard erection pressed against her backside. She pushed against it, telling me that she wanted me as much as I wanted her.

I was battling against my physical attraction to her and my emotional one. I loved her beyond reason and craved her touch when we were apart. I let out an angered growl and pulled back, but Reese turned to face me and kissed me, once more igniting the pent up desire I was feeling for her.

"We shouldn't, baby. You need to rest," I told her.

"I won't break, Walker. We've been here once before, and I will tell you now what I told you then: I am stronger than you think and will not break. I am fully aware of my limitations and how far I can push my body. Making love to my husband is not one of the physical acts I need to refrain from. Therefore, my love, stop pulling away and come toward me. I need you. You need me. Please, Walker, don't make me beg for something we both want."

She clearly stated what she wanted, something I always encouraged her to do. I said nothing, but showed her instead. I pulled Reese on top of me, and she perfectly straddled my body and took what was hers...me. Grasping my hands, she rhythmically rose up and down on me until my eyes were rolling to the back of my head. I was so turned on and wanted to fucking scream her name, but I bit my lip so hard, I swore I tasted copper in my mouth. My Aphrodite bit it too, and I was so close to the edge of my orgasm, I knew I only had seconds to go before I would explode inside of Reese. She let go of my hands, and I sat up to wrap my arms around her waist. Looking into her eyes, her lusty eyes stared back at me.

"I love you, Walker Reed. I will love you forever. Come with me...now," she whispered.

The intensity between Reese and me was like a volcano erupting. She bit down on my shoulder as she rode out her orgasm, and then collapsed on top of me. When she did not move, I was almost alarmed, but then she turned, looked into my eyes, and smiled. She said she wanted to stay connected with me for as long as possible; didn't she know we would always be like this? We shared something undeniable between us. I never questioned us, and neither should Reese.

She peacefully fell asleep as I cleaned us both. I was exhausted but could not close my eyes. I needed to watch her, feel her pulse, and place my hand over heart to feel the steady beats coming from under her skin. This was beyond the realm of possessiveness, but when it came to Reese, I knew no other way. We had come so far with each other from the moment we reunited until now. I could not even begin to think what my life would mean now if I lost her. I didn't believe I would survive a loss like that again. After my son was saved, I put all of my trust in God's hands. He saved Jackson, he saved my wife and child from Henry Townsend—the devil him-self—and now I would throw myself at his mercy again. I would do anything for Reese and our children. She knew this with every fiber in her soul. She doubted that fact and once again chose to keep se-crets from me. We were okay, I was not lying when I told her that, but I was still left with an uneasy feeling.

I wanted to trust her. I needed to believe when she said she was okay that she was truly telling me the truth. I found myself battling old insecurities, and when this occurred, my need to take over came to the surface and I was unstoppable. No matter how I reacted when I discovered she had left, I had to look beyond it, because I loved her so much. Our family was worth fighting for. We chased the dream every day and lived the reality wrapped up in each other's arms at night.

Reese was so still in bed, I feared she was feigning sleep to avoid talking to me, but I could not wait to find out. Looking down to my watch, if I did not leave now, I would miss my first morning meeting and then the shit would really hit the fan with my team. Jen-ny had stayed on top of everything I assigned, but it was time for me to return and get everyone on track. I simply kissed Reese on the forehead and made my way to my waiting car.

"Good morning, Mr. Reed," I heard as I stepped off the elevator to greet Jenny, who was waiting for me with coffee in hand.

"Hello, Jenny, and good morning to you as well. Is Donovan here yet?"

"He is waiting for you in your office. He's with Tom, going over the latest financials of the company you are thinking about ac-quiring. Can I bring you anything before you get started?"

"I'm fine," I said, "but please put through any personal calls. And I need you to schedule a meeting with Dr. Lemay for some time today."

Jenny looked at me with raised eyebrows and was gearing up to ask me questions, but I saw the hesitation in her eyes. She simply agreed and turned to walk back to her desk.

I entered my office to hear Donovan and Tom arguing over the pros and cons of taking over Sandoval IT Group. The company had far reached its founding partners' expectations, but in the ever-changing times of technology, it had gone stagnant and needed to be revitalized. I loved to throw new deals toward Donovan and Tom and then sit back to watch their creativity come to life. They were both extremely good at what they did, competitive and driven with the intent and purpose to claim victory and present it to me on a silver platter. We all shared that glory when the Reinhart Building was complete. It was our crowning achievement, and I was happy to share it with my team. Reed Global was built on solid ground. I vowed to change the way we did our business when I took over as CEO from my father.

"Please don't stop arguing on my account," I said as I closed the door behind me.

Donovan and Tom both stopped talking until I gave the okay to carry on.

"Good morning, Walker, and welcome back," Donovan was first to rise and shake my hand.

Tom, always the reserved one, remained in his seat but said a quiet hello. He was a man of few words but flawless with his work.

"Okay, team, where are we?"

Four hours and several meetings later, I was eyeing the door to make my exit, but knew I still had a full day ahead of me. I had not heard from Reese yet, but that did not stop me from calling the house to check in with Priscilla. I was going crazy, sitting here with all sorts of scenarios running through my mind, but Priscilla was on top of it at home and assured me they were fine. She told me that Reese had come down to get the baby and bring her back upstairs. Reese had retreated to our room and shut out the rest of the world. *Fuck!* I hated feeling this helpless when it came to my woman. I was expecting Dr. Lemay to arrive soon to give me an update on Reese's pregnancy. I had to know, and I knew I would not be satisfied until Rachel confirmed it.

I was so deep in thought that I did not hear Jenny enter my office or see her standing in front of my desk.

"Sir, are you okay?" she questioned as I sat there with my head in my hands.

"I'm not sure what I am Jenny, but thank you for asking."

I responded the best way I could, but Jenny knew me better and sat down, giving me the opportunity to go on. I was not in the mood to pour my heart out to my assistant today. I feared if I did that, I would not stop talking. I was never so open in all of my life; just the opposite, actually. But with Reese back in my life and all the happiness I had been blessed with, my heart was full, and I found myself doing things that a couple of years ago would never have been.

I was about to say something when my intercom buzzed and it was Catherine telling me that Dr. Lemay had arrived. Jenny excused herself to show Rachel in. Before she came in, I went into my private suite to splash some cool water on my face. I could not hide the worry from my face.

I stepped out to see Rachel walking around my office and admiring the artwork that had replaced the old antiques that used to be in here. Reese had chosen some prints from artists whose work was popular in the south.

"Hi, Rachel, thank you for coming by. Please have a seat."

I gestured to her to the sofa. I sat down to face her with my arm resting on the back of the sofa. We had become friends since she began treating Reese, and she delivered my precious daughter into the world, so I felt I did not need to be my usual in-your-face self. I needed a personal connection right now and assurance that my wife was okay.

"What's on your mind, Walker?" she asked, getting right to the point.

"I think you know, Rachel."

"Walker, you know I will not disclose your wife's personal medical file to you. You can try your strong arm tactics, but there is a thing called patient confidentiality and I will not break it, even for you," she stated.

"And to think we could have a friendly conversation about Reese, but you've decided to leave the friendliness out of it. How foolish of me to believe otherwise, Dr. Lemay."

Well, that went well. Here I was, trying to take things slow and on a calmer level, but the feisty Dr. Lemay hit me first with her attack of defiance, making me go in for the kill.

She said, "Walker, I..."

"No, Dr. Lemay, it's Mr. Reed to you, and if you want to keep the pleasantries out of this conversation, then I will get to why I asked you here. First, you do not need to preach to me about confidentiality. Having said that, there is always a way around that rule. I can gain access to just about anything I desire, but I wanted to simplify it by just asking you a few questions. Your refusal has only angered me and now makes me believe there is something I do not know. Care to share it with me before I find out on my own?"

"You are an impossible man!" she shouted.

"So I've been told."

"Mr. Reed, I do not care to argue or upset you, but Reese is my patient and I will not talk to you about her without her consent. You can threaten me all you want, but I will fight you at every turn and win because that is how much I care about my patients. If Mrs. Reed tells me it's okay, then I will give you the answers you seek."

"You surprise me, Dr. Lemay, not too many people challenge me and remain standing. Good for you. But your brave stance will not stop me from getting at what I want. I need to know that my wife is okay and our child she is carrying is healthy as well. Can you give me at least that? Are they what Reese has tried to make me believe...safe from this health scare? Please give me that much."

"Good day, Mr. Reed," she said, and she walked out of my office, leaving me more distressed than ever before.

Damn stubborn woman! The door slammed behind her as she exited my office, and I saw Jenny's shocked expression written all over her face. I walked back to my desk and felt more frustrated than ever, but deep down I knew I was not angry as I let the good doctor believe. This was just my overactive worried mind.

I trusted Reese, at least I wanted to with all of my heart, but this was before she ran. It was my heart that was conflicted with worry. To hear the word "cancer" nearly knocked the breath out from my lungs. I needed to believe in God, in Reese, and trust medical science too. I could not allow myself to ever doubt her. The truth was...I was scared. I was fearful and apprehensive of everything these days, especially when it came to Reese. I lost so much in the first half of my adult life that I could not bear to lose anything else. My wife. My kids. They were my entire world.

When I was growing up under the iron fist of Phillip Reed, his day-to-day focus was building his business, counting his millions, and waiting for me to take over for him as CEO of Reed Global. Well, I did. I changed the face of our company, and I still held out hope that one day my son, Jackson, would see the light and join me by my side. It was a dream, one I kept to myself because I knew my son's heart was focused elsewhere. But a father can dream.

For the rest of the day, it was business as usual. Hours later, I was just about spent, but I had one more meeting with Donovan.

"Where are we with the expansion for the Teller Building on Fifth?" I asked.

"New York has its perks," he smiled a bit too excitedly.

"And? What does that mean?" I asked him.

"Oh, boss, it means that your instincts were spot-on when you suggested this project. With all of Townsend's properties now ours, we will rule New York."

The mention of my former father-in-law's name—my biggest enemy—was not something I cared to take joy in.

"Donovan, curb your enthusiasm."

"Sorry, boss, I didn't mean to be insensitive," he responded.

"It's okay, business is business, and his company was ripe for the taking. He left everything he had to my son in his will, but Jackson refuses it, so it remains in a trust until he decides otherwise. As for the properties, you are right. New York is ours, and there won't be a building in a five-mile radius that won't have the name 'Reed' attached to it."

"Hell fucking yeah!" Donovan exclaimed as he pumped his fist into the air.

"And with that, I think that concludes our meeting."

"How about a drink?" he asked me.

"I'll pass. The only thing I want to do is go home to my beautiful wife and daughter. You know, Donovan; a wise woman once told me to get a life, and that is exactly what I did. You should think of something other than the confines of this building."

"Who said that...Jenny?" he asked.

"Yeah, Jenny, and I've been thanking her every day for that great advice. It was what led me back to Reese, and now look at what I have."

"I'm not there yet, and if and when I am, I will still crave the feeling I have right now. I love everything about what we do here. For now, it's enough."

"Very well," I said, escorting him out.

I flicked off the lights to my office, as I met Jenny at the door.

"Sir, you have a call," she told me.

"Jenny, I'm done for the night. Whoever it is can wait until to-morrow."

"It's Jackson," her tone shifted, and mine went to worry in a matter of five seconds.

I hurried back to my desk and took my son's call.

"Jackson, what's wrong?"

"Take a breath, dad, I'm okay."

"You just aged me ten years. What is going on? You don't sound like yourself."

"Dad, I haven't even said anything yet. How do you know how I sound?"

"What the hell, Jackson! Are we playing twenty questions? Or are you going to tell me what is going on?" My voice grew louder along with my apprehension.

"Dad, I want to come home."

Five words I longed to hear, but not this way.

"Jackson, talk to me. What's going on?" I questioned him again.

"Can I come home?" his voice was cracking, and my heart was breaking.

"You never have to ask. You always have a home here with me, but son, please talk to me? I will not ask again."

"Dad, I'm sorry. I don't mean to worry you. I just need to get out of this city for a while."

"Fine. I will send the plane for you, and you can be here by tomorrow. What about Riley? Will she be coming home as well? You two were not supposed to arrive until the 18th. I have so much planned for the holiday and the special occasions that will follow," I said.

"Plans change. I am sorry, dad. I cannot answer for Riley. I just know I need to get the fuck out of this city, and I mean tonight. I'm not waiting for the plane; I'll book the first flight out of La Guardia, and see you in a matter of hours."

"Jackson, no need to do that. I will charter a private jet for you. You can leave in an hour."

"Thank you, dad. I love you, and I'll see you soon," he said and then hung up.

"Jenny! Come in here, now!" I called out.

"Sir?"

"Call the charter service we use in New York, and book a jet to leave in one hour out of New York/La Guardia. Tell them they have one passenger: my son."

"Right away, sir."

I paced my office in frustration. What the hell was happening with my son and Riley back in New York? He gave me no indication they were having problems when we talked last. But now, he is flying back to California tonight. How am I going to explain this to Reese without upsetting her? I still had to broach the subject with her about my visit with Rachel today. Confidentiality, my ass! That woman was breathing fire toward me today, and I was sure she would fill Reese in on how much of an intrusive husband I was. *Good luck with that, Rachel. I am only willing to bend so much. I am still the beast that Reese married.*

I looked over to Jackson's picture on my desk looking so happy with his arms around Riley. I let out a deep sigh and closed my eyes that they were okay. As much as it thrilled me to no end that my son was coming home, it did not make me happy to know it was under these circumstances.

Jenny called out, "Sir, all has been arranged with the plane. Is there anything else I can do for you?"

"No thank you, Jenny. Go home."

"I will, sir, once I know you're okay."

"Am I that transparent?"

"No, you're a father, a concerned one, and Jackson is damn lucky to have you."

"Thank you, Jenny. Please go home. I'm right behind you."

I did not have a clue as to what was going on in Jackson's world, which was a first for me. I silently prayed for him and hoped he would find a resolution to whatever was bothering him.

CHAPTER 7

Walker

Another test

BY THE TIME I arrived home, I was beyond exhausted. From the minute I ended my meeting with Donovan, all I wanted to do was come home to Reese and our daughter, but due to the lateness of the hour, I had missed dinner and Fallon's bedtime. Reese was waiting for me in the entryway, of course.

"Hi, baby, come here," I said to her.

I opened up my arms for my angel to walk right into. I wrapped my arms around her and relished the fact that she was my home, and at the end of the day, this was all I needed. The tension I felt from Jackson's call slowly faded away.

"You are so late, I was getting worried," she whispered while I still held her close to me.

"I'm sorry, love. I should have called you sooner, but I was preoccupied."

A lame excuse, but it was the truth.

"Come, let me fix you some dinner, and you can tell me all about your day," she said.

I nodded and let Reese lead me to the dining room. I so wanted a scotch but I knew better, so I opened a bottle of my favorite Barolo. I poured myself a glass while Reese plated my dinner.

"It smells delicious. Is that country fried steak?" I asked.

"Yes, it is. Nana's recipe. I'm not sure how it will compare to hers, but I tried."

"Baby, I will love it, and I love you for making it for me, even though you were supposed to be resting today."

"I'm fine, the baby is fine, and cooking dinner for my husband is no hard task. And while we are on the subject of my health, can we not bully my obstetrician from now on?"

Fuck! Thank you, Dr. Lemay, for ratting me out to my wife.

"I didn't bully her," I said. "I simply asked her a few questions."

Yeah, I bullied her. My smile did not go unnoticed by Reese. She misses nothing.

"I love you," she said. "Eat your dinner. Drink your wine, and then we will have a talk. I'm going to check on the baby."

"Love you too!" I called out as my girl tended to our daughter.

It pleased me to no end how well Reese knew me. As worried as I was for Jackson, I still managed to smile when it came to my wife. Either I was transparent, or she had magical powers to be the beacon of my soul. I could not stop smiling as I ate the delicious dinner she had prepared for me. Moreover, no insult to Lila, but this was damn good.

Reese gave me a half hour to myself, which was more than enough time to eat and rid myself of my foul mood. Truth be told, I was better the minute I walked through the door, but she gave it to me anyway. She changed into one of my favorite silk nightgowns and robes that I loved to peel her out of, and I would soon.

"You must be exhausted. Let's go to bed," she said to me.

"I thought we were going to talk," I smiled at her.

"We are, Walker. Don't you know by now our best conversations are discussed in bed?"

Good girl. My girl.

"Lead the way," I said.

"So, my love, talk to me," she said as she began undoing my tie.

"Can we shower first? Then I want to make love and kiss every inch of your beautiful body. And not that I will ever have my fill of you, I will be satisfied just enough to go over my day with you."

"Fair enough. Take off your clothes. What will it be? Shower or bath?"

I replied, "Shower, that is if you're up for some hot, steamy wall sex?"

"Lead the way."

Our multi showerheads were massaging our bodies as the steam filled our bathroom. I lifted Reese in my arms as she wrapped her legs around my waist. I entered her slowly, gently, and took my wife up against the wall. She moaned out her pleasure as our tongues entwined with one another. I loved fucking her in here. We were like two perfectly in sync beings linked to the other.

"I'm so close, Walker. Please go faster, and don't stop."

"We'll get there, baby. I'm right there with you."

And moments later, I spilled my hot seed into Reese and remained there as she bit down onto my shoulder while she rode out her orgasm.

"I missed you today," she said as I dried her, and then myself.

"Come. Let me dry your hair," I said to her.

We sat on our bed and I combed Reese's long tresses. She loved when I did this for her. This was an intimate act we always shared, and it pleased me to no end to pleasure her. I massaged her shoulders as I applied lotion to her back. My dick came to life as I stroked my fingers up her spine, and Reese's reaction to my touch set me on fire for her. I made love to her again and worshipped her body with mine. Reese placed her cheek on my heart and listened to the fast drums of my heartbeat.

"I love you, Reese, so much."

"I know, and I love you. Are you ready to talk to me? Because my vagina needs a little rest."

I laughed aloud to the point of holding my stomach. Oh my goodness, I needed that. After I got my breathing under control, I kissed her forehead, and held her in my arms.

"I'm sorry I didn't call you to say I would be late, but something came up and I lost track. I won't be careless with your feelings again."

"I'm not angry with you; it's just not like you to not call."

"You're right, and I'm sorry. When I left the house this morning, I knew I was going to have a shitload of work to catch up on, but then my focus turned to you and our baby. Reese, you startled me with your 'scare,' and I should have been honest with you. Deep down, I know you're both fine, but it's unknown fear inside of me that makes me take my anxiety to the next level. I love you so much, this you know, and I am the happiest husband in the world. I love that you are pregnant again, and with my child growing inside of you. The feelings I feel are extraordinary, a high I never want to come down from, not ever."

"…but?" she said as she looked up into my worried eyes.

"But…I also know that we are not immune to outside harms, and that is what scares the hell out of me. Reese, it sometimes feels like we are being put through the paces again and again, and I don't know why that is. But I'm over it."

"Walker, I think it's normal to feel like this from time to time, especially for us. We have so many parts of our story that I would like to forget, but we cannot, and I am not sure I want to. It's what makes us who we are, and we are pretty incredible."

"Yes, we are. Thank you for reminding me, even though it still scares me. Does this emasculate me?" I winked.

"Yeah, right! You are one-hundred-percent alpha male and hot as hell. What was our deal? We love all parts of each other, right?"

"Right," I said as I kissed my love.

"By the way, I not only verbally gave consent, but also a written one to Rachel for you to be privy to my medical file and, if needed, to make all decisions on my behalf if I could not."

"Reese, I just assumed that was a given right afforded to me because I was your husband. Why do I get the feeling I am back there again in the dark?"

"You are not, I promise you. Dr. Lemay hesitating was my fault. She, just like Freddy, encouraged me to be up front with you from the beginning, but I kind of threatened her with a lawsuit if she betrayed my confidence."

"You did what?" I exclaimed, now sitting up and totally feeling blindsided by another revelation.

"I did, it was very Reed-like of me—or, let me say—ruthless."

"My God, woman! If you are referring to using scare tactics into getting what you wanted like my father always did, then you have succeeded, because Rachel did not cower down to me at all. As if I heard it all in my life, this one is a new low for you."

"I'm not going to do this with you, Walker, nor defend my reasons to why I chose to keep my health concerns to myself. You forgave me, did you not?"

"You know I have," I replied.

"Okay then, please let's move forward. I apologized to Dr. Lemay, and I'm happy she still wants me as a patient after the emotional stress I put her through."

"She is not a concern nor are her feelings. It's good to take people down a peg or two once in a while. Just promise me that you will never reference my father again in anything you do."

"I promise."

So much for avoiding talking about Dr. Lemay. I closed my eyes, removed the last ten minutes from my memory, and moved on to another subject that needed to be addressed.

"Have you talked to Riley lately?" I asked.

"Only through email. She has been so busy with exams and her film project that needed to be handed in before the holiday break.

Why? Have you?"

"I have not, but I have spoken with Jackson, and there is something you should know. He's on a plane as we speak, and coming here tonight."

"What? What about Riley? Is she accompanying him?"

Now I saw worry and anxiety in her eyes.

"No, she's not. He said he would explain it to me once he arrives, but I imagine he will be exhausted and our talk will have to wait until tomorrow. Stephen will meet him at the airport and bring him straight here."

"Walker, if Riley is not with Jackson, then that can only mean something is wrong between them, and as her mother, I should try to help her through it," she said, now out of my arms and reaching for her cell phone. "I'm calling Riley, and she better answer. I do not understand this. Why is Jackson flying here? And without my daughter?"

What could I say? I knew nothing, and I was just as curious as Reese was.

"Voicemail. She always picks up for me when I call, but it went straight to voicemail, which tells me that her phone is off. Should I call Richard?"

She looked at me as if she already knew I had a watchful eye on the kids via Richard.

She exclaimed, "Well? Should I call him? Do not be coy with me, Walker. You can't tell me that you didn't know their every move they made since the day they left."

She knew me too well.

I said to her, "Before I answer your questions, will you please come back to bed and calm down? Getting excited is not good for you or the baby."

I patted the now cold side of our bed, and her worried eyes softened as she got closer to me. I took her back into my protective embrace and kissed the top of her head.

I continued, "Richard does keep an eye out for both Jackson and

Riley, but not like you're thinking. I trust them completely, but having said that, he is a Reed and needs to be protected. I let my guard down once, and look at what happened. I will not make that mistake again, not ever. When Jackson marries and begins a family of his own, he too will take the necessary measures to protect what is his and what he values most in life."

"I know, and I appreciate how we are protected. You are our shield, and we love you for it."

"I love you too. I do not want you to worry about anything. The last thing you need is stress. We will talk in the morning with Jackson, and I'm sure what we are imagining is far worse than what he will tell us."

I kissed Reese and tucked her in under the duvet.

"I love you. Get some sleep and we will talk in the morning," I told her.

"What about you? You need rest too."

"I will be back soon. I want to check in on Fallon and read her a story."

"Walker, she's sleeping, and you'll wake her."

"I promise I will read quietly. I have not missed a bedtime story yet, and I will not start now. Go. To. Bed."

I kissed her quickly and made my way to the nursery. Our little girl was wrapped in her favorite blanket and holding her teddy bear. She looked at peace. Her lips curved up, and her eyes flickered. *What could she be dreaming about?*

I loved to watch her sleep, and it calmed me. Children always have a way of making the largest of problems seem so small. They are innocent and unaware of any ugliness in the world that can hurt them. As a parent, we strive to be better for them. This is what I vowed the minute I held Jackson in my arms. To love him forever. To protect him. To give him the best life I could. Now I made those same promises to our daughter, and will do the same for our baby on the way. I tried with great effort to tamper down any uneasy feelings about Jackson's visit.

He was a grown man, a point he never stopped reminding me of. As his father, I would listen and try my best to help him with whatever was upsetting him. I would also give him the room he needed to work it out on his own. I smiled a little because I knew what I just said sounded so much better in my head than what my actual reaction would be once he arrived.

I sighed deeply and returned to the matter at hand. I lovingly looked at my sleeping daughter. I read her a princess story, and then held her little hand in mine.

"Daddy loves you."

CHAPTER 8

Walker

Home again ... minus one

AFTER SPENDING SOME quiet moments with our daughter, I checked in on Reese, who was sound asleep. I leaned down to kiss her soft lips and quickly retreated before I lost what little control I had. It took all my strength not to climb into bed and wake her just to hear the sound of her voice. Being in that close proximity to my beautiful wife took my breath away. She would always say yes to me whenever my body beckoned for her. To be inside of her always was what I craved most. After all, I was a man hopelessly in love with his wife.

I closed our bedroom door and made my way to my office. I checked in with Stephen to check Jackson's flight status. He was in the air right now, and I should expect him home in the next couple of hours. I was too wound up to sleep even though I worked from the minute the sun rose. By all rights, I should be in a sleep coma by now, but knowing Jackson had a problem was just putting me on edge.

I looked through my emails and saw one from Rosalyn. I was beyond excited to put together a Christmas surprise for Reese, then a party for our daughter, but now it seemed like the furthest things from my mind. Christmas would be here soon, and if the past had taught me anything, it was to not take one day for granted. Seize the day and be thankful for the time you get to have with your loved ones.

Driving myself crazy was not going to help anyone, so I answered her back and told her that meeting this week in my office would be fine. I just wish I knew what was bothering my son. He did not give much away on the phone, and I doubt he would want to get into a heavy conversation when he finally did get here. Against my better judgment, I phoned Stephen, who answered on the first ring.

"Yes, Mr. Reed."

"Stephen, I'm going to retire for the evening. Will you please tell my son that I will see him first thing in the morning?"

"Of course, sir, as you wish. The winds are with us tonight, and he should arrive ahead of schedule."

"That's great to hear. If he should need me for any reason, please do not hesitate to wake me. Understood?"

"Understood, sir," Stephen replied in his usual efficient manner.

"Good night then."

Returning to our room as quietly as I could, I quickly changed into sleep pants and crawled in beside Reese, who immediately felt my presence and reached for me. I kissed the top of her head as I pulled her close to me.

"Good night, my love," I whispered.

She did not reply in return, but let out at a happy sigh, which in turn ignited my dick to tent in my pants. I willed myself back to calm and finally allowed my overactive mind to fall into sleep.

The next morning, my eyes felt heavy with a sand-like feeling to them. They stung as I tried to pry them open. I was still so tired, but sleeping in on any given day was not my norm. I turned over and tried not to stir too much to wake Reese. I grabbed my cell phone off the side table and saw only one message from Stephen around two a.m.

"Mr. Reed. Jackson has arrived safely in California, and we are on our way back to the estate."

I did a stretch when I heard a familiar voice coming from the baby monitor. It was Jackson talking to his sister. I powered down the device and made my way to the nursery. The door was ajar, so I stayed back to listen before making my entrance. I peeked in quickly before Fallon noticed me. I remained quiet and happily witnessed their reunion. I hated to intrude on his private moment, but curiosity got the better of me and I stayed out of sight.

Jackson had her on a blanket in the middle of the room. She was listening to his every word and smiling up at her big brother. This was the first time they had been together in nearly five months, but even after all that time, Fallon knew her big brother and was smiling from cheek to cheek having him home.

Jackson said, "You have gotten so big, princess. What is your mommy feeding you?"

Fallon gave Jackson the baby look of death. I had to cover my mouth because of nearly laughing aloud. Oh, she is definitely a Reed, and just may have my temper too. As if Jackson quickly figured that out too, he leaned down and kissed her head.

"Now, my beauty, don't give me that look. I am just teasing you. You are perfect. I can lift you in the air and get my work out in. Do you want to try? Let's wipe that drool off your face first. Come here, baby girl. 1, 2, 3, 4, 5 little toes on this foot! Oh, you are so cute!"

"Dada. Dada. Dada," Fallon sang out my name.

Did she sense my presence as easily as Reese did when I was near? It was usually the first thing I heard in the morning, but Jackson was getting treated to the sweet sounds coming from his baby sister.

"I know, princess, you want your daddy. I know how you feel, I need him too." *He needs me. Oh son, I'm here. All you have to do is talk to me.* "Why don't we let him sleep for a little while longer, and then we can wake him up? I cannot believe you are almost one. It feels like yesterday that I was holding you in my arms for the first time. I cannot believe I have a baby sister. I love you, sweet Fallon...so much. I wish I could just smile and drool through my day, but I cannot. I have some stuff going on, and I am not sure how to handle it, so what is the first thing I do? I come home to daddy to fix all my problems. But that's just it, Fallon, I am not sure it is a problem for me as much as it is for Riley."

To listen to Jackson and hear the distress in his voice bothered me, but I also knew this was Jackson working it out, or mentally preparing himself for the conversation he promised me.

"Dada. Dada. Dada."

"I know, baby girl, I know."

I watched Jackson lift and hug his sister a few more times before placing her back into her crib. He sat in the glider that was close to the crib and closed his eyes and sighed in deep frustration. I wanted to go to him, but I was already at fault for eavesdropping on their private moment. I made my way back to our bedroom and closed the door. Reese was beginning to wake, and I climbed back into bed with her.

She turned over and greeted me with a soft kiss to my lips. I returned the gesture and held her in my arms.

"Were you in the nursery?" she asked sleepily.

"I was, and so was Jackson. I woke before you and heard voices coming from the monitor, so I went to the nursery to see Jackson playing with Fallon."

"How cute. It's early though. She usually sleeps a little later than seven. I should go and feed her."

I quickly pulled Reese back and told her to wait.

"What is it?" she asked.

"Jackson is still in there with her, and I don't want to intrude on their time together. I shouldn't have listened for as long as I did, but I couldn't help myself."

She smiled and giggled with that delightful laugh of hers.

"And what is so funny?" I said.

"*You*, Walker, *you* couldn't help yourself? I am laughing because you always listen, and I do the same thing when you are alone with the baby. I love to watch you engage with our daughter."

"She is pretty awesome, but it's what Jackson said that alarms me. He definitely has something weighing heavily on his mind, and Riley is a part of it somehow. I heard him mention her name and needing me to help him."

"Why isn't she calling me? I am her mother, and if she has a problem, I would think she would have let me know by now. Every time we talk, she is always so happy and complains of nothing. School is great. Friends are great. She loves New York and her teachers."

"Yeah, that may be true, but what about Jackson…is he great?" I retorted.

"That remains to be seen. Now that I am thinking about it, his name did not come up in our last few and very quick conversations. Walker, we need to know what is going on with them. Maybe she has confided in Samuel. You know how close they are, now that they have rebuilt their relationship. I could put a call through to him today, and ask him."

Ugh! Just the mention of Samuel, her ex, never sat well with me. I knew I had no reason to ever be jealous, but I was, and probably always would be. He had too many unappreciated years with my woman when she could have been with me. What a fool he was to never see what he had, a precious diamond he took for granted. I hoped he had seen the error of his ways and would be a different man with Dr. Taylor. *WTF? Now I am actually thinking of Briggs and his love life.*

"Walker, seriously? Haven't we moved past this already?"

Reese smiled at me, almost laughing. She hugged me tighter while trying to stifle her giggles, a sound I would normally welcome, but not this morning when she so casually mentioned her ex's name. I played it cool, and talked right over her question.

"Earth to Walker, are you listening to me, baby?"

"Of course I am, love," I responded, kissing her passionately. "You said we need to figure out what is going on with the kids, and we will. I am going to call down to Priscilla and have her take care of Fallon while we shower and dress. Then we will join Jackson for breakfast and talk with him. Sound good?"

She smiled and remained quiet, giving me my moment to get through. I loved her so much for loving and accepting all of me.

"Are we going to tell him our news?" Reese asked me.

"I kind of wanted to wait until Christmas, if it's all the same to you. This way, we are all under the same roof as a family, and we can share the great news together."

"Okay, you're right. Remember the last time we did this? Riley nearly broke the sound barrier with her excitement."

"I do, and it was wonderful even during a stressful time. I want this time around to be different. I can't tell you how much I am looking forward to this holiday with all of our family together."

"All except Nana and granddaddy," Reese said with sadness written all over her face.

"I know, love, but you will see them soon, I promise."

I kissed her to put her at ease and did not want to spoil the surprise of their arrival for Fallon's first birthday. When Thomas and Lila returned home to Georgia after their extended visit with us and all we went through with Townsend, Thomas had undergone a few procedures for his heart. Reese wanted them to remain with us here in California, but they were adamant about returning home. Thomas received a pacemaker for his heart and was doing quite well. He had taken off twenty pounds with healthy eating and exercise. Occasionally, he would sneak a pastry from the shop, but Lila was always one-step ahead of him. She made his favorite treats with healthier oils and organic ingredients. She would laugh to herself about her sneaky plan to keep her husband on track with his diet.

Now with all the positive change in his health, his doctors had cleared Thomas for flying. Reese did not know this; it was part of the surprise I had planned for her. They had made plans with their friends for the holiday but assured us they would be here for New Year's and their great granddaughter's first birthday. I would send the jet to bring them and their precious pups for a long visit. I could not wait to see the look on Reese's face when they walked through the door.

For once, Reese and I actually just showered. She tried with her best efforts to sway me, but she knew I wanted to speak with Jackson.

"Raincheck, my love?" I asked Reese, as I kissed her neck and then continued to dry her off.

"Hmm, maybe."

"Yeah, I don't think so. We have no maybes in our life, just absolutes, and I will collect my raincheck later, I promise."

"I know, baby. You are a man of your word," she said with a wink.

"You better fucking believe it!" I said, picking her up and kissing her passionately. "Get dressed...now, or that rain check will be happening sooner than I promised it would."

Once we got downstairs, Priscilla was there to meet us.

"Good morning, Mr. and Mrs. Reed, breakfast will be ready in five minutes. I am a little behind schedule this morning due to this little princess here. How does one get anything done when this beautiful girl is in your presence?" Priscilla asked, as I wondered the same thing.

I simply smiled at Priscilla's kind remarks about Fallon. She was truly our princess.

"Come here to mama," Reese said, opening up her arms for our daughter, but Fallon only had eyes for me, which made me feel like king of the mountain.

"Dada. Dada," she said as she pounded onto her tray, sending cheerios down to the floor.

My heart was bursting, but Reese's eyes were glazed over with unshed tears. *Never mess with a pregnant woman!* I remember this all too well.

I unfastened the baby's seatbelt and lifted her up into my arms. Her little hands immediately went for my cheeks, and she slobbered all over them. I was in daddy heaven.

"Good morning, Fallon Ryann Reed! You are a sight for sore eyes. Daddy loves you so much, but do you know who loves you too?" Our daughter stared intently into my eyes. "Mommy wants love too. Can you give big kisses to mommy?"

Her brown eyes sparkled as she looked over my shoulder to see Reese making silly faces to make her smile.

"Mama. Mama."

Fallon squirmed in my arms to get to Reese, who was now giggling and hugging Fallon.

"Okay, little miss, I see the game you are playing. Working both sides, huh? You're lucky you are adorable."

Blown raspberries were now on my cheek again. I would take it all. Now that our tug of war was over, Reese and I sat at the table and waited for Jackson to return. While we were upstairs, he decided to go for a run.

"Do you plan on going into the office today?" Reese questioned.

"I am, love, sorry. You know I would stay home if I could, but I need to tie up some end of the year matters before the holiday begins."

"What about Jackson?" she asked.

"Did I hear my name?" Jackson made his appearance and went right for his little sister. "Good morning, baby sis. Did you miss me?" he asked as he kissed the top of her head. "I'd hug you too Reese, but I don't think you want to smell me right now."

"I'll take my chances, Jackson. Get over here. It has been too long since I've seen your face."

She hugged him with so much love as a mother would. I missed Elizabeth for him; something told me he needed her. I stood and waited my turn.

"Hey, dad."

Two words and probably the biggest hug I had ever received from my son.

"Welcome home, son. We are so happy you're here," Reese said as she smiled at Jackson, trying to keep her obvious worry to herself and not ask him about Riley until we had a chance to speak with him.

"Thanks, dad. Reese, I'm happy to be home too. I'm going to go upstairs and shower, and then if it's alright with you, dad, would you mind if I tagged along with you today at Reed Global?"

Did I hear right? My son actually wants to come to work with me today. Yes, of course! I was screaming in my head.

"That would be fine, Jackson. I'll be ready to leave in a half hour."

"Sounds good. I'll go get ready and be right down," he said as he kissed his little sister again, grabbed a croissant, and ran out as fast as he entered.

"What was that all about?" asked Reese.

"I'm not sure, but I promise I will find out. Something is going on, that's for sure, but before we worry, let me talk with him, okay?"

Reese replied, "Okay, but I'm still going to give Riley a call today. She has to know he's here, right?"

"I hope so."

That was all the assurance I could give Reese at the moment. I had been so wrapped up with our life here in California that I feared I may have missed some important stuff going on in my son's life. It was not easy letting go, but I did it for him because it allowed him to live his life outside of mine. His sudden arrival here made me wonder what was going on back in New York and with Riley.

When he was ready, Jackson came downstairs and asked, "Dad,

would you mind if we drove in on our own? I haven't driven in months and would like to take the R8 if you say yes? What do you say?"

His expression was reminiscent of all the times he would excitedly ask me for anything, and he knew all too well that I would say yes to most of his requests. His doctors had cleared him to drive, but living in the city, all he really needed was the rail system, or Richard.

"Okay, you can drive, but no grinding the gears and treating the road like a racetrack."

He laughed, but I could tell he was excited to get behind the wheel. We made our way down the long drive that would take us out of my estate, with Jackson shifting and opening up the engine and me praying we arrived to Reed Global in one piece.

"Easy, son, I want to see your sister grow up, and you marry the girl of your dreams."

With the mere mention of Riley, his joyful expression fell a bit, and he slowed the car, maintaining a controlled speed until we arrived at the office. An attendant met us at the entrance of my private garage and parked the car.

The elevator ride was met with awkward silence until we reached the executive floor. Jenny was at her desk and brightened up when she saw the boy. He immediately rounded her desk and scooped her up into his arms. She always had a soft spot for him, but we all did.

"Oh, Jackson, what a surprise! Your father didn't tell me you were coming home so soon."

I was relieved that Jenny played along. Obviously, she was the one who made the last minute arrangements but still happily smiled and acted shocked when she saw Jackson.

"That's because I surprised him."

What? Was that what my son was calling it these days? His arrival was more like an announcement. I was more determined than ever to find out what had been going on with him. I allowed them to catch up while I made my way into my office. I phoned Richard.

"Richard, I need an update on Riley. Do you have a location on her?"

"I do, sir. She is dining with her father in the student common area. He arrived about an hour ago, and he warmly greeted her."

"Was he alone?" I asked.

"No, sir, he wasn't. He was with Dr. Taylor, who had treated Jackson during his therapy."

"Yes, of course, I heard they took their professional relationship toward a more personal one."

"Yes, sir, I believe you are correct."

"Okay, I didn't call to hear about Briggs' love life. I want to know about Riley. Jackson is here with me in California when he should be in New York with his girl. Do you still have eyes on her?"

"I do. They are having coffee now," Richard answered.

"Okay, stay on them and call me when Riley returns home to the apartment. Once she does, I will phone her myself. Are we clear?"

"Yes. I will be in touch."

My call ended with Richard, but I still did not feel good about this. Did they break up? There was no way Jackson or Riley could keep that from us. It had to be something else. I was praying for anything else than what my mind was conjuring up right now.

My day powered on. While I took meeting after meeting, Jackson stayed in our media room. I just about skipped lunch until he excitedly barreled through my office while I was on an overseas call in England. My eyes gave my son a glaring look, and he mouthed, "Sorry."

I shook my head with the familiarity of this and quietly laughed to myself. He had such a zest for life and never had any issues expressing himself. His eyes seemed brighter than this morning, and he looked like he was on top of the world being here. I was left wondering if he was happy that he was back in California, or being here at Reed Global.

After my call, it was lunch with Jackson and having the conversation he had effectively been putting off all day. I received no word from Richard yet, so I could only assume Riley was still with her father. It was up to me to take on Jackson first. I gestured to him that I would be a few minutes to finish what I was working on, and then we could go. He left my office and closed the door behind him.

I was already done but did not tell him. I quickly called Reese. She indeed called Riley, but only got her voicemail. She tried several times, and to no avail. Her calls were not returned.

WTF? I called Jenny into my office.

"Yes, sir?" she asked, holding her tablet.

"Jenny, I'm done for the day. Please forward any necessary calls to Donovan and anything marked urgent, you may forward to my cell, but again I stress, urgent. Are we clear?" I asked as I grabbed my briefcase.

"Yes, sir. I will take care of everything here; you just take care of him. He needs you, sir."

These were words I had heard before, and after all this time, they still did not sit well with me. I looked over at Jackson and said, "Ready?"

He wrung his hands out, and he simply nodded.

CHAPTER
9

Walker

Talk to me

I HAD NEVER been in this position before where it was silent between us. Jackson was not saying a word as we left the parking garage. I feel it deep within my heart that he wanted to say it, no matter how hard it was, but I needed to lead him there. And the one place that I had hoped would break down his walls would be a visit to his mother's grave. It was not morbid as it sounded. Elizabeth's final resting spot was beautiful and very peaceful.

I could not bear to have Gail and Henry in the same place where their daughter, Elizabeth, was laid to rest. It would never be the same for me if I had done that, so Jackson decided to have them cremated and their ashes scattered on the grounds of their Arizona home. Jackson had fond memories of time spent there with his grandparents, and after all that happened, he could not go through any more pain.

"Why are we here?" Jackson looked up and seemed surprised.

"You know why?"

"No, I don't. I can't be here, dad. Please take me home."

"Home to where I raised you, or home to New York to be with Riley? Which is it, son?"

Clearly, I caught him off guard, but someone had to address the elephant in the room.

"Why are you doing this to me, dad? This is not where I want to be. Please let's go."

"If not here, then where, son? Talk to me, and tell me what is going on with you. As delighted as I am to have you home, something is not right, and we both know it begins with Riley. Stop torturing yourself, and me, and just talk. I may be able to help."

He wiped his eyes and stepped out of my car. I watched Jackson walk over to his mother's headstone and fall to his knees. He was crying and releasing all of his pent-up feelings. I gave him a few minutes before I stepped out to join him. I put my hand on his shoulder, and he covered it with his own.

"Look at me, dad. Here I am, crying like a little boy instead of behaving like the man you raised me to be. I am ashamed of myself. I challenged you so many times on how grown up I was and to let me go. I have been on my own for months now, and I have never felt more alone in all of my life. I certainly don't feel like I'm taking on the world; it's more like being buried under it."

I told my son, "First of all, you *are* everything I raised you to be and so much more. Jackson, I do not know anyone, including myself, who was more focused and knew what he wanted more than you. When I was your age, all I did was fight my father. I pushed him to every limit I could manage, until the day I met Reese, and my world became right. Look at all you've already been though in your young life. You have come out so much stronger for it."

He got up off his knees and turned to me.

"That's just it, dad. I am not strong...not anymore. I thought I was doing alright, but I was fooling myself into believing that I could return to the person I was before my AVM. Everything has changed."

"Jackson, talk to me. What the fuck are you telling me?" Now I was shouting and in all the places to have found my voice.

"Dad, I'm fine! Relax. I am perfectly healthy, you should know. You get all my medical reports from both Dr. O'Larien and Dr. Briggs."

"Wrong. Contrary to what you believe, I do not have access to your medical files. Not since you took control over your life and made it perfectly clear to me that you were an adult, a man on his own that was able to handle his own affairs. Do I want to have that control back? Of course I do. I would be lying if I told you otherwise, but you were right when you declared your independence. I love you, son. I will always protect you and give you anything you need, but we all have to stand on our own, and when you left for your trip with Riley, you did. I was saddened, but so very proud of you at the same time."

"Thank you, dad. I swear to you, I am fine. I'm sorry that I scared you, but I meant what I said: I am not the same. The plan I had to go to film school and be the next Spielberg is gone. I want more in my life, and I don't want to spend my time chasing the dream when I can be living another reality."

"What does that mean? I'm not following you, Jackson."

He took a deep breath, and then said it, something I never expected: "I want to move back to California and work side-by-side with you at Reed Global."

What the hell? Did I hear him right?

"Dad, say something. You are freaking me out. You look like you're going to be sick or something."

He was right about that. I felt like he just turned my world upside down with his announcement. Of all the times I had wished for Jackson to join me at Reed Global, and the fights we had over his school choices, now he tells me he wanted what I wanted him to have all along. *Yeah, son, I feel sick.*

I took my jacket off and loosened the tie that was suddenly feeling too tight around my neck, kind of like this conversation I was about to have with Jackson. I placed my suit jacket in the car and turned back to my son.

"Jackson, something is missing here. You just do not up and change your life at the drop of a hat. What don't I know? Tell me now, or the next call I make will be to Riley."

He turned his back to me and stared back down towards his mother's grave. His head was hanging low in defeat.

"Go right ahead, dad. I won't stop you, and she probably won't answer anyway. She's too wrapped up into her own shit right now to give a crap about me and my feelings."

I turned him around by his shoulders and held my stance for a moment. The light in his eyes has burned out. He looked lost, a look I was all too familiar with. We sat on the bench, and I asked him to explain.

"Start from the beginning, and do not leave anything out."

"It's pretty simple. We've grown apart, and I'm not sure we can get back what we had. Riley and I want different things, and she's made it perfectly clear that she has no intention of leaving NYU, or New York, not even for me."

As I listened to his explanation, the enthusiasm I thought I would feel upon hearing my son wanting to return to California should have made me feel good, but I felt far from it. I could not take joy in something I was wishing for at the expense of my son's happiness, and Riley's.

He went on, "The first few months were amazing. Brandon and Clay moved in, and we were this close-knit family. Then the play-boys of our group met girlfriends and decided to play house on their own, which was fine by me, but with the extra roommates, it was rather cramped. That is when I asked you if it would be okay to move back into the penthouse. Dad, that was hard for me to even ask because I thought you might have been pissed at me for giving up too easily on my own place. I did like it for a while, but as much as I love my friends, I love Riley more, and the frat life wasn't for me."

"Jackson, you know I would never throw your decision to move out back in your face. I would think you know me better than that," I said, trying hard to not show my hurt with my son's distrust.

He sidestepped what I said and continued, "Once we were settled back into the penthouse, I thought we were okay and back on track. I was not pretending to play house with Riley. I wanted us to be real, and be the couple we always were, but she slowly began to change. As she adapted more into the college life, I felt myself withdrawing from it and felt Riley was slipping away from me. Every time I would bring it up, she would deny it and change the subject. I saw Brandon and Clay when I could, and she quickly became friends with their girlfriends. Alice and Evette were great with the guys, but when they were with Riley on their own, something just felt off about it."

"What do you mean? As in not a positive influence on her?"

"I don't know, dad. They did the things girlfriends do, and Riley was experiencing life outside of our relationship. She was going out more and without me. It was as if she was the sorority girl that got excited during rush week, and all I wanted was to be on our own, like what we had before. Brandon and Clay, you met them dad, they're fucking crazy. Their girlfriends... even crazier. I wanted out, so that's why it was okay with me to move back to the penthouse, but I think in the end, Riley resented me for it."

"Jackson, she couldn't have changed that much in all of the six months you've been gone? Please tell me that she is not doing drugs."

"Of course not! She is behaving as a twenty-year-old should, and not one that wants to marry anytime soon. I love you, dad, for accepting my relationship with Riley and never once telling me that I was too young to want what you and Reese have. I just don't know if I will have my happily ever after with Riley, not after the way I left things."

"Which was?"

"It's a long story, dad, and once I begin telling you, I don't know how I will feel about Riley once I relive it. I'm not ready. Please give me a few days."

The pain was evident all over his face. Whatever happened back in New York had devastated my son. I could not push him. He came here on his own without me asking him. He needed me, so I would be ready when he wanted to tell me more.

"Can we go home now? I can't be here anymore," he asked.

"Okay."

What else could I say to Jackson? His heart was completely broken, and pieces of him were all over the place. I wanted to believe him, but something just did not fit. I knew more than ever that I needed to speak with Riley, and I just needed to figure out how to accomplish that feat without causing more trouble for them or damaging my relationship with my son.

I could not believe that Riley would not confide in Reese, especially when it came to Jackson. The insecurities were rearing their ugly head once again. Reese would not keep something so important from me, but then again, she kept her health scare from me, all in the name of not putting me through any pain.

Dammit! She and Jackson are completely the same. They kept their secrets even though they said they would not do it again. They believed it would be for my benefit, but really all it did was cause me more pain in the end.

Was Jackson doing this with Riley too? Was it fair to Riley to uproot her entire life? Now she had reached the point that she was happy, my son pulled the rug out from under her and changed her life once again. Riley never left his side throughout the entire ordeal with his AVM and the rehabilitation that followed. She put off college without hesitation all in the name of loving Jackson. Reed men could be selfish creatures of habit, and when we wanted something, we usually got it. However, with the sacrifices she had already made, Riley deserved the same opportunities that she put on hold.

They were young and should be experiencing everything life had to offer them now, and clearly, Riley was blossoming in college.

She was raised in a restricted environment with limited freedoms. It would only be natural for Riley to have excitement to live on her own and putting herself out there with new friendships. I was going to reserve judgment until I could speak with her face-to-face.

Secrets played a huge role in the ending of my relationship with Reese. No matter what the reasons were behind them, they hurt like hell and devastated us, forever changing our lives. To get her back was nothing short of a miracle. Reese and Jackson could not keep hiding things in the name of protecting us, because in the end, that would only hurt us more.

My feelings about all that he shared with me left me conflicted. I knew there was so much more than what he was saying. It was written all over his face. That was the one telltale my son inherited from his mother: they could not hide their emotion because they wore their hearts on their sleeve. His body language was telling me so as I watched his back stiffen, probably willing me not to ask anything more.

As I stood in front of Elizabeth's grave, my mind retreated back to that day in the hospital when Jackson initially concealed his condition from Riley and then made her swear not to tell me. By lying to me and asking her be silent, he placed her in a difficult situation. I would never forget the rage I felt when I overheard Riley talking to Reese when she thought no one was near.

I could not allow Jackson's problems with Riley to come between my relationship with Reese. I had to believe she did not know. She sure acted surprised enough when I told her Jackson was coming home. I trusted Reese completely. I would not travel down that dark road again. I loathed who I became when I allowed my mind to go there. I was just like *him*—my father—but sometimes worse. I said my goodbye to Elizabeth and drove us home.

Once we got there, I would give Jackson some time to relax and mull everything over while I talked with Reese to figure out how we were going to get the kids back on the right track. We had so much to look forward to in the coming weeks, and I would move heaven and earth to make all of Reese's, baby Fallon's, Jackson's, and Riley's dreams come true.

As I punched in the code to our gate, Jackson never took his eyes off me. Did he think I was happy about all he told me? My head was fucking spinning with all of these new revelations.

"Dad, are you okay?"

"Define 'okay.' How can I be okay, Jackson, when you drop all of this on my lap?"

Breathe, Walker, just take a freaking breath!

The wide wrought iron gate slowly opened, and I drove through until we reached the main house, where Stephen was waiting for me. I waved him off so I could take a minute to talk with Jackson.

This was not where I wanted to begin a conversation after agreeing that I would give him time, but he asked so I was more than willing to share my feelings. I shifted in my seat to look over to Jackson. His head was down and eyes were on the floor of my Audi R8.

"Jackson, look at me when I speak to you."

His eyes met mine, and I did everything I could not to take him into my arms. You never want your child to hurt over anything, but as I was reminded too often, he was a man now. I could not fix everything, as much as I wanted to believe that. Jackson needed to stand on his own. Here's lesson number one: I needed to be upfront and brutally honest, no matter how much it pained me to do so.

"For years, you have wanted film school, and you finally have all that you want. And now...poof! You change your mind and want to work with me at Reed Global. Jackson, that was my legacy handed down to me from my grandfather, father, and once upon a time, I may have dreamed it for you, but I know you don't want it, not like I did."

I went on, "I resented my father to hell for trying to control me and make me into the mogul you see here today, but in truth, I don't think I could have accomplished all that I have if it wasn't where my heart was leading me. I am a Reed, and this company runs through my veins. It never did for you. So to have you tell me suddenly that you do in fact want this, leads me to believe that there is so much more that I don't know."

I continued, "I'm not going to push you anymore tonight, but Jackson, make no mistake, I will find out everything. I always do. Think long and hard before you say anything else to me, because with everything already revealed, if you are leaving out vital parts that Reese and I need to know, then you will not like my reaction. As you are well aware, I demand honesty. I also know that whatever it is must be destroying you on the inside, so I will give you time. But please, do not make me wait too long to hear the rest."

He said nothing in return, which was fine by me.

CHAPTER 10

Walker

The words he did not say

AFTER THE SILENT car ride back home, my heart was craving noise. It did not matter if it was the clatter of pots and pans, or listening to my precious baby harmonize her words. I needed anything other than the silent treatment Jackson gave me after the truth I told him. I couldn't help myself, though. He dropped a bomb on me today with wanting to drop out of school and move back home. He pretty much told me it's over between him and Riley, and then he shut down. Did he know me at all? How was I supposed to let this go?

With Reese's health scare, and then finding out we were pregnant again, I should have been over the moon, but I was not. Very far from it. Our kids meant the world to us. Everything we did was in the name of family, and when one's happiness was threatened, I reacted, and sometimes not in the most positive way.

It wasn't the most positive conversation with my son, and I needed to calm and not react. If Reese was by my side, I probably would have been pulled back just because of the power her presence wielded over me. We had been through too much, and there was no reason why we shouldn't fight to put back together what was broken between Jackson and Riley.

After we walked in together, Jackson took the stairs up two at a time to his room and effectively won this round with me. I knew I said I would give him space, but I was so fucking angry with him at the same time. This was just an example of what happens when I gave up even the slightest bit of control. Somewhere deep inside of me, I knew he was not ready to take on New York on his own, or with Riley. Two young adults in a city of millions, and thousands of miles away from the people who loved them.

I would speak with Riley tonight after I checked-in with Reese and spent some time with Fallon. I said I would reserve judgment until I spoke with her and listened to her side of the story. It was the only way to be fair to Riley and to my son. Jackson brought this to our doorstep, so now I felt in all rights to find the underlying cause of it and to try to help them both anyway I could.

"Good evening, Mr. Reed. Dinner shall be served in ten minutes. I have prepared all of Jackson's favorites for tonight."

"Hello, Priscilla, that was very thoughtful of you, but I'm not sure Jackson is in the best of moods to eat right now."

"Leave it to me, sir. Once he smells the dessert, I'm sure he will be like a bull charging the crowd."

"Whatever works. Where is Mrs. Reed? She wasn't upstairs."

"Mrs. Reed is out on the grounds walking with Fallon," she said as I noticed frowning as she looked down to her watch.

"What is it?" I nervously questioned her.

"Mr. Reed, I've been so busy preparing dinner that I lost track of time. It has been more than an hour since I last saw Mrs. Reed. I would have thought she would have been back by now."

All my alarms were on alert. I needed to find Reese, and I mean now. I bolted through the back door and took the path that led to our meadow and gazebo. My eyes scanned the property; I did not see any signs of Reese or the baby.

Running in quick strides to the gazebo, it was empty. Where were they? I was beginning to panic, and then I heard Fallon crying. I followed the signs deeper into the rose garden, and there she was, secured in her carriage with Reese lying on the ground beside her.

"Reese!" I called out to her.

Once I reached them, I quickly checked Fallon, who had immediately stopped crying once she saw me. Then I tended to Reese.

"Reese, baby, wake up."

A minute felt like an hour, but then she stirred in my arms and opened up her beautiful eyes. They were bloodshot.

"Oh thank God! What happened, my love?" I begged for an answer as I swept her up into my arms.

She felt so light, too light for a woman pregnant with my child. Did she even eat enough?

"Walker, please put me down. I feel sick."

I did as she asked, and then Reese began expelling the contents of her stomach into one of the rose bushes, while I held her hair back. This was killing me, watching my wife sick, leaving me helpless.

I handed her a handkerchief from my pocket. She accepted it with a small smile and hid her face in it. I leaned her back down to the ground and rubbed her back.

"Wow that was a bad one," she said.

WTH? How many times did she get sick in the day? And how bad was she suffering if she was passing out? I pulled out my cell phone and dialed Priscilla, telling her to come outside to bring Fallon back to the house. I could not carry Reese and push the carriage at the same time.

My stubborn wife was insisting she could walk by herself. I ignored her protests and easily carried her back with no effort at all. It seemed like a conversation was due with Reese as well.

"Priscilla, please tend to Fallon. I will be upstairs with my wife."

I carried Reese up the stairs to our bedroom. Jackson came out from his room and looked worried when he saw Reese in my arms and in her weakened condition. She was pale with no color to her face.

"Dad, what happened? Is she okay?"

"Not now, Jackson. Please go downstairs and help Priscilla with your sister. I will be down shortly," I said, dismissing my son and shutting the door behind me.

"Walker, you were very short with him. That's not like you to speak to Jackson in that way," she weakly chastised me.

"Reese, at the moment I do not care how I sound. I just want to make sure you are okay. Now, please, tell me what happened out there? Do you remember passing out? Any idea how long you were unconscious?"

I handed her some cool water and instructed her to take small sips. I did not want to push her with her stomach being so unsettled. I remember Reese being sick with Fallon and suffering through the highs and lows of her blood pressure. It seemed so early now for this to be happening again. I would never forget seeing her in the hospital with an IV hooked up to her, with Briggs by her side. That gutted me to see her ex-husband tend to her care, and so lovingly after how badly he had treated her.

I made my peace with Briggs after he saved my son's life, but at the end of the day, I was still a mad man when it came to protecting my wife. I would never change, and Reese had accepted that part of me, all parts of me.

"How are you feeling?" I asked as I took the glass from her.

She brushed her hair away from her face and sat up against the headboard of our bed.

"I'm much better, Walker. Thank you for taking care of me."

What? It was my job as her husband to do everything in my power to keep her safe and protect her well-being. Reese should have known by now that it was no hardship to care for my woman. I would die for her.

"Please tell me what happened," I requested.

"I was walking with Fallon and felt completely fine. I stopped at the gazebo to feed her and then walked further into the garden. She was beginning to fuss, so I turned around to come back, then my feet gave way and I began vomiting profusely. After a few minutes when I felt it had passed, I began walking with Fallon, and then I must have fainted."

"Reese, I am only going to ask this once of you, so please tell me the truth. How often are you getting sick like this?"

Her expression said it all. *Dammit! Why does she keep this from me?*

"I'm sorry, Walker. I should have been more careful after this morning's round of sickness. I just wanted some fresh air and to play with our daughter."

I had no fight left in me. She was pregnant with my child and had been sick all day, suffering on her own. She had been through enough and did not need me scolding her on top of that.

"I'm going to run you a bath, and then give you a massage."

"Okay," she replied.

Good girl! I was happy she agreed with no argument. Once the bath was ready, I undressed and carried Reese to the bathroom, quickly removing her clothing too. I settled in behind her, washing every inch of her body with her favorite body wash. I tended to her hair next, and then began rubbing her shoulders. She released her pleasure from my touch by grinding herself against my hard erection and letting out sexy moans.

"No," I said.

"What?" she asked, shifting slightly to look at me.

"You heard what I said. I am not fucking you in this tub, so stop rubbing your delicious ass against me. You were sick today and more than once, I might add. I am not that much of a selfish bastard to take you after all of that."

"I won't break, and maybe this is exactly what I need."

Reese effectively made her point by grabbing hold of my dick, which she was now stroking in earnest.

"Oh fuck! Reese, that feels so amazing."

"You were saying?"

In one swift move, Reese straddled my hips and impaled herself on my dick, as she gripped my shoulders for support. Her nails clawed deeply into my skin while she leaned back and screamed my name repeatedly. I could not stop her. She was savagely taking what belonged to her, and I let her. We had our tender moments, and then moments like this where we both became unhinged and hungered for the other in an almost untamed way.

"I'm so close, Walker. Come with me baby," she cried out as I silenced her with my mouth.

Our tongues entwined as we wrestled with domination over the other. Control and submission go hand-in-hand. We both exercised our desires, and took what we wanted. Most times, it was an internal battle for me, especially when Reese pushed me too far.

We climaxed together, leaving Reese to collapse on top of me. I did not want to move as our bodies were still connected. The water was beginning to cool, and I did not want my love to get sick. I stepped out first, and then helped Reese out from the tub. She felt light in my arms as I carried her back to our bed. She looked well-sated, and her eyes were dreamy as she could not take her eyes off my nakedness.

"No, don't even try to tempt me again, you sexy vixen."

"What? A wife can't look at her husband?"

She knew exactly what she was doing, but she did not get to win two rounds against me.

"You can, and I will never stop you, baby," I said as I pulled up my jeans.

She was still wrapped up in her oversized towel, and slowly peeled it away from her body.

"Reese," I sternly warned, "I love you, but no. I need to get you into some warm clothes and put food in your stomach, and then we need to have a talk."

I kissed her quickly and walked over to her closet. She dressed in soft cotton wide leg pants with a body-hugging camisole top with a thin sweater to go over it. She dried her long hair and arranged it in a loose bun on top of her head. I loved her hair and reveled every time I ran my fingers through it.

After my trying day, and then finding my wife passed out from sickness on our property, I would have preferred to stay in our bubble for the rest of the night, but we both needed to eat and talk. We had Jackson and Riley to discuss and the new rules I would put in place for Reese, for when I could not be here with her.

We walked hand-in-hand down to the dining room, where Priscilla had our dinner ready for us. Jackson was seated already and playing with Fallon. She could not take her eyes off him. He would make a wonderful father someday to his own children.

Reese had taken her seat, and I walked over to Fallon to take her from Jackson. She excitedly came to me with no hesitation. Her little hands pinched my cheeks as I leaned in to blow raspberries on her face. She giggled when I did that, a sweet sound I would always welcome.

"Are you feeling better, Reese?" Jackson asked.

"I am, thank you. It must have been something that didn't agree with me," she explained without emotion.

Jackson seemed satisfied with her answer, and the subject changed. Dinner was met with an awkward silence. I had about enough of it when Jackson's cell phone began to ring in his pocket.

"Excuse me, dad, I need to take this."

I nodded, and he left the room. Reese held my hand and noticed the uneasiness between Jackson and me.

She asked, "Are you okay?"

"No, and I really hate those three words. I am far from being okay, and my son is faring no better."

I brought her hand to my lips where I kissed each of her fingers, and then took her index finger into my mouth. Reese slowly closed her eyes, as my sensual assault took effect. She gazed at me, and then I stopped.

"Walker, why did you stop?"

"Tit for tat, my love. Just giving you a little taste of your own medicine."

"Why? You seemed to like it when we were in the tub."

"I did, very much, but Reese, you need to know your limitations of how much you can push your body, especially now, being pregnant. I always want you, you know that, but after seeing you collapsed on the ground, having rough sex with you should have been the last thing on my mind."

"I'm sorry, Walker. I know how you worry about me, but this is part of being pregnant. I can handle it, and if I can't, I promise to tell you."

"That's not good enough, Reese. You should have never been out there on the property on your own. Where was security? We still have it, you know, and will always have it. You do not have a say when it comes to dismissing them when it comes to your personal safety or the safety of our daughter. Do you understand me? Answer me, please?"

"Yes, Walker, I understand," she said, dryly.

You stubborn woman! You will be the death of me, I thought to myself.

"Don't try to pacify me, Reese. I hear your words of promises, but will you keep them and not lie to me? Every time something like that in the garden happens, it rips me apart, and the feeling that is raging through me breaks me down. I hate it, Reese, and you damn well know it. You used me upstairs with sex, something I am all too familiar with, but it will not happen again."

"Walker, please. You are taking something intimate that we just shared and making it ugly. What we just did and where we did it probably contributed to making the baby that I am now carrying. You never hold back when it comes to taking me and allowing me to return the favor. I'm sorry I got sick, but as you can see, I am fine and so is Fallon."

She tried to touch me, but I pulled away as if her touch was burning my skin. I was angry, and seeing my wife passed out was my breaking point of this fucked up day. I tried to calm myself, but I was way past the point of no return.

I said, "You will never tame me, so do not even try. I love you. I will always put your needs before my own. When I feel you need protecting—which is all the time—no one, including you, will stop me from doing that. So please, my love, do not try to make me submit in doing something I do not believe in. You can have your victories in our bed, and clearly you demonstrated that so easily tonight, but do not get used to that. It is not always up to you. I say when, and that is something you have always known from our beginning. It is too late to change the rules now. And one more thing: do not challenge me when it comes to your safety."

The sparkle had returned in her eyes. She knew the fight was gone from mine.

I told her, "Now, come here and kiss me."

"I love you, Walker, so much."

"And I you, my love."

Holding Reese in my arms is just what I needed to end my shitty day.

Fallon called out, "Dada, dada."

"Our little girl wants attention," I whispered to Reese.

We both stayed entwined with the other and smiled over at Fallon.

Jackson never returned to dinner. I left him on his own for a while and helped Reese put Fallon to bed. I was exhausted. It felt so much later than it actually was. After Reese agreed to my new safety protocols in place, I reiterated my instructions to my staff, including Priscilla.

This was our home, and I wanted Reese to feel free in it, but because she ignored what her body told her, I had to take extra measures to safeguard her. Pregnancy was hard on her. I saw that with Fallon. She agreed to see Dr. Lemay in the morning to have a check-up. We would go together, and I would decide then if I would go in or work from home.

"I have some work to do in my study," I said to Reese. "Will you be okay on your own for a while?"

"Of course, I'll be fine."

I kissed her and left her to read while I made a call to New York.

"Richard, what do you have for me?"

"Hello, sir. After Ms. Briggs' concluded her time with her father, she returned back to campus and remained there for the rest of the day. She just arrived back at the apartment about an hour or so ago."

"Was she alone?"

"Yes, sir. She was carrying an armful of books."

"You are certain she's in the apartment now?"

"Yes, sir, I am."

"Okay, I will ring the penthouse phone, and there should be no reason why she does not answer. If she does not, Richard, then I will call you back and you will personally bring her to the phone. I have had enough of this back and forth nonsense."

"I understand."

I disconnected with Richard and then phoned the apartment. It rang for several times, trying my patience. When I was about to hang up, she answered. *Finally!*

"Hello," she said.

Her voice was so similar to Reese's.

"Riley, this is Mr. Reed. How are you?"

There was silence for only a minute, and then she answered in a shaky voice, "I'm fine, Mr. Reed. Why the call?"

"I think you know, Riley. What I don't know is why are you avoiding your mother's phone calls, and why is Jackson here in California and you are in New York?"

"I can't talk about it, Mr. Reed. You are going to have to ask your son."

"Riley, I have, and he will tell me nothing. So now I am asking you. We have all traveled down this road before. As memory serves, it did not end well the last time you or my son kept secrets from me. I do not wish to pry. I just want to help. Please, Riley, let me help."

CHAPTER 11

Riley

Alone

I KNEW IT was just a matter of time before Mr. Reed would track me down. I should have screened the calls, but knowing how domineering he could be, I was sure Richard or someone else on Mr. Reed's payroll was monitoring my every move. After all, I was back where Jackson wanted us, living in his father's big penthouse. Last summer we were playing house here, and it was as if we were already married and living our happily ever after. But now...I didn't know what we were.

My mother may have been comfortable living life under Mr. Reed's rule, where I was not. Jackson lived his entire life surrounded by tall walls built to protect him. I really thought when we finally moved to New York, our life would be so different, but I was wrong. It was almost unrecognizable to me.

Jackson was thousands of miles away when he should have been here with me. He got scared and ran. I stayed, but I was alone. My father hated that I attended school here and never stopped trying to convince me to transfer closer to him. Why would I do that? So I could be ignored like he ignored my mother for all the years of their marriage? No, thank you, daddy, but I was happy just where I was. I would have been perfect if Jackson was here, but he made his choice, as I made mine. Now, how did we live with it, knowing we may never get back what we had?

After we returned from Germany, Jackson and I made our final arrangements to move to New York. We waited so long to be together, and finally our dream was about to come true. All the plans we had made were falling into place. Clay and Brandon were joining us at NYU, after deciding they wanted more than UCLA had to offer. Who were they kidding? They missed Jackson and their friendship! Those three were as close as brothers could be, but so very different at the same time.

Clay and Brandon were wild, where Jackson was more reserved. He never partied or got so drunk that he would forget his own name. They each came from wealthy families, Jackson from the wealthiest. He was heir to the throne of Reed Global International but always said that film school was his passion. It was mine as well. I loved creating something from an idea and turning it into something real that I could play out before me.

The best part was sharing my dream with Jackson. We were a team, united by our parents' love story and promises we made to one another as we fell in love. It was a love story guided by fate and fate alone. Jackson said his mother in heaven, whom he refers to as his guardian angel, was our beacon. When we met on the day of my father's hospital dedication in a building designed and built from his father, we connected from the very first word we shared. I knew when I said those three words to him that he was the one that I knew I would love for a lifetime.

He promised me forever when I accepted his mother's ring. We were young but did not care. I would have married Jackson every day if he asked me to, but being the man he is, he wanted to wait and give me the wedding of my dreams.

I did not care. I just wanted him. I would miss my mother and my new sister terribly, but this was our time to experience life outside the protective walls of the Reed mansion. I felt free for the first time in my life, having experienced nothing like Jackson had in his life. I was sheltered in Maryland. I attended private school all of my school years. I only attended cotillions and other formal school functions.

I loved my childhood. My father and mother educated me about art, music, and things most kids my age never got to experience. I shared many of the same interests with my father. We were close for a long time, and then one day, we were not.

Mr. Reed coming back into my mother's life changed our family forever and created a new one for me. He was madly in love with my mother, and I loved his son. It was kind of crazy how it all came to be, but Jackson promised one day he would write their story, and we would all watch it one day on the big screen. "An amazing and very rare love story," he called it, starring Walker and Reese. What they had was magical.

I heard Mr. Reed say on more than one occasion that Jackson and I were them, just twenty years later. I wanted to believe that with all of my heart, but how could I anymore when Jackson shattered my world by choosing to leave me? I remembered it like it was yesterday.

"You can't be serious Jackson? Why do we have to move?"

"You know why. Don't stand there and pretend you do not know what I am talking about."

It had been a long time since I heard him raise his voice with me, and I did not like it.

"I think you need to explain it to me, Jackson, because I do not have a clue as to why you are suddenly moving us to your father's

penthouse. We agreed to live here with our friends, to experience college life, and to be together. What has changed?"

"You! Riley, you have changed, and not to my liking."

"What? How have I changed?"

"Riley, I love you, and there is nothing more I want than to see you happy, but I can't do this roommate thing for one more day. Clay and Brandon may be my life-long friends, but they are reckless and dangerous at times. They party too hard, and now adding the girlfriends to the equation is a recipe for disaster. This is not our life, and I am removing us from this before it blows up in our faces. Now, we will talk about this, but not here. Richard is waiting outside for us. Gather your things and let's go."

I just stood there in silence and shock. Jackson exercised complete control over me, and I allowed him to do it. My bags were packed, and he was waiting for me to just walk out the door and leave our new life behind.

Clay and Brandon just rejoiced because "Warden Jackson" has left the compound, as they always called him. They now had more room to themselves and for their girlfriends. Once we moved out, I saw less and less of Alice and Evette. My entire world began and ended with Jackson, and I felt suffocated, another unknown feeling I did not like.

He kept his word and we did talk once we were alone, but it was the same discussion. He wanted me to understand his feelings and try to meet him halfway. I told him how I felt, and he disputed what I was saying.

"Riley, I don't want to control you. I love you, beautiful girl. We are in this together, but please do not sit here and tell me truthfully that you loved that circus we just left? It was toxic, and I should have never agreed to allow the guys to share an apartment with us. We are getting married, and couples do not share homes with bachelors."

"They have girlfriends now. What is so wrong for three couples to hang out with each other? I will admit it was somewhat crazy when I needed the quiet for studying, but that is what libraries are for. I was fine with it, Jackson. Why couldn't you just be more open to it?"

"Riley, have you not heard a word I said? It is not for me, and I do not want us to be part of that scene. Now please, let's go to bed, where I can make love to you without interruption."

The discussion was over. Jackson had made his point perfectly clear by suggesting the bedroom. I would always say yes to him, I loved him so much. A part of me deep down knew he was right, but another small part of me wanted to be immature, drink one too many Tequila shots, and maybe hug the toilet once or twice, just to say I did something fun. Nevertheless, even something as small as a party Jackson would not bend on. I knew him well enough to know when he was done talking about something. I was the one that usually exhausted our conversations.

I tried not to think about it as Jackson slowly made love to me. He was tender and knew my body so well. I had freely given my heart and committed my soul to his by accepting his proposal of marriage, one day becoming Mrs. Jackson Reed.

The rational side to my brain was clouded by my love for him. At the time, I truly did not understand what being a Reed really meant and how it would affect my life and the person I was.

CHAPTER 12

Jackson

Following my heart

"**Y**OUR SCANS ARE perfect. Bloodwork all came back in normal range. You gained ten pounds in muscle. I would say you, Jackson Reed, are in perfect shape and health," Dr. O'Larien said as he typed his notes on his tablet. "Anything else you wish to discuss with me?" he asked, handing me a bottle of water.

We sat casually in his office and sometimes it was hard remembering that he was my doctor and not my father's longest friend. Liam never pressured me like my father. He also made it clear to me that he could be trusted with my confidence if I ever should feel like I could not talk to my father. I respected him a great deal and appreciated not only how he took care of me, but also his friendship. There was a time when I doubted him, but that was my fear of being sick. I owed him and Dr. Briggs my life for all they did during my surgery.

Regarding my surgery, something had been weighing heavily on my mind lately, and I always wondered about it. Liam asked me if I wanted to talk, so why put off what I desperately wanted to know.

"Dr. O'Larien."

"Jackson, how many times do I have to tell you? You may call me Liam. I think we are way past the doctor and patient pleasantries."

"I'm sorry, bad habit to break. You should hear how Riley addresses my father. He says the same thing to her, but she still calls him Mr. Reed."

"What's on your mind?" he asked.

"My surgery."

"Oh? What about it?"

"I...never..."

"Jackson, what is it? You know you can ask me anything."

I took a drink of my water and released a few deep breaths.

"I'm sorry, Liam, this is something I haven't thought about in a long time, and maybe I didn't want to tempt fate by doing so now. After I woke from my surgery and was strong enough to talk, I shared something with my father. I told him that I saw my mother. For a few precious moments, I received the best gift in the world, my mom. She showed me a glimpse to my future."

"I remember discussing this with your father. Every patient's case is different. You always had a longing to meet your mother, and you finally did in your dreams."

"It's more than that, Liam. I felt as if I left my body and crossed over into another realm. I thought I was in heaven and my mother was an angel bringing me home. She said I was only sleeping and would wake when the time was right. I guess what I really want to know is how long I was dead for? My heart stopped beating, didn't it?"

He leaned back into his leather chair, and he took his glasses off to rub his eyes.

"Yes, Jackson, your heart did indeed stop, and it was the most frightening seconds of my life. You were not just another patient; you were my best friend's son, and I knew I could never face him again had you not made it. Dr. Briggs and I worked furiously on your brain and heart all at the same time. He took control over his ER, and me for that matter, and then we got you back. The real test would be when you woke up. You surpassed all of our expectations, and although had experienced some setbacks to overcome, you did amazingly well. You sitting across from me is living proof of the miracle we were blessed with that day. I truly have no other way to explain it to you."

"Thank you, Liam, for answering my question."

"My pleasure, Jackson. Are you okay?"

"Never better. Thank you for everything. I'll see you in six months."

"You know you don't have to wait until your next check-up. I keep putting off beating your father in a game of golf. Maybe you can join us?"

"Thank you for the invitation, but I don't like golf. I do enjoy your positive attitude in believing you can beat my father in golf, or anything else in that matter. Reeds don't lose, Liam."

Oh my God, I thought to myself. *I know I heard the words coming from my mouth, but it still took me time to process what I just said. A Reed? Seriously Jackson? I must have sounded like a spoiled, pretentious snob*

"I'm sorry, Liam. I don't even know where that just came from."

"No worries, Jackson, and of course you do. You are one hundred percent correct. Reeds do not lose. Secondly, Reeds never apologize for something they believe to be true. I learned that a long time ago, knowing a man like your father."

After I left Dr. O'Larien's office, I decided to take a walk throughout the city. Oddly, I was mimicking the look of a tourist like when it was their first time to a big city like New York and they stared and looked up at the buildings. What surprised me more was where I ended up.

I had been here before countless times, but today it almost felt like the first time. I had no clue on what I was even looking for but walked in through the main lobby. Suddenly, a feeling of home rained down on me.

The Reed Global building in New York almost mirrored what we had in California, but this was my grandfather's creation, not my father's vision. The interior has been remodeled since my father took over all controlling interest in his family's company, which solely belonged to him now. He grew Reed Global to an international level. My father's personal wealth had crossed over to the billions, but he raised me so differently than how he was brought up.

My father made me work for everything I had, to know the value of the dollar, and to appreciate one's good fortune. I never wanted for anything I desired, but not everything was easily given just because I was Walker Reed's son.

"Excuse me, young man. Can I help you? We don't permit loitering, and this is private property."

The efficient security guard did not know who I was. I almost wanted to see how far I could push him before I revealed myself, but I let him off the hook. I turned to him and was ready to show him my identification when a familiar face walked over to us.

"Jackson! What are you doing here?" shouted the bubbly blonde-haired woman I would know anywhere, Bridgette Johannsen, daughter to Tom, who happened to work directly with my father.

She practically bulldozed over the security guard to get to me. She was tall and towered over me by a few inches in her sexy stilettos. If I were not expecting it, I would have been knocked on my ass. She wrapped her arms around me, pulled me into a tight hug, and kissed me on my cheeks.

"You never called, you ass! Lucky for me I'm not one of those needy girls that wait by the phone while crying into a heaping bowl of ice cream."

"Same Bridgette as I remember."

"Yeah, well you would have had a chance to know me better had you not have fallen madly in love with your current...oh my God! You have a fiancée. You are too cruel, Jackson Reed. You couldn't have waited a few years to take yourself off the market?"

"I am blissfully happy, my friend, and so in love with my girl. But thank you anyway for that endearing compliment."

"You ass!"

"Aren't you supposed to be a rising executive?" I said. "Language please!"

I could not help but laugh aloud. Bridgette possessed no filter when it came to her mouth, but it was one of the reasons why I liked her so much. She was real, and in this world, that was hard to come by.

While we enjoyed each other's friendly banter, the security guard stepped back. It was clear to him that I was no bum off the street panhandling in one of the most prestigious buildings in New York. I did excuse myself from Bridgette's clutches and introduced myself to him along with the five other men who had joined him.

"Hello, gentlemen, I am Jackson Reed, pleasure to meet you."

As if you could hear a pin drop, silence was all around me until Bridgette interjected.

"You heard him, boys, this very handsome young man is the son of the man who signs your paychecks. Please put your tongues back in your mouths and say hello."

Please let me find a roll of tape so I can seal her mouth shut.

Handshakes and greetings were passed around, and I put my hands up to them to tell them: "Relax, I will not tear your heads off." The shorter man who first approached me, his name was Peter. He apologized for overstepping, but I shrugged him off. How could he know? It had been a while since I had been here, and my father only frequented this office a few times a year. Peter made me a special security badge, and I said my goodbyes to them as Bridgette dragged me off.

"Seriously?" I said to her. "Did you have to speak that way to them and embarrass the shit out of me?"

"Oh, come on, Jackson! Lighten up. You have to admit that was fun. They looked like they were about to shit their pants. I will never forget the last time your father made an unexpected visit here. The building was thrown into complete chaos. I think we were afraid to breathe, but he was cool."

"Cool? My father? We are talking about Walker Reed. I hope you mean cool like ice runs through his veins, and not the guy we all want to hang out with?"

"Probably both, but what's the big deal? Are you okay? I know we haven't talked in a while, but I'm still your friend."

Bridgette was one of the few friends I could actually talk with. I missed her terribly when she left for college, but since moving back to New York, I saw her several times before meeting Riley. She was interning for my father's company and hoped to be hired full-time.

I only knew this piece of information because it was I who helped my father choose the candidates for the program. Tom did not want any special favors for his daughter. He wanted her to be chosen without any influence from him. I knew my friend was highly intelligent and would work hard. It was not very often that I assisted my father in anything pertaining to his business. Bridgette interviewed with him, and he of course knew who she was and asked my opinion on what I thought of her.

I responded to her, "I don't want to talk about me, tell me about you."

"Nice try avoiding, but I asked you first. You look good, Jackson. I'm so sorry I didn't get an opportunity to visit you when you were in the hospital, but my father kept me updated."

"I probably would have refused you anyway. It was hard being around my family, let alone my friends. Once I returned home to California, I had to work so hard to get my life back, and then my grand…"

"We don't have to talk about it. I read about it. It was in every New York paper. I am truly sorry."

"Thank you, Bridgette. So, how do you like working for Reed Global?"

"Um…love it! My internship ends in two months. Please pray they offer me a position. I love the marketing department. I even helped with one of the ads that will play during the Super Bowl!"

"Wow, that's impressive. If I can put in a good word or anything, I will."

"You've done enough, Jackson, and do not even try to lie to me. I know you had a hand in getting me accepted into the program, so thank you."

"For a confident woman, you seem to always doubt your abilities to rock out and be a bad ass on your own. Let me tell you something, my friend, if you were not worth your salt, you would not be here. My father has no time to babysit his future executives. You either have it or you don't. There is no in-between when working for Walker Reed."

"I couldn't have said it better," we heard someone say behind us.

We both turned around, and Donovan Tate entered the office we were in to have lunch and talk.

"Mr. Tate, we weren't expecting you until tomorrow," Bridgette said, sounding flustered as she stood to shake his hand.

I was trying to stifle a laugh under my breath until she gave me a death glare.

"Hello, Bridgette, I guess that point is moot now, because I am here and would like to see the projections I asked you to show me."

"Of course, sir, I will be right back."

She turned back to me, said goodbye, and asked me to stay in touch. Donovan just smiled and shook his head.

"How are you, Jackson? You are probably the last person I thought I would run into, and here of all places."

"It surprised me too," I said. "I guess I should be going. Mr.

Tate, would you mind if I stepped into my father's office for a few minutes?"

"Of course not, Jackson. Like you said, it's your father's office. Be my guest."

"Mr. Tate."

"Yes, Jackson."

"If it's all the same to you, would you not mention to my father seeing me here today?"

"Sure thing, son, but I don't fly back to California until the end of the week, so if you wanted to talk, I'm here."

"Thank you, sir. I may just do that."

Walking to his office, I felt like I was on display with bright lights over my head. I felt recognized. I know I looked like my dad, but I was wearing jeans, a plain white t-shirt, and Converse sneakers. My ensemble was not that intimidating, but I guessed just my name alone carried much influence around here. It felt oddly empowering to have such a commanding presence.

Although he was thousands of miles away, I could feel my father all around the room. It was eerie, but I also felt my grandfather. This was his office first. I remembered him telling me countless stories of how he learned the business from the bottom floor up. His own father was driven and determined to groom his son to be the best. My father was the best, and he may not have agreed with my grandfather on many occasions, but how could he not be thankful for who he was today?

My eyes scanned the room. The walls were lined with my father's successes. I felt a lump in my throat as I got closer to his desk. It looked intimidating at first. I sat behind it and suddenly felt like the prince to the kingdom sitting in his chair.

Could this be all mine someday? This was my legacy. I told my father that I did not want any part of it, but I wasn't so sure about that anymore.

CHAPTER 13

Riley

What's changed?

*W*HERE ARE YOU, Jackson? Dammit! Straight to voicemail. You promised you would be here, I thought to myself. I was in a mad panic over the lateness of the hour. I kept checking my phone to see if I missed a call or text, but there was nothing from Jackson.

Professor Connelly gave strict instructions for this latest project. I only had the written notes, whereas Jackson was to present the footage. This would only be a rough draft, so to speak, but our teacher wanted to see how we would outline the subject at hand, and then proceed as if we already had the greenlight for the screenplay. I had run out of time, and I only had half of the assignment to turn in. I was going to fail for sure.

"Ms. Briggs, you are up next," the Professor called out.

I slowly stood up and did the only thing I could do: tell the truth.

"I apologize, Professor, but my partner on this assignment has failed to show and has left me in a very uncomfortable position. I only have my half of the work. He was supposed to bring the actual film footage."

Please do not cry. Please do not cry, I chanted to myself.

"I see, Ms. Briggs, and do you always choose incompetent partners for only my class? I seem to remember an incomplete I handed down to you in the beginning of the semester. I strongly suggest you consider finding a new partner to work with, or I will be forced to fail you with another incomplete. I expect you in my office promptly after class to discuss your future here. Is that understood, Ms. Briggs?"

"Yes, sir," I responded. Two monosyllabic words that made me feel so small. *Oh Jackson! Why did you do this to me?*

Promptly at six o'clock, I found myself sitting across from Professor Connelly. He was hard to read at times. When I first met him at orientation, he was welcoming and kind, but maybe that was just to draw you in. Now I was seeing an entirely different side to him.

He opened up what looked like a file on me. He was flipping through pages and then closed it and used his elbows to lean on his desk. He stared at me intently, making me feel sick to my stomach. I was about to be thrown out of his class for piss poor attendance and work.

"Answer me this one question, Ms. Briggs. Why did you take my class if you are not willing to do the work I expect from all of my students?"

My stomach was in knots, and I felt sick. After I swallowed hard and willed myself to not throw up all over his pristine desk, I sat straight up and answered his question.

"I imagine, sir, I could give you the obvious answer to leave you feeling complacent and maybe forgiving enough to give me another chance. My other option is to just take the incomplete and not waste anymore of your time. But in the end, I need this class to move forward with my requirements. I am here because I want to become a documentary filmmaker, and I believe you could teach me the tools I need to accomplish that. I am sorry I have failed to meet the expectations you require from your students to be worthy enough to be in the same room with you. It was an error on my judgment choosing my partner, and if given another opportunity to redeem myself, I will not make the same lapse in judgment again, sir."

Please, please do not fault me because my boyfriend is an asshole...oh, I mean fiancé.

He continued to stare at me for a minute or two, and then he reopened my file. *Just get it over with already if you want me gone. Why am I being tortured like this?*

"I see here that Jackson Reed was supposed to be your partner on this assignment."

"Yes, sir, he was."

"And you have a personal relationship with him?"

"Sir, I believe that is an inappropriate question, and quite possibly crossing the line."

"You may be right Ms. Briggs, but it will not stop me from asking it. I see potential in your ability to become what you say you want to be. Your file screams overachiever. You obviously are not taking this path to play house with your boyfriend. You actually do want this. I have read Mr. Reed's file as well. His file pretty much matches yours, but I do not see the same fire in his eyes as I did when I first met you two. I understand he went through a major operation, with that delaying your start here at NYU."

He continued, "Whatever the case may be now, I see two very different students, and I am only willing to give one another chance. I do not do this lightly nor often Ms. Briggs, so remember this conversation the next time you fail to hand in an incomplete assignment. You have one week to produce the footage, or my grade stands and you will be given a zero, ending any chance for you to pass this class. Good day, Ms. Briggs."

"Thank you, sir. I promise I will not let you down again."

I grabbed my backpack and fled his office as if I was on fire. By the time I reached the quad, I was out of breath and placed my hands on my knees. I wanted to cry until I had no tears left to shed. I did not understand Jackson at all, and whether he liked it or not, he was in for one hell of a fight when I get home.

Right on time, Richard was waiting for me by the student service building. At least someone knew how to keep to his schedule. I did not want to take my foul mood out on Richard. He has been nothing but kind to me, and he was not the one I was angry with.

"Good evening, Riley," he warmly greeted me.

I loved that he could be comfortable around me, and not so formal like he once was toward me. Mr. Reed had insisted he conducted himself in a certain manner, but I treated him like a friend, and he in turn treated me the same way.

"Hi Richard, is Jackson with you?" I asked before looking into the darkened car.

"I'm afraid not. I have not spoken to him since I dropped him at his morning appointment."

"Richard, that was nearly nine hours ago. Aren't you worried? Should we call Dr. O'Larien?"

I was angry with Jackson for missing our presentation, but deeply loved him at the same time. He was never this irresponsible not to check in with Richard, or me for that matter.

"He's fine Riley, no need to worry. He left a message for you back at the apartment."

"He didn't think just to call me directly? Richard, does he even know what today is?"

"I'm not following, what is the importance of today? Other than his six-month check-up?"

Of course, his appointment would be important today, and take precedence over anything else. No matter what, today was important to me, and it should have been for Jackson. He showed no respect for me today by blowing off class and putting my academic career in jeopardy. I was so angry with him, I could scream off the roof of this car.

Screw it! And screw him. I am going out and maybe give him some time to worry about me for a change.

"Thank you, Richard, but I'm going to see a friend. I won't need a ride tonight."

"Miss Riley, I do not believe it is wise of you to walk the campus this late at night. Please allow me to drop you anywhere you wish to go, but please do not walk."

"Okay, you can drop me at Stewart Hall."

We drove in silence to Evette and Alice's dorm. I was praying they would be home and not otherwise engaged with their boyfriends. I really needed some girlfriend time to vent about my guy.

"Shall I wait?" Richard asked.

"No, I will be fine."

"Any message for Mr. Reed?"

"Nope, not one."

"Miss Riley, can I offer any help to you?"

"I'm good, Richard, but thank you."

He looked worried for me, no more than I was for myself. I had all intentions of confronting Jackson about missing class, but all the fight was gone from me. It just saddened me to discover that even Richard did not know about the presentation and how important it was to me. I was starting to believe Professor Connelly was right about Jackson and how he may not want the same things I wanted.

I knocked on the door a few times before Brandon swung open the door. He was only wearing low hanging basketball shorts and holding a beer in his hand.

"Hey, good looking…beer?"

He went to hand it to me, but Alice walked over and slapped him upside his head.

"Don't be a jerk, and will you please put on some clothes? Or better yet, go back to your own apartment."

I could not help laughing silently to myself.

I heard Evette call out to her boyfriend, "Brandon, get your sexy ass back in here and finish what you started."

Oh, my bleeding ears! When I was done being angry with Jackson, I would thank him for moving us out from party central.

"Come in, honey. We've missed you. With our schedule change, and you guys moving, we do not see you as much. How are you?" Alice asked as she gave me a hug and pulled me down to the couch.

I tried with great effort to hold back my tears, but it was too late.

"What's wrong, Riley? Why are you crying?" she said as she handed me a Kleenex from the side table.

"I'm sorry. I'm just a mess, and I do not know what to do."

"Well, you did one right thing: you came here. So talk to me. How can I help? And whose ass do I have to beat down?"

"You know I love you, right?" I told her. "Calm down, Jersey girl. It has not gotten that far yet, but it is close. I'm just upset because Jackson missed a very important presentation today for Professor Connelly's class, and I was just humiliated."

"Wow that sucks, friend. Did he fail you?"

"Not yet, thank goodness, but if I don't hand in a perfect project by next week, it's over."

"Have you talked to Jackson? What was so important for him to miss class today?"

"I don't know, Alice. I was hoping to talk to him about it, fight about it, something, but I just feel disconnected from him lately. I came here instead."

"Good decision. How about this for a great way to get back at him: dry your tears and we hit a club or something. I can throw these guys out, and it will be just us girls. What do you say?"

"Can I borrow your Gucci mini?" I asked.

"I must really fucking love you because I am going to say yes, but do not spill anything on it. That skirt cost me an entire paycheck."

I already felt better. I borrowed clothes from Alice, and Evette did my hair. We looked hot. I ignored Jackson's seven text messages and two voicemails. I did not even care to listen to them and automatically hit delete. I needed this break, and I was not going to submit to Jackson Reed tonight.

Alice knew of this club called Buzz All Night. It was booming with bright lights, uptown funk music, and filled with VIP-roped off sections for whatever your pleasure. I was not even old enough to be in this place, but of course, our "man whores" knew the doorman. It paid to have mega rich daddies to give in to their whims. I tried to focus on having fun, but my mind kept going back to Jackson. He would not want me in a place like this, especially without him.

I was thankful that the guys ended up joining us. The girls did not seem to mind either, which left me the odd girl out without her man. I shrugged it off, because this was what I wanted, *right? Let loose and have some fun. Yeah, good times. All that I had been wishing for since we arrived is dancing with Jackson.*

"Come on, girl, let's dance," shouted Alice, and Evette followed.

Brandon and Clay were getting us drinks and then found us on the dance floor. We downed our shots, and got lost in the music. The guys could be complete tools sometimes, but protected us girls from the other assholes in the club. Brandon and Clay formed a tight circle around us, and although Jackson was not here with me, I felt safe. These guys were his friends and would not allow anything to happen to their girlfriends or me.

I was beginning to feel guilty for ignoring Jackson. He had to be frantic by now. So much for maturity. My behavior was so not on the lines of that.

"It's getting late, Alice. Can we leave?" I nervously asked her.

"Where's your sense of adventure? It's not even midnight yet. One more drink, Riley, and then I will personally take you home to your hot man."

"Hey, watch it, Alice, I'm the only hot man I want you thinking about," Clay called out.

"Relax, you are, baby," she yelled at him.

"One more drink and then we have to go, okay?" I asked.

"Scouts honor," Alice said, putting her hands behind her back, but I think she was just doing that for show.

She did not have any intention of going home anytime soon. Maybe Jackson was a little right about them. They were awesome but did like to party, and as much as I was trying to fit in, this was not my scene. I had to pee, and then I was going to take a cab home. As I was walking out from the women's restroom, a tall blonde guy approached me.

He said, "Hey baby, I've been watching you all night. You are so fucking hot. Let me show you a good time."

I wasn't sure if it was the three shots I downed, or this guy actually believed the lines he was dishing out.

"Um, no thank you, I'm good," I told him.

I began walking away until he pulled me back into his broad chest.

"I don't think you heard me. I want to dance with you."

He was hurting my arm to the point of pain. Richard had taught me how to defend myself. It was time to put what I had learned to the test.

"Get your hands off of me, or you will be sorry," I screamed.

"A little thing like you is going to teach me a lesson? I don't think so."

He leaned in to kiss me, and that was when I delivered a kick right to his balls. He shrieked in pain and doubled over, holding his man parts. I was not finished with him. As he was screaming out profanities to me and nearly falling to the floor, that's when I raised my knee up to his face, hoping I broke his nose.

"Fuck you, you big ape. Next time when a girl says no, you better fucking listen."

I turned and was greeted by a round of applause from the other girls waiting in line for the restroom. I began walking away, and once again, a strong arm pulled me back. But this time it was Jackson.

I did not have a chance to enjoy the adrenaline rush I was feeling when all the air was sucked out from the room as I took in Jackson's anger. He was breathing fire, as his eyes turned cold, a character trait I had seen before with his father, never with Jackson.

"What the fuck are you doing here?" he screamed at me, using a tone I was not used to hearing. His eyes were blazing with fire, and not the desirable kind. He was beyond angry.

"Do you even know how worried I've been?" he yelled.

His strong hands were gripping my upper arms tightly to the point of pain, which is what I saw in his eyes. I put that look there, and before I had a chance to answer, he was dragging me out of the club. Evette, Alice, and the guys saw the scene unfolding and approached us.

"Hey, man, calm down. We were just having some fun," said Brandon, and then Clay was right behind him.

Jackson gave his friends the "fuck off" look, and it did not go unnoticed by the girls. Jackson tucked me behind him, and then shoved Brandon.

"Some friends, you are. While my girl was about to be attacked by some fucking pig, you all were dancing it up! Thanks for having her back."

They all were stunned into silence, and asked me if I was okay. I said I was and could take care of myself. Jackson just glared at me with my comment.

He grabbed my hand and told me that we were leaving. I had never seen him so angry with me, not ever. The guys said nothing to Jackson. I told the girls I was okay and would see them tomorrow. As we walked away, I heard Jackson mutter under his breath, "Don't count on it."

Dragging me out of the club was the highest form of behaving like a caveman. I could see Mr. Reed throwing my mother over his shoulder and claiming total dominance, but not Jackson. This was not like him.

He never let go of my hand as we arrived at our waiting car. Richard quickly opened up the passenger door as Jackson placed me inside, even buckling my seatbelt. I wanted to scream at the top of my lungs, but who would hear me? This man who was supposed to love me was manhandling me, and Richard was dutifully obeying his every command.

How did this happen? I was the one who should be angry, not Jackson. He was the one that blew me off today, and without a word to tell me he was okay. *This is bullshit!*

I was about to find my voice, and we were already back at the apartment. As quickly as Jackson put me into the car, he was even quicker pulling me out. He ushered me quickly past the door attendant and into the private elevator that would bring us upstairs to his father's penthouse apartment.

"What has gotten into you, Jackson?" I finally screamed at him.

He said nothing but shoved me up against the wall and took my mouth with a punishing kiss. His hands were everywhere on my body. Fuck my betraying body for wanting him so much. I should be so angry with him, but here I was with my legs wrapped around his waist and grinding against his hard dick. I hungered for him.

"I need to see you," he whispered in my ear, taking my lobe into his mouth, trailing wet kisses down my throat, and holding me tightly in his arms.

His hand cupped my sex, and my back hit the cold steel wall of the elevator. He was relentless, fingering my glistening heat until I was screaming his name.

"Riley, I wanted to kill that fucker for thinking he could touch you, but then you kicked him in his balls and I felt an instant relief cast over me. Richard has taught you well. I was proud of you for defending yourself, but beyond angry that you put yourself in that position. You were in direct line of danger. What were you thinking?"

I had no words after that intense orgasm. He slowly put me down and smoothed my clothing. His eyes had softened, but I knew we were not finished talking about this. He took my hand as the elevator doors opened into his home.

We walked straight up the stairs to our bedroom and slammed the door. Anger replaced with desire, Jackson removed the clothing he knew did not belong to me, and tossed them to the floor. He was naked in seconds and carried me to the shower. He took me again and made love to me as tenderly as he could, begging me to forgive him for his earlier actions. Tears were streaming down both our faces as we held each other under the shower, the water washing away our anger.

Jackson storming into the club tonight to rescue me when I did not need it was over-the-top hot, but also a little frightening. As gentle as I knew him to be, he showed a possessive side tonight, and he did nothing to hide it. He might as well have dragged me out by my hair to show his dominance over me.

I did not help matters much when I so easily submitted to him. We were each other's firsts, and every sexual experience I ever had was with him. I was turned on when he exerted control, but angry with myself for giving it to him. My betraying body did not help either. He knew it all too well by now, as I knew his.

The elevator brought me to heel, and his apologies that followed were his regret. I loved him. I loved his touch. Experiencing pleasure even in that state was no hardship.

But this was not us, not by a long shot.

I could not put into words what scared me the most, the real crux of our problem, and something neither of us wanted to admit:

We were growing apart.

And who would say it first?

CHAPTER 14

Jackson

We want different things, but I want you

I FELT LIKE I had crossed over into a different realm. In my wildest dreams, I never imagined myself ever exacting that much dominance over Riley, but I did. And it was in front of our friends, with Richard to bear witness.

Earlier today when Richard returned to the apartment without Riley, I just snapped. I called her repeatedly with no calls returned. I texted and begged her to call me, but again, silence was between us. She was behaving irresponsibly and so out of character. I knew she had to be with her friends, but to my surprise, she was with my friends as well.

Finally tracking down Riley's location thanks to Richard, we raced through Manhattan as fast as we could. I did not want my girl in a bar without me. Anything could have happened. What if I did not get there in time and a guy slipped something into her drink? Her friends and my friends were not paying any attention to her, God knows what could have happened. I would not allow my mind to go there right now.

On their own, the girls were fine typically, but when they were with Clay and Brandon, that was an entirely different story. They changed, I changed, and I was okay with that. I was never involved in the party scene; they knew it and Riley knew it. For her to just go out and not consider me was not going to fly. We did not drink nor do anything else recreational that could harm us. I thought she understood that.

I had to have her again. I needed to show her how much I loved and wanted her. My anger would not have stopped me from taking what was mine. When she called me a caveman, it was usually in play, but tonight it was different. I knew I must have scared her on some level, but my emotions got the better of me. Hell if I even understood them! I'd heard the saying, "The apple does not fall too far from the tree," and the way I spoke to Liam today and behaved with Riley tonight, I was definitely feeling like a Reed. I just didn't know if I liked this version of myself.

I carried Riley out of the shower and did my best to tend to her needs. She dried off with a warm towel and put on her robe. She toweled her hair and kept it wrapped up. I wanted to touch her again but kept a safe distance until we could talk. My apology was right there to be said, but would she want to hear it? I was ashamed of my behavior, and I knew if we were ever going to move past tonight and the last few months, I needed to talk to my girl. This conversation, just like our last one, was not easy for Riley to hear. This one will be no better.

How would I tell her that I had singlehandedly changed the plans for *our* future? I loved Riley, and she loved me. But I knew that if I didn't take this chance to follow where my heart was leading, I would always regret it. And that was one feeling I never wished to feel in my lifetime. When did things become so confusing?

After our amazing summer of showing Riley every inch of New York City, it was time to begin our junior year at NYU. Riley and I both had taken accelerated classes in our junior and senior year of high school. By the time we graduated, we each left with an associate's degree in hand. We knew that was just the first of many steps we had planned for our education. With me recovering from surgery, Riley began taking online classes instead of attending UCLA and then having to deal with a transfer. Once I was strong enough, I also took classes. It took me a bit longer, but I eventually caught up.

Now here we were. We were attending a physical school with each other, just as our parents did. These grounds were sacred. We were walking the same halls, having coffee together, and loving that fact that we just simply loved each other.

Riley consented to be my wife. We agreed we would wait until we graduate. I wanted to give her the wedding of her dreams and bring her back to Big Sur to marry her under the tree where I carved out our names.

I will never forget our first day. Riley must have chewed about a dozen pencils. She was so nervous. I was not sure what I was feeling in terms of school, but I knew I was happy just to share it with Riley. Her smile alone lit a fire deep within my soul. She was incredibly intelligent, driven, and had her eyes on the prize. She wanted to make films on her own terms, something to leave a personal mark on, and a legacy one day for young filmmakers that would come after her.

We took our seats and waited for Professor Connelly to make his grand entrance. A few minutes later, he walked in while carrying a megaphone. We held our ears as he talked, or shouted.

"Hello! Can you hear me? Because if you cannot, then you have a bigger hearing problem than I do. I am Professor Sean Connelly, not Connery. I'm Irish, he is Scottish."

Light laughter filled the room while he continued to shout through his megaphone. He finally placed it down to his desk and removed his suit jacket.

"Now, ask yourselves why out of all the eager students that signed up for my class, you twenty-three are the chosen ones, all handpicked by me? I see greatness in all of you, but it does not happen overnight. It will be achieved over a course of time and hard work. If you all can agree to those simple requirements, then let's begin."

Riley was over the moon, whereas for me, I shrugged off my less than enthusiastic feeling. I convinced myself it was first week jitters. After a month, my feelings had not changed. I was fighting for a connection, a spark, something to get me re-energized for my classes.

I kept my conversations with my father to the basics. He asked question after question, but I was brilliant at evading. I knew all too well my father's feelings, and I was never in the mood for a reminder. I did not want to have a five-hour conversation about the importance of my education and how vital it was for my future.

Living with Brandon and Clay was not my smartest idea and did not help ease my mind. They turned our love nest into a frat house. Now that they had girlfriends, it was a round the clock party. The girls were nice enough, and Riley needed friends. I just was not sure they were the best ones for her. They were wild like their boyfriends, and how they made it to class each day shocked the shit out of me.

Some days I could barely keep my eyes open, thank goodness for strong coffee. I was not supposed to drink an excess amount of caffeine. So instead of putting the crap that everyone loved into my body, I began running and lifting weights. My energy level was strong, but I still struggled in school. I struggled to feel something, anything…what was I missing?

After a month cohabitating with our friends, I had reached my limit of annoyance and called my father. He was too respectful of my feelings to ever say "I told you so" and give me an hour speech about it. Of course I knew he would say yes to me wanting to move back to our penthouse with Riley. I just needed to convince her that it was the best solution. My memory returned to the argument that was the beginning of our down spiral.

"You can't be serious Jackson. I love our place, I love living with our friends, what's the problem?"

"I don't love living with our friends, and sharing our once spacious space with four other people. It is cramped, and we have no privacy. I can't concentrate or study, we have to move."

"You decided for me? Without even asking how I felt about it."

"Riley, we are discussing it now."

"No, Jackson, you are telling me what you have decided and have completely taken me out of the equation."

"You are overreacting as usual and not willing to compromise. You want to believe that I did what you are accusing me of...fine! Your personal things are packed. Richard will pick up the rest. A car is waiting outside to bring us home. Are you coming?"

"Jackson, we need to talk."

Her soft voice pulled me out of my thoughts. She was brushing her long hair and keeping her head down.

I sat down beside her and silently pleaded for her to turn and face me. She asked to talk, and then she shut down. What a mixed message! My girl was stubborn and needed a little coaxing. I put my hands on her shoulders and pulled her closer to me.

"Riley, please look at me," I said.

She allowed me to hold her while I continued to berate myself for being rough with her. I hated that she went to the club and unprotected. This was unchartered territory for us. I did not know how to handle being at odds with Riley. She was the love of my life who I always wanted to cherish, respect, and grovel at her feet if I had to.

Her silent treatment was killing me. I hated when she shut down. With Riley, you would always get the same two reactions when she was upset. The first one would be to overreact, and the second would be to shut down. Both reactions equally upset me.

"Riley, please talk to me," I demanded.

"Why, Jackson? You're not interested in anything that's important to me."

"That is not true, and you know it. You are my priority in all things."

"Where were you today? And I am not talking about seeing Dr. O'Larien. I mean afterwards. Where were you for six hours today? Because I can tell you where you weren't."

I paced the room trying to remember, and then my eyes locked in on her backpack with her binder sticking out of it. *The presentation? Oh my God! How I could have forgotten something so important to Riley, and to me*, I thought to myself.

"I'm so sorry, baby," I pleaded. "I completely forgot about it. What happened with Professor Connelly?"

"Seriously, Jackson? 'I am sorry' is all you can say to me? Because of your disappearing act, I am one strike away from failing his class! I will ask you again. Where were you today?"

Her hurt eyes were piercing my soul with a thousand razor blades. *What is she doing to me?* She walked over to our discarded pile of clothes and picked up the shirt I wore today, examining the collar. Tears were falling from her eyes, and then she threw the shirt at me.

"I guess I have my answer," she stated and walked out of our bedroom.

WTF? I looked down to my shirt and noticed red lipstick. *No!* I guess when Bridgette kissed me, we were too close in the other's space. I tossed the shirt and ran after Riley, who locked herself in our guest bedroom. She was crying uncontrollably thinking I cheated on her. I pounded on the door and begged for entrance.

"Riley, please open the door. You do not understand. Whatever is going through your mind right now, you have it all wrong. Please allow me to explain. Riley!"

I shouted again, "I swear Riley, if you do not open this door in the next five seconds, I am going to kick it down. Please open the door."

I banged and banged until finally had enough and with adrenaline taking over, I kicked the door with such a force, it separated from the hinge. Riley, shaking from her crying, was in a corner with her head in her hands. I took a breath and slowly got down to my knees and crawled over to her.

Her cries were piercing my soul. Regret was making my heart hurt. I had hurt her feelings and made her doubt me and our relationship. Our love was real, but she had trouble overcoming her insecurities, an issue I had thought we overcame once we were engaged.

"Riley, please? I would never betray you. You are the only one I love and want, could ever want. How could you believe for one second that I would ever want anyone else? Moreover, to be with you so intimately, only to take what is sacred between us and share it with another... that is crazy, beautiful girl. You are everything I want and shall ever need in ten lifetimes."

Her tears stopped, and she lunged herself into my arms.

I kissed her all over her face and said, "I'm sorry. I am sorry. I love you so much. I swear we are going to figure this out. Let's get you to bed, and we can talk in the morning."

She said nothing. I carried her back to our bedroom and tucked her underneath the duvet. I held her in my arms and just whispered my apologies repeatedly. I was exhausted but pushed myself to stay awake in fear that I would awaken to a cold bed and Riley gone.

The next day, the morning light was beginning to come through our large floor to ceiling windows. I quickly hit the remote we kept on our side table, and a second later, the room darkening shades came down. Riley was sleeping, not sure how soundly, but I knew she was out.

I wanted to do something special for her this morning but was afraid to leave her alone. I dialed Richard and asked him if he could pick up some pastries, bagels, and her favorite latte she drank every morning before class. Richard agreed, and while he was out picking up breakfast, I took a quick shower. When I came out of the en suite, she was awake and sitting up against the headboard.

"Good morning," I said.

"Is it?" she asked, making my heart pang with guilt.

I climbed back into bed and let my eyes ask permission to touch her. She did not hesitate and let me hold her.

"I am sorry for yesterday. I would never intentionally hurt you, and I am deeply sorry I let you down. I will call Professor Connelly and personally apologize."

She responded, "Why call him when you can talk to him in person on Monday?"

It was time to tell her.

"Riley, I'm not sure if I'm returning to his class…or school, for that matter."

Shocking her into silence, she pulled away from me and shielded her body with the duvet cover.

"What are you doing Jackson? You are breaking my heart, and I do not understand why. Why are we in this place of uncertainty? I feel so far away from you, and all I want is to feel your arms around me and your love surround me."

"Riley, you have me and my love. How can you doubt my feelings for you? You are all I want to share my life with. Please believe me when I say how lost I would be without you."

"If that's true, Jackson, then why push me away? And before you say that I am imagining this conclusion, you would be wrong. I know how I feel, and I am not so naïve not to notice that my fiancé has something weighing heavily on his mind and is hiding it from me."

"I have never lied to you, Riley, especially about my feelings for you."

"You have, Jackson! Have you so easily forgotten our first trip to New York?"

"That was different and miles apart from where we are now. I was trying to protect you and keep something from my father that I knew would hurt him. As you well remember, my bright idea did not work out so well for us. I learned a very hard lesson the day I lied to you and to my father. I promised you I would never be so careless with your feelings again, and Riley, I have kept my word."

"And the lipstick on your collar? Is that keeping your promise of forever to me?"

I responded, "I can see how you easily would jump to that conclusion, but you are wrong. After my appointment with Liam, I just walked the city with no direction in mind. But all of a sudden, I found myself standing in front of Reed Global, as if I was caught in a magnetic storm pulling me in. I had never felt a strong reaction to that place before until that very moment. I could not explain it; I just went in thinking I was going to take a quick look around and then leave. A familiar face quickly changed my mind. You know Tom, who works with my father out in California? He has a daughter who interns here, Bridgette Johannsen, and I haven't seen her in years."

The mention of Bridgette caused Riley to shift in her demeanor. Was it the look of jealousy? Her eyes were dancing with emotion. Her beautiful skin became flushed, which was a clear sign that she was not too happy I spent an afternoon with another woman when I should have been with her.

She shifted again in our bed, making the cover fall down low and exposing her breasts with her perfectly pebbled pink nipples. She knew exactly what she was doing to me. Riley should have known that she never had to work at getting my attention. This girl owned my fucking soul; why did she have such a hard time believing it?

I was not going to play this sexy game of hers, and I was about to turn the tables. As I was about to say something, my phone buzzed with Richard, alerting me that he was back with our breakfast. I rose from the bed.

"Breakfast is here. Get dressed and join me downstairs."

I wanted to punch myself in the face for leaving her there in bed, so fucking tempting. My body felt heated, and the bulge in my pants was pressing hard against my zipper. *Damn girl! You are going to unman me if I am not careful.*

She looked hurt, but I knew if I stayed, we would make love, and I was not ready. Riley needed to communicate with me and not use her body to do so. Her game had effectively worked in the past, but not this morning. We had so much to discuss, and I had to maintain my focus.

A platter was set out with many bakery choices to choose from. I knew I could put away a bagel and a few pastries on my own. I was starving and knew my girl had to be hungry too.

She came down a few minutes later, wearing only sleep shorts and a body fitting tank top. Her choice of clothing left little to the imagination. I was happy Richard was discreet enough to give us privacy.

Her long hair was up in a messy bun with curly tendrils hanging along her cheek. I swallowed deep and took a few calming breaths. She leaned down and reached over to pick up a pastry and then her coffee, giving me a clear shot of her ass. Riley's seductive show she was putting on for me was not going to deflect me from our conversation. My girl was going to have to wait, no matter how my body was reacting to her.

Her show was over for now and she took a seat across from me. Another breath and I was ready to continue our talk.

"She's just a friend, an old one from school."

"Friends with benefits?" she quickly spat out.

Unbelievable! Could she be any more hurtful? I would never betray her.

"You know, Riley, I've changed my mind. Jealousy does *not* look attractive on you. The floor show, as entertaining as it was, also proved unnecessary. I love you, and there is no one else for me. Bridgette is my friend, and for you to imply otherwise just pisses me off."

"What do you expect me to think when I see clear evidence on your clothing?" Riley shouted back.

"I expect you to trust me and never doubt my feelings for you. This is what I expect from you, Riley. You are the only one I have ever slept with. The world I come from, I could have had any number of girls for my choosing, but not one would ever compare to you. You have my heart, my body, my soul. I waited for you. Please do not ever dismiss what we have with each other. And more importantly, please trust me when it comes to my feelings for you. It deeply hurts me beyond reason that you doubt us, and me, for that matter. I have spent all night and this morning mentally punishing myself for hurting you, and you so easily hurt me without hesitation. Why, Riley?"

She stood to come close to me, but I got up and took a step back. I really wanted to know how she could so easily go from one extreme to the next.

"Well?" I asked.

"I don't know, Jackson. I don't know why I do or say the things I do. You knew what you were signing on for loving me. I practically gave you an out back in Maryland."

"You did, and what did I tell you then?"

"You called me baby, and begged me to listen to you."

"And?" I asked.

"You told me you loved me and that you have given me your heart, one that was free from the minute we met."

"And?" I asked.

"And you said that you would fight with me all day long, only if you were able to hold me in your arms at night, something like that."

My fight was gone and so was hers. I was hopeful we could really talk now.

I told her, "I believe I said more to you, but that pretty much sums it up. Come here, Riley."

I opened up my arms, making it easy for her to walk into. Once she was close, I could not wait and pulled her into my chest. She wrapped her arms around my waist and held me tightly to her.

"I love you, crazy girl, so much I can't breathe at times. I know my actions lately have probably confused you, but please allow me to explain them to you now."

We grabbed our coffee and took our conversation into the living room. I sat with my back against the sofa and Riley in-between my legs. She was nestled as close as she could be, and I would pull her back if she decided to run.

I began, "For the past ten years, all I have ever wanted was to become a filmmaker. I fought my father for my independence and choice of school. He hated every part of my plans, but in the end, he conceded and allowed me to live my life on my own. I was very thankful for that, and to your mom for helping him through it."

I continued, "What I wasn't prepared for was the AVM, and how close I came to losing my life. Everything would be gone, and pursuing my dreams wouldn't have mattered because I didn't make it that day when my heart stopped on that operating table."

She shifted in my arms and took my face in her hands.

She said, "But you did survive, Jackson. Where is this coming from?"

"I guess it's always been there, but it's been on my mind since we moved here. At my appointment yesterday, I questioned Liam about those seconds on the table after my heart stopped. What you don't know is that when I was down—or for lack of a better term: dead—I saw my mother."

"You never told me this. Why hide it, Jackson?"

"I guess in a small way, I wanted to have that memory all to myself. But then I shared my revelation with my father, because he experienced something similar and I knew he would believe me without question."

"Did you believe that I wouldn't believe you? Or I would think you were crazy or something?"

"Stop it! Once again, you are questioning me and the love I feel for you."

She said, "No, I'm not. I'm asking you a question, and you are evading."

"No, you don't believe that you are good enough for me, and when you allow your mind and heart to believe that, it takes all I have to convince you that you are wrong. Riley, you are all that I want! How many times do we have to do this dance with one another? I am allowed to have feelings too and sometimes they get hurt, so I am not blind when I hurt yours. I am just trying to explain how I feel without you flipping out and running for the nearest exit."

"I'm sorry if I make you feel that way, but you have told me nothing in the last few months, and now today all of a sudden is about cleansing your soul and being open with me. When did that change, Jackson?"

"I don't know, I honestly don't know. Riley, you must understand coming that close to dying and losing all who were important to me gave me another perspective on my life. The childhood dreams I once had were not as important to me anymore. I am an adult now, and the realities of becoming what I dreamed are very different from what I once imagined. I am not saying it will not happen, because anything can be achieved if you work hard. I just no longer want that dream. I want something else."

"Okay. So what do you want?" she inquired.

I took a deep breath and exhaled a few times.

"I want to return to California and learn the business that is my legacy. I miss my father, and I want to work with him, to learn from him, and to carry on what he has worked so hard to achieve. I am a Reed, and it's time I take my rightful place by his side."

She interrupted, "And by me agreeing to become a Reed, I am just supposed to give up my dreams and be the little missus that yields to her husband's every wish and demand?"

"Of course not. Are we there again? Have you heard anything I have said?"

"I have Jackson, and I believe it is incredibly selfish of you to just drop this down onto my lap and not expect me to have a problem with it. Clearly, last night you had no problem behaving like a Reed when you showed me exactly how to submit. Now, you are doing it again."

"Okay, Riley, if you want to go there, then fine we are there! I love how you can so easily turn things around to work to your benefit. Last night, I was out of my mind, and I took it out on your willing body that craved mine. You always know that you can say no to me, and I would stop without question, but did you? You came at me just as hard until we could not form clear sentences. As much as I loved it, I was still regretful and spent the night apologizing for it."

"Fine, Jackson! I'm a slut that likes it rough. Happy now?"

"God! You are so fucking frustrating at times. How dare you demean yourself like that? What the fuck, Riley? How much more do you want to break me down? You ask for me to talk to you, and when I do, you go dark and cold and turn into someone I don't recognize."

"Look, Jackson, I told you once before that I would change my entire life for you because this ring on my finger makes it alright to do so. I gave you a choice back in Maryland when you were recovering, and you told me no. We would still have our dream in New York. We would be married when we finished school, and then begin our careers together. I'm happy here, Jackson. I love school. I am learning so much from my professors, and I am even in a better place with my father who is only a few hours away from me. How can you ask me to just give it all up to follow you back to California?"

"You already said it, Riley. Wearing my ring and agreeing to marry me makes it okay for me to ask you these questions. I am not going to throw you over my shoulder and put you on a plane tomorrow. This is just something that has been on my mind, and I am finally talking to you about it."

"No, you are telling me. You did this when you moved us out of our first apartment. I did not have a say then, and I do not have a say now. You so eloquently reminded me earlier that you are a Reed. A Reed always gets what he wants, right, Jackson? The strong-arm tactic worked so effectively for your father. Why shouldn't it work the same for you?"

"Riley, please don't go there. I don't know how much more I can take."

"Why *not* go there?" she yelled. "Your dad singlehandedly removed my father from his marriage to my mother without blinking an eye, leaving my father destroyed. I love that my mother is blissfully happy with your father after years of unrequited love for each other, but we are not them. We are Jackson and Riley, not Walker nor Reese. It is fun to joke around, but baby, what we have is entirely different from their beginning. In our story, there is not a person trying to break us up. We have our parents' blessing to be together. We have support and understanding for our choices. We have been through so much, and you don't ever have to remind me how close I came to losing you. I was there right with you. You made it Jackson, and came out stronger than ever before. You make me believe in love. Our parents had their happily ever after in their story, so please let us have ours."

"Riley, I want nothing more than to be your husband and give you the world, but I also cannot deny how I am feeling. Please try to understand where I am coming from. Please just think about it, and I will discuss it with my father when we go home for the holidays."

"I can't go with you, Jackson. Not now, after everything that was said here."

"No! You are upset, and I am so sorry for putting you through any pain. Just please promise me you will think about it, and once we are in California, we can talk about it."

She got up off the couch, and it felt like she was miles away from me. She held her head as she paced the room, and then she turned over to me with tears in her eyes. I wanted to hold her, touch her, and convince her we would be okay. We had to be okay.

The way she was looking at me made me nervous. All sorts of thoughts were going through my mind. What Riley did next, I never anticipated.

She walked back over to me and reached for my hand. With her soft fingers, she opened it, with my palm facing up. She leaned down to place a kiss, and then I felt something small and heavy in my palm.

She gave me the ring back, my mother's ring.

I could not help my tears from falling. I grabbed her and held onto to her before she could run, holding on as if my life depended on it. My life did depend on it…with Riley. She was my heart, and by returning my ring, she was breaking me into a thousand pieces. If my breaking heart could be heard, it would have sounded like a wounded animal begging for death.

"Please, Jackson, let me go," she pleaded with me.

"No! I love you Riley. How could you just give up on us?"

"I love you too, Jackson, and it is you that are giving up on us, not the other way around. I need time to think, and I cannot do that while wearing your ring. In this moment here with you, that ring feels like a thousand pounds on my finger. It is weighing me down and forcing me into an impossible situation."

"A situation? Are you fucking serious right now? What is it, Riley? Our love is now a burden to you? I am not free to change my mind on my career choice? What's wrong with claiming what is rightfully mine?"

"Nothing at all, Jackson. What *is* wrong is that you once again made a decision without me. You already decided to drop out of film school long before this conversation. This is why you did not care that you missed our presentation, because it was the furthest thought from your mind. You think that because I love you and wear this ring, you can just change our lives and not expect me to have an opinion about it. I'm sorry, Jackson, but I will not live like that. It works for my mother, not for me. She is happy with her new life; they both are. Your father and my mother have the perfect life in California. I thought that you and I had that here in New York."

I had to ask, "Are we over?"

"I don't know what we are; only that I love you, and I need some time. Please give that to me."

I had never felt more alone than I did at that moment when Riley walked away from me. I gathered a few things in a bag and called my father to tell him I would be arriving sooner than expected. I kept the details vague with him over the phone.

The ride to the private hanger at the airport was a complete blur. Richard took my bags and carried them onto the plane for me. He gave me a hug and then asked me not to do anything that I would regret later.

"Sir, Riley is worth fighting for," he said, "and she is your match in every sense of the word."

I had no words to return to him, just an understanding between us. The cabin door closed, and the jet was in the air within minutes.

I left without seeing or talking to Riley. Her walking away was enough of a goodbye. My heart was shattered, broken. I may have been returning home to California and to my father, but I knew my real home was with Riley.

Was she right? Did I just expect her to yield at my every wish and command? Riley acted as if Reese was a kept woman that needed my father's permission just to breathe. I did not want that kind of marriage, and it was not one that my father had with Reese.

I was damn proud to be my father's son, and I knew that being a Reed came with an immense amount of responsibility. I tried all my life to live up to it.

I did not believe this was the end for Riley and me. I would never accept it. It broke my heart to leave her, but it was what she wanted.

Somehow, I would fix this and make things right. We had to be okay.

Riley

Facing the future without him

I DID NOT want to believe that Jackson would actually leave, but he did. The realization of his absence and silence throughout the apartment hurt me—no, shattered me. He left me, and I let him.

I was not trying to make him choose, but I thought I was giving him room to think how the sudden change of *our* plans would ultimately change the direction of my life, and our life together. I knew with all my conviction that I had to stand my ground with him, or I feared I would lose my voice in this relationship. I had to be his equal in all areas of his life. If he deemed me any less, then how could we realistically make it? This was my fear, and the slamming of the door drove that point home for me. We were more lost than I ever realized.

It has been one whole day without him, and I was still in the same clothes I was in yesterday when he ordered me to dress and come down for breakfast. My phone was ringing off the hook, no doubt my mother and Mr. Reed calling. I did not feel like talking to anyone, so I let it all go to voicemail.

Richard was up here several times to look in on me, but he was probably just spying for Mr. Reed. God! I hated how I sounded. Richard was so much more than a Reed employee; he was our friend.

I finally pulled myself out of bed and took the hottest shower my skin could tolerate. I ate the day old pastries and brewed a fresh cup of coffee. There was no point in me starving my broken heart. Jackson was the one that left, not the other way around. I had too much to do now because he decided to take a break from life and go find himself. I still needed to hand in a kick-ass project to Professor Connelly, and that was my only priority now.

I took my files and my work into the media room. I made myself comfortable for what I knew would be many hours of viewing Jackson's footage and revising if I had to. This was his work, per sé, but it was *our* project. I only saw parts of it and never had the opportunity to screen it with Jackson. I thought I would see it for the first time at our presentation.

It's so good Jackson. You are so talented. Why have you changed your mind about wanting this? I see your love for it right before my eyes. We would make such a great team, I thought to myself. I wiped a few tears that began to fall, and buried my head in my hands to cry. *I can't do this without you, Jackson! You are such an asshole for leaving me!*

My phone was flashing with Mr. Reed's name blinking back at me. He was not going to stop until I spoke with him. What could I tell him?

Thank you, fiancé, for once again putting me in an impossible situation of going up against your father. Fiancé? I do not know what you are anymore to me, Jackson. You left me.

"The hell with it!" I shouted out to an empty room. Curiosity won over, and I answered the call on the last ring.

"Hello," I said, my voice a bit shaky.

"Riley, this is Mr. Reed. How are you?"

I took a breath before answering.

"I'm fine, Mr. Reed. Why the call?"

Oh, I know why. We have shaken up their perfect world, and now Mr. Reed is probably in "let me fix it mode." Heaven forbid I upset my mother in any way. Again, I felt like kicking myself for my thoughts right now. I was angry with Jackson, and no one else.

"I think you know, Riley. What I don't know is why are you avoiding your mother's phone calls, and why is Jackson here in California and you are in New York?"

"I can't talk about it, Mr. Reed, you are going to have to ask Jackson."

"Riley, I have, and he will tell me nothing. So now I am asking you. We have traveled this road before. As memory serves, it did not end well the last time you or my son kept secrets from me. I do not wish to pry. I just want to help. Please Riley, let me."

"Mr. Reed, I don't need a reminder of Maryland. I was there."

"Then if you learned anything from that time, you should know by now that you can tell me anything, and I promise I will listen. What I will not comply with is lying to me. Your mother is worried for you, and so am I. Please Riley, talk to me."

He sounded sincere and I knew he was telling me the truth, but he was Jackson's father. I could not be one hundred percent sure if he would truly support me. He asked me again to talk to him. What did I have to lose? It already felt like I lost Jackson, so why hold back now?

I said, "Mr. Reed, I'm finding it hard to believe that Jackson being Jackson, hasn't told you anything yet. You must know something. He wouldn't just fly across the country and show up on your doorstep without at least giving you a clue to his reason behind it."

"Okay, Riley, you are right, but I can assure you that your

mother and I do not know much at all. Jackson seems very conflicted and clearly lost without you. He says he wants to work at Reed Global, and his dream of becoming a filmmaker is no longer important to him as it once was."

"There you have it, Mr. Reed. You've been informed," I smugly said.

"Riley, I think I need to know more than that."

"I do not know what you expect from me. I will give you the short version, because I know how fond you are of getting right to the point. Jackson and I were fine up until we began school. I will admit our dynamic of apartment life was not very cozy, but we managed to make it work. I only knew Jackson hated it when he ordered me to follow him back to your apartment. He hates my friends, and if you ask me, he probably hates Brandon and Clay too. He doesn't care for them anymore, and I really do not know why."

I continued, "I have done everything Jackson has asked me to do, and it is still not good enough. A few days ago, we were meeting with our Professor to present him with our film project. I wrote up the documentary, and Jackson was in charge of the film footage. We both completed our parts, but Jackson never showed up for the scheduled time. I was completely humiliated, and if I do not produce a finished project to Professor Connelly, I can kiss my semester grade goodbye. Word will get around with my other instructors that I'm this alleged flake, and I will be fucked, Mr. Reed! And it will all be Jackson's fault. You wanted the truth, Mr. Reed, now you have it. Your son not only has changed his mind with plans that we made together, but his reckless decision has affected my academic career as well. I am so angry and disappointed with your son. Maybe it was right in the end for him to leave. From where I am standing right now, our life is unrecognizable. But know this: with or without him, I will chase my dreams and succeed."

Oh, that felt good! I found my voice and practically screamed it aloud to Mr. Reed. I could not hold it in any longer. I was angry with Jackson and Mr. Reed for pushing me. He wanted to know, so I certainly gave it to him. I was sure my mother would disapprove of my manners, but I refused to be at fault here.

"Mr. Reed, are you still on the line?" I had to ask, because I did not hear anything after my outburst.

"I am. Did Jackson give you any reason why he missed something so vital not only to you, but to him?"

"It was the day of his check-up appointment with Dr. O'Larien. He said after his visit, which I believe went well, he just walked the city until he ended up at Reed Global. He said he met up with some Bridgette girl, who by the way kissed him and left her lipstick on his collar. Yeah, that was fun to discover. He explained they were just friends, and he was merely visiting his legacy."

I went on, "I was angry with Jackson for not showing up for our presentation. It was obvious to me that he had other things on his mind, and with no messages from him, I was ready to blow off some steam. I went to see my friends and decided to have a girl's night. Jackson found me at the club and practically dragged me home. I had never seen him so angry since the time he was recovering from his surgery. This was a different kind of frustration. He wanted to kill the guy that was coming on to me, but I knew how to take care of myself, thanks to Richard. By the time Jackson got to me, the guy was holding his balls in his hand. I was kind of proud of myself, but didn't have time to enjoy my victory because your son brought me home."

I continued, "Do you want to know what happened next? Of course you do. You are the great Walker Reed. Your perfect son fucked me hard against the wall and proved his dominance over me. And what's worse? I liked it, because it was Jackson. I love your son so much, and I would have submitted to him in any way possible just to hold onto him. We cried all night, because we both felt like hell. The next morning, he apologized, and what I thought was going to be a real conversation led to Jackson walking out on me. He has not even bothered to call me, or even have the courtesy to send a text. You know the rest, Mr. Reed, he ran back to you, back to the fortress of Reed. I hope you are happy that you finally have what you have always wanted."

What is wrong with you, Riley Taylor Briggs? You just told Mr. Reed in living color all the naughty details about your sex life with his son. I can only imagine the look on Mr. Reed's face right about now. Thank goodness I am thousands of miles away from him.

Telling Mr. Reed made it sound so bad, especially for Jackson. But who was I kidding…I loved when Jackson took what was his. It was incredibly hot, and although he was mad, I knew he would never intentionally hurt me. We established from the moment we gave ourselves to the other what we liked and did not like, and so far, I loved it all.

Silence was all that came from the other line. This was the reactive side to me. Once I was pushed too far, I was a ticking time bomb ready to detonate. He was just being a concerned father, and I just ripped into him without any regard to his feelings or my mother's, for that matter. I took a deep breath and hoped he was still on the line with me.

"I'm sorry, Mr. Reed. I have been nothing but disrespectful to you throughout this entire conversation. Please forgive me for speaking so crudely to you."

I wanted to just crawl under a rock and stay there. I could only imagine what my mother would think of my behavior, and I hoped they would not tell Grandma Lila.

He still did not say anything to me, but I knew he was still with me because I heard the light tap of his fingers drumming on his desk.

"Riley, how long do you have to turn in your work to Professor Connelly?" he said.

What? After all, I said, this is what he wants to know? About school?

"As it stands now, the project is complete. I just need Jackson to submit it with me. If he chooses not to, then I have a week to completely re-do the project on my own. I know from the footage I just watched, there is no way I will get it done."

He responded, "I will not let you fail. Jackson will be on my plane first thing in the morning back to New York. And so this will not be a surprise to you, I will also be accompanying my son."

"Mr. Reed, Jackson made it perfectly clear that he does not wish to return to film school. I can't have him just going along with a ruse to our professor for the sole reason to get me a passing grade."

"Riley, he has not dropped out of anything; he has only missed one class. You phone your professor today and tell him to expect a presentation in his office on Tuesday morning. Am I making myself clear?"

I squeezed my temples together with my fingers and counted to ten.

"Mr. Reed, this is not just Jackson's life you are taking over; this is my life too. I will not be strong armed to bend at your will because you are, well, you."

"Riley, you are my family. I love you with all of my heart. I will not allow you to fail, and this is not me controlling you. This is your future father-in-law trying to right a wrong and help two amazing individuals find their way back to one another. Please Riley; tell me you understand my true intentions here."

I could not stop the tears from falling no matter how hard I tried. I loved Jackson so much, and if involving Mr. Reed helped us get back to where we were, then I would allow him to assist.

"Okay, Mr. Reed, do your worst. I only hope whatever happens does not push Jackson further away from me."

"Riley, believe me when I say this. My son is in love with you. Contrary to what you think, I believe my son is not perfect. He is going to make mistakes, probably a lot of them, and you will be right beside him making some of your own. As for what he feels for you, I do not doubt a blind man could not see how much he loves you. You are both young and experiencing many changes. You are not expected to get it right the first time out."

I retorted, "Yeah, but you did, Mr. Reed. You planned your entire future around my mother after you first met. If your father hadn't interfered with your lives, you would have had a lifetime with my mother, and I probably wouldn't be here right now."

He said back to me, "The fact remains that no matter what happened, our love remained true, and we are together now. My son knows exactly who he wants to share his life with, and although you are at odds now, believe me, he is faring no better here without you. It took a lot for me to call you today. I promised I would not interfere with my son's life, but I also will not stand by and do nothing when I am in a position to help. Riley, I promise that you and Jackson will be okay."

"I hope you're right."

"I am. I would not make a promise I could not keep. My history with your mother is proof of that. I take it once your assignment is handed in, you can begin your holiday break?"

"Technically, it has already begun, but I'm free once this matter is resolved."

"Good. I expect your bags to be packed and you to be ready to leave for California once Professor Connelly awards you an A on your project. I will see you tomorrow."

After he ended our call in his right-to-the-point manner, I slumped back in my chair and sighed deeply. My eyes found our picture from Big Sur. Jackson and I were both hugging the tree where he said he would marry me one day.

Tears began wetting my cheeks, and I closed my eyes tightly to ward them off, but it was no use. I was in pain over missing Jackson. I wanted him so much to come rushing back into the apartment and take me in his arms so we could make up and put all of this behind us.

The reality was not that pretty. He left, and all the assurances Mr. Reed gave me did not make me feel any better. Jackson and I vowed to stand on our own, but he was not here to lean against. What other choice did I have? I had to trust his father to help us.

CHAPTER 16

Walker

Never count out a Reed

HOW COULD TWO people drift so far apart in such little time? Jackson certainly had some explaining to do.

After my very illuminating conversation with Riley, a drink was in order, something very strong. Scotch was out of the question, and my choices were limited. After my very big misunderstanding with Reese, I drank myself sick after she left me and vowed to never be that indulgent with my body again.

I instead chose one of my favorites: a 1958 Giacomo Borgogno. "Thank you, Priscilla," I happily said aloud when I opened my cabinet. After pouring myself a glass, I let the delicious, rich flavors dance on my pallet before swallowing the first sip. Leaning back in my chair, I was lost in thought, replaying the conversation over in my mind with Riley.

How far Riley had come from a shy, innocent girl who nearly

succumbed to the sound of my voice, to now an angry lioness destroying her prey. Riley did not hold back in the slightest how she felt about the current state of affairs regarding her relationship with my son. Riley was always a heart-on-her-sleeve type of young woman. She would express how she felt in living color, usually by crying or a very animated display of emotions. She was angry, a tone she rarely used. I heard true heartbreak and pain, all caused by my son. It did not sit well with me at all. To think that way of Jackson made my stomach ill.

I pulled out my cell and sternly called out, "I need to see you in my office at once."

I disconnected and finished off my wine, only to quickly pour another glass. This vintage was not to be drank quickly. Ticking off everything one by one after Riley's call was making me incensed, and I saw red.

Stephen swiftly entered my study, closing the door behind him.

"Yes, Mr. Reed, what can I do for you?" he asked.

Skipping the pleasantries, I got right to my point.

"I need the jet fueled and ready to leave by seven tomorrow morning."

I looked down to my watch and realized it was way past midnight. I had been in here for hours after leaving Reese, who was now sleeping alone without me. *Fuck! How many more hoops am I going to have to jump through before this family can enjoy one fucking holiday without drama?*

"The destination, sir? Where am I filing the flight plan to?" he asked with efficiency and phone in hand.

"New York is the place. We are going to bring Riley home, back where she belongs...with Jackson."

He simply nodded and took his leave. I finished my second glass of wine and finished up the last of the work on my desk. I emailed Jenny with instructions for the tasks I would want completed. Next message was to Donovan and Tom to handle any scheduled meetings that did not require my immediate attention. Yeah, right!

Everything required my presence when solely running an empire. *This is the last thing I needed right now, and it is the worst possible time to just pick up and leave.*

What pained me the most was leaving Reese on her own. Her first trimester of pregnancy was always the hardest for her to get through. Her headaches with Fallon nearly gave me a heart attack every time I witnessed her discomfort. Reese would always minimize her pain level for my benefit, but she did not lie very well. I would always be on edge when it came to her health and well-being. Losing Elizabeth did that and forever changed me. I would move heaven and earth to make things better for Reese. Every pregnancy she experienced had met with stress, pain, loss, danger, and the unknown of what was to come next. I would not have her go through anything like that again. She already had one health scare, which aged me ten years.

Jackson and Riley's problems were their own, but I could not stand by and do nothing, so I would take their burdens upon myself and spare Reese anything that would upset her. Now I just had to explain to her about my sudden trip.

I nearly slammed my laptop closed. I needed to sleep a few hours and hold Reese in my arms. I closed the door to the study and walked down the hall to the bedroom. I peeked in on Fallon, who was sound asleep holding her precious teddy bear to her chest. I came upon Jackson's room, where light was coming from underneath his door. I lightly tapped, and Jackson called for me to come in.

"It's late, dad. What are you doing up?"

"I could say the same thing about you son. What are you working on?" I asked as I glanced over to his computer, clearly seeing a letter typed out on the screen.

Jackson noticed my eyes lingering, and he closed his laptop.

"Sorry, I didn't mean to pry," I said.

"You never do, dad. Is there something on your mind?"

Is he being funny? Because I am not amused, I thought to myself.

"Very perceptive of you, son, and yes, I have a great deal of concerns on my mind, you being one of them. Pack a small duffle. We leave for the airport at six, and that will be in four hours."

"What? Why? Where are we going?" he asked.

"Don't you know?"

"If I did, I wouldn't have asked," he said, his tone raising an octave higher than usual.

"Sure you do, Jackson. You have much to answer for, but not now, not here. You will answer every question I ask you when we are on the plane. This is not a request. Pack a bag and be ready to leave at six."

"And if I'm not? What happens then?"

Jackson's defiance played on my last bit of control. Between him and Riley, they were quite the workout for my efforts to remain calm. He sat straight up in his chair aiming daggers at me, clearly issuing a challenge.

Lesson number one, son: If you want to join me at Reed Global, you had better be ready to take me on.

I said to him, "In all my years as your father, I never would predict you would be so bold to challenge me, but here you stand, ready for battle. You believe you have it all figured out, don't you, son? You are mistaken. You will not win, so do not ever try to top me. Your defiance towards me in the past has gotten you nowhere and hurt more people than helped, so pull back now before you say something you will regret. This is my only warning."

"You talked to Riley, didn't you? Dad, this is my life. Please stay out of it. I will handle things with Riley. We just need some space to work it out."

"Time away from the other is the last thing you need. Believe me, son, it serves no purpose. You have hurt that girl beyond measure, and you will do everything you can to repair the damage you have caused to her. Do not even try to stop me with your so-called independence and how you can manage your life all on your own. If that were true, son, you would not have fled the home you created with Riley to come back here to lick your wounds. Grow up, Jackson! You are a Reed, and you will make this right with your girl. I expect nothing less from you. Now, do as I have instructed. I don't want to discuss anything else with you until we are on the plane."

I practically slammed my way out from his room.

"Fuck! Dammit to hell!" I shouted out, waking the baby with my outburst.

Reese came flying out of our bedroom to make her way to the nursery. She stumbled a bit with the sleepiness still in her eyes.

"Walker, what's wrong?" she asked breathlessly, coming closer to me.

"I'm sorry, baby, for waking you. Go back to sleep, and I will tend to our daughter."

"*We* will tend to our daughter," she said, as she extended her hand for me to take.

We walked back to Fallon's room to calm our princess. She was startled awake with the loudness of my voice. I sat beside her crib and rubbed her back in soothing circles. Reese sang a few lyrics to her favorite lullaby, and then our baby was once again asleep.

By the time I finally climbed into bed with Reese, it was close to three a.m. I was exhausted, but my body hungered for her touch. I needed to be inside my beautiful wife so she could take away all that was burdening me. She knew—she always knew—what I needed and began stroking my engorged cock. I arched my back just slightly and grounded my head into my pillow. I was coming undone with Reese touching and then pleasuring me with her mouth. But I did not want to come like this.

I pulled her up and positioned her over my cock, where she could sink down on me. I loved the feeling of Reese riding me hard with no gentleness whatsoever. This was a fiery exchange between us, and I would always take whatever she offered. She topped me with her dominance, keeping me just where she wanted me to be. I knew I was reaching my breaking point and wanted to flip her to her knees, spank the shit out of her, and fuck her from behind. But I gave Reese this round, no matter how much I wanted to up the ante.

I found my release shortly after Reese had reached hers. My eyes rolled to the back of my head in pure ecstasy for my woman. She collapsed on top of my chest, our bodies still connected as one. I would not dream of moving her, not yet. I needed to feel her for as long as possible.

"I love you so much, Mrs. Reed," I whispered closely to her ear.

"I love you too, Mr. Reed," she mumbled while face down onto my chest.

We detached ourselves from each other, and she slightly winced. We were rough tonight. I knew it was too much for her.

I asked, "Are you okay, baby? How sore are you?"

"I'm fine, Walker. Please do not worry."

"I do worry, quite often when it concerns you. Why do you choose to carry on like this if you are in any discomfort?"

She responded, "Walker, is that a serious question? I would never hold you back from taking what you need, because it is the same need I have too. I will never stop you, my love. Haven't you worked that out already?"

"You're pregnant, Reese. We should be more careful with your body."

"It's my body, Walker, and I know it pretty well. Please no worrying your mind over it."

"It's my body too, baby, and it's carrying my child."

"*Our* child."

"Yes, our child, a precious life I need to safeguard with all that I have. I love you so much for giving me yet another child, the greatest gift a man could ever receive," I said with a sigh.

"Talk to me baby, what's going on? You look so tired," she said.

Holding me in her arms, Reese was my everything, my cure to all that ever ailed me.

"I'm leaving in a few hours for New York. Please do not push me for a long explanation to as to why. The easiest way to say it is that I'll be taking Jackson with me to sort out his academics and then to repair what is broken in his relationship with Riley."

"I trust you, Walker, and if you need to go to New York, then do what you have to do. I will be here when you return."

"I promise you, Reese, as I live and breathe, we will have a spectacular holiday surrounded by our family and friends. You will smile so much that your tender cheeks will hurt. Nothing is going to come between us, not this time, and never on another holiday again."

"Kiss me before you make me cry. I love you, Walker."

"And I love you, Reese, so much more than my own life."

We made love once more until my girl was completely sated to the point of exhaustion. I was trailing close behind her. I managed to get two hours of sleep, but they were spent holding Reese securely in my arms.

I kissed her sleeping form and left a note on her side table. I kissed my Fallon goodbye, and then made my way down to my waiting car. Jackson was already seated across from me, looking stoically out of the window.

I was beyond exhausted from the past few days' events. I closed my eyes until we reached the private hanger. The pilot and co-pilot were ready, along with one flight attendant to assist. Jackson did not wait for Stephen to open his door; I, on the other hand, took the extra seconds to sleep.

"Have a good trip, sir," Stephen said as he shook my hand.

Normally he would accompany me on any trip, but I needed him to remain behind to oversee any issues at the office. It also gave me great comfort knowing he could watch over Reese and Fallon in my absence. If I had more time, I would have sent them to see Freddy, but who knew I would be traveling to New York on such short notice?

I handed off my briefcase and took my usual seat. Jackson could not have been further away from me. I gave him the time he needed, knowing we would be talking soon enough.

Once in the air and at the set altitude, I unbuckled my seatbelt and got up to sit closer to my son.

"Look at me, Jackson. It is not a request."

"What do you want me to say, dad? You didn't give me a choice or even allow me to explain my side to you. You once again took over, and the rest of us just have to fall in line."

"Jackson, you don't believe that, do you? I gave you more than one opportunity to talk to me and you refused, so here we are in a situation that I did not create. You did this son, and all on your own. If you ask me what I truly want, then I would say to be back in bed with my wife, but as you can see, I am here with you. Suck it up, and talk to me."

He sighed in frustration.

"Where would you like me to begin, dad? On the other hand, do you know it all already? I know you talked to Riley. She confirmed it to me this morning by a one-word text: '*Walker*.' Dad, my relationship with Riley is mine, and mine alone. We will work out our problems on our own. How many times do I have to say this to you?"

"As many times as I ask you, Jackson, because it is clear to me that you are slowly drowning and so is Riley. Yes, I did speak with her, or do you recall our conversation only a few hours ago?"

I watched my son run his frustrated hands through his thick mane of hair that matched my own. He knew not to have another outburst with me, so he held his head and sighed loudly for me to hear, another move I hated seeing him do. I never knew if he was experiencing pain from a headache or a possible AVM again. Liam and Samuel assured me with all of their knowledge and expertise that Jackson would never go through that again, but it was my fear, and it scared the hell out of me.

I waited another beat. Then he finally looked at me, and I saw the son I had raised. His eyes matched his mother's, but they were full of sadness and pain. He was fighting against what he wanted, what he was dreaming to have, and what he may lose.

I understood this all too well and would never wish this upon my son. My eyes told him that he could tell me anything, no matter how much it cost me to hear it. He needed to trust me and know that I would never purposely judge him. I was his father. I had put him above all things in life and never hesitated to do so. He had to give me the same in return if I was ever to help him.

CHAPTER 17

Jackson

Awakening

FRUSTRATING MINUTES LINGERED on. I knew my father was waiting with his last grasp of patience, but where could I begin? How could I tell him that I might have lost Riley and ruined any chance of reconciling because of my change of heart?

I never imagined ever being here in this place, so divided from Riley, but I was. And I had done everything wrong. I should have trusted her to hear me and really be with me in the conversation that would change the dynamic of our relationship. Instead, I took another approach, one that was so not me. I behaved like a tyrant and took what she had given me and turned it into something dark, with no semblance of us. Riley was right to call me out on all of it, but she still managed to show mercy for me when I was being an ass.

"I'm waiting, Jackson," my father's voice broke me out of my rampant thoughts.

I told him, "I asked her to come to California with me. I asked her to choose me over her dreams and what she wants for her future, and she said no. We got into a huge fight, and she gave me back mother's ring. I had a bag packed, and I told her she could stay in the apartment for as long as she wanted, but I would not be returning. She let me go, dad. She let me walk through the door and never asked me to stay."

"No, Jackson, you let her go. How could you do that to her?"

"She gave me no choice. We were so far from where we began, what else could I do but to leave?"

"You stay, Jackson. For fucks sake, you should have stayed! To tell that girl that you would not be returning…you might as well have just stabbed her in the back with your betrayal. To never return to New York, to Riley? My God! What was going through your mind when you heard those words pass over your lips? I do not understand you, son. How is this happening?"

"Dad, what do you want me to say?"

"Gee, I don't know son, maybe start with how you carelessly cast aside the girl you are supposed to love, the same girl you asked for my blessing to marry. It's no wonder why she sounded the way she did and clearly held nothing back when I asked her for an explanation."

I responded, "You think I destroyed her? Dad, you do not know the half of it. Believe me, I apologized all night for my behavior. Riley and I worked it out, and I had every intention to tell her everything the next morning. But when I did, she lashed out. We argued about a lot of stuff, and then she told me she needed time to process everything that happened. The next thing she did, I never saw coming."

"What happened?"

"Riley took off my ring. She knew it would destroy me, and it did. I never felt so much pain in all of my life after I felt the weight of the ring in my hand.

"And Riley? What about her, Jackson? Did you ever consider for just one minute how she felt? She did not remove her ring for show. She was just as much devastated as you were. That ring would only serve as a reminder for her to what it represented…a future, Jackson! A future with you! Dammit! Have you so easily forgotten how hard you two fought to be together? I know you, son. You would have never given her your mother's ring if you didn't know one hundred percent that Riley was the one."

"She is the one, dad, my only love. I want Riley for the rest of my life. I just don't know how I can get her back."

"Son, in order to get her back, you would have had to lose her. What you have with Riley is so rare. It is a love that was written for you, and it was found when you least expected it. You have found your forever with Riley. You will have all that you have dreamed about, but you just need to remember your beginnings and all that you have that makes you and Riley so special. I never doubted your feelings for her, neither did Reese. We believe in love. We fight for love. We trust in love. What we have together, we know you and Riley share the same in your relationship. It's clear to anyone who meets you or listens to you talk about the other."

"You don't believe I've lost her?" I asked.

"I do not. She is waiting for you, Jackson, and if you would open that heart of yours to catch up with your brain, you would know she never wanted you to leave. Riley wanted you to fight for her, to fight for what you two worked so hard to achieve. That girl loves you. She fought for you during the times you had nearly given up on your recovery. She waited for you to be ready. She never complained during the times you shut her out. She was always by your side and went through every single emotion just as much as you did. Son, you have everything a man could want, and for the life of me I will not understand how you have so foolishly put your relationship in jeopardy."

I felt sick to my stomach hearing my father go on into detail about how much I fucked up with Riley.

I said, "I hurt her, dad, with my distance, and then I did something more. I am not sure how she feels about it or how to explain my actions."

"Oh, you mean the rough sex? Let's begin there, shall we?"

"No fucking way! She did not tell you about that, did she?"

"Believe me, son, my ears are still bleeding, if it matters at all to you. Um, she didn't just tell me…it was more like screaming at the top of her lungs. I am not going to sit here and trade experiences with you. What you do in the privacy of your bedroom with Riley is your business. What troubles me is that the anger you felt when she was out partying affected your judgment in the care of Riley. I will not deny that I have not felt that intense feeling of ownership and the need to possess my lover. Aggression is one emotion I do know and have experienced in bed. It was something we have shared before and enjoyed. What I have always struggled with was how it affected me afterwards."

He continued, "The woman you love should always be cherished beyond anything else in the world. From the beginning of any relationship, expectations need to be voiced. You should always talk and agree without crossing the line. No one is perfect, and sometimes no matter how hard you try not to hurt the one you love, you end up doing just that. I take it that's what happened between you and Riley?"

"That's exactly what happened," I said. "She accused me of being like you. Sorry, dad."

"I make no apologies to who I am, son. I never have. Reese accepted all parts of me without question, and I do the same in return. You and Riley have shared a very rare gift with each other, and I know the love you have holds so much value for you both."

"It does, dad. I swear I love Riley with all of my heart."

"Son, I believe you. Now tell her, and make things right between you two."

"I will, but it's not just the argument we had. It's so much more."

"Jackson, I have to admit you took me by complete surprise when you announced you wanted to work with me at Reed Global. I had a hard time believing you since all you have ever talked about was film school. How can you so easily change your mind about something you know so little about?"

"I'm sure you have many questions, dad, and I will try to explain it to you the best way I can, but I need time to find the right words. I completely did everything wrong when it came to telling Riley, and me showing up in California didn't make anything better. I know I took you completely by surprise, and I am sorry for that. With all that I have been through the past year, the realization never hit me until I was on my own in New York. I had so many reminders of my surgery and recovery, and then having to deal with Grandpa Henry's death was just too much for me. Even in death, he is still trying to pull me to him by leaving his entire estate in my hands. What was he thinking?"

I did not miss the change in my father's demeanor once I mentioned his greatest enemy's name. He murdered my grandmother and made my father lose precious years with Reese. He nearly cost our family the life of my baby sister. He was consumed with madness.

"I'm sorry, dad. I shouldn't have brought him up. I was just leading to what I am trying to explain. Grandpa was just one of many factors to why I changed my mind. Ultimately, I got confirmation at my last doctor's appointment with Liam."

"You're okay, right son?"

"I am. I am in perfect health. Liam will see me again in six months, and then we could switch over to yearly exams. My scans are clean, and he supports my running again."

"As long as you don't overdo it, I'm all for it too. What are you not telling me? Your face has just turned white as a ghost."

"Dad, did you ever really know how close I came to dying? Because I never have."

"I could not bring myself to ever ask. I was too afraid to. Once

Liam and Samuel walked out of the OR doors, I knew you made it. Once they said the words, I saw no need to question it. You were alive, and I had my son."

"It was very close, dad, and knowing all that made me just realize how life is short. I have an amazing gifted father who would hand me the world if I asked for it. I never wanted your life, and when my own was at risk, it just put things into perspective for me. You have accomplished more in your lifetime than ten men in theirs. You have worked incredibly hard to make Reed Global what it is today, and I want to be part of it, if you'll have me."

"Jackson, I want nothing more than to have you join me in California, working by my side, but I just don't think that's truly what you want. You have worked incredibly hard to get here to this point. You have one more year or so of school, and then you will have your bachelor's degree. You still have graduate school to take on, then however you want to pursue your filmmaking."

"Dad, you are not listening to me. I am removing film school from the equation, and I am just going to focus on school. I already have several accredited classes in business management, economics, and financial. With the right mentorship, I know I will learn everything I need to know about Reed Global and what it represents for the outside. I already know everything about the internal structure, the power players, and your dream about the innovation this company stands for. Please, dad, just give me a chance to prove it to you."

"You have made some strong arguments, ones I will consider, but not until we square away your academic standing at NYU."

"Pertaining to…?" I hesitantly questioned.

"Your film project with Riley. You, along with Riley, will present to Professor Connelly. You have a meeting with him first thing tomorrow morning. Once I conclude my meeting with the dean and receive your final grades for this term, only then will we discuss your change of plans and future, whatsoever that shall be, at Reed Global. Have I made myself clear?"

"Yes, sir."

"Good. I'm glad you see it my way."

"Is there another way?" I asked.

"No, son, there is not. If you are to succeed at Reed Global, you would do well to remember that."

CHAPTER 18

Riley

Your dream is my dream

MONDAY MORNING WAS the one day most dreaded, but it was my day off from school. I lucked out this semester with Professor Connelly's class moving to Tuesday. I shouldn't get too excited. Today would be no picnic for me. Jackson would be here soon with Mr. Reed. He told me that he was bringing Jackson home to complete our assignment, but also help us work out our differences.

Walker Reed was like a thunderous storm cloud making his presence known. He had the power to wreak havoc upon you without blinking an eye. He also had a softer side, though, no thanks to my mother and now my little sister. They had him wrapped around their finger and at their disposal.

When I was angry, my thoughts were harsh and unwarranted

towards Mr. Reed. He had been nothing but kind to me. He welcomed me in as a part of his family, not only because Reese was my mother, but also because I was in love with his son.

I had time to think about Jackson and the future I wished to have with him. I loved him very much and wanted nothing more than to marry him. He wanted to wait, but after days without him, the need to be with him had grown so much more.

We would reconcile our differences and come out stronger. I felt sick over returning my ring. I did that in anger, and after processing it, I know I was wrong. That hurt Jackson very much. I saw the look in his eyes when he felt the heavy diamond in his hand. My finger felt naked without it, but I had to prove my point that although I loved him, I could not just take a backseat and ignore my dreams.

I worked just as hard as Jackson had, and my plans had not changed in terms of my career. What I wanted to do, I could do anywhere, but I still should have had a choice in the matter. I had to maintain my independence, and if Jackson was willing to meet me halfway, then I had no doubt we could reach a compromise. We did it before, and it always worked out.

My phone buzzed with Richard's alert. Jackson and Mr. Reed were on their way up.

"Take a deep breath, Riley, you've got this. Go with your heart, and stand your ground." I said to myself, trying with great effort to believe it.

The doors opened to the great room, and in walked my handsome fiancé. My fingers were itching to touch him. I missed him so much and wanted to be enveloped in his comforting arms. Mr. Reed followed closely behind his son, and then Richard was next, carrying their bags.

Jackson made his entrance, while I continued to stay rooted in place until he made his move. I no longer had to wait, because Jackson practically ran to me. As he got closer, he extended his arms wide open. I then knew where he needed me to be. It was what I had wanted too.

Our bodies collided with the other as he held me tightly to him. I could not move if I wanted to. Jackson was caging me in with no means of escaping, which was fine by me. This was what I had wanted all along: to be with the man I loved and to connect with him always, even when he was struggling. Jackson was my guy, and I belonged to him and with him, always and forever.

I made a promise to listen to him first before reacting, as long as he gave me the same consideration. I learned a long time ago back in Pottersville that you catch more bees with honey.

"Hi," I barely got out above a whisper. "I love you."

"I love you too, baby. I am so sorry for leaving you. Will you forgive me?"

"Only if you forgive me for not begging you to stay," I said.

"It was my fault, Riley, all of it. I swear on my life that I will never hurt you again, not on purpose. Please let us not fight. This distance we have between us does not have a place in our life, and I am kicking its ass to the curb…today."

"I couldn't agree more. Thank you for coming home."

I held Jackson with all of my strength. Jackson shielded me with his body like a protective cloak. I was safe when I was with him, and all I could do was to hold him and never let go again. My nails were digging into his back, marking him. I knew he had to have felt a slow burn, but he never complained. It was something I always did when I was scared or feeling lost.

Jackson tickled my side, releasing my hands. He smiled and kissed me gently on my lips.

"I'm really sorry. I know we have a lot to talk about, but can we hold off for a while until we can be alone?"

"Yes, of course we can. And stop apologizing. I love you too."

The realization hit us. We were not alone, and Mr. Reed was patiently waiting in the background.

"Hi Mr. Reed. I…" I said, stumbling over my words. I was so embarrassed with how I talked to him earlier.

Always kind to me, he completely ignored my apology and gave me a warm hug.

"Hello, Riley," he said to me. Two words that packed so much love behind them.

He took me in his arms and gave me a welcome I probably did not deserve. I felt shameful after our call, and I just wanted to apologize for my behavior. What would my mother think?

Before I could speak, he put his finger up to his lips. He did not want an apology from me. He wore the look of understanding, and I knew we were okay. Mr. Reed was clear on his intentions and got right to the matter at hand.

Jackson held my hand as we walked to the media room. Mr. Reed had requested to view Jackson's film before handing it over to our teacher. I had added my voice to some of Jackson's footage, and I was very pleased on how it turned out.

We sat in silence with our hands linked and watched Mr. Reed's eyes brighten with every new shot. He looked in awe from what I could tell. I never felt a more proud moment. As much as Jackson had tried to convince me that we were the only ones that mattered, I still cared what his father thought of me. His opinion mattered too, and I respected his boldness and honesty. Jackson carried the same qualities, one of many I loved about him.

After the film finished, Mr. Reed excused himself and said he had a few matters of business to take care of. Jackson and I looked over to each other with his sudden exit, but concentrated on working out our issues.

Jackson left me on my own while he went upstairs to shower and change. I was tempted to join him, but decided to wait. It would be too easy to just jump in bed and forget all the reasons why we were apart in the first place. We needed to talk and really listen to the other. Sex only complicated things, and once we reached a resolution, there would be plenty of time for making up. Remembering what Jackson promised me made me smile brightly: *"I will fight with you all day as long as you allow me to hold you at night."*

Jackson Reed will be doing a lot more than holding me tonight, that's for sure, I thought to myself. I could not help but to grin like a lovesick puppy.

I called my mom while I was waiting for Jackson. She was another person in my life that I was avoiding at all costs. She did not deserve my distance or silent treatment. She was blissfully happy, and it was not fair of me to take out my problems on her. Her voicemail picked up, so I left a message.

"Hi, Mom. It is your favorite brat calling you. I am sorry we have not talked, but you will see me soon, I promise. Please give Fallon a kiss from her big sister. I love you, mom."

CHAPTER 19

Jackson

Anything is possible

ILET OUT a breath I didn't realize I was holding. I had no clue to how Riley would react seeing me. The minute my eyes found her beautiful ones, I knew the storm had passed between us.

She was part of me, as I was part of her. We sealed our fate back in Georgia when she agreed to love me forever. Our promises were real then as they were now. Nothing changed, as far as I was concerned. She was the one that I loved, and once we talked and heard the other out, I knew this too would pass and we would put it behind us.

We had so much to look forward to in the coming year. We were halfway through our junior year of college, and then with summer classes—if we decided to take them—this time next year, we would be finishing. Our graduation would take place the following May.

I wanted to do something nice for Riley tonight. I turned the shower on and closed the door in case she was close by to hear me on the phone. I was over using my name to gain some advantage, a lesson I learned all too well with Riley. But this was different because it was a surprise for her. I phoned over to La Brasserie and spoke to Andre. He was more than accommodating once he knew whom he was speaking to. I stifled a laugh as he went on and on in his French accent.

It was so easy to trade on my father's name, but I was a man now and had to make my own mark on the world. When I first talked to my father about working at Reed Global, I was not expecting a gold card to the executive offices. I knew I would have to work hard and earn my way on my own merit. It was something I was looking forward to, working in all areas of my father's company. He did not give me an answer as of yet, but I had a good feeling he would soon.

I reserved a private dining room at La Brasserie. I wanted privacy with my girl to treat her like the queen she was. I had been neglectful lately, solely focusing on my own needs, and not considering her feelings. That was all going to change this evening.

I sent Riley a text. I told her in all caps to be ready for romance this evening. We were long overdue, and I wanted to give her the night of her life. She texted back, asking what she should wear. I responded with a winking smiley face, and this text:

"Something that leaves little to the imagination."

I could almost hear her squealing downstairs. The smile I always loved seeing on Riley's face would return tonight. I owed it to my girl to show her how much I loved her and how sorry I was for hurting her. Tonight would be a new beginning for better days to come.

I was ready first and made my way downstairs to wait for Riley. I had a bottle of champagne chilling, along with strawberries and her favorite chocolate. My father had not yet returned to the apartment, and I was grateful for the privacy he gave us. Richard arrived and told me the car was waiting for us downstairs. All I needed now was Riley.

"Thank you, Richard, for taking care of tonight's arrangements. I know she's going to be really surprised."

"You are most welcomed, Jackson. If I may speak out of turn?"

"Of course, go on."

"You are more to me than a paycheck, son. I love you like my own, and Riley too. Even a blind man would be able see the love you have for one another. Young adults your age have not had to experience what you and Ms. Riley have gone through. Your surgery alone probably added ten years to my life. That girl never left your side, and she was there for you every day after."

"Richard, what are you trying to say?"

"Be careful with her heart. It is a fragile one. She loves you very much."

"And I her, Richard. Riley is my life, and I am going to make her feel loved every day that we are together. I know I fucked up, but tonight is about righting that wrong. I know what I am doing when it comes to Riley Taylor Briggs, trust me."

"I do. I wish you two a wonderful evening. I will be waiting for you downstairs."

"Thank you, Richard, and thank you for having my back."

"Always, sir."

My heart began to drum a little stronger. I always felt this way when Riley was near. My father says he had the same sixth sense when it came to Reese. A deep connection drew them close to each other. When I experienced the same feeling with Riley, I was almost embarrassed to share it with my father, but he never laughed or teased me about it. He understood how I felt completely. I looked down to my phone, ready to text her again, when she appeared walking down the staircase. Riley looked breathtaking in her evening gown. She sure did look like Reese. It was no wonder why my father stared in silence when he first met her.

"You take my breath away," I said as I extended my hand for her to take.

Her cheeks began to blush to a soft pink. She was practically glowing upon hearing my compliments.

"I mean it, you know. You look stunning. I love this dress…a Freddy Mac original?" I asked as my eyes continued to roam up and down her body.

"Can you keep a secret?" she asked while smiling.

"I can. Where did you get the dress, babe, because this is the first time I am seeing it."

"It's a Versace, one that is very expensive."

"Yes, I can see that, but who does it belong to?"

"My mother. I *borrowed* it from her closet. Your dad and my mom still keep their bedroom here, so I don't think mother would mind if I wear it tonight."

"You are adorable when you are nervous…you know that, right, beautiful girl? I am only teasing you, babe. I have another secret for you…this beautiful Atelier Versace dress actually belongs to you! *I was the one that placed in your mother's closet for you to borrow.*"

"I love it! Thank you, Jackson."

"Anything for you, and I mean it, babe. Tonight is about us, and I want to see you happy again."

"Oh, Jackson, I am happy. I love you so much. Don't you know that by now? I just lost my way for a while, but I'm here with you because there is no other place I'd rather be."

I want to marry this girl and make her mine forever, I couldn't help but think to myself.

"A glass of champagne before we go?" I offered.

"I would love some."

I handed her a glass and placed a small strawberry on her tongue before she took a sip of her champagne. Her eyes lit up with the combined flavor. She then took a sliver of chocolate and let it melt in her mouth. Her moans of pleasure and enjoyment sent a direct message to my growing erection.

"Stop it, naughty girl, or we will never make it to the car," I said to her. "Shall we?"

"We shall."

"By the way, I'm looking forward to removing you from this dress."

She blushed again and casted her eyes down to where I could no longer see the sparkle in her eyes. I knew she was happy, maybe even a little nervous too.

"Hey, look at me," I said as I lifted her chin. "You look beautiful. How will I ever get through a meal tonight when the only thing I am hungry for is you?"

"Jackson…" she said.

"What is it?"

"I love that you are trying so hard to make me happy, but just having you back is already enough for me. We were both wrong, and in your absence I see that now."

"We will talk later, beautiful girl, but for now I just want to give you a wonderful night. Please, indulge me?" I held out my hand for her to take. She said nothing more and smiled shyly.

Riley was in my arms throughout the entire ride to the restaurant. I was thankful the snow had not yet arrived in the city, but it was cold. I would carry her into the restaurant if she asked me to. It felt too long since I held her like this. We went from a couple that never argued to sniping at each other on a daily basis. It was the stress of living with our friends and trying to fit into a scene that neither of us belonged in.

After meeting Andre and hearing his repeated pleasantries, he finally showed us to our table. He kept calling me Mr. Reed, when I told him Jackson would be fine. I saw him look over his shoulder once or twice, almost looking for my father. The restaurant always seemed to get a mention in the paper when my father dined there.

I held a chair out for Riley and gently pushed her to the table, taking a seat beside her. We were not twenty-one yet, and I did not want to put Andre in an uncomfortable position, so I ordered a non-alcoholic wine. It was one that Riley and I had before.

"A toast to you, beautiful girl. I love you, Riley, and all I shall ever need is you by my side. You are what dreams are made of. You are a dream and a wish come true. I never have to be afraid anymore, because you are here with me."

I wiped a lone tear that escaped her eye, and then we clinked our glasses and entwined our arms without spilling a drop.

We kept our conversation light throughout our feasting on appetizers. I knew once I began talking, I would not wish to be interrupted. I wanted to get everything out in the open and go to bed with a resolution. Facing Professor Connelly would be taxing to say the least, but all he could really fault me for was missing the presentation. All my grades to date had been exemplary.

"Do we have complete privacy here tonight?" Riley asked.

"We do. I can hold off for some more time before they serve the entrees, if that's what you wish."

"I do wish," she said, as I gestured to the waiter for privacy. "We need to talk, Jackson. I do not want to seem ungrateful. I love everything you have done for me tonight, but we also know we have issues to discuss, and they are not going to be resolved unless we talk them out. I would rather go home to make love and drown in your love until dawn."

"From your lips to my ears, I do agree with your plan. Riley, what can I say that I have not already said about our friends and the apartment. I hated living as a group. And while I'm being honest—because that is the only way I choose to be with you—Alice and Evette are not good influences on you. They come off nice enough, but are spoiled, party too hard, and they have no guidance as we have. They are trust fund babies that work the scene for all its worth. Maybe that is how they landed Brandon and Clay. They are all cut from the same cloth, and I do not wish for my future wife to be a part of that."

She responded sarcastically, "Um...pot...kettle...black! Aren't you also a trust fund baby?"

Is she angry about my honesty? I quickly shrugged off her remark and continued.

"You are correct, Riley. I am a trust fund baby, but my father makes me work for every cent I spend. I will never deny who I am or who my father is. I am a Reed and will always be one. I share his name, and one day you will too. My name comes with privileges and responsibility for which my father holds me to a high standard. Brandon and Clay were not raised as I was, and one day they will be expected to grow up, but I do not have the patience to wait for them to catch up. I want more for my life, and every day I get to live is one more day with you. The surgery changed me, Riley. I just didn't know how much until I moved here with you."

She looked down again, and I knew Riley was trying to stay strong and not cry. I lifted her chin once more and held her face to kiss her. The heat radiating off her beautiful lips made me dizzy. I wanted her so much, but this was not the place.

I comforted her and said, "Eyes on me, baby. The sooner we can finish this conversation, the sooner we can focus on you and me, okay?"

"Okay," she said with a sniffle.

"Riley, I have so many feelings about all I went through last year, and they are just now coming together in my head. Now, there was a time when I felt I would never be free of my father's watchful eye or influence, but I was wrong to think that way of him. He was being a father, a devoted one who never let me down. He was always there for me. The relationship we have as father and son, he did not have with my grandfather. It was very volatile at times, and they never seemed to agree. How my father successfully managed to learn the business from him is a true test to my father's character. He was destined to run Reed Global, and I as his son want to join him and bring my vision to the company."

"What about filmmaking?" she asked. "Are you absolutely sure you want to let that dream go?"

"To some degree, yes, I do. But I can still have both and not give up one dream for the other. I am talented behind a camera, just like my father is with his sketchpad when designing an environmentally safe skyscraper. I believe I can do this. My friend, Bridgette, is interning right now in the marketing department, and she gave me pointers about what classes I should take. Next semester, I've already signed up a full schedule of management classes, and most of them are in conjunction with graphic design, marketing, and development."

"So, will you stay at NYU? And graduate with me as we planned?"

"I will, Riley. I promise. All I am changing are my courses, not my girl, and not my zip code. It was selfish of me to think I could leave New York or put you in a position to choose. With all the good that has blessed our lives, I still remember the heartache too. I am not blaming my father, but I did not have the proper time to grieve over my grandparents' death. I loved them very much despite everything my grandfathers did. My father flipped a switch and it was over for him, but not for me. I am not regretting the words I said to my grandfather before I had my seizure; maybe they drove him to the edge to commit his heinous crimes."

"You are not to blame for his actions, Jackson. He could have killed my mother, baby Fallon, and maybe even you. How could you say such a thing?" she said, starting to cry.

"I'm sorry. Please, baby, no tears. I am sorry for even bringing him up, but again, he is part of the story. At my appointment with Liam, I did ask about my heart stopping on the table, and had him explain it to me in detail. I knew it was hard for him to talk about it, as my relationship with Liam is so much more than doctor and patient. Liam has known me since I was born and is a dear friend to my father. He was scared that day, and if it was not for your father, I may not have made it. You will never know how grateful I am for the gift I have been given, a second chance at life and sharing it with you."

I sat up in my seat and continued, "Riley, there is something else I need to share with you, something I have only shared with my father."

"Go on, I promise to listen," she whispered.

"Don't worry, baby. This is a good thing. When I was down on the surgical table, I felt as if my soul was leaving my physical body and I was dying. To some, near death experiences may not be believable once you hear yourself telling the story, but what I experienced was as real as the conversation we are having now. I saw my mother, and she was beautiful. I kept asking if I was in heaven, and she smiled and told me I was simply sleeping and would awaken soon. Riley, I felt her hand on mine, and she led me on a path to what I would be missing if I gave up and let go. I saw you, baby, and our future. She took me back to Big Sur, and I saw our tree, the tree that has our names on it. My heart stopping gave me the greatest gift: I met my mother and for the first time looked into the eyes that matched mine."

I continued, "I knew I could never leave you, Riley, and I am asking you to please forgive me for behaving so foolishly these past few days. I was so wrong to turn away and walk out the door. I knew I broke you, and because I was only thinking of myself, I did not look back. I promise on the second chance I have been given, that I will never hurt you like that again. I know we will fight, baby, but if you allow me to hold you at night, then I know we will always be okay."

"You had to go there, right?" she blurted out, tears falling. "This is why I do not wear mascara when you are always saying the sweetest things that make me cry. Oh, Jackson, I am so sorry. I love you so much, and I promise to always be respectful to you and your feelings."

I took her in my arms and kissed her madly. Riley was the only one for me. I did not let her go and held her close to me. I needed her to see the truth in my eyes and never doubt my feelings for her.

She asked, "Jackson, are you really one hundred percent sure on your new plans?"

"This is very important to me, baby, and I am asking for your support. I have no idea what the future holds for our careers, but I do know what it means for us. We are going to get married and have a family of our very own to love. I want it all with you, Riley. The question is: do you want it with me?"

"Ask me," she whispered.

It took me a second to figure out what she wanted me to say next. And when I realized it, I knew I wanted nothing more for all the days of my life.

"Riley Taylor Briggs," I said as I got down on one knee and pulled out my mother's ring, "will you marry me?"

She looked me in the eyes and said, "I will, Jackson Walker Reed. I love you. I promise to love and be with you for the rest of my life, and if we fight all day, I promise to hold you at night."

She put the ring back on, and I practically jumped Riley right in the middle of the private dining room. I wanted her so badly.

The wait staff picked this moment to bring in our dinner. We blissfully ignored them and kissed until we were breathless. I knew we would be okay. We needed the other as much as we required air to breathe. I pulled back just to look at the beauty that was mine, my forever love.

My father never stopped reminding me of how rare it was to find *the one* to share your life. He thought he was lucky to find and fall in love with Reese the first time. To have lost her, only to be saved by my mother was his second miracle. A son was born from their love, and he found Reese once again to create the family they have today. This was a debt that my father would never be able to repay to God.

I felt the same way when I looked at Riley. She was my miracle, and I knew I survived my surgery to live more days with her. Riley had the ability to make me lose my mind with just her touch. Her piercing eyes hypnotized me.

Riley was my compass. No matter where I traveled, she would

be my guide through the good times and the bad. I had been lost without her, not knowing if we would be able to repair what had been broken between us. The reality was that we dropped the ball when it came to communicating with each other. We promised tonight that we would not do that anymore and be completely honest, no matter the topic. It was the only agreement that we could both live with.

"Can we take this to go? I would rather have dessert instead," she said to the staff, making her sexy intentions clear to me.

I wanted Riley so badly that we never made it to my other events planned for this evening. Operation Get Your Girl Back was in full swing, with Riley taking over. Her appetite was ravenous, and I was not referring to the food. She pounced on me the minute Richard closed the door to the limo.

"Not here, Riley," I said. "I want you in our bed."

I could not believe I said those words aloud, shocking her a little.

"Why not? I do not want to wait, Jackson. I have missed you so much. Please make love to me, right here, and right now."

The privacy screen was already up. I buzzed Richard to ask him to drive around until I tell him otherwise. He agreed with no argument. He must have known what was happening back here in our private bubble. My girl completely took control, and it felt good to let her.

"Ride me, Riley, and do not hold back," I said as my fingers gripped her hips.

She hiked up her dress and to my surprise was completely bare and wearing no panties. How did I miss that? Bearing down on me and using my shoulders as support, Riley turned me on with every move she made.

She took her time to hold off on our release, as I closed my eyes and leaned my head back. She felt amazing against me. Shimmering beads of sweat were on her chest, as I leaned in to kiss her and lapped my tongue from the base of her neck down to her breasts. She let out a gasp as I took her pebbled nipple in my mouth. I bared my teeth and sunk down causing her to jerk slightly, but then taking the pleasure I was giving her, she moved faster.

I slowed her down by holding her hips in place. I wanted this to last between us. This sexy liaison with Riley was beyond erotic, but I knew she was close, so was I. I held off for another minute or two, and then I knew this was it. She tightened her walls around my dick and leaned in to bite my shoulder, muffling her orgasmic screams of pleasure. Hot streams of cum filled her.

Riley never disappointed me, not ever. This was over-the-top amazing and more so because I finally felt we were back on track and in a good place. I was not deluded in my thinking that we would never fight, but I did not want to feel distance between us again. Riley needed to talk to me, and I had to stay to hear her.

Her head was nestled in the crook of my neck as I continued to hold her.

"I love you, Jackson, so much. Can we just put the last few months behind us, and begin again?" she whispered her words to me in-between kissing my neck.

"I would love to, Riley, but we will not do that. It is part of our story. I agree it wasn't the best chapter to get through, but we did and can move on from it, okay?" I looked up to her and kissed her nose.

"Are you still angry with Brandon and Clay?" she asked.

I stiffened a little when she mentioned their names. Having them move in with us was a huge error in judgment, and that was on me. But not safeguarding my precious love in a bar where she could be hurt was on them. I knew I would have to address that soon with them but not tonight.

"I don't want to discuss them, Riley. When I'm ready, I will reach out to them."

"Okay."

I instructed Richard to bring us home. By the time we reached the penthouse, Riley was exhausted. She teased we would make love all throughout the night, but I would not hold her to her promise. It was past midnight already, and we needed some sleep to take on Professor Connelly in the morning. Besides, my body still felt the aftershocks of our tryst in the limo.

Once inside, I carried my sleepy girl upstairs and removed her from her barely-there dress. She was stunning and all mine to love forever. With one zip, her dress was off, leaving her only in her bra, which I quickly removed. I took in the raised blossoms on the top of her breasts, which served as a reminder to our sexed up car ride home. I tucked her under the covers and placed gentle kisses to the marks on her breasts, making my way up to her swollen lips.

I said, "I love you, Riley. Sleep well, baby."

She was out, probably for the night. I changed into shorts and a tee. I was not sure if my father was back yet. I quietly left our room to knock on his door. His bed was still untouched. I went downstairs to his office, where I found him typing furiously on his laptop.

I said, "Hey, dad, you're back."

"It appears so, son, as are you," he replied without looking up at me.

My father looked serious and in deep thought, which sometimes put me on edge to what he was thinking or planning. I waited for a beat, and then he finished whatever he was working on and gave me his attention.

"How are you?" he asked. "Did you enjoy yourselves this evening?"

"We did, dad. Thank you for everything you did to help me give Riley a fantastic night."

"Anything to see that girl smile again is worth every penny."

"What are you working on?" I could not help asking.

"You will know soon enough. Get some sleep. You have a big day tomorrow, and then we are off to California."

Taking the hint not to question him any further, I said my good night to him and then joined Riley, who was sleeping soundly.

I woke before the clock. I quickly shut it off before it blared out music. I leaned up on my elbow to watch her. Riley's hair was a tangled mess. I should have taken out some of the pins that was keeping part of her hair up. I saw a few sticking out and began freeing her hair from them without waking her.

As I pulled the last pin, her eyes opened, and she let out a happy sigh.

"Good morning, playing hairdresser again?" she said, groggily.

"Of course, what gave me away?"

"Your magic fingers massaging my scalp."

"I hadn't gotten that far yet."

"I know. I was just hoping you would," she said with a wink.

Of course, I would not deny any pleasure she asked for, especially like right now when just her smile alone weakened my knees. I massaged her scalp and combed out her long, thick hair with my fingers. Riley began to touch me, making me hard for her.

"Babe, stop. We have to meet Professor Connelly at eight, and we should not be late."

"It will be quick, Jackson. Please? It will calm my nerves about seeing him again. He wasn't too happy with us the last time I was in his office."

Without another word, she took me in her mouth, making all my nerve endings come alive. I did all I could to hold back, but the sensation was too great. I knew I was close to my release, and I did not want it this way.

I tugged on her hair gently to break the suction she had on my dick. Riley was taken aback with the abrupt halt, but she softened when I smiled at her. I sprung up to place her under me and began making love to her.

Wrapping her legs around my waist with her nails biting into my forearms, she screamed my name as I moved faster and harder until we came together. We kissed and kissed until we both needed air. I was panting as if I had just run the New York City marathon.

We met my father downstairs at the car. My hand linked with Riley's as we drove to NYU in a nervous silence. No matter what today would bring with Professor Connelly, I could walk away knowing that Riley and I would be okay, no matter what was decided for our grades.

CHAPTER 20

Riley

Here goes nothing

EVEN WITH THE hot car sex last night and this morning's romp with Jackson, I was still a bundle of nerves. I had no clue how Professor Connelly would welcome me back and now with Jackson by my side.

He counted him out last week when he was a no-show and gave me double hell for it. My confidence was shaken, which I hated by the way. The ratio of successful women filmmakers to men was low. I knew my gender put me at a disadvantage, which made me work twice as hard as my brilliant fiancé.

Jackson was a natural behind the camera and made it look easy. His own father appeared to be speechless yesterday as he watched what Jackson had filmed. Why for the life of me would Jackson want to give that talent up? I knew what we talked about, and I would support him in whatever he decided, but his wayward thinking still bewildered me.

"Riley, you need to relax. Where is my confident girl?" Jackson whispered close to my ear as his hold on my hand tightened. I glanced over at Mr. Reed, who ignored his son's affections.

"I'm good, babe, really."

"Liar! No time to fight with me, we are here. Showtime."

"You got that right," I said.

Richard handed me my backpack as Jackson swung his over his shoulder. We linked our hands and walked over to Reed Hall. *Yeah, Reed Hall...* Of course I was taking a class in a building named after Walker Reed. He was everywhere, which made me nervous. He was well-known for his contributions to the university and served as a member on the Alumni board. Reed Global was also heading up the plans to revamp several wings in the administration buildings.

We arrived outside Professor Connelly's office door. Jackson was going over his notes one last time while Mr. Reed was looking at me expectantly. *Stop looking at me*, I thought to myself. I was beginning to feel creeped out. How did my mother handle all of his dominating intrusiveness?

"Breathe, Riley," Mr. Reed said to me. "You have done excellent work, and I know what I am talking about."

He winked at me, but I was still a nervous wreck.

"Good morning, Ms. Briggs. Already off to a good start by being punctual," Professor Connelly greeted me as he looked down to his pocket watch.

"Good morning, Professor," I greeted him as I quickly entered his office.

Jackson followed my lead and greeted him with his perfect manners. Mr. Reed remained back and did not follow us in, but not before giving us his speech that we would do well. He kept out of sight and away from Professor Connelly's eye of sight. Jackson and I assured him that we would be fine, and would rock the socks off our teacher.

He closed his office door, clapping his hands as a sign he was ready to begin.

"Again, good morning. So nice of you to join us, Mr. Reed. I take it you did not need a map today to find your way to my class and make it on time."

He looked over his shoulder to me and then back to Jackson. *Okay Professor. I get we messed up, but you do not have to be an ass about it.* Jackson was cool with his reply and did not show any signs of apprehension.

"I apologize for missing our scheduled appointment, sir. I will not waste any time here by giving you an explanation. I'm here now, and we are ready to present."

The professor looked satisfied with Jackson's answer and gave us the signal to proceed. The floor was mine, and after a few calming breaths, I began. I was not sure if he was bored because of his expression. I continued with my part of the presentation, and then I sat to hear my portion of the narration that I recorded to roll into Jackson's segment.

Professor Connelly curtly nodded at me when I finished, and then it was Jackson's turn. God! Jackson looked so edible. He was the spitting image of his father, and so confident in the way he carried himself and controlled the room. I had to cross and uncross my legs a few times just at the sight of him. Jackson glanced my way and winked. He knew how to command a room and me so easily just with a simple gesture.

I looked back over to our teacher, and he came alive once Jackson began. Jackson did most of the voiceover work on the footage he had filmed. All he had to do was hit the power button. Professor Connelly's reception of what he was viewing matched Mr. Reed when he watched it. Jackson's work was flawless.

The lights flickered back on and my stomach heaved. *Just kill me now if I toss my cookies in here.*

"Well done, Mr. Reed. Well done. You captured everything I set forth for you. If I did not know firsthand who filmed this, I would think I was watching something from National Geographic. Ms. Briggs, although you explained in detail of pros and cons of the strain on our ecological system, I felt you came up short in what I was looking for. The research was subpar to say the least. You can do better, Ms. Briggs, and if you wish to remain in this class, you will."

Crushed! I worked my ass off on this project, and he sat there and accused me of average work? *Oh hell no!* I was better than that, and I did not get A's all semester long because I dreamed it. I earned my perfect GPA, and I was not going to let this jerk threaten that.

I looked over to Jackson, who looked stunned by his comments and subtle threat. I gave him a assuring look that begged him to stay out of it. I could fight my own battles, and if I was to be a Reed someday, I had better learn now how to deal and take care of business.

I told him, "If I may, Professor, your statement is unwarranted, and quite frankly out of line. You say I have presented subpar work. Do you even know what that word means? And how it can damage my academic standing?"

I received another look from Jackson, but I shooed him off.

The professor responded, "I am well aware, Ms. Briggs, and I would advise you to watch your tone when speaking to me."

"I apologize for speaking out of turn, Professor, but maybe you should go over it again, because I only hand in excellent work."

Professor Connelly appeared to be weighing it over and may have said something if it had not been for the knock at the door.

He called out, "Come in."

It was Mr. Reed.

"Pardon the intrusion, may I come in, Professor?"

"Of course, Mr. Reed." He swiveled around in his chair to look over to Jackson and completely ignored me. "Jackson, you did not mention your father was on the grounds today. If I had known, I would have invited him in to observe."

"My apologies, Professor, but students usually do not bring their parents to school."

Boom! Take that Mr. Stuffy Pants. I had seen greater men try to schmooze Jackson, and they always failed. Jackson had been around this his entire life and learned from his father how to handle himself.

Mr. Reed ignored our teacher's fake compliments and talked right over him. I loved it.

"Now, Professor, I did not mean to intrude, but I have been called away to handle an issue down at my office. I just wanted to check in with the kids to let them know I will be leaving, unless your meeting has concluded."

Mr. Reed looked over only to me and gave me a look of understanding. He was in my corner and believed in my work. I think he was about to hand Professor Connelly his ass.

Mr. Reed continued, "If I may be blunt in asking...what did you think? I had the pleasure of viewing the documentary yesterday, and I found it to be quite informative. A very up-close and personal assessment of how companies of the world are polluting our air, waters, and land by not taking proper measures of protecting what we all should be more vigilant to. Would you agree, Professor? Now, I may be a bit biased when it comes to these two, but what can I say? It is brilliant. Award-worthy, if the public were judging it. I could not be more proud and look forward to hearing your opinion. Oh, listen to me prattle on, Professor. Well, I guess my business could wait a few minutes more. Your opinions, sir?"

Jackson and I were both stunned to silence how his father was going on about our work, and for that matter, so was Professor Connelly. I was prepared to continue to argue my valid points to him, but with Mr. Reed coming to my rescue, I remained silent and waited for Professor Connelly to speak. He cleared his throat and adjusted himself in his seat. He was taken by surprise by Mr. Reed and was not showing a good poker face.

Jackson was now sitting beside me, holding my hand to calm me. This was not how I envisioned this morning turning out to be. He looked over to Mr. Reed, who patiently was waiting for the professor to address his question.

"This project was to be divided into two separate parts. The members of the team would take on one part each and submit the project as a whole. The film footage was outstanding."

"And the written portion?" Mr. Reed questioned.

Looking a bit ashen, the professor simply stated that it needed work to be more engaging to the audience.

"I respectively disagree with you Professor. This film was more than a class assignment; it carries heart with an innovative mind that is sure to capture any viewing audience. Before issuing a grade, perhaps you should sit on this for a few days and then view it again. I truly believe your opinion will change after seeing it with a new perspective. Just my two cents. That should have no merit on your decision, but it has been my experience not to judge in haste."

"Mr. Reed, I can assure you that this project will be graded fairly."

"I'm sure it will, Professor. I was just stating an opinion. I am sure that lesson is taught on day one. Well, I must be going now. Thank you so much for your attention, Professor. It was a very enlightening morning. Jackson, Riley…farewell."

We watched Mr. Reed leave, and then our eyes returned to Professor Connelly, who appeared to be speechless. I might have thought he wet his pants after the tongue-lashing he just received from Jackson's father.

"If there is nothing else you need from us professor, we will be on our way," I said as Jackson still held my hand in a death grip hold. We began to rise from our seats, and he stopped us.

"I have something to say, Ms. Briggs, and I will ask you to give me a few more minutes of your time."

I nodded and sat back down.

"My first question is to Jackson. Do you wish to continue with my class once school resumes in January?"

"I do, sir," Jackson responded.

"You missed our meeting last week, which told me that you

were not serious about your commitment to this class or to your partner here. I gave you both a second chance to redeem yourselves, not knowing at the time if you would. Your footage was perfect, Jackson, and your father giving me his opinion on your project does not sway me in the least, no matter what his role here is on this campus."

"I never asked for special treatment, sir, nor will I ever."

"I am happy to hear that, son. Now, Ms. Briggs, you immediately took what I said as a derogative comment, but really it was to show you that your work needs...well, work. If it had not been for Jackson's narrative parts, the rest would have been choppy conclusions. This was a big assignment, and you both did very well, but having said, that it was not perfect on all fronts. Ms. Briggs, this is why we have the red pen technique. It has been around for ages and one that will probably always be. It is to help, guide, teach, and just maybe after all is said, you will turn the negative to a positive and improve."

Professor Connelly continued, "Ms. Briggs, a word of advice: If you are to remain in this field and hope to someday make it as a documentarian, then I suggest you listen to good advice when it is given. You show a strong potential, and I will teach you if you leave here with an open mind and willingness to learn what I know. These tools are valuable, and you cannot go further without them. For Jackson's part, he receives an A plus. For yours? You receive a B minus, and with all grades considered, you close this semester with a B plus average."

"Thank you, sir, that is generous of you," I said, sulking.

"Not *generous* at all, Ms. Briggs. The word I think you are looking for is *fair*. Had you given me the opportunity to explain it earlier, we would have saved a lot of time here. I will see you both in January. Good day."

I never wanted to run so fast in my life, but Jackson maintained control and we casually left his office, and with passing grades. My heart was beating very fast to the point I needed to take some calming breaths.

"I am so proud of you, baby. You did great back there."

"Jackson, how could you say that and actually believe it? Your father interrupting probably saved me from making a bigger fool of myself than I already had with Professor Connelly."

"Riley, you are no fool, but your passion speaks volumes on who you are. I love everything about you, but take a breath. You passed his class and will do it again come spring."

"Easy for you to say, Jackson, you do one thing and say another. Are you returning with me in January?"

"Is that a serious question? After all we talked about, you still doubt my intentions?"

"I am trying not to, Jackson, I want to believe every word that comes from your mouth, and I am just scared to lose you."

"You will never lose me. I told you that I do not have to give up one dream for the other. In this world, we need to learn everything we can to be great. Please let us table this conversation for now and enjoy the holidays with our family. I promise I will never make another decision without discussing it with you first. We are a team, Riley, and will forever be."

"I love you," I said to him.

"And I you, beautiful girl. Let's go."

We walked over to the student coffee station to get lattes for us, and one for Richard, who had been patiently waiting for us to return. I knew Mr. Reed was anxious to get home to my mom and baby Fallon. Christmas was right around the corner, and I did not have a chance to even shop yet. I also felt weird about leaving New York without seeing Evette and Alice first, but Jackson assured me that all was fine with our group.

He had phoned the guys earlier to clear the air, and the girls too, but he never apologized for protecting me. Brandon and Clay each apologized for not taking better care of me while I was out with them, and they promised to do better in the future. I heard Jackson laugh aloud because I knew that there would never be a next time going out to a club without Jackson by my side. If the ice did thaw where the girls were concerned, I could almost guarantee a security detail would be watching me from a safe distance.

I thought the Reeds were over the top at times, but when marrying into a high profile family, I knew there would be some adjustments to my independence I would have to agree to. All of it came with Jackson as a package deal. As long as we were together, I would learn how to adjust to my new life, *our* life, together.

Walker

Legacy

ONCE I VIEWED Jackson and Riley's project, an idea hit me. I left immediately for my office at Reed Global. My team back in California—available to me at a moment's notice—was waiting for instructions via the video conference I asked Jenny to set up for me.

Tom had been subtly dropping hints of returning to New York. His daughter, Bridgette, was currently interning for us and doing a spectacular job on our marketing team. She also shared a friendship with Jackson. They both had natural talents that would be beneficial for my team, and what is even better is that I could assign Tom to mentor them both.

I phoned Stephen immediately once I arrived in my office. I briskly walked through the bay of elevators, catching my front security team off guard. They were always alerted when I was in town, or at least most of the time. I never wanted anyone I employed to have too much confidence and predict what the boss would do.

They all stood in attendance as I walked by, keeping pleasantries to a minimum. I walked on to my private elevator that would take me to the executive floor. I entered my code and the doors closed immediately, taking me up quickly. I stepped off and was greeted by Mara, my New York assistant, trained by Jenny to meet every one of my requests with diligence.

"Mr. Reed, so good to see you again. Everything is ready for you in your office. May I bring you a refreshment?"

"Good afternoon, Mara. Please bring me an espresso and a bottle of sparkling water. Order lunch in for me from La Brasserie. Andre will know what I want."

"Very good, sir."

My pristine office was just as I had left it the last time I was here. It was designed to suit my taste, but the room still felt cold. My father spent most of his adult life behind this desk building the business and controlling every aspect of my life. This desk was one of the few pieces I could not part with.

I remember visiting my grandfather on the few occasions my father allowed me to accompany him to the office. My nanny was always close by; it was never solely with him. My grandfather was different from Phillip. He was generous with his time and always treated me with warmth and love. My father was hard, cold, and unforgiving. He was strict with me, which only pushed me to defy him until it was my turn to take over at the helm of Reed Global. Now under my charge, it was known as Reed Global International.

The word "legacy" was heard often during my childhood and teen years. From the time I could walk, my father groomed me to be like him, but we were different. I knew I needed to stand on my own if I were ever to be successful enough to sit in his chair.

My eyes scanned the room and felt the past as it became clearer to me. It was right here in this very spot when Henry Townsend charged through the door to call me out for treating his daughter badly. She was pregnant with my child, and it all hit me: I was going to be a father and needed to step up to the plate.

Now, all these years later, my son was asking to work beside me and to take his rightful place as I did with his grandfather. I never believed this day would happen. Jackson never showed interest enough to want to be here, and I never pushed him. It was important for me to know he was happy in making his own choices for his life. A part of me was disappointed that I would be alone at the helm, but I made a promise on the day I held him in my arms that I would do anything and everything in my power to make him happy. Today, I had the power once again to give him something that he desired most that would ultimately change his life.

This was not a decision to be taken lightly. I had to be one hundred percent certain that this was what my son wanted and would not change his mind on a whim later. I spent the last twenty years of my life working around the clock to build my business to what it is today, a legacy that would one day be passed down to my children.

"Excuse me, Mr. Reed," Mara said, standing in front of me holding a tray with my espresso on it. She placed it down on my desk and waited for me to respond. I was so deeply lost in my memories that I did not hear or see her enter my office. With my senses returning, I finally answered her back.

"Thank you, Mara. Do you have Stephen ready to go?"

"I do. He's ready when you are."

"Fine. That will be all for now."

With my thoughts clear and focused, I was sure that this was the best course of action for my son. I connected my call with Stephen and began making arrangements.

"Mr. Reed, how's New York?"

"All is well, Stephen. I am anxious to leave for home, which will be as soon as we wrap up this meeting."

"Donovan and Tom just arrived. Hold for a moment."

While I waited, my eyes found my beautiful Reese holding our daughter in her arms. I had their pictures all over my office, but this was one of my favorites. Reese was on a swing holding our daughter while we were in Germany.

"Good afternoon, Walker," Donovan greeted me, followed by Tom, also joining our meeting.

"Gentlemen, I trust all is well at the office?" I asked. "The reason why I called this impromptu meeting is that I would like your thoughts on one of you relocating here to New York, short-term."

I knew that Donovan was happy in California, but he would go wherever I asked with no questions. I was actually directing my question to Tom to test the waters.

Donovan was first to answer: "Sir, if I may, I thought we had agreed to keep Lars Sapien in the role of overseeing our interests in New York?"

I responded, "First of all, it is not *our* interests, Donovan. All interests are *mine*, and *mine* alone. I believe that point was established a long time ago. Was it not clear to you?"

"My apologies, Walker. Please go on."

I actually enjoyed that. Since Jackson unexpectedly arriving in California, I had been out of my usual tense mood, so messing with Donovan brightened my spirit.

"As I was saying," I continued, "this arrangement would be temporary. I would like the transition to happen quickly, say mid-January. Moreover, this would continue through the end of the year, possibly continuing into the next calendar year, at which time we would revisit the timeline. Let me be clear: this move is not to remove Lars from his role. This is more of a personal request, and one that I would only trust in either of your capable hands. We will discuss this in more detail once I return to California. I wanted to give you both the opportunity to consider a relocation. Obviously, this move will be a change and affect the balance you have established here in California, as well as with your family. I will be back in the office on Thursday. We will reconvene at nine a.m. Any questions?"

Both Tom and Donovan were quiet throughout but agreed to continue this conversation and consider my proposal. What I was waiting for was Tom to engage, but he was the more reserved one of the two, and I expected he would require more of a one-on-one meeting.

"Stephen, are we all clear?" I asked.

"We are, sir. Both men have disconnected from the call."

"Very good. So, my friend, what do you think? Have I come up with the best possible solution to make everyone in my life happy?"

"You always do, sir. This could mean a new life entirely for Jackson and Riley, if they agree."

"Trust me, Stephen, he will agree. I'm about to give him the brass ring."

"In small doses?"

"Absolutely. I should be in the air in a few hours. I will see you when I land."

"Yes, sir. Have a safe flight," Stephen said before hanging up.

"Mara," I called out.

"Mr. Reed."

"Call for my car."

"Right away, sir."

I phoned Jackson to make sure he and Riley were ready to leave. They were already waiting for me to return. I told them to go on ahead with Richard, and I would meet them all on the plane. I then phoned the other half of my soul.

"Hello, my love," Reese answered in her smooth as silk voice that completely brought me to my knees.

"Hey, baby, how are you?"

"Missing you terribly. Fallon has been out of sorts since both of her princes left."

"Correction, my love. *I am the king*, and Jackson is the prince."

"Oh, my apologies, my lord," she responded.

"Smart ass! I need to be home with you...now!"

"You will and soon. How are Jackson and Riley? She called me, but I wasn't feeling all that great and was lying down."

I said, "I hate that I'm not there with you. How's the morning sickness today?"

"Tolerable, but I haven't been able to hold anything down, only a few crackers."

"The anti-nausea medicine is not helping?"

"Not really. I'm trying to stay hydrated, but I'm vomiting as quickly as I take in the fluids."

"Reese, where is Priscilla? Allow her to care for Fallon until I return. Are you in bed?"

"I am, and Fallon is beside me, napping soundly. Priscilla is close by, so please do not worry."

"Have we met? I believe your memory is failing you. I will be home as soon as I can, and the kids are great. I will tell you everything tomorrow. Rest assured, they are fine and back on track."

"You are my hero. I love you, Walker, so much."

"I love you more. Kiss our daughter from her daddy. I'll see you soon."

I disconnected my call with Reese, and grabbed my things, looking back to my vast office. *One day, son, this will all be yours*, I thought to myself. I smiled in confidence that the dream of my son working by my side would be real, something I would revel in. This was his legacy, and a part of me was eternally grateful that he knew that too.

My assistant met me at the elevator, and we exchanged formal goodbyes. The elevator doors closed as my team waved goodbye.

I let out a deep breath. My chest literally hurt being away from my wife and daughter. I never believed I would ever feel this way again after losing Elizabeth and finally coming to terms with the fact that I would raise Jackson all on my own. Now that boy was a man, so ready to take on the world, marry the love of his life, and follow in my example. My beautiful Reese completed me. All of our time apart and it felt like it never happened with all the good fortune that replaced the once dark parts in my life. We had a beautiful daughter and a new baby on the way. Life did not get any sweeter than that.

I believed that what I planned for Jackson would give him the best of both worlds. He would remain in New York with Riley, and without disturbing the new balance in their lives. This time next year, they would both leave NYU as graduates with degrees in hand. I would share my plans with Jackson once we were all home in California and under one roof.

I climbed the stairs to my plane, and Richard was there to greet me. I was exhausted. All I wanted was Reese to hold me. I looked over to Jackson. He believed I could move mountains, and most of the time I could, but at the end of the day, I was still just a man who was incredibly in love with his woman and needed her every second of the day to breathe.

"You made it!" Jackson walked over to greet me.

He pulled me into a tight hug and whispered "thank you" for only me to hear. Riley waved to me and went back to her phone. I pulled back from his embrace and wondered why he was thanking me.

"Jackson, let's get in the air, and then we will have a chat."

He was satisfied with my answer and joined Riley. I smiled and took comfort in knowing I had a small part in their happy reunion.

I stayed in my office longer than I should have, but I needed the time to relax my mind over the past day's events. Jackson and Riley seemed more than okay with the private time I gave them.

We were approaching LAX as I took my seat for landing. The kids were engaged in conversation, and my mind was on Reese. I hated to be away from my wife, and with her being pregnant, I hated leaving her even more. She had been sick and kept it from me. Thank God I still had eyes at home to keep me informed. I married such a stubborn woman. I would have to make sure to give her extra TLC when I got home.

The landing was perfect as usual. I quickly gathered my things and exited my plane. Stephen was waiting to bring us home. I handed my things over and climbed into the backseat, with the kids following. I did not want to delay my homecoming with pleasantries and conversations. I wanted Reese.

"You two look happy to be home," I said to them.

Their hands linked together with huge smiles on their faces.

"We are, Mr. Reed. Thank you for all of your help back at school."

"Whatever do you mean, Riley?"

"With Professor Connelly. You walking in when you did probably helped us more than you know."

"Thank you for saying that, but you were judged and graded on your merit, not mine. I believe the professor was fair, and I am happy he gave you both a second chance. Not all professors would be so giving, Riley. Remember that lesson for the future, and I am not only giving this advice to Riley. Am I making myself clear, son?"

"You are. Thank you, dad."

We finally arrived home. I did not wait for Stephen to open the car door. I practically leaped out like a super hero. The kids were excited too. Priscilla met us at the door, and then stepped back as we entered. In the entryway stood a beautifully decorated Christmas tree trimmed with colorful lights and ornaments. Not only was the foyer beautifully decorated, but it appeared the entire house was too. *Did Rosalyn decide to carry out our plans without telling me?*

"Welcome home, Walker."

There was my beautiful wife, dressed in red and holding our daughter, who matched with her beautiful mother.

"Dada. Dada." Fallon was squirming in Reese's arms trying to get to me.

I enveloped them both in my arms and I said, "Home."

"Yes, you are my love," Reese said. "We missed you so much."

Reese kissed me on my lips, a chaste one at that, but I knew we would have a proper reunion later when we were alone. I held our daughter while she blew raspberries on my face, and I watched Reese hug Riley and Jackson.

Our family was all back together and under the same roof. Reese had tears in her eyes, and Riley followed suit. Jackson smiled over at me, and then once Fallon saw her big brother, I was soon handing her over.

"Hello, sweet girl. Did you miss me?" Jackson said as he hugged his sister, and then Riley took her turn with Fallon.

Receiving wet raspberries on their faces, they smiled and took turns kissing their sister in return. Reeds rarely cried, but if I did, this would have been the time to do so. Watching our kids so happy was all we ever wanted for them.

Reese took my arm and walked us into our great room. The house looked exactly how I planned it out with Rosalyn. *How did Reese manage to do this?*

"Do you love it?" asked Reese.

"I do. Our home looks amazing. I thought you were sick. How did you manage to pull this off?"

"I had help. Please do not be mad, but I phoned Rosalyn and asked her if she could put together a spur of the moment surprise for you. I know we talked about our decorating ideas, but I really wanted the house to be ready for the kids. And I wanted to do something for you for a change. Did I overstep?"

I took Reese in my arms and held her as tightly as I could manage.

I responded, "Baby, this is perfect. You are perfect. I love it so much. There is nothing you do that does not make me love you more. I will have to make sure Ms. Rosalyn Baker receives a bonus for her efforts. Have the grounds been taken care of as well?"

I was almost nervous to ask. I was still hopeful that I could give Reese a surprise of my own.

"Now that you are home, I can show you," Reese signaled over to Priscilla and then took my hand to follow her outside. "Close your eyes, Walker. No peeking."

I did as I was instructed, but I was dying of curiosity at the same time.

"Okay, my love, open your eyes."

I slowly did, and the grounds and our home came to life with thousands of lights shining all around us. *How did she know?* Reese arranged everything I planned to do for her, down to the last perfect light strung on our gazebo. If Santa's winter wonderland existed, I was looking at its twin before my eyes.

Fallon's eyes were sparkling with the glimmering lights all around her. The kids were walking the grounds, and Riley picked up some snow and made a snowball.

"Real snow, Jackson! Can you believe this?" she said.

A snowball fight followed, and Reese was positively glowing. Reese was great. Our kids were happy. I was home, and I knew this time around, our holiday would be perfect. My love held my hand and grasped it tightly.

"Well? What do you think, Walker?"

"It's beautiful, sweetheart, it all looks spectacular. I do not know how you managed to accomplish all of this, but it is amazing. I could not be more surprised! Merry Christmas, Reese."

"Not yet, my love. We have many presents to look forward to," she said with a wink, my devilish vixen.

"Oh yeah? Well, the only present I care to open right now is you, my love. Say goodnight. It's time for bed."

"Good night, Jackson and Riley. See you in the morning," she called out over shoulder as we left to carry Fallon to her nursery and tuck her in for the night.

I had never seen Reese look so happy, she was beyond beautiful and radiant. I could not wait to show her how much I missed her.

CHAPTER 22

Riley

Finding our way

"FALLON, CAN I tell you a secret?" Jackson said. "You won't tell anyone, will you? I know you have big bro's back. Who loves you, baby girl?"

"Dada. Dada. Dada."

Jackson responded, "He's one of many, baby girl. Our dad loves us very much and would move mountains if it meant our happiness. He already did with Riley and me. I messed up big time with her and hurt Riley's feelings. I made a promise a long time ago that I would love Riley forever, and I hurt her. You see, baby sis, even with the best intentions, you can still hurt the one you love."

He did not know I could hear every word he just said to our little sister.

He continued, "I apologized, and she has forgiven me, at least I believe she has. I love her so much, Fallon. You know how daddy always says, 'You are my whole world,' well that is how I feel about Riley. She is my everything, princess. We hit a rough patch, but we are okay now. We will always be okay. So, sweet girl, let us keep this little talk between us, alright? I promise I will always be here for you, and for Riley. I promise, Fallon. I love you so much."

God, I loved him. I thought to myself: *I am not mad, Jackson. How can I be? All you do is try to make me happy and fight for our love when I stop believing in it or fight against it. I am the one that feels undeserving of your love, but I made a promise a long time ago to trust my heart in your hands. I love you forever. We will find our way and will be okay. We will always be okay.*

I wish I had my camera to capture this moment between Jackson and Fallon. They were so cute together. She was grabbing his cheeks and drooling all over him. He loved every minute of it. I wiped my tears and walked in to join the happy duo.

"Hey, babe, I didn't know you were there," Jackson said to me.

"I just got here. Good morning, love."

"Good morning to you. How did you sleep?"

I responded, "I slept well, knowing you were there to hold me. I have missed you Jackson. God! I am such a girl. Sorry to be so weepy."

I watched Jackson place a kiss upon Fallon's head of chestnut brown curls, and then he secured her in the baby bouncy. He was so beautiful to watch. I could not help but to imagine how he would be with our own kids when we had them. He smiled down at our little sister, and then he rejoined me on the carpet.

"I'm not going anywhere, Riley. You're the one. You drive me insane, crazier than anyone in my life, but it is a good crazy. A crazy that I crave. A crazy that makes me want to do better for you and for myself. A crazy that makes me feel alive and so in love with you. You are the one. I love you, Riley Taylor Briggs! You are my one and only."

"How do you know for sure? This could be just a passing fly-by-night romance. You do know how good looking you are, right? Seriously, Jackson, you should be on the cover of a magazine."

"I'd like to think I am not that shallow. It's just a face," he said back.

"A face that I want to kiss right now."

"I'm not stopping you, babe."

His strong arms wrapped around my body. His lips touched mine, and my insides felt like they were on fire. It was an intense shock, as if I just touched a live wire. I wanted to make love to him.

I told him, "Make love to me, Jackson. I want you so much. Please let me show you just how much you mean to me."

"Riley, I know. All you have to do is stay with me. Trust me. Believe in us, and I'll take care of the rest. Okay, beautiful girl?"

"Okay. Now make love to me." I repeated my request.

Our bodies began to tangle with the other when a sudden squeal from Fallon reminded us exactly where we were. We broke out into a fit of laughter, and then we saw our parents standing in the doorway. *Kill me now!* I nearly had sex on the floor of our baby sister's nursery, and I was once again under the stare of Mr. Reed. My mother was not helping with her half glare. I could not decide if she wanted to reprimand us or laugh with us.

"Good morning, Riley, Jackson," mom said to us. "Good morning, baby girl," she said to Fallon as she actually stepped over us and then picked up Fallon.

Mr. Reed kissed mom and then Fallon. He was still glaring at us.

"When you two decide to get up off the floor, we will be downstairs. Breakfast is ready," mom said.

Jackson started giggling as my mother, Mr. Reed, and Fallon left the room.

"Stop laughing, babe. Your father still scares the shit out of me."

"He loves you Riley, and I love you. Hungry?"

"Not for food."

"That's my girl," Jackson said as he pulled me up and put me over his shoulder.

"Jackson, put me down! Oh my God! Do not drop me."

He slapped me on my ass, taking me by surprise. I loved when we played like this.

"I can walk, you know," I screamed.

"I know, beautiful girl, but I will never pass up an opportunity to hold you."

"Caveman."

"Only for you." He slapped my ass again, and making me want him more. What a difference from where we were a week ago. *Twist my arm. He can do this anytime he wants*, I thought to myself. Jackson put me down just as we reached the kitchen. I think I had reached my quota of embarrassment for one morning.

"You are not even out of breath. You do realize how many stairs you just carried me down?"

"Riley, you weigh like, what, 110 pounds? I can toss you around like a rag doll. Babe, I love when you are in my arms. Get used to it, okay? I'm hungry."

"Let's go join the parents," I suggested.

I kissed my sweet man, who once again picked me up and twirled me around. We walked into the kitchen, where our parents were waiting on us. Fallon had oatmeal all over her rosy cheeks. She picked up the bowl, and then…bam! Slam! More oatmeal all over her.

"Hi, mom. I think you may have to soak her in a bubble bath."

Mom said, "You may be right. She loves bath time. Priscilla, can you take Fallon upstairs for me?"

"Of course, Mrs. Reed," Priscilla responded.

"Bye, Fallon," I said as I blew kisses at her.

Once the baby was gone, mom turned back over to me.

"Thank you for coming home, Riley. You have made me very happy," she said.

"You never have to thank me, mom. I should be apologizing to you for not returning your calls."

"No need, my daughter. Can we talk later?"

"Absolutely," I told her.

We enjoyed a delicious family breakfast. Priscilla made amazing pancakes. We all engaged in catching up with one another. Jackson's hand never left my thigh. He never stopped smiling throughout the meal. Mr. Reed was quiet but looked happy to be home and back with my mom.

Mr. Reed made spa appointments for mom and me while he and Jackson went out on their own. I had so much to tell mom and still felt bad for shutting her out. I was going to tell her everything, even the naughty stuff that made her blush.

"Ready, sweetheart?" mom asked me.

"Spa day, here we come! See you later, boys," I said as I winked at Jackson and waited for mom to kiss Mr. Reed goodbye.

Soaking my feet in the heavenly lavender soak was amazing. The Swedish massage was magical, and I was already working on my second mimosa. *Thank you, Mr. Reed!*

"Talk to me, my daughter. I am going to try very hard not to give you a guilt trip, but seriously, Riley…where have you been?"

"Lay into me, mom, I deserve it. I'm sorry."

"Riley, we are not here to argue. I miss my daughter and want to know what is going on in her life."

"Thank you, and arguing with you is the last thing I want to do. I think New York surprised me. It was one thing exploring the city with Jackson when we were vacationing, but to live there is an entirely different story. I lost myself for a while and the reason I was there in the first place."

"How so?" mom asked.

"I guess I lived a pretty sheltered life back in Maryland, and when it was time to finally be out on my own, I felt free. You've met Clay and Brandon. They are wonderful guys, but wild. They make no apologies for their antics and just want to have a good time. When they got girlfriends who are equally crazy, our quiet life became loud and unbearable for Jackson. He hated living with them and kind-of played the 'I am a Reed card.' And before I could blink, I was living back in the penthouse."

"Is that a bad thing?"

"It can be when you give up control and go silent in your relationship. I didn't like myself too much, and I was not thinking the nicest thoughts about the Reed men. Sorry, mom."

"I am well aware of the Reed dominance, Riley, but you must know it comes from a good place. You have to establish early on what works in your relationship and what does not. Having said that, life is not without its challenges. You have grown so much in the past year, and so has Jackson. He is his father's son, no matter how much in the past he denied it. He emulates his father in all things while maintaining his own individuality."

"Sounds like us," I said.

"It usually happens that way when you are close to your parents. Jackson loves you and will always protect you from anything he feels will harm you. You may have seen him as being too possessive and exercising control over you, but it was his way of protecting. I have been down this road with Walker many times. They cannot help themselves but be protective, and will never make apologies for doing so. No man on this planet has the ability to make me feel safe like Walker does. I will not compare one relationship to the other, but what you have with Jackson is special. Be careful with him and his feelings, Riley. He wears his heart on his sleeve, and when you lead with your heart, it sometimes takes the brain a while to catch up."

"You speak Reed very well," I said, jokingly. "Mr. Reed gave Jackson similar advice."

"I have years of practice, my daughter."

"Do you know about Jackson wanting to work at Reed Global?" I asked.

"A little. I have not caught up yet with Walker, and I know they are going to talk about it today. The bigger question is: how do you feel about it?"

"At first, I was angry with Jackson for changing his mind without discussing it with me first. We fought and then he left, which nearly destroyed me. When he came back, I listened for the first time in months. Mom, I miss you every single day, and Fallon too, but this is your life out here on the West coast, not mine. When Jackson mentioned going to California, I thought I was going to die. His words gutted me, and I truly believed he was choosing his first life with his father, and forgetting the one he was making with me. I know how foolish it sounds, but that is what I believed. He gave me no time to process his change of heart, and I did not react very well to his news."

"Are you okay now?" she asked me.

"We are. Sure, we have to continue talking, but we are a lot better than we were a week ago.

"Just keep talking with each other, and you will find your way."

"Exactly. We will always find our way."

The rest of our afternoon was less of the heavy conversation, and more girly stuff. After the spa, we hit Rodeo drive and gave Mr. Reed's credit cards a workout. The best part of the day was stopping in to see Freddy, mom's longtime best friend. He let me choose anything I wanted off the secret rack he kept in his office. I left Freddy's with two knockout dresses that made their debut during New York Fashion Week. I was in heaven. We would see Freddy and his husband, Fabrizio, over Christmas.

It was a perfect day with mom. I loved every minute with her. Before heading for home, we stopped at Starbucks to grab coffee for me, tea for mom. We would always save the topic of my father for last.

"Daddy is doing well, in case you were wondering."

Mom surprisingly, yet noticeably, relaxed after I told her dad was fine.

"Have you seen him lately?" she inquired.

"I have, but just for lunch when he comes into the city. He is

busy working on his research with Gillian and splitting his time between London and Maryland. He's happy, mom. That's all you
wanted for him, right?"

"Of course. Divorcing your father was very hard on you and me
for many reasons. After all we went through with Jackson and finding out I was pregnant...well, it was a mindfuck of a situation."

"Mom! Language."

We both laughed until we had tears in our eyes. It was nice to
know my parents finally had an amicable relationship.

"Will you give your father my best the next time you speak with
him?"

"I will, mom, but you know that you can call and tell him yourself."

"I'd rather not, and let's leave it at that. Anyway, there is one
more thing I would like to discuss with you. I promised Walker I
would wait, but we are all together again and need to keep the happy
going."

"Are you okay, mom?"

"I am better than okay. I am pregnant and due in July!"

"Wow! I was not expecting that. Congratulations, mom! Another sister for me to love."

"It could be a boy," she said.

"Yeah, but girls are so much more fun."

"I am so happy to finally have shared this with you. You did
surprise me with the no-screaming reaction."

"I cannot believe you're pregnant again, mom."

"It was a shock for me too, but a welcomed surprise. Walker
had been hinting that he wanted more children, and then to come to
find out that I was pregnant again made me beyond happy."

"Well, I'm happy for you. You never looked more beautiful
than when you were carrying Fallon. I should have guessed just by
looking at you last night. You were glowing. Mom, not to be a
downer asking the tougher questions, but are you...healthy? And the
baby...is all okay?"

"We are now. I had a little scare in the beginning, but I promise you that I am fine, other than the morning sickness I have been dealing with."

"What kind of scare?" I asked. I took my mother's hand and held it in my own, reassuring her that I would not freak out with whatever she would say."

"Riley, I'm fine, I promise."

"That may be true, but I still want to know."

"Okay, but please believe me when I tell you that I am fine, okay?"

"Okay."

"After I gave birth to Fallon, when my body and hormone levels returned back to my pre-pregnant body, I went in to see Dr. Lemay for a full work-up. I was long overdue for the usual tests, but no need for concern. I am in very good shape, as you can see, and Dr. Lemay was not worried while performing the usual breast and pelvic exams."

"And…?" I asked, a little nervous with mom's explanation. My palms were beginning to sweat.

"They found that I had some pre-cancerous cells and performed a biopsy and some tests."

"Oh my God, mom!"

I disconnected from her hand and covered my mouth to stifle my cries. We were out in the open in a Starbucks, where I already felt eyes on me.

"Riley, listen to me. I am fine. I would never keep anything about my health from you. Yes, it was scary, and when Dr. Lemay called me with my tests results, I will admit I did not handle Walker very well. In fact, I ran away."

"Why? You must know that probably drove him insane."

"I know, Riley, believe me. My fear of hearing that I might be sick and compromising the health of this baby made me behave impulsively. I did not go far, only to Freddy's. He was the only one I shared this with until I was ready to tell Walker. On the night I planned to, Fallon came down with illness, and I was exhausted. It was also the night Walker told me his desire for more children. I just checked out for a while until I heard what Dr. Lemay would say."

"I am so sorry I was not here for you. You called and called for weeks, and like a brat, I ignored you."

"All is forgiven, sweetheart. We are all fine and healthy."

"Thank you, God! I need you, mom, and Fallon and this baby need you too. I cannot imagine for even a second what Mr. Reed would do if something were to happen to you. I was there to witness it all when Jackson's grandfather kidnapped and hurt you. It is something I will never forget for as long as I live."

"Neither will I, but it's over and in the past. No more sad talk, okay?"

"Okay," I said. "Our family is growing by leaps and bounds. This will be me and Jackson one day."

"It will, but not now. You two need to finish your education and get married first."

"I hear you, mom. So for now I'll just have fun living in sin and enjoying all the non-baby-making sex!"

"Riley! TMI. TMI. Oh, my ears are bleeding."

"Sorry, mom, you make it so easy. I love you so much."

"I love you too. Let's go home and see what our Reed men have been up to."

CHAPTER 23

Jackson

What have you decided?

"**S**URFING? YOU WANT to go surfing, dad?" I blinked my eyes in surprise.

Surfing was not at the top of my father's to-do list, and we had not been out on the water in over two years. He looked a bit offended when I scoffed at his suggestion.

"Why is that so hard for you to believe, Jackson? Last time I checked, I was in pretty good shape."

"Dad, I'm sorry. Can you blame me for asking? It's been a while since we last surfed, and in the past when I did suggest it, you always said no."

"Well, I'm saying yes today, so are we going or not?"

"Going! Let me get my stuff," I replied.

"No need for that. Everything is in the car."

It was a gorgeous day with the temperature rising close to eighty degrees. The water temperature would probably be about twenty degrees cooler than that. It was mid-week and our usual spot was empty. We had the water to ourselves, and I could not wait to get out there. We changed into our wet suits and grabbed our boards.

"The swells look good today. We should be able to catch some good ones," dad said.

"Try to keep up, old man."

"Less of the old, son. Watch and learn," he retorted.

Dad and I raced each other to the shore, with him gaining some yardage on me. My father worked out every day, not only in his gym, but also with his trainer. He was in fantastic shape, and although I could hold my own against him, I believed I was about to get my ass handed to me.

By the time I caught my first wave, my father was paddling out for the second time. He waited for me to catch one, and we rode in together, side by side. We were out there for a good hour. I caught some good waves, but dad looked right at home and in his element. It was good to see him smile and be carefree. It was not often I got to see that side of him. After surfing, we took a ride up the coast and grabbed lunch.

"That was fun. Thank you for surfing with me today," he told me.

"I enjoyed it, dad. Thank you for asking. Are we going to talk about New York?"

"We are, but I thought we might want to have a day to ourselves before getting into a heavy conversation."

"I want to talk, dad, if it's all the same to you. I need to be able to give Riley an answer before we go back to New York."

Our waiter interrupted our conversation several times before my father halted his eagerness. He took our order and quickly brought us our drinks before retreating to the kitchen.

"Jackson, you must understand by you dropping the bombshell on wanting to work at Reed Global, frankly it took me by surprise. I will admit I have had time to process your suggestion, and I believe I have come up with a reasonable compromise. Now, I have not discussed any of this with my team as of yet. That meeting will be on Friday."

"What have you decided?" I inquired.

"For one thing, you are not leaving NYU. You will continue your education until you receive your MBA in Business Management. I have checked with the dean, looked over your course load, and have confirmed that you will need sixty credits to achieve that goal. I could not have asked for better grades. It is clear that you have worked very hard to get as far as you have. Now, as for your film classes…what do you intend to do? It's obvious to me that Professor Connelly appreciates your work, and with the right guidance, you will be successful."

"Dad, I already told you that I am not pursuing a film career. I want the degree in business. This is why I have taken double the course load if I wish to graduate on time."

"That I understand, Jackson, but did you or did you not assure Professor Connelly that you would be returning to his class in January?"

"I did, dad, but…"

"But what! Jackson, you are trying my patience. Do you even grasp how much natural born talent you possess? Did I watch someone else's film? You heard your teacher and the feedback that followed."

I sighed heavily and was thanking my luck that our waiter brought out our lunch. I had lost my appetite over this conversation. He placed our dishes in front of us, and my father told him to not disturb us. The poor guy looked green after my father's instruction. He usually had that effect on most people. I was not feeling too hot myself.

"Yes, dad, I did agree to go back and finish his course. Having said that, I do not plan to take on anything new."

"Okay, Jackson, I can work with that, but if I am being honest here, I would encourage you to give it more thought before completely dismissing the idea. Now, from what I have seen with your past documentaries and the newest one, I do believe I could use your skills on our research development team."

"No disrespect, dad, but I am better than that, and I believe I would be better suited for marketing."

"You may be right, son, but it is not your decision. It is mine. I will assign you to what I feel your skills are best suited for, but for now, this conversation is over. At this time, I cannot tell you anything else until I meet with my team."

"May I ask a question?" I inquired.

"You may."

"Forget it. Thank you, dad, for considering me."

"Jackson, look at me."

I felt so small sitting here with my father. I felt like I was choking with a noose around my neck. I ignored him the first time, and that was something you did not do when talking with Walker Reed. He asked again in a more forceful tone.

"Jackson, look at me."

Riley was right to fear him at times, and as his son, yeah, he scared the shit out of me from time to time. I looked into his eyes and tried not to breakdown in front of him. I expected to see coldness in his eyes, but all I saw was pride and his love for me.

"You are my son," he said, "and I want nothing more than for you to join me at Reed Global. How could you believe I would not want this for you and for us? I am so proud of the man you have become. I believe you will do extraordinary things in your life. The goals you have set forth for yourself are achievable. I am a very proud father. I know you will do great in anything you do, but son, you need to walk before you run."

"Is that what grandfather told you?"

"Quite the opposite. I never walked, only ran. I did not want to follow my father's example when raising you. I always encouraged you to follow your heart and not push you into something you did not want to do."

"Thank you for that, dad, but working at Reed Global is what I want. I will not fight you on anything. I just want to be part of it, dad."

"That is the best thing you have said all day, son."

"I have my moments."

We both laughed and let out a breath. Going round and round with Walker Reed is exhausting, but he was right. I had to walk before I ran.

We went on to finish our lunch with no tension lingering around after our heavy conversation. I trusted my father with all of my heart and soul.

"Thanks for today, dad. I needed it."

"I did too. It is not often I get the chance to let go like this, maybe not ever."

"If I move back to California, I will make sure to add surfing to my day planner," I told him.

"Nice, but you can also surf on the East coast as well. Walk before you run, Jackson. I promise you will not be sorry for it."

"Okay."

"Now, with all of that out of the way, I have something to share with you. I know I told Reese I would wait, but I can't keep something so fantastic from you. If I know my lovely wife, she is probably also breaking her vow of silence with Riley."

Curiously, I asked, "Sounds big, what is it?"

"Reese and I are going to have another baby!"

"Wow! I guess the Reed men do come from strong stock. Congratulations, dad."

"You better believe it. We are very happy. Your brother or sister will arrive in July."

"You really think Reese is telling Riley your big news?"

"Why do you think I'm telling you? I guarantee Reese told Riley. We will not say anything when we get home. Let me see Reese first before we celebrate."

"Yeah, good luck with that," I said. "If Riley does know, I'm sure she will not be silent about it."

"This is true. One way to find out: let's go home to the women we love."

"Lead the way, dad. Can I drive?"

"No!"

We drove home, laughing and reconnecting. The weight of the world that had been burdening me was now lifted with the help from my father. He raised me to be strong and to stand on my own as a man worthy of the Reed name and the legacy attached to it. I also knew without a doubt that he would always be there for me if I needed him. I should be so lucky to be a good enough father as Walker Reed has been to me.

Walker

Christmas wishes and birthday surprises

"**J**ENNY," I BARKED into my intercom, "I need Rosalyn Davenport Baker on the phone, now."

"She's holding on line two, sir."

Praise the Gods for the best assistant ever.

"Ms. Baker, I would like to discuss how all the plans that you and I discussed privately were somehow all carried out while I was away in New York. Imagine my surprise when my car pulled up to my front door and I was welcomed home with my entire estate decorated with thousands of lights, right down to the tree I ordered."

"Mr. Reed, I can explain."

"I'm waiting."

This was fun. I kicked up my feet and leaned back in my chair. Reese would not approve of my torturing tactics on Ms. Baker, especially so early in the day.

The truth is I loved it all. My home never looked more spectacular in all the years I lived there. Sure, I made every effort to impress Jackson when he was little, but I never had anyone to share it with me. Now married to Reese, and adding to our family, I had never been happier to celebrate a holiday.

I guess it was time to put her out of her misery. After she rambled and stammered on, I finally interrupted her.

"Ms. Baker, thank you for your very colorful answer to my question, but I have heard enough."

"But, Mr. Reed, I was only following the request of my client. Please do not fire me. I have a reputation to protect, and I am damn good at my job. Oh my goodness! Mr. Reed, I am so sorry. I feel sick."

"Ms. Baker...Rosalyn, if I may. Please. Stop. Talking. Listen carefully, because I am not one to repeat myself. You are a very talented individual, and I would be a fool to let you go. And we both know I am no fool. So thank you Rosalyn. I'm not sure how my lovely wife managed this surprise before I had the chance to, but nonetheless, I loved it."

"Mr. Reed, thank you. I am so happy you approve, and actually, it was quite simple to pull off. See, Mrs. Reed phoned me while you were in New York and hired me to give you the surprise of all Christmas surprises. She was quite specific on what she wanted, which made my job easy because you both share the same taste. It is very rare in my line of work that I meet two people that are so in love with the other and are always in harmony that is you and Mrs. Reed. I can assure you, it is an amazing thing to witness."

"Thank you, Rosalyn."

I would never tell her how much I loved hearing all the lovely things she was saying to me about my wife. I believed her too. Ms. Baker was an overzealous individual, but she was right about one thing: she was damn good at what she did.

"So, Mr. Reed, I take it you still would like to move forward with the rest of your holiday surprise for Mrs. Reed?"

"Absolutely, I cannot wait."

"That's great to hear, sir. Would you like to discuss this now? Or should I email you on it?"

"Ready when you are, Ms. Baker."

Nearly an hour later, everything I planned for Reese was now confirmed, which delighted me to no end. My day carried on with no major issues to raise alarms until Donovan and Tom barreled through my office, with Jenny attempting to halt them. She was about to scold them when I raised my hand, signaling her that all was under control. Tom, always the reserved one, began loosening his tie, a rare move on his part. He was usually so put together and quiet, but not today.

"Sir, if I may have a word."

"You are overreacting, Tom. Nothing has been decided yet," said Donovan, who was standing behind him.

And to think I just said a few minutes ago how great my day was going, I thought to myself. *Time to put an end to this nonsense. I am running a business here, not executive daycare.*

"That's enough!" I yelled. "Sit down and be quiet. All of your yammering is giving me a headache."

They both stopped immediately and looked at me with apprehension while taking their seats. Tom sat up straight and readjusted his tie.

I said to them, "Now, need I remind you whose name is on the door you just crashed through? Because the last time I checked, I was the fucking boss! Am I not?"

Both men were now quiet with eyes cast down to the floor. I slammed my fist onto my desk to get their attention, looking for a reaction from them.

"You can speak," I shouted at both men, who were now looking three shades of foolish. They quietly nodded and I carried on. I leaned back on the desk with my hands crossed over my chest and looked at both of my top executives.

"Tom, since you so animatedly graced me with your entrance,

you have the floor. Please explain to me what has you so upset?"

"Mr. Reed, my apologies. Donovan and I were simply having a disagreement that was taken to a higher level, and I was coming by to speak with you. But as you witnessed, that did not happen the way I originally intended."

I said, "Okay, Tom, you have my attention. I am a busy man, explain yourself!"

He looked over to Donovan, who was just about grinning and taking too much enjoyment at his friend's discomfort now. I issued a warning to Donovan, which had him once again casting his eyes to the floor.

Tom said, "I would like to further discuss the conversation that began in New York. Have you made a decision on whom you are sending to New York?"

"I have not," I responded.

"Will a decision be made soon?"

"Why? Do you have a better offer somewhere else?"

"Of course not! You did mention relocation, and if that is what your intentions are, then I would like to know as soon as possible in order to accommodate the needs of my family."

Not happy with what he was hearing, Donovan was quick to interrupt him, "Tom, why do you think it's going to be you? I do more business in New York on behalf of Reed Global that would make your head spin."

I interrupted, "Okay, that's enough. I am not sure how all of this began, but it ends now."

I gestured my hands between the two men. "As I explained during our conference call, this relocation would not be a permanent one, and if you remember, I said it was on the lines of a personal favor to me shall you agree. Due to the lateness of the hour, this discussion is tabled for now. When I am ready, we will meet and iron out the details, understood?"

"Yes, sir, thank you," Tom said as he stood to shake my hand, while Donovan was still in his seat. Tom bid me goodnight and took his leave.

"Donovan, something to say?" I asked.

"I apologize. I should have never brought my disagreement with Tom to your door. It will never happen again, and I will make things right with him before the beginning of our day tomorrow."

"See that you do, because you bet your ass that juvenile display will not happen again, nor will it be tolerated," I reiterated.

He stood to leave, and I gestured to him that I was not finished.

"Have a seat Donovan, or better yet, go fix yourself a drink," I told him, as Donovan poured himself one and took a seat in front of my desk. "Donovan, it has been a trying couple of weeks for me and my family. What is most important now is to enjoy the holidays with my wife, my children, and extended family. I do not have the patience for any inside quarreling you have going on with Tom. Am I getting through to you? Or do I need to speak slower?"

"Walker, as I have already stated, I apologize. The display you witnessed will never happen again. If I may explain?"

"Go on," I told him.

"I was in meetings all day, and then Tom joined me in my office to discuss tomorrow's meetings with you. Then he took a phone call. He ended his call, and his mood shifted to anger."

"How so?"

"I guess with Jackson making an appearance in the building, and then your arrival a few days later, the staff is wondering what is going on."

"Hold up," I interrupted. "May I ask how you knew that my son visited Reed Global? I never told you, Donovan, which means either someone else did, or you saw him personally when you were in New York to meet up with Lars Sapien. Now, if memory serves, I believe I told you to never keep anything from me again, a lesson you quickly learned after Reese reunited with me. So, which is it?"

I felt my jaw tick with rage. Donovan was my number one, and I expected greatness from him, but even the slightest infraction made my blood boil especially when it came to something as personal as

Jackson.

"Walker, I did not keep anything from you. You sent me to New York to meet with Lars, and it should not be a coincidence to run into Jackson from time to time. After all, he lives in New York. What I did not expect is to see him in the building. He was in conversation with Bridgette, Tom's daughter, who we hired on as a marketing intern. My time with Jackson was less than a minute. I said hello and goodbye to him, and then I went on about my day."

"The fact remains is that you did see him and did not tell me. Why go round and round on this? You should know that I would want to know about this; thus, you should have mentioned it to me."

"He asked me not to," Donovan said.

"Come again?"

"He asked me not to mention running into him, and I agreed. Walker, because he is your son, technically he is an extension of you, and that makes him my boss too! I respected his request and offered my time to him if he needed to talk about anything that is all. Is everything all right with Jackson? Because he seemed fine when I saw him."

"No need for concern, Donovan. My son is fine. You, on the other hand, are not. Whatever is going on with you and Tom needs to be resolved by morning, and I promise you this will be the last time I say this to you. You are right about one thing: Jackson is a Reed, and this company that I have built is a part of him and a legacy that will be his, and hopefully one day he will run it with his siblings. Until then, I am the only boss around here, understood? I do not care what you deem as important or inconsequential. Do. I. Make. Myself. Fucking. Clear?"

"Yes, sir."

"Fine! Get out."

He said nothing more, which was fine with me. Fuck! I hated to go round and round with Donovan and be at odds with him. He probably did not deserve my wrath, but it felt justified after the week I had with Jackson. He decided to change the course of his future without ever sharing his change of heart with me, and then he was reminiscing at Reed Global without my knowledge. Of course, he was welcomed there, but Donovan was right, when a Reed was on the premises for any reason, the staff was always on red alert. *Am I that fucking intimidating?* I looked over to a mirror, took a hard look, and answered my own question. I let out a heavy breath and grabbed my briefcase.

"Are you done for the day?" asked Jenny, as I closed my door behind me.

"Yes, and after tomorrow, done for the rest of the damn month."

"Everything has a way of finding its place, sir. You of all people know that all too well."

"Stop channeling Lila. You're freaking me out."

"That's just life experience, sir. Your family is waiting. Let them make your day better."

"Not just my *day*, Jenny. They make my *life* better. See you in the morning."

As Stephen drove me home, I remained quiet and reflected on all that occurred over the past week with Jackson. I believed I had figured out a way to keep him in school, in New York, and groom him to take his rightful place at Reed Global. The ideal resolution for me would be to have my son join me in California, but that would not be fair to Riley.

Jackson made a heartfelt commitment to that girl when he presented her with his mother's ring. We were selfish men to a degree, but we never used that selfishness to hurt the women we loved. He did just that, and if I knew my son, he deeply regretted it.

I always hated silence in my relationship with Reese. The Mitchell women were just as stubborn as the Reed men, maybe even more so. My love had the ability to completely shut down and never blink an eye, whereas I would lose my ever-fucking mind and allow it to revisit dark places I had since put behind me.

Both Donovan and Tom were overachievers. They strived to perform at their best. Donovan exceeded all of my expectations when it came to his commitment to Reed Global. Tom was the passive one and more of a father figure with just the right amount of leadership qualities that I believed Jackson would benefit from.

Jackson had been chomping at the bit awaiting my decision. After dinner this evening, I would test the waters and his new commitment to the company I built. It was his legacy, as well as his sister's and our future child that would bless our family next year. With the right mentoring, I believed Jackson would achieve amazing accomplishments in his life. As time went on, I only hoped I would get to see it, with Jackson joining me at the helm in California.

Tom and Donovan could teach him a great deal, but there was one greater. Just like his grandfather and father before him, a Reed was the only one that would properly serve, as the key to that legacy would one day be his.

As my car came to a stop, I admired our home, now decorated like a wonderland of Christmas. Knowing the love of my life awaited me behind those doors, I quickly exited the car with renewed spirit and hope. Of course, she beat me to it, she always did. The front door swung open, and Reese was standing there beautifully glowing with our child growing inside of her. She depleted all of the oxygen in my lungs with just a smile meant only for me. How did she know that was exactly what I needed?

"Welcome home, darling. I missed you today," she said to me.

"And I you, Reese. Allow me to show you how much."

I took her in my arms and crushed my mouth down to her plump ruby lips, with Reese inviting me in to her delicious mouth. She let our soft cries of pleasure as I delved deeper, claiming every inch of her, as if I hadn't a thousand times before. We disconnected, leaving both of us breathy and me with a raging erection inside of my trousers. She knew exactly what she was doing, and I loved and welcomed every bit of it.

"I have a surprise for you my love. Call it an early Christmas present," she said as she placed her hand in mine and walked me further inside our home.

"Reese, you do not have to give me anything. It's my job to spoil you."

"Oh, Walker! You give so freely to every single person in your life. Will you allow someone to do something nice for you? Now, please do not spoil my surprise. Come!"

"I love you, Reese."

"I love you more," she responded.

"Impossible."

"How did I know you were going to say that? You are my world, and in the eyes of your children, you are their hero. Therefore, your son decided to give Priscilla the day off and took over as commander in her kitchen. She was literally biting her nails down to the cuticle until Riley whisked her away to the spa. Priscilla was long overdue for some pampering, and Jackson insisted she take some time to treat herself."

"The apple does not fall too far from the tree, does it my love?" I laughed while winking at Reese.

"No, it does not. He is a Reed with all of his heart and soul, and today he wanted to pay it forward with some kindness to our loyal friend who never asks anything of us."

I smiled and closed my eyes for a brief moment. I was always generous with my staff, but Priscilla had been the one constant in our lives since Jackson was a small child. And now she had bestowed all of her love on Fallon.

With Reese still holding my hand, we stopped at the door that would lead us to the dining room.

"He worked really hard today and made all of the arrangements all on his own. Your son loves you very much," she explained.

"Lead the way, Mrs. Reed."

I was one lucky man and thanked the universe every single night for all the blessings I had in my life. As I walked into the dining room, I took in the great gifts that made my life complete.

"Welcome home, dad!" Jackson called out.

He was at the foot of the table with Riley seated beside him, and our precious baby girl was seated on his left in her chair and blowing raspberries at me, along with her chant of "Dada, dada, dada." It was a beautiful lyric to my ears.

"Thank you, son, and hello to you, princess," I said as I hugged Jackson and kissed my baby.

"Hello, Mr. Reed. I hope you are hungry, because you are in for a treat," Riley called out as she beamed at Jackson. She praised him for what I was about to enjoy.

The large silver domes were lifted, and I was presented with my favorite meal, one I usually enjoy at my favorite restaurant, La Brasserie Les Halles.

"Dinner is served," Jackson said with pride.

Treated with course after course, my eyes never took in a more delectable meal: Filet de Boeuf, Béarnaise beef tenderloin, accompanied with my favorite Bordeaux, a 2004 Chateau Pape Clement, Pessac-Leognan. I might have licked my lips at the sight of this mouthwatering meal. It looked amazing and smelled just as good.

I cleared my throat and asked the obvious question as my family happily enjoyed my expressions. "How did you do this, Jackson? Are secretly hiding another talent I do not know about?"

My comment was meant to be funny, but his smiled turned down for a brief moment. I immediately regretted my choice of words, but Jackson talked right over it.

"It was not easy, and I had a lot of help to prepare this meal for you."

He gestured to the door, and I braced myself for what was coming next. Reese could not stop smiling, nor could Riley.

"You can come out now," Jackson called out.

In a flash, Andre entered and greeted me with his overzealous pleasantries.

"Thank you, young Mr. Reed for allowing me to assist you this evening. My apprentice has made me very proud, Mr. Reed. Please, enjoy your dinner."

Before I could utter a word, he left as quickly as he entered.

All eyes were on me as I picked up my fork. No knife was required as my fork pierced the tender meat with no effort at all. I sampled a piece as it melted on my tongue, causing me to let out a response of pleasure.

"Jackson, this is amazing. Thank you for all of your hard work in preparing this meal for me."

"You are welcome, dad. It's the least I could do for you. Okay, let's eat!"

We enjoyed the meal my son had prepared for all of us, and then we were delighted to dessert prepared by Riley.

"You can never go wrong with Crème Brulee," she said as she passed around the decadent dessert.

"You two are amazing," I told them. "Everything was wonderful, and you pleased me very much. You will also note how stuffed I am. I may have to put in an extra hour with my trainer tomorrow."

"I have one more surprise for you, Walker," Reese whispered into my ear. "It's not that kind of surprise, though. This one is G-rated."

She gave me one of her sexiest winks and walked us into our family room where Jackson was on the floor with Fallon. The baby was squirming in her brother's arms, anxious to crawl to her daddy.

I noticed that Jackson had his camera positioned on a tripod. I was not sure as to why, but my little girl was calling out for me with one of the happiest smiles I had ever seen. I knelt down with my arms wide open, awaiting my little princess, but I was surprised with another treat.

Riley stood up behind the camera and signaled to my son. Jackson stood his little sister up and kissed her cheeks, almost giving her a boost of encouragement. As my arms were still open for her, she slowly took her first steps into my waiting embrace. She made it four steps before I swept in and caught her. She gave me two slaps on my cheek with more wet kisses to celebrate her newest milestone. Our baby Fallon was walking, mere weeks before her first birthday.

"Are you happy, Walker?" she asked as she wrapped her arms

around me.

"Immensely. Oh Reese, I've never been happier. Another amazing moment with my family and a milestone for our little girl!"

I smiled over to Jackson and Riley for capturing it on film. I would always cherish this night spent with our family.

"Merry Christmas, my love," I told Reese.

With Fallon nestled between us, I took Reese's mouth and kissed her madly. For all of my planning with Rosalyn to surprise Reese and the children, they turned the tables on me yet again. My heart was bursting with so much love. To see Fallon take her first steps just made my life perfect. This wonderful family of mine gave me the best Christmas surprise ever. All that was missing were Thomas and Lila and my mother, who I hoped would be here for Fallon's first birthday…unless Reese sidestepped me again, and they were all hiding behind another door.

We said our goodnights to the kids, and after putting Fallon to bed, Reese put me to bed. She slowly undressed before me as I laid back waiting for her. With so much they all did for me today, I closed my eyes and took in all of the pleasure she was giving to me, allowing her freely to love on me as only Reese could. We made love slowly, gently, and fell asleep tangled in each other's arms.

Yes, my family made me better, as I endeavored to always be better for them.

CHAPTER 25

Jackson

Sons and fathers

AFTER MY SURPRISE dinner went off without a hitch, I asked Riley if she would take a walk with me through my father's prized garden. Who knew he had a green thumb? I guess there were many things I was still discovering about Walker Reed: his passion for architecture; his love for beautiful things; his love for Reese, our family, and me.

Having to grow up without a mother was at times unbearable, but I never felt alone as one would think. My father was always a constant presence in my life. He never left me for more than a day when he needed to attend a business trip, and if it was any more than that, then he took me with him.

We were a team, always and forever. I knew this now and really understood what that truly meant. My father wanted me to stand on my own, but he was never too far away if I ever needed him. That was what I wanted, to be a success and earning it all on my own merit.

"What are you thinking about?" Riley asked me.

"Life," I told her.

"Can you be more specific?"

"I want to make my father proud."

"You do. Why would you ever doubt that you don't?"

"Riley, it is very easy to trade on the Reed name. I did it today by requesting Andre. Without hesitation, he dropped everything and left his busy restaurant to hop on my father's private jet, so he could teach me how to cook Walker Reed's favorite meal."

"And don't forget, he was paid handsomely for that service. Jackson, what is the problem? You made your father so happy tonight with your surprise. Don't second guess yourself now."

"I'm not, Riley. I am very happy that he was pleased. He is never one to ask for anything for himself, so this was the least I could do for him. This is hard to explain."

"I have time, talk to me."

"Can I kiss you first? And hold you for a little while before I do?"

"You never have to ask Jackson."

I took Riley's hand and brought it up to my lips to place a chaste kiss on it. I missed her so much and wanted nothing more than to make love with her, but out in the open was not possible. As we walked on, when it came into sight, Riley pulled back.

"Jackson, we can't. Not in there."

"Riley, no one will bother us out here, and believe me, it's soundproofed."

"Stop making jokes. There is no way I am going up in there."

"Yes you are, beautiful girl, and I assure you everything will be fine."

I unlocked the door and flicked on the lights. The room came alive with thousands of sparkling lights that lit the dome of the glass ceiling of the gazebo. This was my father's and Reese's special place, and now on loan for Riley and me to share for at least a few hours.

"If the walls could talk in here, I think my ears would bleed," she said.

"Yeah, you're probably right, but maybe we can add some stories of our own in here. I love you, Riley Taylor Briggs, so much. I am not perfect but endeavor to be as close as I can. We are going to fight, but what was our deal? I know you remember. I see it in your eyes, but I do too. *I will fight with you all day long, as long as I can hold you at night.* Back in New York, I forgot that rule, and I failed you, but I promise I will never repeat that mistake again."

"Jackson, I thought we were past this."

"We are; however, I still feel the need to share my feelings with you about it, so please beautiful girl, listen to me. This is where I failed in New York. I kept my feelings to myself and acted on things that I thought I could just tell you about and expect you to be okay with, and not argue with me about it. Seriously, babe, what fucking planet was I living on? We are equals in this relationship, partners for life, and above all, I respect you so much. I want nothing more than to marry you, and I want to make that a reality as soon as we finish school. The coming year is going to be busy and intense for the two of us, but when it is over, I hope to celebrate our accomplishment by marrying you. We will marry under our tree in front of our family and friends. How does that sound to you?"

"It sounds perfect. I want all those things with you, and thank you for calling me your equal. I know marrying a Reed comes with a huge responsibility, and I promise I will try to live up to the prestige behind your name every single day as your wife."

I pulled her close to me and crushed my lips to hers. Her fingers entwined in my hair, bringing me closer to her. We broke apart, and I held her face. She was beautiful and all mine.

"Riley, all I want you to do is love me. You never have to worry about becoming someone else because your last name is Reed. You will always be Riley Taylor Briggs Reed first, and the rest of it we will learn together, okay?"

"Okay. Has your father mentioned anything about New York? And you working for Reed Global?"

"No, but that conversation is coming. In fact, it happens tomorrow. I don't want to push him, I have learned that lesson all too well, and I do not wish to repeat that mistake again."

"Oh, I get that, my love, with your father you get these brief moments of courage, and then when it passes, you are on the edge of wetting your pants," she said.

"Sadly, I can relate. It would be so easy to just sit back and trade on his name and have anything and everything handed to me, but he did not raise me that way. I want so much more than to be just a trust fund kid. Hell! They make reality shows with kids like the ones I went to school with. I want more out of life. I want more for me, and for us."

"Are you talking about Brandon and Clay? Once upon a time, they were your friends, Jackson."

"They still are, Riley, and I will speak again with them soon. They are great guys, but they can be reckless, and their girlfriends are worse. I don't want to talk about them anymore. Let's change the subject."

She suggested, "I'm up for concluding tonight's conversational part, and move on to the physical one."

"And what did you have in mind?"

"Well, we're already here, and it *is* romantic."

"You read my mind."

She smiled and let out a delight of giggles that made me so hard, I thought I would come just by the sound of her voice. She slowly unwrapped the tie to her dress and let it fall down to her feet, carefully stepping out of it. Riley was lovely. Every inch of her was perfection, and I was going to kiss every bit of her before the night was through.

No time for foreplay, I wanted her and she wanted me. We

could play later. I was naked before she could blink and swept her up into my arms with her legs wrapping around my waist. I placed her gently down onto the soft surface and kissed her to the point of her ruby lips beautifully swelling. I nipped, bit, and devoured her delicious mouth.

My two fingers twisted and pulled at her nipples as Riley cried out from her orgasm. I slowly made my way down to her aroused pussy where I wasted no time and plunged my fingers in. Another cry rang out, hitting the right spot to make Riley come undone, again.

We no longer used condoms. She was on the pill, and we had been making love bare ever since. We trusted each other, and although we knew that no birth control was 100% effective, we were together and neither one of us was going anywhere.

"I love you, Riley."

"I love you too, Jackson. Now please fuck me before I truly do break these soundproofed walls."

"Impatient much?"

"Yes. It's your entire fault with how you tease me and my body," she said.

"Oh baby, you haven't seen anything yet."

I knew she wanted me to take her now, but I was not ready yet, not when she tasted amazing on my tongue. I pulled out my fingers and held her hands in place as I delved my tongue inside her.

"God! That feels fantastic," she moaned.

I smiled listening to her words, because this was all I wanted, to make Riley happy in every sense of the word, and this act I had down to a science. I knew her body just as well as she knew mine, and they were meant to bring the other pleasure. I stopped just as she was about to release her third orgasm. She screamed out, but I silenced her quickly with my mouth and then entered her just as she liked it: fast, deep, and hard.

"God, I love how I taste myself on your lips. It is beyond erotic," she whispered.

Her words were my undoing as I pumped faster into her small frame. Riley arched her back into the perfect position, meeting me with all fire and passion that makes her sexy and irresistible.

"Eyes open, baby," I told her. "I need to see you as we come together. Hold on, I am so close."

With swiping her tongue across her lips and a sexy wink that followed, I gripped her hips and we both shouted out our releases, with me filling her to the brim with my hot seed. We might have made a baby of our own if she was not on the pill, and I really did not care. I knew it was too early to entertain these possibilities with Riley, but I could not seem to help myself when I was buried deep inside of her. She was the one that I loved and would want forever.

I held my beautiful angel in my arms and looked up to the glass ceiling above us. The stars were fake, but my wishes are real. Everything I promised Riley here tonight would come true and soon she would be my wife.

"Jackson! Oh my god! Wake up!"

My body was suddenly jerked around the comfortable mound of plush blankets and pillows when my eyes opened with Riley's morning wake up call. I could think of better ways to begin the day, but she sounded positively freaked out. I sat up to see my girl in action. Riley was tossing the room to find her abandoned clothes from last night's escapades.

"Holy shit!" I screamed.

Now I knew why Riley is freaking out, it just took me a minute to catch up. We fell asleep out here last night. No doubt, she was out of her mind with worrying over my father's reaction to finding us here. The truth was, this was my father and Reese's place, and we just borrowed it for a while and never intended to stay as long as we did.

"Your father is going to freak out! Jackson, get up now!"

"Riley, will you stop screaming at me for a fucking second? My head is pounding."

"Screaming? Oh, you have not experienced me screaming yet.

This is just great, Jackson. After all we shared last night, here we are fighting again. Gee thanks for the memories."

She stepped out from my reach, with me catching her by her waist before she fled the gazebo.

"Let me go, I have to get out of here," she said, struggling.

"No, and stop it right now. Wow! You are a fired-up beast in the morning, but one that I love very much. So please, calm down and put your claws away. We fell asleep, that's no crime. You are behaving like we crashed his prized car, and even if we did, my father's first reaction would be to make sure we were okay first."

Her breathing slowed and the fight was out of her, at least for now. I wrapped my arms around her and breathed her in. She smelled of sex, roses, and me.

"What's this about? My father is not as scary as you make him out to be, and it is not as if he doesn't know we have sex. We live together, Riley, and sometimes we are not very discreet about it. This right here is no big deal, so please calm down."

"Jackson, I feel like we violated their sacred place or something. We have to get out of here before we are caught."

"Okay, beautiful girl, but you have quite the imagination."

I finally got dressed after kissing the shit out of Riley, making her agree to a raincheck later on. I fixed up the floor, and as we made our way outside, there was Reese holding Fallon with my father standing beside her. He glared at me, while Reese did the same with Riley.

"Good morning, dad. We were just on our way in for breakfast," I said as I tried to be as lighthearted as I could, but they were not buying it.

"Jackson, Riley," he said, greeting us with a curt tone, never a good sign. "I believe you are mistaken, son. You have not only missed breakfast, but we are closing in on lunch. After my early run this morning, I decided to go in and begin my day so that when you arrived for our meeting, I would only have to focus on you and your future place in Reed Global. Therefore, according to my watch, you have exactly one hour to shower and get downtown to Reed Global."

"I'm sorry, dad. I'll make it."

I reached for Riley's hand, but Reese asked her to stay. I could not afford to waste another minute. I quickly kissed Riley and whispered sorry in her ear. I made a mad dash for the house and knew I would be facing my father's wrath soon enough. *Way to go, Jackson! That's showing him your responsibility and dedication.*

I made it to my father's office in just under a few minutes before my appointment, taking the shortest shower of my life. I was not sure how to dress, so I went with my best jeans, a solid white t-shirt, and a checkered dress shirt over it. You can never go wrong with black Chucks.

Who was I kidding? I looked like I was going to a Starbucks to meet up with friends, not a meeting with one our country's richest CEOs who privately owned his own company. Yeah, he was also my father, but behind those doors, he was the master of his universe.

"Hi, Jenny, is he ready for me?" I asked as I made my way to his office.

"Stop right there!" Jenny called out.

"What's up?"

"Per Mr. Reed's instructions, you are to wait here until he is ready to meet with you."

"So, he's in there?" I asked.

"He is."

"Okay, then why can't I go in? I made it in time for our meeting, so why do I have to wait?"

"That will be a question for the boss," she told me. "Take a seat."

I wanted to say more, but Jenny's expression held me back with a warning. Going a few rounds with Jenny would be only a warm-up with my father. I reluctantly sat down and put my headphones in my ear.

After exhausting my playlist, I watched executives come and go for hours on end, as Jenny went about her day. She never left her desk, not even for a bathroom break. Was this my father's way of teaching me a lesson? Was he that pissed off? I was in deep thought over this, until I heard my father's voice over the intercom.

"Jenny, please come into my office."

"I'm on my way," she quickly replied.

I stood up to say something, and Jenny waved me off. This was getting ridiculous, but if I was ever to have a role here, then I had to suck it up and take it. I guessed if it were anyone else, the chance at working here would have been blown already. Therefore, being the boss' son had some merit to it.

Fifteen minutes had gone by when Jenny resurfaced.

"Jackson, your father is leaving for an out of the office meeting. Mr. Reed sends his apologies for the change in his schedule. He will not be able to meet with you today. I can check his calendar for another day to have your meeting."

"Don't bother, Jenny. I get the message loud and clear."

I grabbed my bag and huffed to the elevator, hitting the button rather hard.

"Oh, Jackson, a word."

I turned around to face my father's longtime assistant, and the closest to a family member I ever had. I did not want to take my foul mood out on her.

"No offense, but I'm tired Jenny and hungry too! See you around."

"Jackson, I swear to the high heavens, if you get on that elevator, it will be the biggest mistake you make today."

"Jenny, I already messed up today. How can things get worse?"

"You get on that elevator, and you will find out," she said.

"Alright, you have my attention. Why will it be a mistake to leave?"

"Are you a Reed?" she asked me.

"What kind of question is that? Of course, I am a Reed."

"Do Reeds quit?"

"Never," I replied.

"Never. Right. Reeds never quit. They go after what they want, and they always get it. You did something to make your father's head spin, and not in a good way."

"Jenny, you just told me that he could not see me today, so I thought leaving was best."

"For anyone else, it would be. You will stay and prove to that growling bear in there that you are serious about your commitment to him and to his company. You will not leave. And that, young Mr. Reed, is lesson number one: He will respect you more if you stay."

CHAPTER 26

Walker

Father and son

T HAT MORNING OF the gazebo incident, I got out of bed early. I had such an amazing dinner the night before with the family, but I couldn't sleep.

"Come back to bed. It's five a.m.," Reese said to me.

"I know, baby. So sorry to have awakened you."

"I thought you wanted sex," she said, wiping her eyes.

"I always want sex with you; in fact, I crave it daily, but will you accept a raincheck for later?"

"I suppose I have no choice, but why are you up and leaving this early?"

"I have to get my run in, and then I am going to the office. Baby, if we want the Christmas and all other celebrations we are dreaming about, then I have to go in early. Do not forget I am meeting with Jackson today. He is not going to know what I have in store for him, but I promise, it's a good thing."

"I love a happy Walker. You haven't stopped smiling since your surprise last night."

"Correction, I haven't stopped smiling since the night you walked back into my life. I love you, baby, so much. Now, go back to sleep for a little while before our daughter wakes you. I will call you soon."

Damn, I love running! Eight fantastic miles, and I could still do more. I have never felt more energized. Today was going to be a great day. I knew exactly what would work for Jackson, and I had no doubt that Tom would not love it too. I took a lightning shower and made it to the office in under an hour. By the time I sat behind my desk, my breakfast had arrived, and I enjoyed a rare moment of peace and quiet. I knew my presence here this early would shock Jenny, but it was necessary if I wanted to begin my holiday break after today.

It was just half past seven, and Jenny would arrive at any moment. All of my pressing matters were complete. I kicked back and waited for Tom and Donovan to join me. As I closed my eyes, Jenny entered my office with a tray of pastries and fresh brewed espresso. *Always on top of everything. I love her.*

"Good morning, Mr. Reed," she said. "Here are the documents you requested. Tom and Donovan are on their way up. Will there be anything else?"

"I'm good. Thank you. Hold my calls, and let me know when Jackson arrives."

"Good morning, Walker," Donovan said, followed by Tom with his pleasantries. Both men chomped at the bit and awaited my answer to the new direction their roles would take.

"Good morning to you both. Take a seat, we have a lot to cover and in a short amount of time. My son is due here in four hours or so, and I would like to finish up before then."

"Now, I understand you two have come up with your own scenarios to what this meeting is about, and what I will say that will change the day-to-day around here. Rest assured, whatever you are assuming, you will be wrong on all counts. You two are my leads, and after a considerable amount of thought, I realized that to lose one of you—even in a short time frame—would be detrimental to our very smooth running ship. Do I have your attention now?"

They nodded, looking relieved.

I continued, "Good, let's proceed. As you know, my son has expressed interest working here at Reed Global, which pleases me to no end; however, he needs to complete his studies first. His goals have also changed. He no longer wishes to pursue a career in filmmaking, but has committed to completing his current class schedule with his professors. It would be not in his best interest to transfer out of NYU to resume here at UCLA. He has made a commitment to complete and earn his degree in New York."

I went on, "I believe we can utilize Jackson's knowledge and skill of filmmaking for our needs here at Reed Global. He is beyond talented in this field, and I am not only speaking as his father, but as a fan as well. He just submitted a superb project that he collaborated on with his fiancée, Riley. With my heart of hearts, I truly believe my son could be an extraordinary filmmaker, but he assures me that is no longer where his heart lies. As a father, I will support him, and as the CEO of this company, I will welcome his talents."

I addressed Tom, "Your daughter, Bridgette, is currently an intern in our Marketing/Development department in New York. I have perused her file and am very pleased with the latest assessment of her work from Donovan, as well as from her team lead, Joan Bancroft. It goes without saying that everything from this conversation must remain in this room, but I wanted you to know that I plan to approve her hiring if she chooses to stay on with Reed Global."

Tom proudly stated, "That's fantastic! I know firsthand that Bridgette wants this. She has worked incredibly hard."

"I do not disagree," I responded. "Her work has been exemplary. I have also given some thought on Bridgette not only working for Reed Global, but also appointing her as an advisor to Jackson. They have been friends for years, and I think that will smooth the transition and help calm the whispering ears of inquiring minds. He is a Reed, and nothing will change that. Reed Global is his legacy and he has every right to be there; however, it will not be just handed to him. I want Jackson to learn every aspect of this business, and that will take time. There will be no cutting of corners. Am I making myself clear?"

"Yes, sir," the two men agreed in unison.

"As you know, I have appointed Lars Sapien to oversee my New York interests, but to a degree. I have eyes on every project and no one fully takes the lead, because that position is held only by me. Donovan, you have a good rapport with Lars, so I trust you two will work effectively together. I am going to have you check-in with New York at least once a month, possibly two if needed. This way, it keeps all the players on alert, giving away no illusion that we are ever too far away."

I went on, "Tom, I also will be sending you to New York at least once a month, possibly two, if needed. I cannot afford to have both of you away from the office at the same time, so I feel this would be the best possible solution: to operate on a rotating schedule. The added bonus is that you get to see your daughter if her schedule allows. Marketing is primarily Donovan's area of expertise; however, you play a large role there as well. I figure this will not only benefit our New York team, but Jackson will learn a great deal from each of you. When Donovan is in New York, he will oversee any of Bridgette's projects, and when you are in New York, you will be in charge of Jackson. Am I clear? Any questions so far?"

Tom interjected first. "What you propose sounds great and I am quite positive looks good on paper, but I would like to know where Jackson stands on these proposals."

"Great question and nothing I would not expect from you, Tom, but to answer your question, Jackson does not know yet. As I mentioned earlier, my meeting with him is later today."

"Okay, so how will you utilize his skills to benefit Reed Global?" Tom questioned.

"Just his presence alone benefits Reed Global, but I see where you are going with this. One of the very reasons why I want Jackson to collaborate with Bridgette is because I feel they are compatible and will work very well together. She is outspoken, whereas he is more reserved but not afraid to speak up when necessary. They each can contribute their unique talents to furthering our Marketing and Development department. Creativity does not come by easily. You have it, or you don't. Your daughter has what I am looking for, and Jackson is hands down brilliant. This powerhouse duo will bring fresh talent to my company, I have no doubt. Now, if you have an issue with your daughter working alongside my son, then state your grievances now, or drop it and we move on.

"My apologies, Walker, I am very pleased. As a father, I am quite proud of my daughter. Thank you for giving Bridgette this opportunity."

"She earned it, Tom, it is that simple," I said to him. "Going the distance in Reed Global will be up to Bridgette. I pride myself in hiring the best, and I do not give out second chances to those who fail me. So far, I am very pleased with her work ethic."

I took a sip of water and walked around to the front of my desk with my arms crossed over my chest. Tom was vocal so far, but I was curious to hear what Donovan thought about my plan. He and Tom were two very different individuals who brought many valuable assets to my company. It was the norm for Donovan to speak with me privately if he had anything of merit to discuss with me and with no outside opinions. This could have been one of those moments, but I had no time to go there now. I waited a bit, took another sip of water, and then addressed Donovan.

"Donovan, you are quiet. Do you have anything to add here?"

"I agree with your ideas for Jackson and for Bridgette. I have had the pleasure of observing Bridgette in action with our team. She carries herself well and brings a lot of energy to the room."

I interrupted, "And what about Jackson? What do you think he will bring?"

"If you don't mind, sir, I would like to take some time to think about my answer. We will confer at a later date."

"I do mind. As a matter of fact, I highly mind. I would like an answer to my question *now*. If you are unable to answer my question, then I will draw my own conclusions and you will not like what I say in return."

"Walker, may I have a word with you in private?" Donovan requested.

Here we go! I thought to myself. My jaw clenched, and I looked over to Tom.

"Tom, let's take a break, and we will reconvene in thirty minutes. Will you conference with New York and have Joan join us on the call? Let's say one hour from now?"

"Right away, sir." Tom said as he took his leave and left me to deal with Donovan, who looked a little green now.

I said to Donovan, "Okay, once again, you have cleared the room. I'm listening."

He inhaled a few deep breaths and got up to walk around my office, closing in on a framed photo of my father and me.

Donovan said, "He would have been very proud of you for all you have accomplished for his company. I remember graduation day when he put his arm around my shoulder and congratulated me on a job well done. The only thing I ever wanted to do was work for Reed Global. When you took over as CEO and offered me my spot, I was ecstatic."

"I remember. Why the sudden revisit of memory lane?"

"I was just trying to remember how I felt back then, and then I imagine Jackson and his reaction when you tell him."

"I would hope he would be happy and feel proud," I said.

"Let us hope for that."

"You do not sound convinced, Donovan. Why is that?"

"I think very highly of Jackson. You know I do. When we talked in New York, his face was bright and something of wonderment when he entered your office. I felt something shifting within him, but I was not sure what at the time. Now I know. He emulates you, Walker. How could he not?"

"Is that a bad thing?" I asked.

"Of course not! I just want to know that he is one hundred percent committed, because you cannot do this job if you are not."

"I agree with you. Is that all?"

He responded, "For now, yes. I was afraid you had decided that one of us would be going to New York on a full-time basis. I am happy to know that we will be splitting our time instead. Don't get me wrong, I love New York, but you are here, and this is where I want to be."

"Fair enough, Donovan. Thank you for your honesty, but why did you feel you could not say this in front of Tom?"

"I guess after my last disagreement with Tom, I did not wish to rock the boat."

"Is everything resolved between you two?"

"Yes, we are fine," he said.

"Okay, I think that is all for now. Let us reconvene on our conference call to bring Joan up to speed, and we will cc Lars through email. He has taken a personal day and will return to the office tomorrow."

"Sounds good," he said as he reached for the door.

Something compelled me to say more.

"Donovan," I called out.

"Sir?"

I extended my hand out to him, and he shook my hand in return without hesitation.

"You are a good man. Thank you for continued service to Reed Global. I am confident that Jackson will learn a great deal under your leadership."

He nodded respectively and closed the door behind him. I knew I was harder on Donovan than most members of my executive team. Not everyone was under the guidance and the iron fist of Phillip

Reed. I may not have agreed with my father on certain directions for our company and my personal life, but it goes without saying that he did teach us a great deal. Now, it was my chance to pass on my knowledge to Jackson.

I took a small break after speaking with Donovan, and then it was back to business. I joined in with Donovan and Tom on their call with Joan in New York. She was excited and ready to begin the New Year with my son added to her team. I would introduce him slowly, so he could familiarize himself with the day-to-day operations, and there was school to consider. His education had to come first, or all bets were off.

Jenny ordered in a light lunch for me, which would hold me over until I could take Jackson out to celebrate. I was just about done and wrapped up my end of the year tasks that Jenny had put together for me to approve or put off until the first of the year. Working long days was not unusual for me, but I was in need of a break and wanted nothing more than to be locked in with my family for the holiday celebrations.

Just then, my private line came to life with Reese's special ringtone. Jenny made her discreet exit, and I took my call.

"Hello, my love," my voice almost purred into the receiver.

What I did not expect was Reese sounding upset.

I asked, "What's wrong? Are you sure? Okay, please calm down, I am on my way."

Stephen was already on his feet, with me barreling through my door.

"I'll be back," I called out to Jenny, as I made my way onto the elevator.

By the time I got home, Reese had settled and was holding our beautiful Fallon.

"Oh, darling, what has you so upset?"

"I am a foolish woman, and very embarrassed to bring you all the way home for this."

"Nonsense, you know you should always call me. Talk to me,

please," I implored Reese to explain the situation as I reached for Fallon.

I kissed the top of my daughter's crown of curls and gestured to Reese to sit down.

She said, "After you left this morning, I slept for a little while and then began my day. After tending to Fallon, I wanted Riley to join me for breakfast. I went to her room and knocked a few times, but when she did not answer, I went in. Her bed was empty and not disturbed. Of course, I was worried. I then walked to Jackson's room and found the same thing. The kids were not in the house, and I had not seen them since dinner last night."

"Sweetheart, did you consider that maybe the staff had already cleaned their rooms and made up their beds?"

"Walker, I am not stupid!"

"Hey, now, I would never think that, and I do not want to hear you mention that word again." I let out a few breaths before continuing with Reese.

"Have you checked today's video feed yet?" I calmly asked her without causing her anymore stress.

"I have not. You know I don't go into Stephen's office."

"Well, Stephen's office is in our home, and you have every right to go anywhere you please. Now, let us go check the feed, and I am sure we will solve the mystery to where Jackson and Riley are. Do not forget, my love, Jackson is due in my office for our meeting, so I know he is probably nearby.

I handed Fallon back to Reese, and brought up all the current footage. We did not see Jackson or Riley on them.

"Okay, no worries. I will locate them," I reassured her.

I pulled up last night's footage from after we went to bed, and sure enough, I spotted them walking hand-in-hand out in the gardens, ending at the gazebo.

"Reese, here they are."

"Oh no, please do not tell me what I am thinking right now," she said nervously.

"Okay, I won't. Judging that the feed shows them entering and not exiting, I will bet they are still in there, which will not bode well for Jackson."

"Nor Riley! I don't want to sound—oh hell, I don't know what to say—but I know I am not comfortable with Riley and Jackson in there and doing what my mind is picturing right now."

"Let's go," I told her. "Do you want to leave Fallon with Priscilla?"

"No, she is the perfect buffer I need at the moment."

"Fair enough."

Fallon bounced up and down happily in Reese's arms, while I guided her through the garden. The gazebo was soundproofed and had no cameras for obvious reasons, so we just entered at our own risk. Luckily for us, Jackson and Riley were clothed and about to leave when we opened the door. Riley appeared nervous, and Jackson was quiet.

"Good morning, dad. We were just on our way in for breakfast," Jackson said, trying in earnest to cover his tracks.

"Jackson...Riley..." I curtly responded, "I believe you are mistaken, son. You have not only missed breakfast, but we are closing in on lunch. After my early run this morning, I decided to go in and begin my day, so when you arrived for our meeting, I would only have to focus on you and your future place in Reed Global. Therefore, according to my watch, you have exactly one hour to shower and get downtown to Reed Global."

"I'm sorry dad, I'll make it." He attempted to take Riley with him, but Reese, gestured for her to stay.

I was beyond livid with Jackson. Other than myself, only three other people had the key to our place—and Jackson is not one of them—which means he took the key without my knowledge nor permission.

"Darling, I hate to leave, but I must get back to the office. Will you be okay here on your own?" I said to Reese.

"Of course, I will. I am so sorry for bothering you with all of this. Call it crazy pregnant hormones."

"I would never, and you are never to apologize for needing me, especially when it comes to the welfare of our kids."

I looked over to Riley, who ducked her head in shame. I was not angry with her, per sé, it was Jackson that I had the problem with. Throughout my drive back to Reed Global, my mind kept retreating to this morning's conversation with Donovan. Was he right about Jackson? *Is my son ready to take on the responsibility I have set forth for him?*

"We're here, sir," Stephen said.

"I looked around the private parking garage and did not see Jackson's car. I went upstairs to contemplate what I would say to him.

I sat behind my desk with my head in my hands. I hated to feel unsure, a rare emotion for me to exhibit. Nonetheless, it happened from time to time, especially with my son. I understand why he did what he did, but he also showed irresponsibility with his actions not returning home, and most importantly, disrespecting Reese and me.

Reese had every right to show her agitation when she saw her daughter this morning. The kids came a long way since they left our home together last summer to be on their own to begin their new life together. I was their age once, and so was Reese. We understood they wanted to be together, but they also needed to show responsibilities in the choices they made. The opportunity I was giving Jackson took years to achieve, and he was getting it without putting in one day of work. *Am I doing right by him? That is the question of the day, and I am too weary to overanalyze it.*

As I nursed my growing headache, Jenny entered my office to inform me that Jackson had arrived. I let out a sigh and leaned back in my chair.

"Shall I send him in, sir?"

"No, have him wait."

Jenny looked down to her tablet, and then looked back to me.

"He's right on time for his meeting with you. What shall I tell him?" she said.

"You tell him nothing! And have him wait."

"Yes, sir."

"Jenny," I called out to her, "I apologize. I do not mean to snap at you."

"Accepted. Is there anything I can do?"

"No, thank you. Jackson needs to learn a lesson, and with having him wait, I should hope he understands."

"Yes, sir."

My day went on as scheduled with meeting after meeting. I would have thought Jackson would have tried to step in to my office since he has always had free reign to do so, but I was sure that Jenny has him secured. My day was finished and my calendar was clear. I managed to accomplish everything I set forth to do. Now what to do about Jackson? I buzzed Jenny and had her come into my office.

"Jenny, please inform Jackson that I will not be able to see him today, and reschedule him for another time."

"Sir?" she asked.

"Yes, Jenny? Something to add?"

"Sir, I can see you have something weighing heavily on your mind, and Jackson is wearing the same expression, but I believe he gets the point you have made here today. He messed up somehow, and that has you riled. But sir, do not allow anger to guide you. He's twenty-years-old, and he's counting on you to show him the way."

"So noted, thank you, Jenny. That will be all."

After dismissing Jenny, I sat back to think. I knew she was right. I hated to be at odds with my son, but this was necessary. The ball was in his court.

CHAPTER 27

Jackson

Humility

"WELL, JACKSON, WHAT are you going to do?" Jenny questioned me.

"Stay, for as long as it takes."

"Good answer. I'll leave you to it then."

"You're not staying?"

"No, I think I am done for the day." She walked over to me, brought me in for a hug, and then stepped back to look at me. "You are a fine young man. And that man in there," she pointed toward my father's office, "he loves you more than anything in the world, but you disappointed him today for whatever reason. Staying is just the first step. What you say or do next is up to you. Good luck, Jackson."

The elevator doors closed, and I was on my own. I paced the

floor several times before finally entering my father's office. He was on a call and gestured to me to be quiet. I dropped my bag and took a seat in front of his desk, and he never took his eyes off of me.

He ended his call and then shuffled some papers on his desk.

"I believe I informed Jenny that I was unable to meet with you today, and yet, here you are. Do you not take direction well? Not a good beginning, Jackson, if you want to work here at Reed Global."

I straightened my back and showed him that I could take what he was dishing out. I knew I screwed up with my father today, although it was more on a personal level. The thing with Walker Reed is that everything in life he comes across he considers as personal.

I told him, "I am fine with direction, sir, and will have no issue following orders if given the opportunity to work for Reed Global one day, sir."

My father continued to study me, and if this was a test, I would make sure not to fail again.

He said, "Okay, Jackson, so you want to work for Reed Global."

"I do, more than anything."

"Fair enough. Why? I do not wish to hear a textbook answer or something you believe I want to hear. I want the truth—your truth—to why you now want to be here. Jackson, consider this your official interview."

I shifted in my seat and tried to keep myself in check. He might have been the great and mighty Walker Reed, but underneath the suit of armor he showed to the world, to me, he was my father.

I cleared my throat and began, "Dad, I am sorry for my actions this morning. It was wrong to take your key and bring Riley to a place I had no right be in, and without your permission to do so. Riley did not want to be there in fear of your reaction, but I assured her that it would be okay. Clearly, I was wrong."

I continued, "As a Reed, I have nothing but respect for our family and the business you built. As your son, I knew you had hopes and dreams for me to join you here at Reed Global, but for many years, my dreams were set on another course. You respected them, maybe not always agreed, but you respected my choice and gave me room to grow. I am sure those who are close to you probably have their concerns about me, and already have questioned my commitment to coming on board here. If I were in their shoes, I probably would do the same thing. It would be very easy to label me as the, 'boss' kid' or 'golden boy.' Believe me, dad, I have heard them all. I never want to be defined by those terms. I want to be better than those judged labels that people feel they could stick on me."

I said, "This was not a knee-jerk change of heart. I have spent many days and months looking at my life, what I want for my future, and who I see sharing my life with me. I know without question that I want to marry Riley and build a life with her. I love filmmaking, I probably always will, but it is not where my heart is leading to right now. I have given you my reasons to why I want this, and you said you understood them. I am hoping I still have your understanding. I guess the only thing I can do now is to show you with my actions moving forward. I do not expect special treatment. If given the chance, I will dedicate one hundred percent commitment to Reed Global and prove to be worthy of the opportunity afforded to me."

I continued on, "Dad, I came very close to losing my life, and then in recent days, I nearly lost the girl who owns my heart. I never knew I had a selfish bone in my body, but I was proven wrong when I believed she would just roll over and submit to me without question. I was lucky she forgave me, and last night was my small way of showing her how much she means to me. I would never knowingly disrespect you, or Reese. I am sorry for worrying Reese and angering you."

I implored him, "I am asking for a chance, dad, a chance to show you what I can bring to Reed Global. I know I will have to work harder than I ever had in my life, but you did, as did my grandfather before me. I swear to you with all of my heart that I have given this a great deal of thought, and I promise my intentions are genuine. I am ready to take my place at Reed Global."

I knew I could not say anything more without sounding like a broken record. I also did not want to come off as presumptuous and call my place "rightful." I knew my father and his work ethic. He would make me earn it every step of the way. I stated my reasons repeatedly to my father when he asked me, and now I had done it again without bringing up the past. For some reason, he needed to hear me explain it to him again, and now I had.

If he felt I was not ready, then I would accept his decision and go about enjoying the holidays with my family. No matter what he decided, we needed to have this conversation. I ran from Riley when she disagreed with me, and I was about to run from my father today. I would do better and prove it to him. Reeds did not quit. Reeds did not run. Reeds stayed.

This was what he did best. My father processed, and when he was ready, he would go off like the Fourth of July. The silence in the room was so thick you could cut it with a knife. I was trying with little success not to sweat as if I had just ran a marathon. *Come on, dad, I can take it.*

I watched my father walk over to a cabinet and pour himself a drink. I remained quiet and did not judge. He sat back down and swirled the amber liquid in his glass. He looked at me and took a sip of his drink before returning it back down to his desk.

"It's not scotch, if that's what you are thinking," he said.

"I wasn't thinking anything."

I lied. I knew scotch was my father's go-to drink, and he vowed never to drink it again after he made peace with his past.

"Sure you weren't, and I don't breathe. Jackson, I run a multi-billion-dollar company, a privately owned company, I might add. Do you think it is easy being me? It is not. So, when I decide occasionally to pour myself a shot of Bourbon, believe me when I say, it is warranted. Now, while you were sleeping all cozy with Riley this morning, I was here changing your life. I have put in place a plan that I believe will not only give you the stepping-stone to begin your career here at Reed Global, but will also safeguard your relationship with Riley. You do not have to move back to California to be part of

Reed Global. Our hub is in New York where it all began, beginning with my grandfather and my father. I took our company to California where I could build it with my own vision. I believe I made the right call, don't you agree?"

I nodded.

He went on, "Now, what I have planned for you is not negotiable at this time. I feel you will benefit greatly in our Marketing/Development department. You will be working with a solid team made up of individual talents, including Bridgette, who I plan to hire on full-time once her internship ends. It goes without saying that piece of information is confidential as well as everything else that is said in this office. I would like you to begin sometime in January, but exactly when, I am not sure yet. I still need to iron out some details with my New York team, and that will not take place until after the first of the year."

He said to me, "Nothing changes in regards to your education. You will fulfill the commitment to Professor Connelly and to Riley. Once you do, whatever direction you choose to take in regards to filmmaking will be entirely up to you. I have looked over your current grades, and all were excellent. Congratulations on making the Dean's List. I am very proud of you, son, despite what you may have thought of me today while you sat in the waiting area."

"Dad, I deserved it, and I get why I needed to be there," I said.

He responded, "I hope you do, because upsetting my wife will not happen again. On my way back to the office, I questioned every decision I ever made for you. I was angry because Reese was upset. Today was a learning tool for you to learn patience. I was not sure what you would do, but I hoped you would have stayed. This act pleased me, and yes, it was a test. You are right, son, about judgments. My best executives did question me, and I assured them of your abilities and talents. I believe in you, son. Unfortunately, even a Reed does not escape the rumor mill. You will rise above it and work at a level of excellence. I expect nothing less from you."

He continued, "Getting back to earlier today, I understand that you and Riley need to be together and on your own, but you were wrong in what you did. Jackson, that space represents so much more than you realize. I replicated that structure and that garden because it represented a piece of my history with Reese. It serves as our safe place, where we married. I will share everything I have with you, but that gazebo is off limits. Reese calls it her pregnancy hormones. You may believe her reaction was over the top, but I do not. You and Riley are lucky Fallon was with us, or I would have reacted a hell of a lot worse. When she could not find you this morning, Reese was scared. Jackson, look at what our family had to endure. I lost your mother, and I nearly lost you. Just when our family was getting back on track, fate stepped in and tested us again. I nearly lost Reese again and your sister she was carrying. Now with Reese pregnant again, we have already endured a scare. I think we are done with all that."

"Dad? What scare are you talking about?" I said as I watched him run his fingers through his hair and sigh deeply.

"I hadn't meant to share that with you, Jackson, and I am not sure if Riley knows about it. If she does, please do not be upset with her. Girls talk, and what Reese shares with Riley is not for me to know, okay?"

"Okay," I responded.

He said, "She's okay, and our baby is too. When Reese discovered she was pregnant again, her doctor discovered some pre-cancerous cells and performed a biopsy and other tests. Reese was terrified to tell me and ran. She took Fallon and hid at Freddy's while awaiting the news from her doctor. I was beside myself as all kinds of crazy went through my mind, and I retreated to a dark place. I found Reese, and we worked it out quickly. You have to learn how to walk before you run, Jackson. Reese gets scared, and she runs. It terrifies me every time she does it, and I am grateful she at least called me today when she got scared again."

He told me, "Jackson, your life with Riley is just beginning. You are going to go through a thousand emotions, and you will mess up, like today. The important thing is that you own up to it all, and then we move on. Today's lesson applies to not only your professional life, but your personal life as well. Our family means everything to me, Jackson, and securing everyone's happiness is always my top priority."

"Dad, I know you do. I…"

"Son, allow me to finish, please. As I was saying, our family's strength has been tested over and over again, and we have come out stronger for it. I do not wish to have any conflict in our family, especially when it comes to our relationship. Nothing will please me more for you to come on board and work with me. I am elated over it and will support you as much as I can throughout this new path you are traveling on."

"Thank you, dad. Thank you. I promise you with all that I am, I will not let you down."

He walked around his desk and took me in his arms.

"I love you, dad, so much," I told him.

"I love you too, Jackson. You are a good man, and I have no doubt in your commitment. Now, I don't know about you, but I am ready to call it a day."

"Me too! And dad…. we are okay, right?"

"We are okay, son. Always," he answered me over his shoulder as we reached the door. He pulled me into a hug, and I believed it.

I was looking forward to going home to tell Riley the good news.

Riley

Mother and daughter

ANOTHER THING I discovered today about my soon to be husband: he can run…and very fast when he wanted to. My mother had her new scare stare tactic down to a science, as I sat here with my head in shame.

Mr. Reed said two words to me, and that was enough. I warned Jackson, and he silenced me with his kisses. I did not want any more drama. We could have gone anywhere, but he wanted to make love under the illuminated stars. I warned him that it was not a good idea, but did he listen? Not a chance. Now I had to deal with the fallout. Lucky for me, my mom was still holding Fallon, or she would have really let me have it.

"Mom, I am so sorry."

"I know you are. Here, take your sister."

I made funny faces and blew kisses to Fallon as she cooed back and happily came to me. I kissed her rosy cheeks, and she immediately went for my tangled, sexed out hair. *Oh god! I need a shower. Jackson and I had dirty sex last night.* Mom grabbed a pillow and sat down while I joined her with the baby.

She said, "Oh, Riley, this is not an inquisition, and I am certainly not the firing squad. You scared me this morning, and I panicked. I thought by now that I was past the anxiety of past events. I went into protection mode and wanted to safeguard my family from harm. I guess Walker is rubbing off on me, but do not tell him I said that."

"Do you want to talk about it? I was there, mom, and I know how I felt when Jackson's grandfather took you."

"No, I moved on from him and what he did to me. When you are a parent and become responsible for someone else, everything shifts. You have a new perspective on the world and the world you will be raising your child or children in. You put them before yourself and your needs. You always want to make sure they are safe and okay. This morning when I could not find you, feeling safe was the furthest emotion I felt."

"Mom, I keep driving you crazy, and I am so sorry. I…"

"Shhh, you do not get to apologize to me for making me worry, as if you could stop me. It comes with the territory, and one long day from now, you will get to experience this feeling for yourself."

"No worries there, mom. I am covered."

"Yeah, thanks for that. Since you brought it up, you do have to apologize for breaking and entering." Mom smiled as she gestured around the gazebo. "I have come to terms that you are sexually active with Jackson, and you want private moments with him, I get it. What I do not appreciate are the methods you took to accomplish that. This is my place shared with Walker, and we treat it as if it is sacred ground. Please do not ask me to explain why, it just is. For you and Jackson to use it and without permission is what I was angry about this morning. It was an invasion of our privacy, and you were not respectful to me and Walker."

"I tried to tell Jackson that it was not a good idea, but he said it would be fine. I should have held my ground and not fall under his charms. It's not easy when you are madly in love with a Reed."

"I understand completely," she said.

Fallon let out a happy squeal and we broke out into laughter.

Mom asked me, "Are things okay and settled now with Jackson?"

"Yes, we are fine."

"Good, I am happy to hear that. Riley, this blip in the road is just one of many you will share with Jackson. You two are still learning so much about the other and learning to respect boundaries, which takes a lot of time and patience."

"He's changed, mom."

"Growing up will do that."

"I know that, but it is so much more," I told her. "He was afraid that I would not understand or believe him, so when he changed direction for our plans, he shut me out. At first, I believed it was some diabolical plan to control me, but that was irrational thinking on my part. I accused him of so many things, and of course, in a childlike manner I told off Mr. Reed in full Riley crazy mode. Oh no, that's something else I need to apologize for."

"Go on," she encouraged.

"I said some not-so-nice things about you, mom, when I was fighting with Jackson. I said that I did not want to be like you, and now I am ashamed of myself for it." Just a moment ago, she was smiling, and now tears were beginning to fall down her beautiful face. "Mom, please don't cry. This is coming out all wrong. Please let me explain."

"Okay. Let me have my daughter, please." She reached for Fallon.

Ouch! That hurt. The way mom said "my daughter" just made me feel so small.

"I'm your daughter too, and I'm sorry for hurting you…again."

"You don't need to remind me of that fact, Riley. I carried you in my stomach for nine months and went through many hours of painful labor bringing you into the world."

"I deserved that, mom. I know it sounds awful, but I was angry and I just lashed out at the first person who was in my path. Jackson left me mom, and then Mr. Reed swoops in and saves the day. Jackson wanted me—no, expected me—to just fall in line with his new plans. I was beginning to really come into my own in New York. I was making friends, and I loved my professors and classes. I knew it would be an adjustment at first, but I really enjoyed living with the guys. And then their girlfriends became my friends and it was great."

"Not so great for Jackson, though?" she asked me.

"He hated it and had enough of the partying, so he moved us out. Before I could even process it, my suitcases were packed, and he ordered me to follow him to our waiting car. Mom, he might as well have clubbed me and threw my lifeless body over his shoulder."

"I see. Therefore, I really do not need to hear the exact words you used, but I think I can figure them out on my own. You see me as weak…right, Riley? A submissive being that bends at her husband's will and has no voice. This is what you believe? Because I married a Reed, this is how women are expected to behave. Am I close?"

I was the one crying now. Her words were ugly and cruel. To hear my mom talk this way gutted my heart.

"Mom, you are the strongest woman I know. I would never call you weak. You are amazing and smart, and…" I was going to go on, but mom raised her free arm to stop me.

She pulled out her phone and hit a button. Two minutes later, Priscilla was here with a stroller to take my now sleeping baby sister. We had been out here for a while. Once Fallon was nestled in her stroller, Priscilla smiled and walked back to the house. Mom took a minute, with her back turned to me. *Can this day get any worse?*

She said, "Okay, I get it. You are not exactly wrong either. For years when I was married to your father, I was his submissive in a way. I played my part very well. Being a doctor's wife, or like I used to call myself: a 'trophy wife,' came with many responsibilities. I looked good on his arm while at hospital functions. I hosted the luncheons with the other wives and chaired the charities that, of course, my husband supported."

"Did you really feel that way while married to daddy?" I questioned.

"Yes, I did. It was not always like that, but for most of our marriage, I did yield to his command. By admitting these things to you does not mean that I did not love your father or want to do these things for him. I married your dad at a time that I was so lost and dead inside that giving up control to someone else was just easy. As the years went on, I truly felt that I was losing a part of myself and did not recognize the reflection staring back at me in the mirror. Your father was there for me in my darkest hours, and he was a good friend. He will always be a part of my life. We made you, our beautiful Riley."

She went on, "But I was ready to begin the next chapter in my life, and finding Walker again when I did was fate's way of showing us who's the boss. Walker Phillip Reed is one hundred percent alpha male. He is dominating, steadfast, and always in control. To love him is to love all parts of him. Riley, I do with all of my heart and soul. Having said that, I am not that broken girl I once was, and my will is my own. You may have strong opinions of what you feel submission means, and what role it will play in your relationship with Jackson."

She continued, "My marriage to his father is private, and I am not so eager to kiss and tell about my intimate moments with Walker. What I will say is that I'm loved by my husband and know without a doubt that he would walk through fire for me. When you love someone so much, it is so easy to give yourself over to that person completely. Moreover, sometimes you can lose yourself over that crazy love, but for me, I would take that gamble over and over again. I am very happy, Riley. I exercise my free will every single day. You do not have to worry about me."

Mom said, "You have to decide on your own what works for you and your relationship with Jackson, okay? He is his father's son, and not just in the looks department. He loves and loves hard. He will walk through fire for you, Riley, as sure as you would do the same for him. Just take a breath and enjoy each other."

I could not wait another minute and lunged for my mom. She hugged me back and lovingly stroked my hair. She always did that when I was upset.

I told her, "I love you so much, mommy. I am sorry for hurting your feelings."

"I love you too, Riley. You do not have to figure out everything all in one day. You have time. You have to learn to walk before you run, okay."

"Now you sound like Nana Lila. She says that all the time."

"Well, your great grandmother is the wisest woman I know and has taught me many things. I only hope I have done right by you and that one day you will pass on my words of advice to your daughter."

"You have, mom, you have. I have screwing up down to a science. How do you put up with me?"

She said, "Stop it. I will not sit here and listen to you break yourself down like that. Riley, you are an incredible human being. You have so much love in your heart and natural sparkle that shines like the sun. You are growing up, and believe me, it is not a race to the finish line. Do you remember what I told you before we left for our trip to New York?"

"Every word," I said.

"Okay, so if that's true, then you remember me telling you that this is your time, a time to get out in the world and live in it. Have fun with your friends. Love being in love. Laugh when something is funny, and blush when the person you love makes you feel beautiful. Just be you, Riley. Jackson loves all parts of you, as you love him too. You two will find your way as individuals and then as a couple."

I hugged my mom with all that I had, and then we walked arm-in-arm back to the house.

"I'm starving, mom. Is it too early for ice cream?"

"Oh, my daughter, it is never too early for triple chocolate fudge."

"Don't forget the toppings too!" I added.

"Never. You get the bowls, I'll grab the spoons."

"Mom, we're okay, right?"

"You never have to worry about that. We are always, okay."

Mom enjoyed the decadent treat before her morning sickness kicked in again. We spent the rest of the morning talking about everything and laughing too. She was right about so many things, and I was so lucky to have her as my mom.

Priscilla brought Fallon in to join us when she was up from her nap. She smiled and banged her hands on her highchair tray, as mom made funny faces. I was in awe of my mom and felt bad for shutting her out when I was fighting with Jackson. No matter how many times I screwed up, she would always be there for me to catch me when I fell.

CHAPTER 29

Walker

Unexpected surprises

AFTER WHAT FELT like the longest conversation I ever had with my son, we finally reached an understanding, and things between us were better. Reese and Riley had their talk as well, and mother and daughter are back on track too. And with not a minute to spare, because today was my wife's birthday, and I intended to give her the best day ever.

I left my gorgeous wife sleeping soundly as I crept out of bed, as quietly as I could. I was wide-awake at five a.m. and needed to burn off some nervous energy. Normally, I would wake the sexy vixen who slept beside me, but the beast in me kept her up for many hours with our lovemaking. I knew she was spent.

After Reese hijacked all of my holiday plans for her, I had to do some rearranging of my own. My last day in the office I spent on the phone with Rosalyn confirming all the new arrangements that were in place. It was no easy task arranging for Lila and Thomas to come to California. They originally were going to join us for New Years and Fallon's birthday party, but with how things have been with the kids and their dramas, I convinced Lila to join us now. Once the party was in full swing, I would have the grandparents make their grand entrance.

Riley would keep Reese busy today. I had arranged time for them at their favorite spa, and then it would be off to see Freddy for her dress fitting. Freddy arranged a private showing in his Beverly Hills showroom for Reese and Riley to enjoy. He had racks of dresses to choose from, and he was to convince Reese to choose one for this evening.

I had not stopped smiling after forty minutes on the treadmill. I was beyond excited for tonight. Reese had given me a lifetime of happiness, wrapped up in her love and protection. She made me want to be a better man, better in all areas of my life. She never asked or expected anything in return, just to love her forever. Done and done. I would always love Reese until I took my last breath, and then eternity would take over from where we left off.

I showered and dressed before returning to our bedroom. Priscilla had prepared everything I requested for Reese this morning.

As I carried the silver tray into our bedroom, I heard cries from our master bathroom. I placed her breakfast down and rushed to her side. Reese was doubled over in pain on the floor. She had thrown up and was holding her stomach.

"Reese, baby, talk to me," I said with concern.

She was crying, wincing, and looked as white as a ghost. She had a glistening sheen of sweat on her forehead. I placed my hands under her knees encouraging her to wrap her arms around my neck so I could lift her. She felt so light in my arms. I placed her down gently onto our bed and phoned Stephen to bring the car up to the door. Reese was only wearing a baby doll nightgown. I grabbed her robe to cover her body up.

"Reese, I'm going to take you to the hospital. You don't look well."

"Walker, something's wrong. I'm spotting."

All the euphoric feelings I felt were gone and replaced with fear of losing our child and what it would do to Reese. I wanted to curse the heavens. Why was this happening now? And on her birthday. I reassured her as best as I could without letting on how scared I was.

Stephen met us downstairs as I carried Reese in my arms to the waiting car. I buckled her in and covered her with a blanket that Priscilla handed to me. I climbed in next to Reese, and Stephen hit the gas. He had already called Dr. Lemay to meet us there.

Hospital staff met us at the ER entrance and took Reese away on a stretcher. I ran alongside the gurney until we reached where Dr. Lemay was waiting on us. The nurses took Reese in, and I felt paralyzed where I was standing.

"Rachel, please, she's my life. Please don't let her die," I croaked out the last words before my tears fell.

"Walker, let me get in there and tend to Reese. You stay here and wait for me. She's in good hands. I promise you."

She turned and quickly ran to join Reese in the examining room.

I heard her call out, "Okay, people, let's get her on a fetal monitor" along with labs being ordered. The door closed and I was left…waiting.

Time seemed to stop until I heard someone say, "Dad, I'm here."

I looked up from my prayer position to see Jackson and Riley. They were holding a tray of coffee and bags of food. I tried to be strong but I could not, not with Reese and my baby in danger. More tears fell, and that was when Jackson grabbed hold of me.

"Dad, you look like you are going to fall over. Come, sit down here."

I patted him on the back and took a seat. Riley put her arms around my neck and assured me that her mom was the strongest person she knew and would be fine.

"Thank you both for coming," I told them. "I am sorry I did not call you sooner. I have just been out of my mind with worry. How is this happening to us? After all we have been through, when are we going to stop being tested?"

"Have the doctors come out yet?" Riley questioned.

"No, not yet. It's been hours. A nurse updated me earlier before you arrived and told me that she was getting an IV for fluids and was on a monitor."

"Dr. Lemay is the best, right?" Riley asked.

"Yes, she is, Riley. And I am counting on her more than ever. Where's Fallon?"

"She's with Priscilla. I didn't think you would want us to bring her here."

I responded, "No, of course not. I would rather know you two were with her. She has to be missing Reese and me by now. We have a morning routine with Fallon."

"I know, dad, but she's fine. We played with her this morning before we even knew what happened."

"And I took care of breakfast and dressed her," Riley said.

I was going to thank them both when Dr. Lemay came out to join us. She did not look her usual polished self. She was dressed in scrubs and looked worried. We all stood to greet her, and she put her hands up to calm us.

"Walker, she's going to be fine," she told us.

"And the baby?" I nervously questioned.

She hesitated.

I repeated, "Rachel…and our baby? Did he make it?"

"They made it," she assured.

"Oh, thank God! Reese and the baby are going to be okay. I need to see her."

"Walker, before you go in, I would like to speak with you first."

"Rachel, I need to see my wife. You just told me that she will be fine."

"Yes, I did, but I still would like for you to sit, take a breath, and allow me to talk with you."

"Dad, come on," Jackson interrupted. "You look like you are going to pass out. Dr. Lemay is right. You need to get yourself in check before seeing Reese, and you will only worry her if she sees you like this."

"I like him," Rachel snickered as we all sat down.

"It was a cyst that ruptured on her ovary which caused the bleeding. Usually they are common in pregnancy, but with Reese's history, this is something that will need to be carefully monitored for the rest of the pregnancy. And now with the new development, we have to be vigilant with her care. I would recommend Reese to be monitored today with a stay tonight. If all looks good tomorrow, she will be discharged and on bedrest for at least a week or so."

I wearily said, "Dear God, today is her birthday, Rachel. I cannot believe this is happening again. Every time we are in reach of something great, we are tested once again."

"Oh Walker, something great did happen today, but I will let Reese share that part of the story with you. Her body is dehydrated again because of the morning sickness. She's going to feel like crap for a few days, but with the proper rest, she will be fine."

"Rachel, can I have a word with you in private?"

"Of course," she said.

I told the kids I would be back in a moment.

"What is it, Walker?" she asked.

"Rachel, it's no secret that we have a very active sex life, and last night was probably a bit extreme for Reese to handle. Did I do this to her? Could I have endangered Reese and our baby?"

"I have spoken to Reese about this already, for that matter. Your sex life does not have to change because you are pregnant. It is actually encouraged, but in Reese's case now, I would have to recommend abstaining for a while. She has been through a lot and is at a fragile point in her pregnancy where she will need to slow down a bit until she progresses more. For now, she is fine, and that is what you need to focus on. Go in and see her, I promise you will feel better once you do."

I surprised Rachel by pulling her into a hug. She smiled and wished Reese a happy birthday. Jackson and Riley were already in with Reese when I entered her room. Riley hugged her mom and told her she would be back soon. Reese wanted them to be with Fallon, so she would not be scared. Jackson gave me a hug and then took Riley's hand and led her out of the room. I wanted to climb in bed with her, but she had tubes coming out of her arm. Reese instinctively slid over, as if she read my mind.

"I can't, baby. You need to rest," I said to her.

"Just for a minute. I want you close."

I kicked off my shoes and slid in as gently as I could. Reese turned to face me and whispered, "I am so sorry for scaring you."

"Shhh, you didn't scare me," I said. I lied.

"Okay, caveman, whatever you say."

She kissed my lips and smiled brightly at me. Her color was slowly returning and sparkle was back in her green eyes again.

"You're really okay?" I asked her as I caressed her face and wiped away her tears.

"We are fine, more than fine," she said with a smile.

"I didn't get a chance to tell you earlier, but Happy Birthday, Reese. I love you so much."

"I love you too, Walker, and I already received quite the birthday surprise."

"Oh really?" I said. "All of your presents are at home, unless you sneaked one."

"No, nothing like that. I've had this present for a while now. I just didn't know of it until today."

"What are you saying?" I asked. As Jackson had put it earlier, I tried to keep myself calm and in check, bracing myself for what Reese would say next.

"We are having twins," she said.

"Twins? As in two babies?"

"Yup, unless there are more in there, I saw two on the screen."

"Oh my God!" I screamed aloud, startling the staff to check on us.

"We're fine. He just found out that we are having twins." Reese smiled at the nurse.

I asked, "And they're okay? I mean really okay?"

"Yes, both our babies are fine. Our appointment was not scheduled until another week from now. I had no idea I was pregnant with twins. After Fallon was born, Rachel put me on hormones to regulate my cycles. And then with the cysts and health scare, I had to stop taking them. I never knew if another child was possible, and then to learn I am having twins is miraculous news."

"Happy Birthday, Reese!" I smiled at her.

"Yes, it is. Best birthday ever, even knowing I have to spend it here in the hospital."

I kissed her once more, and then I kissed her little baby bump and told our babies to take it easy on their mama today. I would still give Reese the best birthday ever. I just needed to make some calls first.

"I love you. Don't go anywhere. I will be back."

"I'll be here," she said.

After conferring with Rachel about my change of plans, she assured me that Reese would be okay. She was doing much better on the IV fluids, and her pain was minimal from the cyst rupture. Reese was always strong and had gone through worse. Rachel assured me this was a happy blip on her radar—no, make those *two* happy blips.

I could not believe my good fortune. Our family was growing even more. As I thought earlier, Reese was my love and reason for breathing. She had given me everything a man could want in ten lifetimes.

Not only would Rosalyn get a bonus for all of her hard work, but I was throwing in a vacation as well. She took a moment of pause while she listened to me change all of her plans for this evening. Once she absorbed it all, she congratulated me and assured me that she could pull it off.

I asked Rachel if she could keep Reese where she was for a few hours until Rosalyn's team could prepare a private room for her surprise. Rachel had no issues with it, nor did the board, considering the amount of money I donated each year to their hospital.

I called Freddy, and he said he would choose something that Reese would love. The grandparents had already arrived, and Riley told me they were back at the house. I asked her not to share anything about Reese being in the hospital with Lila, nor Thomas, for that matter. They flew all this way, and I did not want them upset before I had a chance to speak with them.

Before I left the hospital, I checked back with Reese, who was sound asleep. Rachel had just finished her exam and stepped outside to speak with me.

"She's going to be sleeping for a bit. To air on the side of caution, I did put her on antibiotics. Her levels have returned to normal range, but her body is exhausted from the dehydration. Now that she is carrying twins, it will be vital to absorb as many nutrients she can."

I inquired, "What about the morning sickness? Isn't that one of the reasons why we are here? It never seems to stop. Half the time, she doesn't tell me how bad it gets until I find her passed out or worse, like this morning."

"The pregnancy changed a great deal today, and now that we know more, we could treat her more with precaution. I know you have much planned for her this evening, and I encourage you to make her as happy as you can, but within limits. You will have all the privacy you need to give Reese a great birthday surprise; however, this is still a hospital and care still needs to go on, okay?"

"I understand and thank you, Rachel."

"You are welcome, Mr. Reed. Save me a piece of cake."

Once I arrived home, I was greeted with the sweet smells of Lila's cooking. *I swear that woman never stops baking.*

"Welcome home, Mr. Reed."

"Thank you, Priscilla. I guess everyone is in the kitchen?"

"Yes, sir. I have been removed from my kitchen. It is now Lila's until the rest of her stay with us."

"Good, you need a break, and I want you to take one too. Priscilla, you have been the glue that keeps this home together and running smoothly. I don't know what we would do without you."

"Thank you, Mr. Reed, that is kind of you say, but no need to. I love working for you and your family. Fallon keeps me young and energetic."

I responded, "Well, that is good to hear, because we will be adding to your duties."

"Sir?"

"We just found out today that we are having twins."

"How wonderful!" she screamed. "I am so happy for you. The staff is going to be overjoyed with your news."

"Thank you, Priscilla, but let's keep it quiet until we share our news with the rest of the family."

"My lips are sealed," she whispered.

She gave me a quick hug of congratulations and left me on my own. I entered the kitchen and was nearly knocked over by Lila, who was covered in flour.

"Well! It is about time, Walker Reed," she announced. "You have my head spinning faster than a hot summer's day in Georgia."

"Hello, Lila, and I am happy to see you too!"

I returned her hug and then she kissed me on my cheek. Thomas was next. He gave me a big hug, and I swear I thought he lifted me off the floor.

"Thomas, you have been working out," I laughed.

"Just good living, son, good living. My ticker is working just fine, and the pups keep me busy with the daily walking."

"I am in awe of both of you," I said to them. "Kids, take lessons. You will learn a great deal hanging around these two."

"Okay, Walker, where is my Reese? These two sneaky conspirators have kept me busy long enough with pastry requests, not that I mind my baking, but I would like to visit with my granddaughter."

"Nonsense, Lila, it's been a long day, and I'm sure they were hungry," Thomas said.

"Never mind, where is Reese?" Lila asked.

Before I answered her, I lifted Fallon from her highchair and handed her to Lila. Our daughter was an excellent buffer to calm people when the situation called for it. Today was one of those days.

I said to them, "Lila, Thomas, thank you for changing your plans and coming out here sooner. Reese is going to be over the moon once she sees you."

"I'm waiting, son," Thomas spoke over his wife.

I looked over at Thomas and then back to Lila, who looked worried.

I spit out, "Reese is in the hospital, but I promise you that she is fine."

They both let out a collective gasp upon hearing my news. I took Fallon from Lila, who wiped away her tears.

"Please Lila, Thomas, I know this is not the news you were expecting to hear today, but please believe me that Reese is fine, and our babies are too!"

"Babies?" Riley squealed.

"Surprise!" I yelled, "I was going to surprise Reese with your arrival for her birthday, and she goes and surprises me with news of her own."

"Oh, my dear sweet lord! My baby is having more babies, and not just one, but two. She never said a word to me," Lila said.

"We recently found out and wanted to wait until you arrived for Fallon's birthday, but with all the changes to our holiday plans, we would share our news with you sooner. She has been sick again, and early this morning she was so sick that I took her to the hospital. She had a cyst which ruptured that caused her some pain, but no risk to the baby. Once they did all of their tests and performed an ultrasound, we discovered it was twins."

"This is blessed news. Come here, you wonderful man," Lila said as she and Thomas both bear hugged me, while Jackson hugged Riley, who was crying happy tears.

"Can we visit with her?" Lila asked.

"Absolutely. We are bringing Reese's birthday party to her. Now, let's all get ready, so we can get this party started!"

CHAPTER 30

Walker

Happy Birthday, Reese

O UR FAMILY WAITED outside in the hall until I signaled them to join us. I entered her room dressed in a Freddy Mac tuxedo and carrying a bouquet of long-stemmed red roses, her favorite.

"Happy Birthday, baby. You look stunning," I told her.

"Thank you, Walker, and for all of this," she said as she gestured around her private suite. Rosalyn had her room decorated in the colors that matched our holiday theme at home. "I don't know how you did it, but thank you, my love. I could not be more surprised, and this dress... Freddy has outdone himself. When he and Fabrizio arrived earlier, I thought it was for a visit, I had no idea they were going to transform me into Cinderella attending the ball."

"And why not? Are you not my queen? You look beautiful and deserve this and so much more. I am blessed to call you my wife and

278

the mother of my children. You are my world and the sun that gives my heart light."

"Now, you are going to make me cry," she said.

"All happy tears, I promise. Get ready for some more," I said as I opened the door and stepped aside for the party to begin.

"Surprise!" our family shouted as they made their way in. Lila and Thomas greeted her first with kisses and hugs, then it was Jackson and Riley, and finally, I handed Fallon to Reese.

Fallon's arms and legs were bouncing in excitement to see her mommy again. They had never been separated until today. Freddy and Fabrizio were the last to wish Reese a happy birthday. The two men hugged her while she continued to hug Fallon.

The party was in full swing with toasting to Reese and then everyone congratulating us on our happy news.

With sparkling water in her hand, Reese clinked her crystal flute to get everyone's attention: "Thank you so much for sharing my birthday with me. I could not have asked for anything more. I love each one of you so much. We are family forever and always."

We clinked our glasses and finished off the last of the champagne. Everyone said his or her goodbyes one by one, and then it was my girl and me alone at last.

I divested of my tuxedo jacket and removed my tie. Reese always loved to watch me undress. I knew her eyes were on me now, so I took my time. I opened a few of my top buttons where she could see my skin, and I swore I saw her eyes brighten. She sexily bit her bottom lip and crooked her finger for me to come closer.

I took a knee to her bed and leaned in to kiss her, resulting in Reese grabbing me by my lapels to bring me closer.

"Stop it," I told her. "I know what you are doing."

"Oh really? And what am I doing?"

"You know exactly what I mean, sweetheart," I said as I kissed her plump lips and sat back.

I hated to say no to Reese, and the look in her eyes was her telltale sign that she wanted to make me happy for all that I gave her today, but it was not that way. All I wanted to do is make her smile. I did that today. That was all I wanted.

"I don't care, Walker. Please come back here."

"Is it up to you?" I asked.

She then smirked and patted the side of her bed. I kicked off my shoes, and now with her IV's tucked to the side, I took her in my arms. I lovingly held her as close as we could be.

"Thank you, Walker. I loved my party. Everything was perfect, just like you."

"Oh, my love, it is you that is perfect. You are welcome. I have something for you. Close your eyes and no peeking."

I pulled out the gift-wrapped box I had in my pocket and placed it on the palm of her hand. She carefully removed the paper and opened up the Tiffany blue colored box. When her eyes connected with what was inside, she held it in her hand and looked back to me.

"This is beautiful. How did you know?"

"A little birdy told me," I admitted. "Actually, it was you."

"Me?"

"Yes, you. Do you remember telling me how your mom had given you a charm bracelet when you were younger, but somehow the clasp broke and it was lost?"

"How could you possibly remember that story? I shared that with you over twenty years ago."

"I remember everything when it comes to you. I speak Reese for a living. Therefore, I figured it was time to replace that bracelet. Each locket contains a memory from your past, our past, our present, and our future. Go ahead, look."

She opened the first heart, and it was a picture of her parents. The second heart was of us when we first met. The third heart was our family today, and the last one was empty. It was waiting for a picture of our twins. Reese held out her arm, so I could place the diamond platinum bracelet on her dainty wrist. I kissed each heart and then slowly and sensually made my way up her arm, neck, and eventually on her lips, where I took her mouth gently with my clear message of intent…to be continued.

"Now my love, you need to close those beautiful emerald eyes of yours and go to sleep. I have another beautiful lady waiting on me at home."

"A few more minutes, please," she pleaded.

"No. Tomorrow is Christmas Eve, and I want tomorrow to be magical for you. In order to give you that, you need to be well rested, okay? I love you, Reese. All of me loves all of you with every fiber of my being. You are my gift in this life and the next. I am forever blessed to call you my wife and the mother of our children. You have made me incredibly happy. Please just allow me to give you the same in return. Go to sleep. I will be here first thing in the morning with Fallon in my arms."

I hoped I got my message across for my love to understand. She kissed me passionately in return, and I knew she finally conceded. I slipped my shoes back on and gathered my jacket. I turned to leave and only took two steps before she called out to me.

"As much as it was a pleasuring tease to watch you undress before me, I, on the other hand, am still wearing my dress. Shall I call someone to assist me?"

That's my girl! She is a tease and knows exactly how to make my body react. Okay, Reese, that point goes to you.

"Now, I cannot have that, now can I? Can you sit forward for me?" She moved not even an inch, knowing I would have to put my two hands on her to get to her back zipper. "Reese, please."

"Begging? Ooh, I love it, Walker. Please continue."

She will be the death of me. We loved to play the art of seduction, but not tonight, or the foreseeable future.

"Reese, you know no bounds, and it is about time I teach you. I will remove this gorgeous dress from your amazing body that is carrying our children, and you will cooperate and do as you are told. I am not that much of a bastard to try to have my way with you after everything you have been through."

"Oh, Walker, when you put it like that…I was only teasing, and you know it. Obviously, I can't make love with you right now, but it doesn't mean we can't have a little fun, right?"

"You are adorable, and of course we can have fun…when you are stronger. Dr. Lemay has requested that we abstain for a while, and I am agreeing to her request. Your well-being and the lives of our babies are my only priority, so please, my love, cooperate."

I kissed her again, and she finally agreed. Reese kept me with her for another half hour, but now I was the one conceding.

We playfully touched the other in between kisses, and she even managed to land a bite or two. She was now changed out of her dress, her sexy as sin silk stockings and fuck me now heels. This was no easy task, but one of us had to be mature. *Fuck my life! God, I wanted her.* I gently lifted her and placed her under the cover.

"Now, behave and allow me to leave with the angriest set of blue balls ever."

"Okay, you may go. Kiss our daughter for me. See you in the morning, Walker."

"That was too easy. What are you up to?"

"Nothing, I am just saying good night to my husband, who by the way is devilishly handsome and wears a tuxedo like no one's business. I love you, Walker Reed."

"Good night, Reese. I. Love. You. More."

Stephen drove me home, and I could not stop smiling. I was getting good at praying for things, especially in times when I needed the Man Himself to hear me without judgment. I hit the button for the privacy screen so Stephen would not hear me. What I had to say was meant only for God, and I hoped he would hear me tonight:

"Tonight I wanted to curse you because my wife and the welfare of my babies were in danger. Why do I continue to do this? I have been here before, throwing myself down at your mercy so a loved one of mine could be saved, in this case, three lives. It is not up to the mere mortals here on earth to question you. We will never know why you choose the ones you take, to be with you in your kingdom. The living ones that are left behind forever wonder the big question…why?"

I went on, "I silently begged you again today to save my Reese and my baby. You did, and I was blessed with a gift of not only one baby, but two. I am a selfish man, this I know, but my heart is good and beats only for my family."

I continued, "Thank you for protecting them today. Another debt I will never be able to repay, but nonetheless, I will try to honor the gifts I have received."

I said another prayer on the memory of the son we lost and asked him to watch over all of us.

Tomorrow was a new day, and one that I would get to have with Reese and our family.

CHAPTER 31

Jackson

A surprise of my own

THE LAST TWENTY-FOUR hours had been a blur. With Reese admitted to the hospital and my father and Riley out of their minds with worry, I was more than spent. We expected my father to remain with Reese at the hospital, but she wanted him to come home to be with Fallon. They had never spent time away from her, so Reese did not want my little sister scared. Big brother had everything under control, but I was not going to argue with my father over it. I knew they were worried and had enough to deal with.

He came home later than expected and once settled, had spent the night in the nursery with Fallon. It did not surprise me at all. Anytime when I was sick as a child or even in my younger teen years, my father was never too far away. I remember one time when my fever broke after having the flu, I turned over on my side, and there was my father watching me with concerned eyes. I think I was eleven. When he knew the fever had passed, he looked relieved and happy. I would always remember those moments, because that was Walker Reed simply being my dad. Now, he was taking on fatherhood all over again with Fallon, and soon with the twins.

As I laid watching Riley sleep soundly, I could not help falling in love with her more. Her bare back slightly exposed under the sheet that carried her intoxicating scent brought me to my knees. Her long thick hair was spread out over and down her shoulders. I saw tangles where my fingers were entwined throughout her hair as we made love last night. As tired as we were, we needed and craved each other's touch.

In the last few weeks we had been through many tests in our relationship, most of them my fault, and I deeply regretted them. Now, I was given a second chance with Riley and a leap of faith with my father. He had every right to be upset with me over my changes that I did not prepare him for. I expected both my father and Riley to just agree and move on. I was wrong. Although he advised to introduce me slowly to Reed Global, my father was practically shoving me in at full force so I could prove the doubters wrong. All I ever needed was my father to believe in me, and he did with his whole heart. I knew choosing Reed Global over film school was the right decision, which brought me back to the sleeping beauty beside me.

Riley wanted other things for her career, and as her future husband, I only wanted what would make her happy. Who knew, maybe someday she would join me at Reed Global? We did not know what the future held for us, but one thing for sure was that we would find out together.

I thought back to our first summer in New York when Riley wanted to marry me with no hesitation and no care to what anyone would think. It was not so crazy, now that I thought more about it.

I wondered what she would think of getting married now instead of waiting until we graduated and began our careers. My career was going to begin in a few short weeks while I was finishing the last two terms to earn my degree. Riley was right behind me, and if we stayed on course, we would graduate by December of next year.

Why wait to marry? I could not think of any reason to put this off any longer. Would she still want to?

"Jackson," she groaned out half-asleep, "turn off your brain and relax."

I pulled her body closer to me and kissed the top of her shoulder blades, where goose bumps immediately lined her porcelain skin.

"Hmmm, that's better baby." She smiled while her eyes remained closed.

"Good morning, Riley. Look at me, please."

She did a full body stretch before doing so and then turned to do as I asked.

"Good morning, baby." She leaned up to kiss me. "You look tired. Are you okay?"

"Just fine, and you?"

"If you are fine, then why are you biting the heck out of your thumb and scrunching your eyebrows together as if in deep, deep thought," she inquired.

"I will never know how you know these things, but I will not deny that I secretly love it too. You are right. My mind is in overdrive right now, but I assure you that it is a good thing. How about we get some breakfast, and then I would like to take you somewhere for a little while before Reese comes home and the holiday festivities begin," I suggested.

"Sounds perfect. I will go shower and meet you downstairs in about thirty minutes. I love you."

"I'm hurt, my love. No invitation to join you?"

"Sorry," she said, "you know we will never make it out of this room if I allow you to shower with me."

"You know you are cute when you are right. See you soon, and hurry."

I kissed her hard and then soft as we got our breathing back and under control. I loved this girl so much, and I knew where my heart was leading. I just hoped she would follow.

By the time I made my way downstairs, my father had already left for the hospital. Fallon had breakfast and her morning playtime already. She was trying so hard to stay on her feet to get to one point to the other without falling. Dad said I had walked by my first birthday, but my little sister here might beat me by a couple of weeks.

"Come here, Fallon. You can do it."

She was holding herself up all on her own next to the oversized ottoman. I was in a catcher's squat with my hands reached out for her. She looked confident that she could do it, but I think I needed to give her a little encouragement. One big smile from her brother was all she needed to see. Her eyes looked as if they were sparkling. She immediately let go and nearly baby sprinted right for me. I helped her a little bit by inching closer, but it was the coolest four steps ever. I had my camera positioned on the tripod to capture the moment for us.

"Good girl, sweetheart! You did it! I am so proud of you, baby girl. Wait until mommy sees your video."

Fallon laughed as I made silly faces and then hugged her. She was so precious and such a blessing to our family. She was wiggling out of my arms, and I thought she might want to try walking again. I placed her down and sure enough, she took off like lightning, but right to Riley, who was behind me the entire time.

"I should have known," I said. "Hey, baby."

"What? You think you are the only one this little girl loves? Sisters have to stick together now."

"Don't I know that. Let's hope Reese has boys this time around, and then you will be outnumbered. Are you ready to go?"

"I am, but I want to hug this little one for a few more minutes."

"Babies look good on you," I said to her.

"I know that look, Jackson. We have plenty of time to practice before we do this."

"I can't help it. You are always beautiful, but when you hold

Fallon, you are positively stunning."

Her eyes became glassy as she placed Fallon down in her closed off play yard.

I continued, "I mean it, you know. I cannot wait until you are pregnant with my child."

I dropped to my knees and lifted her shirt just enough to expose her flat stomach. I placed a few kisses there and looked up into her eyes.

"Someday, our child will grow right here, and the day you share your news with me will be the happiest day of my life. Don't freak out," I said as I slowly got up on my feet. "I love you, and a man can dream and want these things with the woman he loves."

I kissed her gently, and then Priscilla entered the room, inter-rupting our moment. We said goodbye to Fallon and made our way to my truck. I opened the door to my Hummer and helped her in. I drove us down to one of my favorite beaches I like to surf at when I am back in Cali. The weather was on our side today, with the sun shining brightly and a light wind. We walked hand-in-hand along the water, where Riley remained quiet.

"You're freaking out, aren't you?" I asked.

"Not exactly, just a little taken aback with it all. Jackson, I never know which way the wind is going to shift with your mood swings. As much as I believe I know you, somedays you take me completely off guard, and it's those rare moments where I'm left a little speech-less like today."

"You don't want children?" I could not help but to ask her.

"Jackson, you know I want babies with you, just not today. A few weeks ago, we did not even know if we would make it, and now you are wishing for babies for us. Don't you see how confusing you can be?"

I took her hands and brought them up to my lips. I kissed each of her knuckles one by one, and then my mouth found hers. I took that kiss—no, I owned that kiss—just like the beautiful girl who owned my heart and soul.

"Riley, I love you, and if you will have me, I want to marry you and make you mine forever."

"I am already yours, baby. See the ring?" She wiggled her finger at me while smiling.

"No, you don't understand. Riley, I do not want to wait anymore to make you mine. I want to marry you now, before we return home to New York. I was biting the heck out of my thumb because I wanted the moment when I asked you to be perfect. But every moment spent with you is perfect, so I am asking you here, right now, to marry me. Will you?"

"Jackson, if you are doing this because you think you have something to make up for, then you are wrong. We have moved past it and we are fine."

"Riley, you misunderstand. I know we are fine, better than fine."

"If that's true, then why the sudden urgency to marry now? We agreed we would wait until after we graduated. Jackson, we are almost there, baby. One more year, and then I am all yours, forever."

"What if I want forever to start now?"

"Why is it so important to you?" she asked. "You need to help me understand."

"It took almost losing you to make me see what I had, and I was so fucking selfish to take you for granted. Do you remember our time in Georgia?"

"Every moment," she said.

"Me too. Every single word is in my heart. We made promises to each other that night, promises of forever. It was a promise of the future we dreamed of having together and wished upon the stars for a life together. When you accepted my ring, you chose to love me and to be my wife someday. Well, that day has come. In my heart, I know you are mine, just as much as I am yours, but I need more, Riley. I need more than knowing what my heart feels. I need to hear you say the words to me, with God as our witness as we truly become one as husband and wife."

I dropped down to one knee and pulled out the Cartier ring box. I had redesigned my mother's wedding band for something unique just for Riley. She covered her mouth to hold back her excitement. Soon, I knew she would have difficulty holding back her tears.

"Riley Taylor Briggs, will you do me the honor of marrying me in Big Sur, under the giant redwood tree that bears our names on it? As we made love under the stars, protected by the trees at night, I knew with all certainty that I would marry you there someday. I don't want to dream it anymore. I want to live it with you if you say yes."

She dropped to her knees and wrapped her arms around my neck, kissing me fervently until we were out of breath.

I asked, "Well, is that a yes?"

"Yes, I will marry you. I will marry you under our tree."

We rose on our feet, and I lifted Riley into my arms to twirl around and dance in the water.

"You have made me so happy. I promise you, Riley, with all that I have that I will love you forever."

"I know you will, Jackson, as I will love you just the same for all the days of my life."

We shared a picnic lunch and celebrated what was next to come in our lives. Riley sat beside me with her head on my chest, and my arms wrapped around her.

"Jackson," she whispered. "What will you tell your father?" she nervously questioned.

"Riley, I won't lie to him, not ever again. After what I put him through when I got sick, I promised my father that I would always be honest with him. As much as I would love to keep this private for us, there really is no way I can do that without hurting him, and there's your mom and your father to consider as well."

"Jackson, I wasn't asking you to lie, far from it. When I wanted to marry you back in New York, I was as truthful as I could be but also scared of losing you. I needed to know that we followed through on the promises we made to one another. After going through what we did, I'm thankful we did wait, because I really do want my father to walk me down the aisle, my mother to help me with my dress, and Nana Lila to give me something special to hold when we marry."

I said, "Thank you, baby. I have waited so long to hear these words from you. I knew you wanted more and would be willing to do anything to make me happy, but the truth is, just you with me is enough. You have my heart, and I have yours, and soon we will tell the world too!"

"Okay, let's get through the next few days, and then we will tell the parents."

"Okay. Anything you want."

"I have everything I want, Jackson. I love you."

"I love you too!"

I gathered our things, and we walked along the beach until we reached where I had parked my truck. Once again, I helped Riley up and then made my way around to the driver's side. Just as I was putting the car into drive, my cell buzzed in my pocket.

Dad: *Where are you?*
Me: *Beach with Riley*
Dad: *Come home. Reese is home and settled in. Lila is cooking up a storm and wants Riley to help her.*
Me: *On our way.*
Dad: *Good. See you soon.*

"That was my dad," I told Riley. "Your mom is home and doing well. Nana has requested your help in the kitchen…something about cooking up a storm."

"Yay! I hope she puts me on desserts."

"That's fine. Just don't hide under all that baking flour so I can't find you."

She laughed, "Ah, that reminds me of the time when we had the cookie battle with Brandon and Clay. We beat their asses with chocolate chip bombs."

"Yeah, but it took us two days to clean the kitchen."

"That was fun. Do you miss them at all? I'm sure they would love to hear from you, Jackson."

"I'll call them soon. Let's get through the next two days, okay?"

"Okay, my forever love."

CHAPTER 32

Riley

What will he say?

I DID NOT wear my poker face well, and I think Jackson was worse. How were we going to break the news to our parents that we wanted to get married before we returned home to New York? We did not begin our next term until nearly the end of January. Professor Connelly always took an extended leave of absence during holiday break.

I wanted our wedding to be simple. Everyone that mattered in our lives was here with us now, all except a few friends and my father. He long accepted my relationship with Jackson, and the tensions that were once there were no longer evident when we were all in the same room. Mr. Reed vowed to be cordial with my father after he saved his son's life. My father was busy at his hospital, and he now was in a serious relationship with Dr. Gillian Taylor. They travelled between their two homes. She was in London, and my father still resided in Maryland, though I was not sure for how much longer.

The last few conversations we had, I believed he was leaning toward moving to London, but he also had a building back at Johns Hopkins for him and him alone. He dedicated his life to that hospital and made many sacrifices along the way, my mother being one of them.

We'd all moved on from that time in our life, and all I wanted my father to do was be happy. If Gillian accomplished that, then I was happy too. Having said that, I wanted his support for my choices.

After saying our hellos to the great grandparents and his father and my mother, I quietly retreated to my room to make my call to my father. It was Christmas Eve, and I knew he was spending the holiday with Gillian back in Maryland.

The last time we were together, he promised he would see me once I returned to New York. He was my father, so I should not have been nervous about calling him, especially on Christmas Eve. I was going to just call him and feel him out. Before I chickened out, I hit his speed dial number on my cell. I was not surprised when he answered on the second ring.

"Hello, sweetheart, Merry Christmas," he said.

"Hi, daddy! Merry Christmas to you."

I was going to say more when I heard holiday music in the background and Gillian calling him back to their guests.

"I'll be right back, darling," he said to Gillian. "I have Riley on the phone."

"Wish her a Merry Christmas, and ask her if she received our gifts we sent," I heard her say.

"I will. Riley, are you still there?"

"Yes, daddy, I am here. It sounds like you are busy. I can call you back."

"Nonsense, I am never too busy for my number one girl. It feels like we have not talked in ages, but I know it has only been a few weeks. I miss you, sweetheart. I wish you and Jackson could have joined us out here for at least a weekend before returning back to school."

"Well, that's why I am calling. Something big has happened, and you may be seeing me sooner than you think."

"Riley," he enunciated my name showing concern, "are you okay? Is everything well between you and Jackson?"

"Yes, daddy, we are fine. In fact, wonderful. He asked me to marry him."

"Yes, I know this. You have been engaged for a while now."

"No, daddy, you misunderstand. Jackson wants to marry me now while we are here in California. I have not talked with mom yet, so please keep this between us for now."

"Riley, you are twenty-years-old, soon to be twenty-one, but still very young to marry. I accepted the engagement because you promised me that you would wait until you graduated, which is more than a year from now, so why the rush? Are you pregnant? Is that why there is a rush to the altar?"

"Gee, thank you, dad. A woman my age cannot possibly get married without being knocked up first? Sorry to disappoint you, but you are not going to be a grandfather anytime soon. I sure do love the faith you have in me."

"Riley, that is enough. I do not intend to argue with you on Christmas Eve when I have a home full of guests. I apologize if I crossed the line, but what do you expect me to think?"

"I expect your love and support, which is what you should have offered. Nevertheless, as usual, you always think less of me and more so of Jackson. Get over it, daddy! I am marrying a Reed, just like mom did. Deal with it."

Before he could say another word to me, I ended the call. *Nice going, Riley. You probably just ruined his Christmas and the relationship you worked so hard to repair.* Of course, he called back, and I allowed it to go to voicemail. The tears began to fall when I looked up to see Jackson leaning up against the door with a disappointed expression on his face.

"I know you heard that. Sorry," I said to him, sobbing.

He quickly made strides to get to me and without hesitation took me in his arms and sighed in my ear.

"Riley, I am sorry too. I should have phoned him myself and asked his permission to marry you sooner."

"Jackson, I am an adult. Now, I know it is not evident now, but I am. You did not hear him, Jackson. His mind always goes negative when it comes to our relationship. He accused me of racing to the altar because he thought I was pregnant."

"Okay, he should have not assumed anything but believed how happy you are...*we* are. I am going to phone him right now before this escalates any bigger than it should be. Hand me your phone, please."

Jackson extended his hand, wearing an expression of seriousness. We shared a beautiful day, and I was not going to challenge him. I handed Jackson my cell phone, and he kissed me in return. As usual, my father answered on the second ring.

"Hi, Dr. Briggs, Merry Christmas. Yes, Riley is here with me, but I would rather speak with you. Thank you, sir. Yes, today was a big day for us. We are very happy, sir. I apologize for not phoning you first. It was inconsiderate of me to not ask your blessing beforehand. Thank you sir, I appreciate that. Yes, I will speak with my father and Reese, probably tomorrow. Once we have a date confirmed, I know it would mean the world to Riley and me if you could join us out here. Yes, sir, that is still the plan. I am going to marry your daughter in Big Sur. You have a great night, sir. Please give our best to Dr. Taylor. Okay, here is Riley."

I took a deep breath before accepting my cellphone. Jackson kissed me on my cheek and sat beside me.

"Hi, daddy. I'm sorry. I should have never spoken to you that way."

"Riley, I love you," he said to me. "You are my daughter, and your happiness means the world to me. I am still a father and allowed to be concerned for your well-being, despite what you believe. Give your old man a break, okay."

"You are not old, far from it. Will you give me away, daddy? I cannot imagine marrying my prince without my hero by my side."

"Thank you, darling, and yes, I would not miss it for anything in the world. After you speak with mom, call me back and we will talk, or even Skype, and we will all join in."

"Okay, daddy, I love you. Merry Christmas."

"Merry Christmas to you," he said back.

"How do you feel?" Jackson questioned me.

"How do you think? Foolish."

"You are not foolish—crazy sometimes—but never foolish. Oh, my crazy girl, I love you madly and your father does too. I guess this was a preview for what's to come when we tell the parents and grandparents."

"I love you, Jackson, for the faith you have in me, but I lost my temper with my father. As much as I believe we have to move forward from the past, something always seems to creep up and kick me back ten steps. I love my father very much and hate myself for arguing with him."

"There is a simple solution to your problem," he said.

"Oh yeah, what do you suggest?"

"Do not argue with him."

"Okay, my love," I told him. "I will make sure to write that down the next time you argue with your father."

"Riley, the past is the past, and we cannot change it for either of our parents. My father once told me that he could never go back and rewrite history because that would mean so many other things in his life would not have mattered or existed."

"My mother said the same thing," I agreed.

"Exactly, because it was true then as it is now. Our life today is what matters. Our future matters and all we have planned for us as a couple and family. Your father now knows our news, so there is no point putting it off telling Reese and my father. I want to share our news with them, and I am hopeful they will support us in our decision."

"And, if they don't? What will we do then, Jackson?" I asked.

"We will marry under our tree in Big Sur."

"You would still marry me even if you did not have your father's blessing?"

"Absolutely. Riley, he asked me once for my approval for his marriage to your mom. I thought at the time that I would be betraying my mother's memory, or hurting you. Do you remember we talked about this in Georgia? Well, my father never asked of anything from me, so to give him my blessing to have a life with the woman he loves was the least I could do in return for all he did for me. Sure, he may not understand why we are choosing to marry now, but it is not up to him, and I do hope we have his blessing. Either way, Riley, it will not change our plans. I love you, and I want nothing more than to call you my wife. I need this more than you know."

"I know, Jackson, and I want nothing more than to be your wife. We are a team, right?"

"We are. Now, the party awaits downstairs for us. Are you okay?"

"I would be better if you would make love to me first. I need you, Jackson, forever and always."

He said nothing but placed a kiss on my lips and then turned to lock my door.

He said, "I love you, and I need you too. Lie back and put your hands above your head."

I immediately did as he asked and was breathless with anticipation. Jackson hovered above me as he put all of his weight on his elbows. I wanted to touch him, but he gave me a look that stopped me.

"This is for you, Riley. Just let me love you."

Slowly unbuttoning and opening my blouse, his mouth immediately covered my pebbled nipples through my lacy bra. The sensation was building, and I wanted to scream his name in earnest. He removed my bra quickly and gave my breasts equal attention from his mouth.

Jackson took his time as he made his way down to my pussy, which was already dripping with my arousal. One skillful move and my skirt was pulled down, another pair of panties shredded with one pull. My pelvis jerked when his mouth found my entrance. With his right hand holding my two, he used his left to insert two fingers inside of me, and silencing my cries with his mouth.

"Shhh, do not make a sound," he whispered as he took me again, this time with his tongue circling my clit. "Riley, this is going to be intense. If you need to, scream into the pillow."

I did exactly that, because Jackson plunged his tongue so deep into my pussy, I thought I saw stars. He released my hands for me to touch him, and they instinctively grabbed on to each side of his head, tangling my fingers in his hair. I pulled him closer, deeper, until I could take no more. I screamed his name with muffled cries of pleasure until I felt his knee part my legs, and before I could open my eyes, he was inside of me.

His mouth was on mine as his tongue entwined with mine. His breathing became ragged, as he took me faster, harder, and then again and again until he crushed his lips on mine again. We both shouted our orgasms, this time with no pillow to hide our pleasure.

"Whoops, my bad," Jackson winked when I just let out a fit of giggles. "Let's shower and join the others before they put out a search party for us. To be continued."

"God, I love you, Jackson Reed. Will you marry me?"

"That's the plan, my love, and I love you more. Forever and always. You are my home."

Some did not believe in fate, but we did. Meeting Jackson was the universe bringing our hearts together.

I could not wait to become Mrs. Jackson Reed. He is my happily forever after.

Walker

The perfect holiday

I LOOKED UP at the Christmas tree that filled our great room. This was our family tree, decorated with ornaments that held special memories for our family. Before we married, Lila had not only given Reese the home movies of her parents, but also boxes of ornaments that had been passed down, dating back to their early days in Ireland.

Lila saved everything, from handmade ornaments that Reese had made in school, to the heirlooms that were priceless. We all had a special place on the tree, and now it was Fallon's first Christmas. I had given Reese a Baby's First Ornament last year when she was still pregnant, and now it hung amongst the memories and the sparkling lights. This time next year, we would add two more for our twins. Our family was blessed.

"Are you happy, darling?" I asked my wife as she smiled watching Fallon bounce on the lap of her grandfather, Thomas.

Our baby daughter was smiling and giggling as Thomas played with her. Meanwhile, Lila snapped photo after photo, another memory that would soon find its way onto her wall back home in Georgia.

Reese said, "Walker, you make all of my dreams come true. Surprising me with a visit from Nana and granddaddy, I could not ask for anything more. Thank you."

"You are welcome, but it is nothing compared to what you have given me." I placed my hands on her stomach and then kissed her ever so gently. "I love that my children are growing here. I cannot wait to meet them. Speaking of children, I am giving Jackson and Riley one more minute before I go get them."

"You will do no such thing. They need this time together. It's Christmas. Let them have their fun."

"Reese, your definition of fun is different from what I am imagining right now."

"I am not blind, my love. I am well aware of what those sneaks are up to. Let's change the subject, shall we?"

"Okay, but they still have one more minute," I joked.

"I'm sorry your mom could not join us. Have you had a chance to speak with her?"

"I have, and she is well. I told her about the babies, and she is thrilled. Of course, I miss my mother, but I want her to be happy too. For years, she was my father's shadow, and now it is her time to shine. Hopefully she will make it for Fallon's birthday."

"Will you be okay if she misses it?"

"I'll get there eventually. Okay, time's up," I said as I stepped out into the hall and shouted as loud as I could. "Jackson!"

"I'm here, dad."

I turned around to see my son and Riley smiling at my expense. The two sneaks entered from the other door. He immediately greeted the family, and Riley sat beside Reese. They had all of their bases covered, and I held my hands up in defeat. *It's Christmas. Let them have their fun.*

My phone buzzed in my pocket, signaling me that it was time.

I announced, "May I have your attention please?"

All pairs of eyes were on me, including Fallon, who repeated my favorite word, "Dada."

"Thank you, baby girl," I said, blowing her a kiss. "Let me begin by saying thank you to each and every one of you for joining us in our home for Fallon's first Christmas, and soon her first birthday, especially Lila and Thomas who made the long trip."

I looked over to Reese, who was smiling up at me.

"My lovely wife here stole my thunder by hijacking my holiday surprise for her," I blew her a kiss. "I don't know how you knew, but thank you for our home and all you have done to make it sparkle for our very special Christmas. Now, I do have a surprise of my own, and I would like all of you to follow me out to the garden."

I helped Reese with her coat, while Priscilla tended to Fallon. It was a beautiful night here in California with temperatures in the mid-sixties, perfect for what I planned. Rosalyn met us at the entrance to the garden and assured me everything was in place. I held Fallon in my arms and kissed Reese on her cheeks.

"Close your eyes, Reese, and do not open them until I tell you."

"What are you up to?" she asked.

"You'll see," I told her. "Keep them closed."

With one arm wrapped around my daughter and the other on Reese, I guided her to where she would see her surprise.

"Merry Christmas, darling. I love you with all of my heart. This is for you."

She slowly opened her eyes and clapped her hands over her mouth. Rosalyn had truly transformed our property into a winter wonderland, even including an ice skating rink and a real amusement carousel for all of us to enjoy, including Fallon. Christmas music played throughout the speakers, and lights were sparkling on every tree, shrub, and structure.

"Oh, Walker, this is amazing. I love it."

Rosalyn had chairs in place in front of the makeshift rink, where we all took a seat. She managed to bring "Disney on Ice" to us. All of the Disney princesses came out one by one, and skating in perfect figure eights. The Disney theme song played as the ice dancers danced in unison, each of them waving as they passed Fallon. Our little girl's beautiful eyes sparkled at the sight of them. She was not afraid of the loud music or all of the decorations.

"You did good, son," Thomas said, clapping his strong hand on my back, giving me his approval.

We clapped when our private show ended. The princesses each took photos with the baby and all of us, another memory we would cherish as a family. Jackson and Riley took their baby sister on the carousel, and we joined them after a few times around. I did not want to tire Reese, but she was holding her own and assured me she was fine.

A snowball fight followed, and I declared war on Jackson, who got me when I was not looking. Reese and the grandparents smiled and cheered on the kids.

"Hey, what about me?" I called out.

I had to call a truce when Reese released Fallon to walk to me.

"Dada, dada, up," Fallon said to me.

"We love you, angel," I told her.

I lifted my little princess in my arms and twirled her around. She was done. Before one raspberry to my cheek, her eyes began to close, and she was down for the night on my shoulder. I hugged her with all of my love, and Reese and I left to tuck her in.

After dinner, we opened one present each and then filled up on Lila's delicious desserts that she prepared for our celebration. I could not be more pleased with all that Rosalyn had accomplished.

My relationship with Reese was tested from our very beginning. We survived our losses, were reunited by chance, and now here we were. We were all together as a family and whole, and happy to look forward to another day together. I looked all around and smiled at everyone. My eyes found my son, who whispered something in Riley's ear. He held her hand in his and turned to address me.

"Dad, Riley and I would like to tell you some news of our own, and we hope you will all be happy for us."

Reese covered my hand over hers, and we waited to hear what our kids were about to say.

CHAPTER 34

Jackson

Our turn for forever

IT WAS NOW or never to share the news with our family. The one emotion that was clear to everyone in this room was love, and I hoped our news would make tonight even better.

My dad looked over to Reese, and then back to me with almost a knowing look. I had seen it before when he didn't act surprised when I told him how much I was in love with Riley. Therefore, if I knew my father as well as I believed, then the next part should have been easy for him predict what I was about to say.

"Go on, son," he said and gave me an encouraging look while Reese smiled at Riley.

They knew, of course they knew, I thought to myself.

"Anyone up for more Christmas cheer? Because I have—no—*we* have something to tell you. While our family are together, Riley and I have decided to get married sooner than we had planned."

I paused for a moment and waited for some reaction, anything from our family telling us this was a bad idea, but all they did was smile and encouraged me to continue. So I did, but not before bending down to kiss the love of my life.

I began, "Our parents' love story is like nothing I ever had a chance to witness before. If fairytales were still written, then their story should be published someday for lovers to swoon over and maybe even get inspired over to find everlasting happiness. I certainly was inspired, and Riley was too. Like Dad and Reese, our love was tested, and we became stronger and more in love than ever before. We left our homes to share one of our own, and this time around, it was I who tested us. You can call it a twist of fate, or a destiny I had yet to realize. The only persons I have shared this story with are my father and Riley, and now I will share my experience with you."

I continued, "During my surgery when my heart stopped, I thought I died. In those few seconds while the doctors furiously tried to bring me back, I drifted to another place in my dreams, where I met my mother for the first time. She was beautiful and young, and admitted to watching over me my entire life. She showed me a glimpse of what my future looked like and whom I would share my life with. I kept asking if this was heaven and I was dead, and she just smiled and told me I was sleeping and would wake soon when I was ready. The only person I saw was Riley, the love of my life. When I survived the AVM and what followed, I no longer held the same passion I once did for filmmaking, but I forged ahead and thought I would feel differently. But I did not. I wanted to take my rightful place alongside my father at Reed Global. Now, I messed up with how I broke the news to Riley, and I expected her to agree to all of my plans and not have an opinion about it."

I went on, "I was wrong to believe that, and if it was not for my father here setting me straight, this beautiful beauty may not be holding my hand right now. I messed up, but I guess we are supposed to occasionally, right, Nana? You once said that it keeps you humble and honest. In just the few short days Riley and I were separated, I knew I was missing the other half of my heart. Generations of love stories are all around this room, and I have seen dad and Reese get their happily ever after. Now it is time for me to make good on a promise I made to Riley one night while in a meadow in Georgia: my promise of forever to Riley Taylor Briggs. We are asking for not only our parents' blessing, but for yours as well. We love you Lila and Thomas, and we do not think we can get married without you. I promise that I will make your great granddaughter happy every single day of her life. And, whenever we fight all day, I vow to make sure I hold her at night and promise her a better tomorrow."

Riley squeezed my hand and wiped away her tears. Reese was crying. Lila was in tears. Priscilla was sobbing. I looked over to my father, and I knew we were given what we asked for.

He walked over to us as Riley stood beside me, and he said, "Your mother would be so proud of you for the man you have become. Yes, you have our blessing to marry Riley. We love you very much and want nothing more than to stand beside you as a family and witness you become one too."

We embraced each other in a group hug, and then the grandparents joined in with Thomas calling Priscilla to join us. It was at this time that Thomas pulled me aside, lifted me in a bear hug, and then reminded me of his vast shotgun collection. *Message received!* Dad was no help at all, as he held Reese and laughed at me.

The champagne was passed around, and we all celebrated together. We sang carols and listened intently to Thomas as he shared a love story of his own. I could not wait to make Riley mine and love her for the rest of my life…forever.

Riley

A father's love

AFTER SHARING AN amazing Christmas, we were down to days before I would say "I do" to Jackson. Baby Fallon was about to turn one-year-old on New Year's Day, and we did not want to take anything away from her special day. So we agreed to marry on December 30th and spend the holiday in Big Sur before coming home to celebrate our little sister's special milestone birthday.

Mom and I had a long talk following Christmas, and the sensitive subject of my father came up. I told her how I argued with him and how I deeply regretted my behavior. Jackson was right and my mother was too: it was time to move on from the past. He was a good man who deserved just as much happiness as my mother now had. He loved me, this I knew, and only wanted the best for my life.

I never questioned his motives before the divorce, and I vowed to not jump down his throat when he did so now. I had the opportunity to chat with Gillian. She had been great for my father. They had been together since after Jackson's surgery, first in a professional relationship and now a personal one.

Mr. Reed sent his plane for my father and Gillian. At first, my father declined the offer but quickly reconsidered, because he could not book a flight and make it in time for our wedding. They were to arrive later this evening, which meant I had the day with mom and Freddy.

"Okay, junior peach, are you ready for the dress?" Freddy asked me.

I jumped up and down and screamed "Yes" while Fabrizio shook his head at his husband. Fabrizio talked to Freddy in Italian, and my mom laughed. I did not want to know. When these three got together, it was a reunion of great stories.

I opened my eyes and my breath hitched in my throat as he brought it out. How did he do it? Mom called Freddy and requested a dress as if it was no big deal to make the dress of my dreams. Freddy had chosen a design from his couture line. It was breathtaking and made for a queen. It was a long sleeve gown of appliqued pearl and champagne tulle, and the best part was the open back. I could not wait to try it on. After wiping my tears, Freddy took my hand and guided me over to the makeshift platform set up in my mother's dressing room.

Freddy and Fabrizio watched me as I did a turn for them. Fabrizio jotted down some notes and placed a few pins near my waist. I never felt more beautiful. Freddy told me that when he completed the dress and placed it on display, he felt it would need a special woman to wear it. He told me that although he never knew it at the time, this dress was meant for me. After all the measurements were done, it only required a few minor adjustments. Freddy was pleased with the final look. It was perfect. He suggested I wear my hair up in a classic sleek updo to compliment my bare back. My father would probably have a heart attack seeing me in this dress. It certainly did not scream daddy's little girl.

"Thank you, Freddy. How can I ever thank you for this?" I said, overjoyed.

"Are you happy?" he asked.

"Yes, with all of my heart."

"Okay then, which is all the thanks I need. You are a beautiful and most graceful young woman. You remind me so much of your mother. You know when I first met your mom at college, she took pity on a thin and lanky Jewish boy from the Bronx. I had no clue where I was going, and I shamelessly flirted with her too. She helped me find my way. And once she smiled, I knew we would be best friends forever. Now, you, my junior peach, have so much sparkle to your personality that people need to wear sunglasses when you enter a room."

"I bet it was so hard for you when she left."

"It was Riley, and I missed her every single day until she walked into my studio and asked me to forgive her."

"She loves you, Freddy. She just didn't have too many choices back then."

"You always have a choice, baby girl. In your mama's case, she did what she felt was right for everyone and never questioned what effects it would have on her life. Allow me to tell you something that I never had the chance to tell your mom. Whatever road life takes you on, never be afraid to let yourself shine. You are going to have a great life with Jackson. It's a true gift to be part of your story and your life."

"Thank you, Freddy. I love you so much," I said as I practically lunged at him with the biggest hug I could give.

"And I love you, princess. Now, how about I go charm Priscilla into giving me Walker's combination to his wine vault? I could use some Cristal right about now."

"Freddy…" Fabrizio slowly enunciated as he packed up their things.

"Oh my, love!" Freddy yelled back. "Where is your sense of adventure? You know Walker won't mind."

Fabrizio let out a huge laugh and smiled back at his husband. He said, "Sure he won't, but I could use some champagne too!"

"Okay, guys," I told them, "follow me."

After a perfect day with Freddy, it was now time for my father to arrive. Mom had offered the guesthouse for dad and Gillian to use while they were here for the next couple of days, but my father politely declined. I knew he would say no, but it was mom's way of making him feel welcomed.

"Are you ready, baby?" Jackson asked. "Stephen is at the gate with your dad. They should be here any minute."

"Jackson, I am so nervous. What if something goes wrong, and daddy and I end up arguing again?"

"That is not going to happen. We talked about this, remember? All you have to do is be his daughter, and the rest will fall into place. Now there they are. Show me your beautiful smile."

He took me in his arms and kissed my neck, which made me very happy and full of smiles. He said, "That's my Riley, I love you."

"I love you too!"

The door opened with my father entering hand-in-hand with Gillian. His eyes found mine, and he smiled lovingly at me. Jackson nudged me out of his hold and toward my father, who did the same.

"Thank you, daddy, for coming," I told him.

"Wild horses could not keep me away. I've missed you, sweetheart."

And just like that and with only a few words from my father, I felt as if I were his little girl again. He lifted me in his arms and hugged me close to him. Once he set me down, he shook Jackson's hand and then pulled him into a congratulatory hug.

"Welcome to our family, son," he said to Jackson.

"Thank you, sir."

"You remember Dr. Gillian Taylor?" My father turned and held out his hand for her.

Jackson said, "I do. It's nice to see you again, Dr. Taylor."

"It's Gillian, and happy almost New Year and wedding day."

"Thank you. We are very excited. Come, the rest of the family are in the great room."

Although my father was very happy with Gillian, I could see his expression change with the thought of seeing mom again. We followed Jackson, and all eyes were on us when we walked into the room. With his manners in check, dad said hello to everyone, and then introduced Gillian. Mr. Reed shook his hand, and Nana and granddaddy greeted my father warmly. Even though they had their differences, Nana was always kind.

Fallon, never missing an opportunity to drool, half crawled and then pulled herself up to walk to my father.

"Up!" she said.

Dad looked over to Mr. Reed and mom before picking up their daughter. Mom gave my father permission with her eyes. Mr. Reed remained quiet, no thanks to mom, who probably told him to behave today.

Dad said, "Hello little one, you have gotten so big since the last time I saw you. You look just like Riley when she was a baby."

Fallon kissed his cheeks with wet raspberries and laughed in her baby voice.

"Okay, my sweet girl, time for your bath," Mr. Reed said as he took his daughter from my father. "Priscilla!" he called.

"Yes, sir?" she asked.

"Please take the baby upstairs for her bath, and get her ready for bed. We will be up shortly."

"Yes, sir," Priscilla responded as she took Fallon, and we waved goodbye.

Mr. Reed announced, "Welcome to our home, and thank you for coming on such short notice. It means a lot to Riley for you to be here."

Dad said, "She's my daughter, Reed. Where else would I be?"

And, so it begins…, I thought to myself.

Mom caught my expression and walked over to Mr. Reed and dad to defuse the situation. She said, "Samuel, Gillian, may I offer you anything to drink? Wine perhaps?"

"Thank you, I would love a glass of Cabernet, and Samuel could probably use a brandy," Gillian said as she smiled over at my father.

"Thank you, Reese," he said, and they all took a seat.

The grandparents talked with dad for a little while and then went up to bed while we continued to talk about the wedding. My father then talked directly to my mom. He did not know she was expecting again, and with twins, until she shared her news with him. He placed a kiss to her hand and offered his and Gillian's congratulations to mom and Walker. The rest of our evening went smoothly. I was thankful he was here with me, and happy on how far we had come as a family.

We explained to dad that the real wedding ceremony would take place here at the house. With mom's delicate condition and along with my grandparents, they could not make the hike down to the redwoods, so we came up with another plan. Jackson and I would marry out in the garden, and then after celebrating with our family, we would leave for Big Sur and have a private ceremony with just us, under our tree. We had written vows just for the occasion. Dad agreed with no issue, and we spent the rest of the evening catching up.

CHAPTER 36

Jackson

Mending fences

WE HAD ONLY spoken once since the night in the club, and I had avoided their calls ever since. They apologized repeatedly for all that went down that night. I had long since calmed down and moved on from it. It was not right on my part to freeze them out. Brandon and Clay were my best friends my entire life, and I knew I had to make things right with them again.

They were both here in California visiting their families, so it was not hard tracking them down. When I called them, they were together with their girlfriends, Alice and Evette. I asked them to come to the house for lunch, and to my surprise, they immediately said yes.

Riley and the girls jumped up and down when they saw each other. I was not a big fan of the girls, but Riley liked them and she needed friends in her life, so this was me…trying. Brandon and Clay cautiously approached me, knowing how things ended the last time we were all together. I stuck my hand out to both of them, and then they tackled me into a bear hug.

"Thanks for coming guys, I missed you," I told them.

"Do you think we would miss your wedding? Not a chance," Brandon said.

"Jackson, thanks for calling. We thought we lost you after how pissed you were at us," Clay said behind Brandon.

"Yes, I was angry, but only a small part was directed at you, so for that, I am sorry too. Our lives are going into different directions, but you are still my friends. Brothers for life, right?"

"Right!" they responded.

Of course, the guys wanted to give me a bachelor party, but I declined that disaster. Instead, we went down to our favorite beach and surfed the day away, while the girls spent the day at the spa.

Later that evening, I took a walk around the property. The winter display had been taken down, and now all was set for my magical day with Riley. The stars were out tonight. I took it as a good sign that maybe my mom was watching over me. I said a silent prayer to her in heaven and wiped a tear or two that managed to fall. I turned to see my father.

"Are you okay?" he asked.

"I am. I was just thinking."

"About your mother?"

"How do you always know?" I asked.

"Years of practice, son. Do you want to talk about anything?"

"No, not really. In the quiet moments, the memories are easier to think about. I wish Grandma Gail was here. It is not fair. At least when she was alive, I felt as if I had a piece of mom always with me."

"I am so sorry, son. I miss Gail too. She was an amazing and extraordinary woman."

"I hope she's with mom."

"Of course, she is," he said. "You have two beautiful angels always looking over you."

"Do you think Grandfather Phillip would have approved of Riley?"

"Jackson, why are you asking?"

"No reason. I just wondered."

"Your grandfather looked to you as if the sun radiated off of you. He would have done anything for your happiness, because you were his second chance. Yes, he would have approved of Riley, because he would know how much you love her."

"He knew you loved Reese, but yet he did not approve," I said.

"For many different reasons, and ones I do not wish to ever revisit. Jackson, we cannot change the past. I was done trying that a long time ago, so let us focus on the reason we are all together. You are getting married tomorrow. Marrying Riley should be the only thing that matters. Come, how about a game of basketball before we turn in?"

"Seriously? I've been practicing, dad. I may beat you."

"Have fun trying, son."

We played a few games and he was right, I did feel better.

"Thank you, dad, for everything. Are you really okay with me marrying Riley now?" I asked as we made our way back from the courts.

"I am. Life is too short, son, and when you are lucky enough to find the one you want to share your life with, why wait? Yes, you are young, but I have never viewed you as the age you are. You are a hell of a lot wiser than I was when I was twenty, and you have your head on straight. You have come so far in such a short amount of time. I have never been more proud of you as I am right now. I wish you a lifetime of happiness with Riley and all you do in your life. I love you, son."

"Thanks, dad. I love you too!"

Somewhere inside of me was a need to hear my father's words of approval. It was always there since I was young. My father had always been there for me. Even when we disagreed, he always loved and supported me. I could not imagine how I would feel if I did not have that support now, but thankfully, I did.

It was a great day spent with friends and closing the night out with my father. After my shower, I stepped out on my balcony to take in the stars one more time. I knew my mother was watching over me as the stars twinkled in the dark night sky.

I watched the exchanges Riley had with her father. They had come a long way and were still trying to get back to where they once were, but he loved her, that was clear. She could be stubborn down to her core, but I knew having her father here on her wedding day meant the world to her. I sent a kiss up to heaven and closed the balcony door behind me.

I told Riley we would marry no matter what, and I meant that with my all of my heart. Tomorrow, I would marry Riley in front of our family and friends, and it would be the first day of our forever. It was what I had promised her back in Georgia. I loved that crazy girl in an epic lose-your-mind kind of love, and meeting her was fate delivering an angel to me. She was, and was so much more. The steps we took alone did not measure our lives; what mattered was the ones we took together tomorrow and the days that followed.

Destiny led us here for the moment we would become one. Tomorrow, we would join in marriage and become a family. It was not just one love story that guided us, but it was our story too! I found my forever with Riley.

I could not wait to make her mine.

On the day of my wedding, my eyes opened to see my father sitting beside my bed and watching me…sleep.

"Dad, are you okay?"

"I am fine, son. Sorry to startle you. I was checking on Fallon, and before returning to get a few more hours of sleep, I found myself here in your room, doing what I did practically every single day while you were growing up."

I rubbed my eyes and sat up against the headboard.

He told me, "You were so little when I brought you home from the hospital, a little piece of immortality with my looks and your mother's eyes. You scared the shit out of me, but I think you knew it somehow and never gave me any trouble. A perfect baby. You slept through the night and hardly had a cold, until you began nursery school, and then that was a completely new set of worries. Where does the time go? Here you are, about to marry the love of your life, and I'm sitting here watching you sleep just to make sure you are okay."

"Dad, you sure you are okay with me marrying Riley today?"

"Absolutely. After how you asked for our blessing? I probably would have been chased around with Lila leading the pack with her rolling pin if I denied you anything. Reese still has puffy eyes from all the crying she did listening to your speech. You have my blessing. You have your family's love and support."

"Thank you, dad. I promise to make you proud."

"You already have, Jackson. I love you. I'll see you down at the altar."

"Dad, how can I ever thank you for allowing Riley and me to marry where you married Reese?"

"You are welcome. The gazebo is a place for love stories to be told. It will now tell yours with Riley, and some day very far into the future, it will again for your siblings and maybe your children. You are my greatest joy, Jackson, and I am very happy you found your heart with Riley. Always put her first. Protect her heart always and forever. Be the man that says "I love you" at the beginning and ending of each day with her. They say to be a good father to your children, always be a good husband to their mother. I have no doubt you will be both. Now, I suggest you get ready. You do not want to be late for your own wedding."

He smiled and opened my door. I sprang from my bed and hugged my father with all that I had. I had never been more proud to be Walker Reed's son than at that moment. With all that I was, I would strive every single day to do right by the Reed name, and my father, who deserved nothing less.

CHAPTER 37

Riley

Wedding day

"YOU LOOK BEAUTIFUL, Riley. You are getting married today, and I am pregnant with twins. How did all of this happen?" my mother asked as I smiled back at her from my dressing table.

"The universe, right?" I told her. "Fate leading the pack and making sure we get our happily ever after."

"Yes, exactly. How could I forget?"

She wrapped her arms around me, and I took in how beautiful my mother was, not only on the outside but on the inside as well.

"Thank you, mom. None of this would have ever been possible without you."

"Riley, all I have ever wanted for you is to be happy. You are an amazing, bright, and accomplished young woman who is about to marry the love of her life. You will be fine. I do not doubt it for one second. Every minute of today, live it to the fullest with Jackson and page mark it in your story that will continue for the rest of your life."

We both were crying, and I said, "Thank goodness for water-proof mascara, right?"

"I was happy to have it on my wedding day."

As mom helped me with my veil, my father knocked on the door and asked to join us.

"You look like a princess ready for the ball," he said as he placed a kiss to my forehead and held my hands to his heart. "It feels like yesterday when these hands held yours for the first time. They were so little next to mine. Now, here you are on your wedding day, about to marry. I believe I recall a conversation we had once where I told you not to grow up."

"When was that?" I smiled.

"I believe you were four," he said, "but in hindsight, I probably began saying it the moment I held you in my arms. I love you, Riley. Although you are all grown up, you will always be my little girl. Please know you can always come to me if you need anything."

"I know, daddy. As I begin a new chapter in my life today, can we begin one as father and daughter? I promise, daddy, I will never hurt you again with my words. You deserve to be happy too, and anytime you ever questioned me, I know now it was always from your heart because you love me so much."

"Thank you, Riley. That means a lot to me. You are beautiful just like your mother here, and if I ever did anything right in this lifetime, it was having you to bless our lives. Right, Reese?" he asked as he lovingly looked over to my mother, who was wiping away her tears.

It had been more than a year since I watched my parents embrace one another. They looked beautiful together, but I knew their hearts belonged to others, and that was okay.

He then took his hand and held the side of her cheek, whispering something in her ear. Mother once again looked lovingly at my father and whispered something back to him. I may never know what they just shared between each other, but I was happy to witness it.

As they continued to embrace, each of their arms opened, inviting me over to join the hug. I would never forget this moment with my parents. Just then, the door opened, and standing in the threshold was Nana and Mr. Reed.

"Riley girl, are we getting married today, or what?" Nana said.

"We are. I'm ready."

Mr. Reed smiled and walked over to my mother to have her join him by his side. She did, smiling back to my father. Mr. Reed kissed her and then extended his hand for my father to take.

"Congratulations, Briggs," Mr. Reed said to him.

"Thank you, Walker, and congratulations to you too."

Nana clapped her hands, and we were front and center. I took a deep breath and checked my appearance once more. I was ready to marry Jackson Walker Reed. My father kissed me on both sides of my cheeks and then slowly pulled my veil down.

"Come, your prince awaits."

This is it. I am about to get married.

Freddy was waiting by the entrance and said to me, "Okay, junior peach, this is your moment. You look lovely."

"Thank you, Freddy. I feel like Cinderella in this dress," I whispered back.

"No, not Cinderella, but a queen," he said as he kissed my cheek and gave one to my mom too.

The doors opened to the path that would lead me to Jackson. When I reached Jackson, he wiped away a tear. He looked so handsome standing next to his father. Brandon and Clay looked on as his groomsmen.

My mother hugged me, and my father lifted my veil to kiss me on my cheeks. He placed my hand into Jackson's and said to him, "Take care of my little girl."

Jackson responded, "Forever."

CHAPTER 38

Jackson

I love you, Riley

WHEN I SAW her at the beginning of the path, I thought my heart was going to stop beating. She looked stunning from the top of her veil to the bottom of her kill-me-now stilettos.

Her arms linked with her parents, who could not look happier. Samuel and Reese may have not gotten their happily ever after with each other, but I sure got mine with their daughter. Our love story was never designed by just any standards, especially not when it was a spin-off from the original: Walker loves Reese.

We did not want the traditional wedding march, so I left it to Riley to pick the song meant for our story, and did she ever. I told her my song choice would be a surprise, so in turn she kept her choice to herself also, "Yours" by Russell Dickerson. It was hard for me not to be choked up after hearing the lyrics, nearly bringing me down to my knees.

The song says how she came to life when we first kissed. I made her better with my best self and my arms around her. "Thank God, I am yours," the song went.

Yes, thank you, God, for giving me Riley. You will never regret your decision to align the stars on the day we met. Our life together has been one adventure after the next, and all the promises we made to each other have now come true, beginning with our wedding.

Riley was my living and breathing angel, swaying in my arms as we listened to the song I chose for our first dance, "Die a Happy Man" by Thomas Rhett. I did not have to go through hundreds of songs before finding the one that would convey what I wanted Riley to hear. As the song ended and the applause began, I whispered to my wife, "I love you, Riley."

She had not stopped smiling all day. She had been the gracious guest of honor, dancing with any guest who asked her to. To watch her with her father made me want bigger things. I could not help but see our lives decades later, with our daughter dancing with me on her wedding day.

I wanted children with Riley, but I needed us first. The way she looked at me right now, I swear she was reading my mind, hell! I could not wait to peel away the layers of her dress and lose myself inside of her. My wife…my life.

CHAPTER 39

Riley

I love you, Jackson

"I LOVE YOU, Jackson Reed, my husband," I answered him back as he twirled me around one last time before we said our goodbyes to our family.

The plane was waiting to take us up to Big Sur, where we would recite our private vows to each other under our tree. We promised our parents we would not miss Fallon's first birthday, so this trip would be quick, but the memory of it would last us a lifetime.

Jackson had been hiking in Big Sur since he was young enough to walk. He and his father always pretended to be on a wild adventure where you never knew what you would encounter over the next hill or around the bend. I loved when he shared stories of his childhood with me. It made me wish I had known him then.

The weather was a cool sixty-four degrees, and the sky was

clear. Our guide met us at the entrance where we would begin our hike. Jackson was so excited to reach our tree. He pulled me along as quickly as my legs could keep up with him. When we found the tree, he picked me up and twirled me around as he kissed me soundly.

We wrote our vows for the wedding in front of our family and friends, so we did something different for here, surrounded by the redwoods tall enough to reach heaven. We each chose a quote to tell the other how we felt. After kissing me repeatedly, Jackson finally pulled out his notepaper and read aloud to me. He took my hand, and his smile made me weak in the knees, how I loved him so much.

"I picked a quote to read to you, but I truly don't believe even a timeless quote can convey how much I love you. I thought about our time in Maryland, the day we visited with your father, and you asked me why I was with you. My crazy girl, I thought back then how those words could ever pass your lips. I promised you forever back in Georgia and every day that followed. I have not regretted one minute spent with you. I asked you to not doubt my love for you, and I hope today, on our wedding day, you finally believe it. You do deserve me, and I you. I love you, crazy girl...even your crazy mood swings. You cannot pick parts of a person to love. You love them all. You are my soul mate. Here, under our tree, I freely give my heart over to you without condition. Today, you accepted that love, and now we are husband and wife. I love you, Riley Taylor Reed. You are part of me. And I am part of you. You are the best thing I want to hold onto in my life and a thousand lifetimes after. You, Riley, are my *happily forever after.*"

He kissed me gently, and then softness turned into wanting as my mouth met his and we kissed.

"That was beautiful, Jackson. Who was that quote from?" I asked as he winked back and kissed me again.

"Some lovesick fool named Jackson Reed. You see, baby, he is crazy in love with this beautiful girl that makes him lose his mind anytime she is near him. Now, your turn."

"Not sure how I can follow that, but I will certainly do my best.

You're right about how I questioned not being good enough for you. I know it upset you, but at the time, it was how I felt. I look at you and believe you are invincible. You can do anything, Jackson, and when you told me that you loved me for the first time, I said to myself, *why?* You could have any girl you wanted by your choosing, but you chose me. You made me believe that fate led me to you that day back in Maryland, and again a year later in New York. I fell in love with you over coffee; by the way, your hand hit the small of my back when you helped me into the cab. I fell in love with your eyes and how brightly they sparkled when looking back at mine. By loving me, you proved me wrong, and I no longer felt that way because I knew what we had was real and everlasting. I'll fight with you all day long, as long as I get to hold you at night."

"Hey, you quoted me too! That's my line," he cutely interrupted.

"It's mine too, and it is okay because I am borrowing it from my husband. It feels so right to say those words to you. Thank you, Jackson, for loving me the way you do. I promise forever and always to be worthy of your love you so freely have given to me with no condition. You are my soul mate, and I am forever yours."

Together, we pronounced ourselves husband and wife and kissed as if it were our first time. The sun had set over the mountains, and the moonlight and stars were witness to our union. We arrived back at our private plane to celebrate not just one wedding, but two. Candles and flowers filled the room as we made love soaring through the clouds.

William Shakespeare said it best: "When I saw you I fell in love, and you smiled because you knew."

Jackson always knew, and he made me believe it too!

CHAPTER 40

Walker

The best is yet to come

I T WAS NEW YEAR'S DAY and my baby girl's first birthday. The last few days had been a blinding blur of celebrations, ending with my son getting married. *Wow, my son is married*, I thought to myself. I thought I would have more time for that to sink in, but Jackson always led with his heart, and his heart was leading him straight to Riley.

How could I blame him? Like father, like son. After today, they would leave for their honeymoon before continuing with their school commitments back in New York.

I returned to a still quiet house after my early morning run. Reese was exhausted and on her feet longer than she should have been yesterday. I needed her well for today, and for Fallon.

Yesterday, she said she was thankful it was a good day for no morning sickness, and that she was taking full advantage of feeling great. Her first born was getting married, and that was a call to celebrate. After witnessing one too many dances with Freddy and Fabrizio, I called a definite time-out for the remainder of the reception. My Reese was a stubborn one, and she never knew her own limitations. Riley was more than happy to take Reese's place when Freddy began the Electric Slide. Even Lila joined in on the fun. It was a perfect day for our family, as today would be too.

After the backyard extravaganza Rosalyn put on for Christmas Eve, and with the wedding that followed, my little princess was more than overstimulated, so I felt it was best to tone it down for her party. She loved music and the classic characters from Sesame Street. Rosalyn had a small stage set up near her play area with chairs placed down in front. A team of puppeteers were hired to put on a show for us today featuring Elmo, Big Bird, and Cookie Monster. A musical number was planned first, and then we would bring Fallon on stage to meet the characters. If she wasn't frightened, then we would have Storytime with Elmo. It was overboard on my part, this I knew, but I could not help myself. I loved to make my daughter smile, and in turn, that made Reese happy, so it was win-win all around.

After my run, I quickly showered and dressed. I wanted to see Fallon before she would wake so I could be the first to wish her a happy birthday. Reese had given up trying to understand me and let me have these moments with our daughter. Reese was sleeping so peacefully, I did not have the heart to wake her. Jackson and Riley would be arriving this afternoon for her party. Everyone who mattered in our little girl's life would be here today, all except for…*you know what, she made her choice, and I am not going to be upset over it.*

I turned the knob as quietly as I could, and then I heard talking from inside of Fallon's room. The door inched opened, and to my surprise, my mother was here and with Fallon. *How?* I never checked the monitor when I left our bedroom or I surely would have seen her. I wanted to go in, but I remained back and eavesdropped on her moment with Fallon.

My mother was always loving to Jackson when he was younger and still remained close with him today. Losing my father suddenly, it was very important for my mother to stay involved in her grandsons' life. I had my feelings when it came to my parents, and would never allow them to come between what I shared with my son. Jackson loved them both very much, and as long as he was happy, then I was fine with their relationship. My mother was still one of the most beautiful women I had ever known. She took great care of herself, and even in her sixties, she was flawless. Sitting with my drooling daughter in a Chanel suit was beyond anything I ever thought I would see, but she was smiling lovingly at Fallon, which made my eavesdropping worth it.

"Happy birthday, my sweet girl. I cannot believe you are one. I am not sure you know this, but you are one special little girl who is loved very much. Your father is my baby, although he has not been that way for a long time. I still see him as the little boy who tugged on my skirt wanting just to play with me, but I was too busy so I sent his nanny instead. I should have been a better mother to him. When I learned I was going to be a grandmother, I was thankful when given a second chance to get it right this time. I fell instantly in love when I held Jackson for the first time, and now he has you. I promise to be the best grandmother I can, Fallon, and this is why I am here. I could never miss your first birthday, one of many I sure hope to be part of. I love you, sweet girl. Happy birthday."

"And she loves you too," I said as I made my way into the nursery.

I knew my mother regretted many things in her life, but to hear some of them broke a piece of my heart. The past was something I promised to put behind me and move on from. Today was about celebration.

"Hello, son. I am so sorry I was not here sooner."

"You are here now, and that is all that matters. When did you arrive?"

"Just a little while ago. With my plane delayed with rain and then the fog that followed, there was no way I was leaving London on time. I am so sorry I missed Jackson's wedding. He may never forgive me for it."

"Nonsense," I said. "You called him, and you had time to speak with him and Riley too."

"I know, son, but it is not the same. I nearly balled my eyes out when your sweet Reese sent me the pictures to my phone, along with the short video. I do not deserve your kindness, but thank you anyway."

I took Fallon from her arms and kissed my baby girl.

"Happy birthday, my love. Daddy loves you so much. We are going to have so much fun today."

I kissed the top of her head and called down to Priscilla. She arrived moments later to take care of the baby.

I told her, "Priscilla, Reese is still sleeping. Please take care of Fallon this morning while I take some time with my mother."

"Yes, sir," she said to me and then cooed to the baby. "Come here, little one."

"Come, let's take a walk," I asked my mother as I invited her to accept my hand. She did with no hesitation, and we walked out into the gardens.

"So, how was Europe?"

"Europe is Europe, and I have grown tired of it," she sighed.

"And what of the handsome male suitor of yours…have you grown tired of him as well?"

"Walker Phillip Reed, have you lost all boundaries of discretion?" she huffed as she walked slightly ahead of me.

"Mother, please wait. Come on, I was only teasing. Why are you upset?"

"You don't see it, do you?"

"See what? I'm sorry, mother, but I am not following."

"I miss your father, and no amount of traveling is going to change that. I am not interested in beginning any new romances with gentleman callers. And it is not nice to mock me. It hurts me, Walker."

She held her head down as to fight off her emotion. I wrapped my arms around her back and held her close.

"I am sorry, mother. Please forgive me. I would never hurt you on purpose. My failed attempt at a joke was insensitive, and it's okay to miss father."

She turned, hugged me back, and said, "Do you, Walker? Do you miss your father at all?"

"Sometimes, I do. Mostly when I am alone with my thoughts at work and sitting in my office. His memory is all around that room, no matter how much I try to change it. He's been on mind lately because of Jackson."

"I'm sure he has. Your father would be so proud of his grandson. The next generation taking his rightful place at Reed Global."

"How did you know?" I asked.

"We talk, Walker, all the time. I could not be happier for you two. This is what you have always wanted."

"Yes, that's true, but I never thought it would be Jackson who wanted it more. He took me by complete surprise, and I needed some time to process it all."

She said, "Everything will work out as it is meant to be, just you wait and see. I wish your father were here. He loved Jackson very much. Anyway, I have dozens of presents for Fallon. I am looking forward to this party I have heard so much about. Yes, I speak with Reese just as much."

"I know I do not say the words as often as I should, but I do love you, mother. And I am very happy you are here with us today."

"Thank you, son. That means a lot."

We walked hand-in-hand back to the house feeling a bit lighter than before.

"Grandma!" Jackson called out as soon as he saw my mother.

I swear she lit up anytime he was near. Jackson lifted her into his arms and hugged her tightly. Riley joined in next, and they had their reunion. Lila and Thomas greeted my mother, and then they were all off in their conversations.

"Hey you, are you okay?" Reese asked me as she stepped up behind me.

"More than okay. Our family is blessed," I told her.

"We are, Walker, and the best is yet to come."

"I could not agree with you more."

After breakfast, we shared most of the morning talking and catching up with one another. Fallon was surrounded by piles of presents. She was interested in ripping the paper more than anything else. Fallon was one lucky little girl, but with all of her new presents now opened, it warmed my heart to see her holding the bear that Jackson had given to her. She crawled to him with her bear in tow. He picked her up and kissed her head. She loved her big brother so much, and then it was complete when she said, "Bear."

We all smiled. Best birthday moment ever! *Reese was right*, I thought as I watched Jackson play with Fallon. *The best was yet to come.*

CHAPTER 41

Jackson

...one year later

MY FATHER ONCE told me that my mother loved to write quotes down on paper or in a journal. She believed that even a few words held the power to change your life. When I left home and was out on my own, I kept her journal close by whenever I needed some inspiration.

On the day I began working for my father at Reed Global, I flipped through a few pages until I found the one I was looking for. My mother marked this quote on the day she graduated from college and began designing professionally.

Every accomplishment starts with the decision to try.
-Olympic Gold medalist Gail Devers.

Looking back now, I would forever be grateful for reading that quote and asking my father for the chance to prove myself to the legacy I was born from. I never assumed it would be easy.

On my first day of work, I was thrown into the deep end by Donovan Tate, my father's second-in-command. It was just under six weeks before the Super Bowl, and Reed Global had secured a commercial to air right before the half-time show. The thirty-second spot cost four and half million dollars and needed to highlight Reed Global and our innovative approach to designing and building the structures that carried our name. What my father and Donovan asked me to do was take it a step further.

Now a full-time member of the Marketing and Development team, Bridgette wasted no time showing me the ropes. Together, Bridgette and I showcased Reed Global as a company that believed in innovation, taking design and building to the next level. We showed the New York skyline and called it the "ground floor," and Reed Global was the way to elevate and take those buildings to a higher level. The commercial was a visual and financial success.

My father was invited to address the NYU May graduating class and give a keynote speech. He honorably accepted and then approached me with an idea. As my last film project for Professor Connelly, my father challenged me to create and write a film that would show the next generation of engineers what the future would hold for environmental technologies. Riley was my collaborative partner for this final project. After our professor approved our concept, we got to work.

I never felt more alive working for my father and using my knowledge of filmmaking to merge both worlds together. Was this his plan all along? He worried that I would regret my decision to put filmmaking behind me to pursue a career at Reed Global, but the way I saw it, I had the best of both worlds.

Riley and I both graduated with honors, and after receiving our final grade of an A from Professor Connelly, Riley never doubted herself or talent again. When I had bailed on our first project, her confidence was shaken and she was unsure of herself. Our teacher saw real potential and drive within Riley, and he pushed her hard to achieve her goals. Now, here we were, college graduates and about to celebrate our first year wedding anniversary.

We celebrated our honeymoon around the world. We had three weeks before returning to school, so we left for parts unknown. Our last trip was all around the United States, so this time around, we chose to go to Europe. We used Instagram as our photo album, capturing picture after picture of all the destinations we explored. We skied in the Alps of Switzerland. We shared a kiss on the Millennium Bridge in London and crossed the Thames River. Our favorite and last night before traveling home was laughing over pints of beer in a pub in Ireland. The locals welcomed us warmly after we told the owner who we were. Niall Daugherty, a friend of Thomas and Lila, shared stories with us about their younger years. It was a magical trip, and our first trip as husband and wife.

We celebrated our anniversary back in Big Sur. We loved where we married and promised to always return to the place where we carved our names in our tree. Fallon was about to turn two years old, and our baby brothers were just about to turn six months old. Daniel Mackenzie Reed was born first, followed by his twin, Cameron Reese Reed. Both boys weighed close to five pounds, and their heads were covered in dark brown hair.

Our baby sister definitely lived up to her name as "little ruler" of the house. At only two years old, she was fiercely protective of the babies. We sat around the huge Christmas tree with Riley and me holding each of our brothers, and Fallon in the middle. My father and Reese stood behind us as the photographer took our pictures, shot after shot of smiles and laughter.

Three generations of Reed children were in this room, each one of us with meaningful purpose to do great things in this life. The only thing my father ever wanted for me was to be happy. Well, I was. In return, all I ever wanted was for him to be proud of me, and he was. I wanted to join my father by his side, and one day teach my younger siblings as he taught me. Yes, we were all part of the legacy my father had built for us. His years of sacrifice and hard work were footprints on the path that would lead us into the future.

I was where I wanted to be, and with Riley as my wife, we too have found our…Forever.

The End

Sort of…

EPILOGUE

Riley

...five years later

TODAY WAS THE day. I knew I was going to hear good news. I tapped my fingers on my thighs as if they were drums. I was nervous, so nervous to hear what my doctor would say, but then again, I already knew because of the two pink lines on the pregnancy stick.

I was pregnant! All I needed now was a confirmation from Dr. Lemay. Although we lived in New York, Jackson split his time between the two coasts. He loved when he had the opportunity to work out here because it meant he would be working alongside his father and Donovan. We had come so far in the five years since we'd been married.

After we graduated from NYU, Jackson began working for Reed Global International full-time, while I began my production company, Big Sur Films. Jackson loved it, with the name holding so much meaning to our relationship. Working with young and inspiring filmmakers was exciting and exhilarating. I loved their passion

338

for the arts, and their creativity was off the charts amazing. Jackson sometimes assisted me when I needed his input, but he mainly focused on Reed Global, and I worked hard to get my company off the ground

Three years into producing my documentary work, my film, "Hidden Truth" caught the attention over at NBC. *Dateline* had done a segment of my film and its message of bullying that centered around five young individuals, all with a unique story to tell. Growing media attention surrounded the film, and it was noticed by the Tribeca Film Festival. "Hidden Truth" was voted one of the top fifteen independent films that debuted for the festival. I could not be any happier, but something was missing, and that was a baby. We had always talked about beginning a family, but Jackson wanted to wait.

We married young and had plenty of time to have babies, but with mom having the twins, the baby bug was itching to bite me too! I knew he was right, and if I had gotten pregnant early on, maybe my film career may have taken a backseat to motherhood. Now, I was a woman who believed she could do anything, and I would not want to set the women's movement back, but I wanted to be a mom first. I had years of filmmaking ahead of me and I truly loved it. But I loved Jackson more, and I so badly wanted to tell him that I was carrying his child.

Dr. Lemay entered the exam room a few minutes later, and she looked happy.

"Hello again, Riley. Thank you so much for waiting on me. I had an emergency with one of my moms, but all is well now. So, let us talk about you. I see you took a pregnancy test a few days ago, and that is when you phoned my office. Let me just pull up your blood test results."

I could not stop fidgeting on the table. Here I was, with my bare ass out and in a cotton cover-up. *Come on, already! Tell me that I am pregnant!*

"Okay, your HCG levels are quite high according to your

bloodwork. When was your last menstrual period?"

"I believe it was after Thanksgiving. I stopped taking my birth control right around my yearly check-up. My doctor back in New York gave me a clean bill of health and told me I could begin trying to get pregnant. Am I, Dr. Lemay?"

"According to your bloodwork, yes, Riley, you are. Lean back onto the table, and let's take a look."

I adjusted my legs into the stirrups and positioned myself down low to the table. Dr. Lemay used the vaginal probe to perform the ultrasound. I went to enough appointments with mom to know that was not the most comfortable thing to do, but if it showed what I believed was true, then probe away.

"Are you okay?" Dr. Lemay asked as I winced a bit.

"Yes, just getting used to it."

"Now, take a breath Riley, and exhale slowly." I did and began to relax. "You are most certainly pregnant. I am measuring about twelve weeks, give or take a couple of days. Once you begin further progressing, I will get better measurements. Now, are you ready for the fun part? If you look right here," she pointed to the screen. "You will see baby A, and baby B."

What!? I thought to myself.

"Congratulations, Riley! You are expecting twins, which brings you to a delivery date around September 24th."

Tears were flooding my eyes as I no longer could see the screen. I couldn't even find the right words to say at the moment. I was so happy and could not wait to tell Jackson.

"By the way, Happy Valentine's Day. If your Jackson is anything like his father before him, I say it is going to be a night you two will never forget."

"Oh, Dr. Lemay, the apple does not fall too far from the tree. The Reeds are very much alike in the swoon department."

She laughed and said, "I figured. Therefore, I will write you a prescription for pre-natal vitamins and send everything over to your ob/gyn doctor in New York. You are a marvel, Riley. I cannot believe you do not have any morning sickness. Your mom did not fair all too well in that department."

"I remember, but so far, I am okay. I feel fantastic."

"You should be. Congratulations again."

I quickly dressed and reapplied my make-up. Jackson would be at Reed Global for most of the day, but I could not wait one more second to share my news. I was going to surprise him at the office.

"Hi, Jenny," I said happily as I stepped off the elevator.

"Well, this is a pleasant surprise! How are you Mrs. Reed?"

"I am well, thank you, but please call me Riley."

"Sorry, tough habit to break. Are you here to see Jackson?"

"I am. Is he available?"

"For his wife? Always. That is a number one rule around here."

I smiled knowing that was the truth. Walker would not care if he were in a meeting with the President of the United States, because when my mother called, everything was put on hold. Jackson was the same way and made that point quite clear on his first day.

"You can go in. He's in there with Mr. Reed," she told me.

"Thank you, Jenny."

Now, I was nervous. Do I just blurt it out? On the other hand, do I ask to speak with him in private? I took a deep breath and entered Walker's office. The two were talking with their heads down looking over a mountain of papers. I stood there for a moment before Jackson looked up to see me. He smiled brightly and immediately got up to walk over to me.

"Hello my love, what a great surprise. I was just going to break for lunch, care to join me?" he asked as he kissed me soundly in front of his father and not caring one bit. I came up for air and that is when my tears began to fall. "Baby, are you okay? Why are you crying?" he asked as he held my cheek. Walker also stood and now looked concerned over seeing me cry. They never liked when they saw us cry, not ever.

"I am fine Jackson, never been better."

"Why the tears then?"

341

"I want to tell you something, something I hope will make you as happy as I am."

"Okay, tell me." I nervously looked over my shoulder to look at Walker. He got the message real quick and made his discreet exit. "Dad, you can stay." Jackson called out.

"No, I think you need some time with your wife. I will go call mine and give you a few minutes to yourselves." He smiled and winked, probably already knowing what I would be telling Jackson.

"You cleared the room baby, so now tell me."

"Come, and sit down with me." I took his hand and we sat on the sofa. I turned to speak and his phone buzzed. He held up his hand to take the call. Ten minutes later, he apologized and asked me to continue. "Okay, so this morning I had an…"

"Baby, hold on a second. I need to take this. He walked over to his desk and hit the intercom button to speak with Jenny.

"Sir, Mr. Tate would like you to conference him on the Devane call at three, are you available?"

"Absolutely, I was expecting that, thank you Jenny."

"Okay, you have my attention. Sorry love, it has been a crazy day."

"I see that, Jackson, I guess I will let you get back to your workday."

"Riley, don't be like that. I am sorry honey. Let me tell Jenny to hold my calls, okay?" oh! I could not resist him if I tried. "I love you, won't be a minute."

One minute turned to another ten, I was going to scream my news at him, and then Jackson took me in his arms and kissed me. With his forehead to mine, he told me he loves me and sorry he was being an ass by ignoring me. He wasn't, not on purpose. I was the one that interrupted his day. "So, I had an appointment this morning and I found out something amazing."

"What appointment, and who with?" he asked.

"It was with Dr. Lemay, and I found out that…" before I could finish telling him, Donovan, Tom, his daughter Bridgette who was now permanently based in New York all walked in, followed by Walker. Jackson immediately scowled at the interruption because I think he was finally getting that I had something important to tell him. The others were oblivious and began all talking at once until Jackson stepped out of our hug and shouted, "Everyone, quiet! My wife here has something to tell me and with the constant interruptions, she has not been able to. Not one more word until I hear what Riley has to say." The group was stunned to silence while I watched my father-in-law smile, he knew and I was sure my mother was on her way.

"Go ahead baby, talk to me," he said.

I nearly died with embarrassment as all eyes were on me. Jackson was smiling over at me with his very sexy, panty-dropping smile. I was already weak in the knees. I looked around and could not find my voice.

"Breathe baby," he said, as I took in a few calming breaths.

With one deeper exhale, I looked over to Walker, and then saw my mom enter and join him. She looked beautiful as always, with her hair long and wavy with curls.

I turned back to Jackson and simply said, "Happy Valentine's Day."

He smiled and kissed me with some laughter behind it. He said, "I did not forget, but is that all?"

"No, there's something else."

"I figured."

"Surprise! I'm pregnant, and with twins."

There was silence…complete silence. Well, until I turned around to see my mother crying and hugging Walker. I looked at Jackson, who still had not said anything yet. Was he in shock?

"Jackson, are you okay?" I asked.

He still was mute. Everyone congratulated me and then slowly exited the room, leaving just my mom and Walker with us.

"Son, do you need a drink of water?" his father asked him.

Jackson slowly got down to his knees and kissed my stomach.

His hands were on my hips, and he placed his cheek against me, a romantic move I once witnessed his father do with my mom back in Maryland all those years ago.

"You're pregnant with twins. Our baby…two babies…twin babies…are growing inside of you?"

"Yup, that's what I was told this morning. Here, take a look for yourself."

I handed him the ultrasound photo and his eyes filled with tears. It only took a second for Jackson to get up and lift me into his arms.

"God! I love you. I'm going to be a father!" he shouted and kissed me soundly.

After putting me down, our parents congratulated us and pulled us into a group hug. Jackson grabbed my hand and said goodbye to his father. I quickly waved to my mother, and he rushed me to the elevator.

"Where are we going?" I breathlessly asked.

"Home, so I can make love to my beautiful wife and worship your body for the rest of the night."

"Lead the way, my love."

Bonus EPILOGUE

Jackson

"**J**ACKSON, I WOULD like you to come out to California. We are having our annual meeting and your presence is required," my father said to me.

"Sounds good, when will this meeting take place?"

"Friday."

"As in Friday of this week?"

"Is there a problem?" he asked.

"No, sir. I am sure I can clear my schedule. I will have my assistant change around a few things. The dedication of the Arts and Science building is in a few weeks, so needless to say, I have been under a deadline."

"And, my grandbabies will be here soon. I cannot believe I will be a grandfather, and with three children of my own, all under the age of ten."

"Yeah, it is pretty amazing. Riley is stunning, even in sweat pants. She looks beautiful."

"The Mitchell women usually are. Thomas always used to say they come from strong Irish stock."

"Even though, Riley is part Briggs," I corrected him.

"Yeah, I don't count that," he laughed.

"So, what's up, dad? And why do I need to be in California on Friday?"

"So I can appoint you a new role in the company."

My heart nearly stopped.

I asked, "And? That would be?"

"How would you like to be Reed Global's Chief Information Officer? I know your heart lies in Marketing and Development, which by the way, Bridgette will also be getting a promotion. She has done fabulous work and has earned a top spot. With Joan assisting Donovan for overseas projects, this was the perfect time for a change in command. She will be the department's head, while you as CIO will oversee the entire operation in New York. You will report directly to me, but from your side of the country. Roles will not change here in California, and now with Lars retiring, there is no better time to place you in the role you were meant to be in."

"Dad, I don't know what to say."

"Thank you will suffice."

"Thank you, dad. You will never know what this means to me. To have your trust is everything."

"I know, son. Believe me, I do. I know my relationship with your grandfather was volatile most of the time, but I have to believe he was happy on the day I took my place at Reed Global, and I know he would be just as proud of you as you take yours. I love you, son. I will see you on Friday."

A few days later, I was back in California for a meeting with all the executives that worked closely with my father. I was on a tight schedule, but I had a stop to make before heading to the office.

"I wish you were here, mom," I softly said as I placed two dozen pink lilies on my mother's grave. "Thank you for showing me my future. I may have not understood it then, but I do now. Life with

Riley is a daily blessing. She has made me so happy, and now with our babies soon to arrive, my life is complete. The only thing that would make it perfect is if you were here to hold my children, but knowing you will be watching over them gives me peace. I have to be going. Dad is waiting on me. I love you, mother, always and forever."

As I made my way into the vast conference room, my father was first to greet me, followed by Donovan Tate, Vice President and my father's right hand in command here in California, and Tom Johannsen, Vice President and another key player who works a number of Reed interests all around the world.

The company experienced a shift in command when Lars Sapien suddenly resigned from his role of Reed Global's New York operations. My father assured me all would be righted soon, and what was a little chaos for but to keep you on your toes.

My transition early on was not easily accepted around the office. Employees would sometimes glare at me or run the other way when they saw me coming. Some did not like change and had a hard time adhering to it. I was the boss' son, and I knew I had to prove myself not only to my father, but also to his team on both coasts. It would not be easy, but I was one never to back down to a challenge.

Now, here I was, standing next to my father as he introduced me as Reed Global's new Chief Information Officer. Life was great, and I was about to become a father to twins, a son and daughter, in a matter of weeks.

"Thank you all for joining us here today," my father announced. "As you know, Lars Sapien has decided to retire and spend his time out on the golf course. He knows he has to practice if he is going to beat me. Anyway, we cannot thank Lars enough for all of his years of dedication and service he has brought to Reed Global International. He will be dearly missed, and we wish him all the best."

He continued, "Now, Jackson, my son, has worked in our New York office for the past five years or so. He has instrumentally broadened our reach throughout the world with his innovative and unique brand of marketing. Along with Bridgette Johannsen, this team has been unbeatable. We value their creativity and look forward to seeing what they can do in the years to come. Bridgette Johannsen will be appointed to Vice President of Marketing and Development in our New York office. My son will step into the role as Reed Global's Chief Information Officer and ultimately oversee every aspect of operations and reporting directly to me. Please give a round of applause to Jackson Walker Reed."

My father was clapping the hardest. His smile was infectious as I made my way over to the podium. He pulled me into a tight hold and whispered how proud he was of me. I tried with all my effort not to cry in front of the team. Reese attended, along with Fallon and the twins. My grandmother had made the trip and was wiping away her tears.

I said, "Thank you very much for that warm welcome. I am not one for speeches, so I will make this as brief as possible. Have you seen the spread out there? My pregnant wife would love it."

Applause was all around as I continued, "As I stand here today, I feel a sense of pride swelling up deep inside of me. I am standing exactly where my father stood on the day he accepted his new role from my grandfather Phillip, more than twenty-five years ago. When most young men are just beginning to begin their lives, my father, one of our country's youngest CEO's, had huge shoes to fill, as I do now. I will continue to work hard every single day, not only as your CIO, but to continue the legacy that two amazing Reed men began. Thank you."

A few weeks later, as I sat behind my desk back in the New York office, my eyes were transfixed on two framed photos. The first one was of my grandfather and father on the day he was newly appointed CEO of Reed Global. The second was a photo of my father embracing me on the day I accepted my new role as CIO. He looked proud, like my grandfather.

It was a day I would never forget. I smiled thinking back. My babies were not here yet, and I envisioned my children one day taking over for me. It was a great dream, and a great legacy. I could not wait to live it, but one-step at a time.

My father once told me that you have to learn to walk before you can run.

Walker

Full circle

TODAY MARKS OUR tenth wedding anniversary, and what better way to celebrate than on Thanksgiving. I asked Reese where she wanted to celebrate our anniversary. She could pick anywhere in the world, and the only place she wanted to be was in Portersville, Georgia. My heart melted when she said the words. It was the one place she truly felt at home, and it was the place where we put the past behind us and began again as we were always meant to be.

Jackson and Riley found love here as well. I always said Pottersville was a magical place. It was true then as it is today. Lila and Thomas have now passed on, but their legacy of love and family lived on. Reese could never part with the home she grew up in, so with some renovation without disturbing the simplicity of the house, we now used it as a vacation home. Freddy and Fabrizio loved it too.

They had adopted two sons and a daughter, shortly after Fallon's second birthday. All the children were around the same age, so when we were all together, it was quite the celebration. I loved that our children would be growing up with Freddy's.

Thanksgiving this year was one big picnic at Clover Lake, the same spot I proposed to Reese. All of our family was here, with Lila and Thomas smiling over us from heaven. My wife was breathtaking with our children in her arms: Fallon, a mirror image of Reese, but with my eyes; Daniel and Cameron, both strong, creative, and passionate just like their older brother; and Jackson, now a father of his own. His children, Jackson Jr., and Elizabeth, were riding on his back and pretending their daddy was a horse. We celebrated our blessings and were thankful for this time together.

I held my beautiful Reese after making love with her under the stars out in our meadow. Reese was the one, the one who captured my heart from the moment my eyes found hers that day in the library. Her beauty beguiled me as I struggled to find my voice. She laughed, of course. How could she not when I was practically drooling over myself?

"What are you thinking about?" she asked as she snuggled closer to my body.

"Oh, nothing much, just remembering the time you practically fell over yourself when we met back at NYU."

She laughed aloud and buried her face in my chest.

"Oh really?" she said. "I believe you have your facts mixed up. It was you, Mr. Sex on a stick, who was drooling over me."

"Sex on a stick, huh?"

"Yes, among other great nicknames you have had throughout the years. My favorite is Mr. Wall Sex."

"And, what about you? My sexy vixen?"

"Am I still sexy?" she asked.

"Is that a serious question?"

"It is. I really want to know."

Oh, my word, even after all these years, my beautiful Reese is still the same innocent Georgia Peach I fell in love with. She was beyond adorable.

"You are and so much more," I assured her. "I guess if you have to ask, then I am not doing my job correctly, and you need a reminder to how much I love you. Worship you. Hunger for you. Desire you, and dream of making love to you every chance I get."

"Prove it," she said.

"Challenge accepted."

I wrapped my woman up in a blanket and carried her inside the barn. She loved me unconditionally, all parts of me, that was our deal. Reese Mitchell was my forever love. And I was hers.

"I love you, Walker. You have my heart always."

"I love you, Reese. My heart was always yours. Now, pick the wall so I can once again live up to my nickname...what is it again?"

"You have no shame, Mr. Wall Sex, and it was Freddy who originally called you that. If memory serves, we were quite loud."

"Baby, I remember everything. I will breathe you until the last breath I take."

"Walker, make love to me," she said as she smiled as only Reese could do.

"Where, baby?"

"Everywhere," she whispered.

"That can be arranged. After all, we have...*Forever*."

Once upon a time...
Right in the middle of living an ordinary life,
two people found an extraordinary love.
Their story was a fairy tale,
and through that love,
another couple was inspired to find their way.

...And they all lived

Happily
FOREVER
After

The End

OTHER BOOKS BY MARY A. WASOWSKI

A Changed Life (standalone)

Forever Series:

Forever: Book One
Second Chance at Forever: Book Two
Our Forever Promise: Book Three

All Roads Lead Home (standalone)
An Unfinished Life (standalone)
Return to Kildare (standalone)

ACKNOWLEDGMENTS

THANK YOU TO my close-knit circle who make up "Team Sparkle" My accomplishments would not be complete without the very talented professionals who help me make my work come to life.

Every book idea begins with my editor, Joe Marron. He gives me that little push that I sometimes need to delve deeper into my characters and develop the extra that I need to make my story great. Your encouragement keeps me going at times when I get frustrated, although your red pen continues to scare me. Per our conversation, moving forward with edits, I prefer sparkly purple. LOL!

When the book is edited and read a hundred times, the next step is formatting. The very talented and creative Julie Titus of JT Formatting takes over and creates a beautiful interior that sets the tone for the words you will read.

Sara Eirew of Sara Eirew Photography – you are insanely talented and creative. My messages must drive you crazy, but when I look at the finished product, I am in awe of you. You take my many ideas and make it original, beautiful, and in a league of its own. Thank you to Mindy Guerreiros for bringing us together and I look forward to many more fantastic covers to come.

Kylie McDermott of Give Me Books – You did an amazing job sharing the love for Happily Forever After to the blogging community. Sending all my thanks to your dedicated team. To all the bloggers who support me – thank you with all of my heart. To Kiki Chatfield, and her team at The Next Step PR. It was a pleasure working with you, and I look forward to working together again in the future. Ruth Martin…you are awesome! The book world has thousands of books that debut every day, and you all have TBR lists that are too long to ever catch up on. Knowing you take time out of your busy day to read and share my work makes my heart so happy. This is a job that I love with all of my heart. Thank you so much for being part of my journey.

I hope you all enjoyed Happily Forever After! Until we meet again...

For the sisterhood, thank you for remaining true and never changing. The best friendships happen when you don't see them coming. Thank you for finding a place into my heart. That's where you will forever remain. I love you all.

Lastly, to my family. Thank you does not even begin to sum up how much I appreciate your love and support. You may have not understood in the beginning why I needed to follow my passion for writing, but you certainly do now. Eight novels later would never have been possible without your love, support, and encouragement that kept me moving forward. Chasing the dream with you by my side has been an amazing adventure. I am so happy that I get to share my dreams with you. Henry, Zachary, Christopher, and Cameron. You are my world. I love you with all of my heart and soul.

ABOUT THE AUTHOR

MARY A. WASOWSKI IS A Best Selling Author who writes adult contemporary romance. Best known for her Forever Series, this is her eighth publication. Proud to be an Indie Writer! Mary loves writing romance and creating sexy alpha book boyfriends for you to swoon over. When she is not writing her happily ever after love stories, she is reading on her Kindle. A romantic at heart and an avid reader of all romance.

She shares her zest for life with her husband, Henry, and their three sons. She lives in North Carolina and works as a full-time writer.

STAY IN TOUCH

I would love to hear from you. Please stay connected wherever you are.

EMAIL:
AuthorMaryAWasowski@gmail.com

FACEBOOK:
https://www.facebook.com/Author-Mary-A-Wasowski-332971356804341

TWITTER:
https://twitter.com/wasow6

INSTAGRAM:
https://instagram.com/authormaryawasowski/

WEBSITE:
http://authormaryawasowski.com/

GOOGLE +:
https://plus.google.com/+MaryWasowski

TSU:
http://www.tsu.co/authormaryawasowski

www.ingramcontent.com/pod-product-compliance
Lightning Source LLC
Chambersburg PA
CBHW071246250626
47163CB00002B/352